THE OUTSIDER

Emily Hourican is a journalist and author. She grew up in Brussels, where she went to the European School and learned how to fake it as a Eurobrat, and now lives in Dublin. She has written features for the *Sunday Independent* for fifteen years, as well as for *Image* magazine, *Condé Nast Traveler* and *Woman and Home*. She was also editor of *The Dubliner* magazine.

www.emilyhourican.com
@EmilyH71

Also by Emily Hourican

Fiction
The Privileged
White Villa
The Blamed

Non-Fiction
How To (Really) Be a Mother

THE OUTSIDER

EMILY HOURICAN

HACHETTE
BOOKS
IRELAND

First published in Ireland in 2019 by
HACHETTE BOOKS IRELAND
Published in paperback in 2020

1

Cataloguing in Publication Data is available from the British Library

ISBN 978 1 4736 8112 5

Typeset in Garamond by redrattledesign.com

Printed and bound in Great Britain by Clays Ltd, Elcograf S.p.A

Hachette Books Ireland policy is to use papers that are natural, renewable and recyclable products and made from wood grown in sustainable forests. The logging and manufacturing processes are expected to conform to the environmental regulations of the country of origin.

Hachette Books Ireland
8 Castlecourt Centre
Castleknock
Dublin 15, Ireland

A division of Hachette UK Ltd
Carmelite House, 50 Victoria Embankment, EC4Y 0DZ

www.hachettebooksireland.ie

For Bridget (both Bridgets)

CHAPTER 1

Algarve, Portugal, August 1998

Miriam watched the hat from behind her sunglasses, looking down along the length of her body with its covering of streaky tan and past the tips of her coral-painted toenails to keep it in sight. Blue and white, with a flap at the back to keep the sun from Sarah's neck, it bobbed out there in the distance.

The hat moved slowly, around the edges of the pool. Sarah was playing safely, just as she had been told to.

Miriam lay back, thinking about the time when she would be actually tanned and could let the fake stuff fade away to nothing. She imagined the new skin that would emerge, smooth, glowing, the golden sheen that some of her friends came back with year after year from their trips to Spain, to Italy, France. Miriam and Paul hadn't been away in years, not since Sarah, nearly twelve now, had been born.

'Not this year,' Paul always said, when she suggested it was time to take Sarah farther than Wexford or Cork. 'We can't manage it this year. Maybe next.' He said it so often that Miriam had been surprised to get a different answer. A tentative 'maybe' that she had quickly turned into a 'yes' by finding them a deal, many deals. Deals on flights, on their hotel, the transfers, but only if 'we do it now'.

And so they had two weeks there, beside the pool, a blank blue surface surrounded by pale green deckchairs, with tables discreetly positioned for drinks the hotel hoped they would buy to compensate for the deal they were on. Beyond the pool, the deeper, more changeable blue of the Atlantic beckoned and repelled at once.

Miriam squinted down her legs again, looking for the blue and white hat. There it was, still close to the edge in the shallow bit.

She felt hot and prickly and knew she was burning, but she wanted that tan so badly. The hat was now on the other side of pool and Miriam shifted slightly on her recliner to keep it in view. She wished Paul would come and take over the watching, but he had gone to talk to someone about golf; apparently if you started at the crack of dawn and promised to be finished by the time the big groups arrived there was a better rate.

Sarah could swim – Miriam had made sure of that, taking her for lessons every Thursday in the local pool, even though she always came away with a headache from the noise: a build-up of children shouting and splashing, instructors yelling, hemmed in by the glass roof and thrust back by the tiered concrete seats so that it concentrated into a violent ball. But her daughter wasn't confident in the water – wasn't confident anywhere – and Miriam knew well that she was liable to panic if out of her depth. Panic and flail and possibly sink, rather than staying calm and putting into practice what she had learned.

And so she watched as the little hat bobbed beyond her. But she observed the people around her too, comparing herself, her family, against them.

Most seemed to be English or German but she had heard one or two Irish voices. Paul had nudged her at breakfast that morning, jerking his head towards the centre of the room where a group sat in a beam of early-morning sunlight.

'Luke, for god's sake, stop it,' the woman snapped in a voice that was surprisingly deep, with an unmistakably Irish accent. She seemed to make no attempt to lower her voice and Miriam wondered was she talking to her husband or to one of the four teenage boys who sat around her. None of them responded, so it was impossible to tell. There was a girl too, Miriam saw. About Sarah's age, head bent over a bowl of exotic fruit, the same kinds – pineapple, melon, grapes – that Sarah was eating.

'Step on it,' the woman said then, followed by something snappish about eggs. She had long dark hair and long brown legs and was wearing a frayed and faded denim skirt and a black vest top. She had pushed her chair back from the table and put one of her feet on the bottom rung of the chair beside her so that she sat at an angle to the table.

'Foxrock-Fantastic,' muttered Paul, leaning in to her. But Miriam didn't think he was right.

'Uh-huh,' she muttered back. 'West. Came up to Dublin to do nursing. Met a rich doctor, married him and never went home.'

It was a game they played – making up stories about the people they saw around them – to pass the time, but also, Miriam knew of herself and suspected of Paul, to make themselves feel better. Keep other people in their places; places Paul and Miriam allocated them, that were small and not too threatening.

The woman looked like the kind Miriam might need to work hard at making up stories about. There was something assured and definite in the way she moved and spoke that made Miriam feel that she herself wavered; a carefree indifference in that frayed denim skirt that made Miriam look at her own neatly ironed sundress without the satisfaction with which she had put it on. She wondered had the woman really just thrown on whatever clothes she had first seen, or had she worked for that impression, trying on and discarding other combinations? Miriam wished she knew the answer. It mattered to her.

She leaned in towards Paul. 'Not a doctor. A lawyer. Barrister. The pompous kind.'

CHAPTER 2

Sarah stayed at the edges of the pool as she'd been told, dipping in and out of patches of shade, even though she had her hat on, keeping obediently away from the sparkling centre where the water was deep and the sun shone hot and bright. Where she was, the water slapped the blue-tiled sides in greeting, high-five after high-five. She crept one hand over the other, inching along through the water's thin resistance. She could swim, but she didn't dare, not there, where everyone else seemed to cut through the blueness as if they belonged in it, shouting, splashing, jumping.

One girl was even turning handstands in the water, throwing herself down again and again, bottom up like a duck, then legs emerging straight up like two giant fingers held aloft, before she flipped over and righted herself, swooping back up to the surface with her eyes shut and water streaming from her face.

Sarah thought her name must be Jenny – she had heard a

woman, her mother, shouting something at her at breakfast, something loud, but much less cross than you would expect from the loudness. 'Step on it,' the mother had called at her, down a table where everyone except the two of them had been boy or man; brothers and father, Sarah supposed. 'I didn't come all the way to Portugal to sit and watch people eating fried eggs.'

'I'm eating fruit,' the girl had said, not seeming to mind the shouting.

'I didn't mean you,' the mother said. 'I meant all these other people.' She gestured around the room, didn't seem to care who could see or hear her. 'Come on, hurry up.'

'Horrible fried eggs,' one of the brothers said then. 'Greasy and flat. No yolk.'

'That's the way they make them here,' the father had said. 'Be glad you get anything at all.' He had shaken his newspaper as he said it, angry or joking, Sarah couldn't tell.

She had been fascinated. Her own parents, when they spoke to each other in places like restaurants, did it in a whisper. They leaned close in, heads nearly touching, and said things quietly to each other. Sometimes they gestured with a shoulder or discreet inclination of chin or roll of eyes towards another table, and they often laughed at whatever it was the other had said, in a way that Sarah could see was a bit mean.

'Never you mind,' they said when she asked what they were talking about. As if she were too young, too little a part of them, to be told.

As she watched, the girl – Jenny? – pulled herself out of the pool in one go. She was wearing a navy two-piece, a bikini.

Sarah knew *her* mother would never have let her wear such a thing. Even though really it was only a top and shorts, her mother would say it wasn't suitable for a girl of eleven.

The girl had long messy blonde hair that fell down past her shoulders, nothing like Sarah's neat square bob. The girl's hair was thick and curly, with something of the glow of gold to it. It made Sarah think of the story of the Miller's Daughter, only in reverse, as though the captive had gone backwards in her fear and confusion – the kind of thing Sarah could imagine herself doing – and spun gold into supple, shining straw.

The girl went to the diving board and Sarah watched as she dived off. It wasn't that her dive was good – it wasn't much of a dive, more a tumble – but that she did it without hesitation, and came up gasping but smiling, brushing water impatiently off her face with both hands. Sarah would have been terrified.

Sarah set off again, hand over hand, around the edge, wondering if they would go to the beach that day, the beach that could be seen from the end of the terrace: a line of brown that was the sand, then a thicker line of deep, sparkling blue. They hadn't the day before – her parents had kept saying 'later' until finally they said it was too late, that they would go tomorrow, and wasn't Sarah happy with the pool? She was, but it was boring, with no one to play with. Her mother just wanted to sit and 'get a tan', and her father spent all his time playing golf or fussing about when to play. At least at the beach, Sarah thought, there would be waves to jump over and sand to build into castles with moats, stones and shells to collect, not this going round and round the edges of a pool.

The shallow bit was full of babies and she hated the way

their nappies filled up with water and hung soggy around their knees. And she felt that people stared at her in the shallows, wondering why she was there, why she wasn't in the middle, being brilliant and diving for goggles and plastic wristbands like the girl in the bikini.

The pool filled up as more and more people finished eating and came outside. There were rubber rings and armbands and one boy with a blow-up crocodile big enough that he could lie right across it. They shouted and laughed and called to each other and in between the grown-ups swam up and down, some slowly with their heads far out of the water like turtles looking for land, Sarah thought, others fast, doing fancy crawls and seeming annoyed when one of the kids got in their way. Others again sat around the edges with their feet dangling in the water, chatting and swinging their legs. There were so many of them now that she couldn't drag herself around the edge any longer because the interruptions to her hand-over-hand were too frequent.

CHAPTER 3

The blue and white hat was still making its slow way around the pool and Miriam felt briefly guilty that she wasn't the kind of mother who invented loud, exciting games, with water and stones and five different buckets. Probably the mother from breakfast was. Or at least the type to kick a ball or organise rounders. But it was so hard with just one – no whirling centrifugal excitement that could build and sweep everyone along. Just Sarah saying 'OK' quietly to whatever Miriam suggested.

The child preferred playing alone, Miriam told herself, making little families out of bits of sticks or leaves that she collected: a father, mother, daughter and siblings; always siblings. Sometimes a sister, more often brothers, giving them names and personalities. Often, she sucked the middle two fingers of her left hand, a habit left over from early childhood, between whispering her little plots and narratives, so that she looked much younger than she was.

Miriam went back to thinking about the things she'd seen in the market the day before. The heavy linen tablecloths embroidered in bright thread with gorgeous swirling patterns and knots of colour, the bold ceramic dishes in yellow and blue and orange. How she had longed to buy them, but Paul had said no, that they could barely afford the hotel and certainly couldn't be going around buying plates and bowls, and, anyway, how would they get them home?

The hat was closer now and Miriam watched as it rose out of the water. She sat up to wave to Sarah, call her over to put a T-shirt on – the girl was so pale, 'milk-bottle white', as Paul said – then realised that it was the wrong hat. It wasn't Sarah under the stripes, but a different girl, younger, dark-haired where Sarah was light, who hauled herself out of the pool even as Miriam watched and ran over to a woman with a baby on her lap and an untidy bag at her feet. Where was Sarah? Miriam scanned the water rapidly, wondering how long had she had the wrong hat in sight.

Only as she flicked her eyes from one side to the other did she realise how crowded the pool had become since she had been lying, sun-drugged, on the recliner. When Sarah had gone in, it had been an expanse of smooth blue broken by occasional groups. Now, it boiled, frantic with people. Swimming, laughing, splashing, shrieking, diving in and out of the water, crossing Miriam's line of vision, shifting perpetually in front of her so that she saw only in snatches, not clearly, like trying to read a page that had been shredded. Not one of them was her daughter. Sarah's pale shoulders, the pink swimsuit and the right blue and white hat were nowhere.

Knowing she was looking too fast, not properly, eyes skipping from group to group, Miriam forced herself to slow down, go back, scan carefully.

Nothing. She went back again, even slower, checking sizes, shapes, colours for the familiar, the correct, form: No. No. No.

At what point, she wondered, already standing up, would she start to scream? To run and wave her arms and shout 'My daughter!' 'My daughter!' She began to walk, but slowly still, pulling against the frantic thump of her heart that urged her to go faster, ready to stop and smile once she caught sight of Sarah's earnest little face, creased into the expression of wary concentration the child brought to everything she did.

She saw the lifeguard, the only one who seemed to be on duty, at the farthest end of the pool, chatting – of course – to a girl in a high-cut hot-pink bikini. Around them stood more young men, also laughing, stomachs taut, shoulders back. In the pool, a kid with a blow-up crocodile was trying to stand up on it and wobbling madly. Beside him, two men threw a gaily striped ball back and forth between them.

Not one of them would have noticed if her daughter had slipped quietly below that boiling surface. Sarah, Miriam knew, would not make a fuss. Would not thrash and scream, would be too embarrassed to draw attention to herself even if she needed that attention to stay alive. That small and shuttered face would simply dwindle, falling further and deeper, fading into the empty wet.

Miriam started to run.

CHAPTER 4

Sarah squinted upwards, even though she knew she wasn't supposed to look at the sun in case it burned her eyes. She wanted to see if the sky was still entirely blue – everyone went on about how great that was, but Sarah found the never-ending blueness of it made her upset. Imagine if everything was reversed suddenly and you had to live there, she thought. There would be nowhere to hide, no bit of anything – no cloud, no mist or fog – to pull around yourself. It was like a desert, where the stretched-out yellow of sand became blue, and just as pitiless. She wanted to get out of the pool, go to her mother, but knew that there was nothing to do there either. She had already finished the three books she'd been allowed to bring with her.

'I'll swim underwater to the steps,' she decided, 'then I'll get out.' She needed to earn her release from the pool, where she knew she should be enjoying herself but wasn't. If she managed to make it to the steps, it would be OK to go and sit beside her mother for a while. Then maybe it would soon be dinnertime.

She pulled her goggles over her eyes, even though they were loose and let in water, and slipped under the surface. The knocking-out of noise was wonderful. It wasn't gone completely, but it slid into a dim background boom that was more like waves crashing on a beach than the sharp screaming and shouting when her head was up above the surface. She ducked up and down a few more times, liking the contrast: sharp, dim, sharp, dim, then set off, avoiding the thrashing legs around her, weaving through columns of bubbles, tumbled white and frothy. Down here, the pool was cool and mysterious. A place where things moved at different speeds, where something strange might approach, then swerve away, as if she had a protective force-field around her.

Sarah swam, trying to kick her feet like a dolphin tail, neat and together, in case that propelled her faster, more smoothly, along.

She blinked at the water that snuck in around the not-tight-enough edges of her goggles, then closed one eye as that side filled nearly completely.

She reached the steps, shiny metal in all that blue, with her lungs bursting, and had reached a hand for the lowest rung, when someone jumped between her and it and spun her around, and when they were gone and she reached out again, she found she didn't know where the rail was that she could grip onto and pull herself up. Her goggles were so fogged and filled with water that no metallic gleam came to her through them. She spun again in case she saw something that would tell her what to do but there was nothing, only deeper fog. Around her on every side were legs and bottoms in togs, a cage of thrashing limbs, but she couldn't see the edge of the pool, the place where water might end and the air she needed could be found. She turned more frantically now, trying to understand where was up and where was down and her heart was throbbing too big and too slow inside her as if there wasn't room for it and it must burst; her lungs were hurting, searching through the little air they had for something they could use and there was nothing, just the stale bits already squeezed of oxygen and used up.

She reached out and grabbed at a leg, an ankle, belonging to one of the people sitting on the edge. Behind the leg, so that the heel drummed against it, was the hard end-wall of the pool but Sarah no longer knew what to do to make that something she could use. The wall was there, but she didn't understand how to reach it, or what to do if she did. She was lost, down there in the sly blue where bodies thrust themselves in front and behind her without warning. She couldn't tell which way she was meant to go. Where was up? How could she get to it? The water held her as surely as if it were made of a million tiny transparent hands.

The owner of the leg kicked her off and she grabbed again, desperate now, knowing that she didn't have time, couldn't afford the shame that stopped her from asking things of strangers, not even a biscuit of a friend's mother in a strange house. Knowing that if someone didn't solve the spinning in her head and pluck her up, then she would drift slowly down and down, like a plaster come unstuck from a grazed knee.

Another hard kick of the leg and she was shaken loose and this time she was falling to where the pool floor sloped towards the deepest middle, where even the boom from above was more silent and the thrashing and swishing of water was less. Where it was smoother and thicker and more difficult to pull against and so she didn't try, just let herself fall as the water wanted her to fall, slowly, quietly, bumbling along the bottom into the drifting well of the deepest point.

And then a hand grabbed at her, missed, grabbed again and hooked around the shoulder of her swimsuit and pulled. Weightless still, she rose upwards as surely as she had fallen downwards and then her head broke the surface and she gulped in air desperately, all the panic that had melted away as she fell to the bottom rushing back over her so that she made a ragged gasping sound that was fear as much as the need for air. She was tugged towards the side so that she could hook an arm over the pool edge, but she couldn't let go the hand that had grabbed her, squeezing it so hard the owner flinched and pulled away, then scrabbled at her goggles, tearing them from her eyes as if they were connected to the pool bottom and might try to drag her down again.

'You don't need to squeeze my hand off.' It was the girl from breakfast, from the diving board, the girl in the navy bikini. Sarah didn't understand what she was saying because of course there was a need. She looked around, for her mother, for someone to whom she could cry and shudder and tell the tale of how she'd nearly died. There was no one, except the incurious, and this girl.

'Lucky for you I'm good at diving,' the girl said. Sarah couldn't answer, could still only gasp, as the thrumming noise in her ears settled from frantic to subdued and she fought the urge to vomit.

'You did need help, didn't you?' the girl asked.

'I nearly drowned,' Sarah managed to say, the enormity of this fact like the slap of a wet towel.

'I thought so,' the girl said happily. 'You grabbed hold of my brother's leg and he thought you were messing. I thought you were too, but then when you did it again, I thought you might not be.'

'You saved me.' Sarah said it wonderingly, because she had been saved. Because it was this girl who had saved her.

They stared at one another, standing in the shallows, both considering. Then the girl turned, as if to go. Sarah thought quickly how to keep her. She wasn't sure she could bear it if the girl left, back to her somersaults and her diving and her brothers, while Sarah went back to creeping round the pool. She imagined them bumping into one another later, maybe in the restaurant, and the girl looking away from her, embarrassed by the memory of Sarah's plight and her own heroics.

'Sarah!' Her mother's voice cut through the screams and yells, as it always did, no matter the competition it faced, hitting Sarah's ears as surely as something aimed from a catapult. 'Sarah!' She was standing by her deckchair, waving urgently. Sarah waved back and the girl turned to look. 'Come here,' her mother's voice came to her, insistent.

'Better go,' the girl said with a smile.

'Come with me?'

'OK.'

Sarah couldn't believe it was that easy – that she had asked, that the girl had said yes.

'What's your name?'

'Jamie. Janine, really,' she made a face, 'but Jamie. You?'

'Sarah.'

'Race you.'

CHAPTER 5

Paul saw his wife sit up, suddenly, and lean forward, hand to her forehead, palm down, shading her eyes as she stared eagerly in front of her. He started to walk faster – she seemed alarmed – and broke into a run when he saw her stand in a sudden movement, sweeping the broad straw sunhat off her head and start forward urgently, at speed, but even as he reached her, she had slowed, then stopped.

'Everything OK?' He tried to sound casual, didn't want her to know that he had seen fear in her movements. Didn't want the people on the chairs around them to feel justified in their eager curiosity.

'Fine.' She smiled at him. 'I couldn't see Sarah for a moment, but I see her now.' She lay back down, arms stretching above her head, seeming relaxed, although he could see a pulse twitching in the hollow of her collarbone, and the red flush across her chest seemed more than just the heat of the day.

They tried to hide from each other how much they worried. Not that either was in any doubt about how the other felt, but in case the open admission of their fears, the naming of these constant terrors – of loss, accident, injury, abduction – should let them loose to roam too freely.

'She'll be fine,' they said to each other when Sarah climbed something, walked along the top of a wall, sped downhill on her bicycle. They smiled when they said it, to show they were at ease with these most usual dangers of childhood, but they were not. Their only child had been too long awaited, had remained too resolutely without brother or sister, for either of them to be other than anxious, for her safety, her happiness. Her self.

'Where is she?' Paul asked now, casually, trying to follow the line of his wife's vision.

'Over there.' She pointed. 'She seems to have made a friend.'

Paul looked to where she was indicating, to where Sarah balanced at the edge of the pool, facing a girl with long blonde hair. The girl was tanned and sturdy where Sarah was pale and thin.

'Great,' Paul said. They both pretended that that, too, was normal. 'What have you been doing?' he asked, easing himself onto the recliner beside her. His shorts, baggy khaki ones that Miriam had bought him barely a week ago, embarrassed him, the way they showed his knees when he sat down. Standing, they were OK, coming almost to his calves, but sitting, they rode up and he had to confront the hard red roundness of his knees that looked, to his eyes, somehow obscene.

'Reading, dozing. It's so gorgeous here. This is the life.' She stretched out and Paul admired the compact leanness of her, the way not an inch of spare flesh crumpled the line of her body. She worked hard at staying fit, with the same driven intensity she brought to everything – an ordered house, the smooth emptying and filling of fridge and freezer, timely arrivals and departures – and before which nearly everything fell into place. Miriam was good at getting what she wanted. Only more children had eluded her, frustrating that ability she had to want so hard that all barriers gave way.

They had wanted and hoped, both of them, for years, until eventually, in the face of a never-ending No, the determination of Miriam's pursuit had been turned aside, onto the house, her hair, her figure, Sarah's clothes and activities. And when Paul tried to find the words to ask if she was sad, to tell her that he was, in ways he didn't really understand, she had made it difficult, assuming an attitude of cool efficiency that he did not dare to disturb.

He reached a hand out now and placed it, flat, on her bare stomach. She moved to shrug him off. 'Too hot.' But she smiled, in a way that made him think of later, of the cool dimness of their hotel bedroom, the casual anonymity that was so much more of a turn-on than the crowded familiarity of home.

'Sure you're not burning?' he asked. 'The sun is very hot. The guy at the clubhouse said it was hotter than usual this week. And your shoulders look a bit red.' It was the wrong thing to say – he knew it as soon as the words left his mouth. She turned away from him, turned her face right away so that she faced the other side of the terrace and all he could see was her ear and the set of her jawbone. She got up, still not looking at him, and called, 'Sarah!'

He saw their daughter turn immediately, as if Miriam had yanked at a thread that connected them.

'Sarah, come here.' Sarah said something then to the blonde girl, and both of them hauled themselves out of the pool and ran over.

'This is Janine.' Sarah gestured, drops flying from her wet arm, to the girl beside her, then fell silent and stared at the ground where puddles were forming from the water that dripped down her thin legs. The girl smiled, at Paul first, then at Miriam.

'Hi.' She grinned at them both and did a kind of half-wave. 'Jamie.'

CHAPTER 6

Why had she said 'Janine', like someone who didn't know her? Why had she not said 'Jamie', like a friend? What would it mean, Sarah wondered, for when they met again later? Would the girl treat her like someone who called her Janine?

She hadn't seemed to mind. Had corrected Sarah in a friendly way, then answered politely when Sarah's parents asked her so many questions that Sarah didn't know how she could bear it. She did bear it, but Sarah hated it. Hated that her parents kept quizzing this girl, because the girl might get cross and hot and want to leave. If only she and Jamie had had time to talk, to make friends properly, before her parents got involved and started asking and asking. Now there was no way to show Jamie that she was on her side, not her parents' side, because she couldn't give her a secret look which would tell her that. They weren't friends enough for secret looks.

The thing was, Jamie was from Dublin, same as Sarah. Was

even from somewhere close to Sarah. Which meant, well, it meant so much that Sarah could hardly bear to think about it.

'What school do you go to?' Miriam had asked, then stiffened so slightly that only Sarah would ever have noticed – she noticed everything her mother did – when Jamie said 'St Assumpta's', because that was the paying one where the girls wore green uniforms with a blazer and a coat, and not just blue polo shirts like at Sarah's school.

'How old are you?' her mother asked next, and Sarah held her breath in case the age was wrong. But it wasn't.

'Eleven,' Jamie said. 'Nearly twelve.'

'The same as Sarah.' Miriam smiled. It turned out their birthdays were only a few weeks apart, both September.

'My mum says it's the best month, because everyone's back from being away on holidays but it's not Christmassy yet.' Jamie turned a cartwheel, so effortlessly that she looked like a puppet tumbling through the air and landing lightly on her feet again. Then she turned another one. She wasn't very good at standing still, Sarah decided.

She couldn't believe Jamie was eleven too, and even though she was excited at that, it worried her. If Jamie was eleven, and she was eleven, why was Jamie able to chat easily to Sarah's parents, whereas Sarah couldn't, while Jamie was there, raise her eyes further than the floaty pink-and-yellow scarf-thing her mother had tied round her waist, staring at the knot, snaking in on itself so the material billowed out on either side, and wait for the talking to stop.

As far back as she could remember, Sarah was used to hearing the word 'shy' around herself. Sometimes it was said outright – 'there's no need to be so shy', as if *need* had anything to do with it, as if she had control over it – sometimes it was mouthed, almost silently, between adults, but somehow Sarah always seemed to catch it as it travelled over her head – and sometimes it wasn't said at all, but hovered in the air around her, changing the way grown-ups spoke to her and the girls in her class played with her.

'You're shy,' the bolder of her classmates said, as if they were saying, 'You have blue eyes. You're tall.' Both those things were true, and unchangeable. And shy was true too, but not unchangeable.

Sarah knew that this word, 'shy', was hers, but she hoped that it wouldn't always be.

'You'll grow out of it,' her mother said, comfortingly, so that Sarah believed her. That she just needed to be a bit older, and the word would drift away, leaving her free to not be it anymore. To be something else. But now here was this girl, Jamie, without anything of 'shy' to her, and she was Sarah's age, even a few weeks younger. Maybe she'd 'grown out' of it already? Maybe Sarah had somehow missed that moment?

Jamie chattered on and Sarah said nothing. She certainly didn't say the main thing that was still in her mind: that Jamie had saved her. That without Jamie, she would still be down there, in that dim and silent place, except that now she would be part of it, bits of her pulled into it so that she dissolved and became water too. She knew that saying it would spoil everything. That the grown-ups would start to fuss and her mother would screech and they would take the secret away from her, take Jamie away by thanking and congratulating and making her tell the story again and again. They would introduce her to people – 'the girl who saved our daughter's life' – and she would be theirs, not Sarah's.

So she said nothing about it, and Jamie said nothing either. Not of that.

At last her mother stopped asking questions and Sarah could see she'd run out of things and there was a pause that made Sarah feel hot and red, and then Jamie asked if Sarah could have dinner with her and her family, just as if it was normal. Sarah had stared at her mother, willing her to say yes, and her mother almost had.

'Well, we'll see,' she had said. 'Maybe I'd better check first with your parents.'

'Oh, they won't mind,' Jamie had said, completely confident. 'My brothers have a friend with them and I was supposed to have as well, but she got sick and couldn't come. Celine. She got chicken pox.'

Sarah blessed the germs that had found their way to this Celine and made her stay at home.

CHAPTER 7

Miriam asked questions, quick and cheerful ones, because she could see that Sarah was unable to. Her daughter stared at the ground, sucking the two middle fingers of her left hand. Her wet hair stuck to her head, so that she was, Miriam thought, like a half-drowned kitten, while this stranger, this new friend with her buoyant curls, looked at Miriam and Paul with frank interest, answering everything asked of her with ease.

Miriam hoped that once the questions and answers flowed, Sarah might conquer her awkwardness and join in, but she didn't. She allowed the conversation to tumble back and forth while she kept her head bowed, scuffing at the green covering of the ground that wasn't grass – more a kind of thick, creeping weed, Miriam had decided, with short, almost fleshy leaves. From a distance, it did a perfect job of being grass, but close up, it was disconcertingly off. Like going to the beach and finding sawdust instead of sand.

'How long have you been here?' Miriam asked.

'Since the day before yesterday,' Jamie said. 'We stayed a night in Lisbon on the way so my parents could make us see a museum.' She rolled her eyes.

'You must have been on the same plane over as us then,' Miriam said. Jamie, she noticed, might look older than Sarah, but the slight hiss to her S's made her sound younger. 'We arrived three days ago. We came straight here. How long are you staying?'

'Two weeks,' Jamie said.

'Same as us.' It was the first time Sarah had spoken since introducing Jamie, and she lifted her head as she said it. Her face, Miriam saw, was filled with hope, and fear. And just as Miriam wondered, a little desperately, what she could do, say, to help her daughter make friends with this self-possessed and confident child – how she could show her daughter in a light that would attract, when so often she had tried and they had both failed – Jamie said, without any encouragement at all, 'Can Sarah come with me and have dinner? We're going into the town later, and my dad said we could have dinner there, that it would be more "authentic"' – she was careful with the word – 'than here. Can Sarah come with us? Please?'

And even though this was moving faster than Miriam had wanted or expected, the way Sarah stared at her then, the silent pleading in her eyes, forced Miriam to say, 'Well, we'll see. Maybe I'd better check first with your parents.'

'They're over here,' Jamie said. 'My mum and my dad. He's back from golf. Come on, Sarah, let's ask now.' She grabbed Sarah's hand and Sarah, instead of looking back or seeming uncertain, let her, even grabbed back, and the two ran off so fast that Miriam had to call after them.

'Wait! I'm coming with you. Just let me get changed.' She pulled a cotton dress out of her bag and stepped into it, then picked up a sunhat, determined that Sarah should put it on – the girl's skin was pink under the white suntan lotion, like the peeled flesh of a prawn.

She should have known, Miriam thought, as she watched Jamie make straight for the woman with the long dark hair from breakfast. Who else could it have been? She slowed her pace, hesitating now. The woman, by doing nothing more than casually admonishing her family earlier, had made Miriam feel that she – the woman – belonged there, would belong everywhere, and Miriam didn't. She imagined the maître d', so smiling to all of them, being extra warm with this family, murmuring, 'Welcome back, Madame,' at her, even as he agreed that, no, nothing had changed, and he hoped they would have as wonderful a holiday as last year.

Miriam wanted to retreat to the safety of her deckchair and Paul, where she could continue to look around her and work it all out – what people did here, how she might do the same things – and where Paul could make the kinds of jokes they both enjoyed and that made them feel better, but she recalled the look on her daughter's face, that mix of hope and uncertainty that had touched her with its hesitancy. So she forced herself to keep moving.

She picked her way through and past other family groups

and all the eager debris of their activities: buckets, rackets, balls of every size from tiny to ridiculously big, past discarded books and towels flung off in haste. Some, those with younger children, had retreated into the shade now, improvising nap times on sunbeds with cool cotton throws, but most disregarded the growing heat of the day and continued to tumble about. Around the smell of food from the hotel kitchens, like an oil slick on water, lay the sickly scent of coconut suntan lotion.

The group Jamie and Sarah had approached and now been absorbed into had arranged themselves in a kind of star shape, so that they seemed to radiate outwards from a central point. It was, Miriam could see, done to keep their faces in the shade of a small tree while their bodies lay in sun, but the effect was strangely defensive, almost militaristic in its formation.

Her daughter and Jamie were now kneeling by the base of the scrawny tree, digging at its roots with sticks. As she watched, Sarah whispered something to Jamie that made them both laugh, and Miriam thought how unusual it was to see so bright an expression on her daughter's face, which normally presented only a careful blank to the casual watcher.

'Hi, I'm Miriam,' she said, approaching the woman with the dark hair, hating that she was standing, leaning slightly forward, while the woman lay at her ease. She wore a black bikini, hair tied back from her face now with a red and white kerchief. Beneath her was a towel of deep moss green, and the way she lay, languidly and half on one side, flesh loose, made Miriam think of a painting of a reclining nude by someone famous. The effect was so studied: the towel, the kerchief, and beside her – prop or real? – a thick and very battered book, pages swollen and sticking out as if someone had pumped them full of air. She snuck a look at the title. *In Search of Lost Time*. Definitely a prop, she decided.

'Maeve.' The woman stood up. She was taller than Miriam, but at least they were both standing now, Miriam thought, deciding she liked this woman for understanding the subtle affront of remaining in her chair. But then the woman didn't say anything else, just looked at her, with a small smile, and Miriam decided that perhaps she didn't like her after all.

'I'm Sarah's mother,' she said, putting out a hand, conscious of the absurd formality of the gesture when they were both in swimwear and around them children flung beach balls and shrieked, babies cried and waiters spun past with trays of cool drinks. 'Our daughters seem to have . . .' Seem to have what? Made friends? Decided to play together for an hour, after which one of them will move on, back to her brothers and her cartwheels, and the other will be left with a small but stubborn wound?

'. . . Seem to have made plans without consulting us,' Maeve finished for her. But she was smiling properly now, so Miriam smiled back.

'They do, and I'm sorry. I should have stopped it in its tracks, but somehow the plan got made before I realised it.'

'That sounds like Jamie alright,' Maeve said, proud, not bothering to hide it. 'She's pretty strong-minded. It's fine with us, if you don't mind? We thought we'd go into town soon, wander round for a bit, then have dinner in one of those fish places on the seafront.'

It was a plan just exactly as Miriam longed to make, down

to every detail. Except Paul had said the seafront restaurants were too expensive, and if they ate away from the hotel, they needed to find somewhere cheap, like the *tascas* that were down grimy backstreets, never in pretty squares or where the crowds were.

'Sounds lovely.' She worked to keep the wistful note out of her voice. 'I'm sure she'd love that, if you really don't mind?'

'Not at all. It'll be nice for Jamie. Too many boys, you know . . .' Only then did Miriam really take in that the chairs around them were filled with sprawling youths, some almost men.

There were four of them and all had slightly longish hair, in shades of dark blond and light brown, and were, she thought, like a pride of lions, golden, indolent, watchful, with their mother, protected and protective, at their centre. One, the youngest by the look of him, observed her through a half-open eye, though he made no move to acknowledge her.

'Can I give you some money?' she said. 'To pay for Sarah's meal?'

'Goodness, no.' Maeve recoiled a little so that Miriam knew it had been the wrong thing to say. 'She does eat fish, doesn't she?'

'Actually, she doesn't eat much of anything,' Miriam said, looking at her daughter's thin back in the pink swimsuit. 'But yes, she quite likes fish.'

'Good. We won't be late back. Come and meet my husband, Simon.'

CHAPTER 8

'This is Sarah. Can she come for dinner with us? Her mum said she could if it's OK with you. They live near us, and I said it would be, that you wouldn't mind.' Maeve was half-asleep, lulled by heat and food and the wine from lunch and Proust's endless sentences, when Jamie burst into demands beside her without explanation in that way she did.

'What?' Maeve struggled to sit up. Her back was bad since the plane, and moving position, especially from lying to sitting, caused it to tighten into an angry knot just where neck moved into shoulder.

'Sarah. Can she come for dinner?'

'But, darling, we haven't even decided where we're going yet . . . ' Jamie was holding onto a pale girl in a pink swimsuit who looked as if she could do with a T-shirt on, Maeve thought. She had seen the child earlier, on her own with bits of sticks she was arranging by size into little groups, and had thought of sending Jamie over to see if she wanted to play. But there had been something about the girl's playing, something so complete in the self-containment she showed, that Maeve had decided not to. It would, she thought, have been like breaking one of the spider webs you found in the early mornings in Kerry – covered in dew so that every thread glistened and what was no more than mess to be swept away from an inside corner of a house became, outside, a tiny, painstaking piece of beauty.

Now, the girl, Sarah, didn't look at Maeve. She kept her eyes on Jamie, as if Jamie were something strange and wonderful she had read about but had never expected to actually see.

'Jamie, I don't know . . .' Maeve wanted to stop this thing, scotch it, before it began. But she caught sight of the dismay on Sarah's face, the rising flush of red and the way the child turned, ready to run away at the first hint of 'no', and found she couldn't continue. Instead she veered into, 'Why don't you give your dad and me a minute to decide, then come back and we'll see. Here' – she reached for her bag – 'go and buy an ice-pop in the meantime. You can both get one.'

Jamie grabbed the money – far too much, Maeve knew, wondering how much change would make it back – and said, 'OK, come on, Sarah.'

Maeve lay down again, hoping they would get bored of each other and the silly dinner plan would be abandoned. She picked up Proust again and wondered when she had lost the ability to read for longer than a few minutes without her thoughts veering away – to what she needed to do or buy or sign, or to someone who had to be collected or dropped off or reminded about mouthguards and shin guards. The boys boarded during the week, but even so, she never felt free of their demands, the thousand necessities of their schoolboy lives. Some mothers she knew relished this – as proof of their usefulness, perhaps – but Maeve did not.

She looked across at her husband. Simon lay asleep on his back with his mouth open. His stomach rose up out of his shorts like an anthill, sudden and surprising. He had put on so much weight that now, when they made love, she moved to lie on top of him.

'You'll crush me,' she had murmured, trying to laugh, knowing how much he would hate what she said, what she implied.

'Hi, I'm Miriam.' It was the girl's – Sarah's – mother.

CHAPTER 9

Simon rolled onto his back, trying to block out the sound of his wife talking to the mother of Jamie's new friend. Everywhere they went, Jamie made friends, dragging them back to picnic blankets and park benches, like a cat with a bird or mouse, for her family to admire and exclaim over. And the friends, he reflected, were often as bedraggled and limp as a mauled mouse or bird. This one, he thought, looked worse than most. So white, she was see-through, thin enough that even walking looked like it was an effort for her, and silent beside Jamie's energetic chatter.

The mother, he thought, lying deep in the day's heat, was thin too, probably just as pale under that streaky layer of orange, but there was something coiled and sprung about her that gave her edge where the daughter was just a meek blur.

And now Jamie wanted the girl to join them for dinner, and Maeve had said yes. The problem with Jamie was that she tired easily of her birds and mice, abandoning them abruptly. Which might mean another ten days of avoiding the reproachful gaze of the mother as they skirted pool and dining room.

He wished Maeve had said no, and some excuse as to why 'it would be nice, but not this time, because . . . ' Except that he knew Jamie would simply have come straight to him and asked, 'Please, Dad?' with that look that said she knew he wouldn't let her down, and so he would have said, 'Fine,' rolling his eyes at Maeve as he silently pretended to deplore all the ways in which his daughter was 'just like' him.

Jamie threw herself at everything as though catching a moving train: fast, hard, urgent. The Girl Who Knew No Fear they called her, after a story Maeve knew about a boy who could not feel fear, until someone tipped a bucket of goldfish down his back and he finally learned the physical sensations – the squirming feeling of flesh that creeps – and then was frightened of everything.

'Simon, this is Miriam.' He lifted his head. Was Maeve mad? Why must he, too, be dragged into this friendship? He needed to make a phone call, she knew that. He had told her at breakfast. There was a deal he had to keep an eye on. An offer made that he expected to be accepted, that needed his word in order for the next stage to begin.

'Hi,' Miriam said. She was smaller than his wife, lean where Maeve was round, with careful hair and make-up. He wondered was the make-up waterproof – Simon prided himself on noticing small things – then decided that no, she simply wouldn't ever swim.

'Hi.' He half sat up but she seemed to expect more, standing there in her jungle-patterned cotton dress, so he got himself into a sitting position, conscious suddenly that the effort was more than it should have been. Maeve was right, he was getting fat.

'Having a good holiday?' He didn't know what to say to her, couldn't remember the name of her daughter, even though Jamie had introduced them just minutes earlier. He hoped she wouldn't be chatty, keep them all there too long while she enthused, or complained, about the hotel.

'Yes, thanks,' she said. 'You?'

'Oh yes. We love this place.' He was conscious that he sounded like the kind of man he disliked, someone insincere and hearty.

'Thank you for taking Sarah out. I hope it won't be any trouble.' Sarah, that was her name.

'Oh, no trouble at all. Don't worry, she'll be safe with us.' Why had he said that, he wondered as she smiled and walked away. Why say she would be safe, when all it did was admit the possibility that she might not be safe?

'Did you have to?' he muttered to Maeve as he lay back down.

'You didn't see her face,' Maeve said. 'Poor little thing. I couldn't say no.'

'She'd get over it,' he said. 'Jamie's tough.'

'Not Jamie. The friend. Sarah.'

'Right,' he said. 'Well it's your funeral.' Again, something in him winced at the words he chose. 'I mean . . .'

'I know what you mean,' she said. She smiled, her face warm in the shaded fuzzy glow of afternoon sun. 'It'll be fine.'

CHAPTER 10

Jamie's brothers were as loud as fireworks, shouting at each other and wrestling like explosions. Sarah felt frightened of them at first, but when she saw Jamie pushing through them casually, as though they were sheep in a field and she a farmer, Sarah decided to try the same approach.

'Get off,' she said to one brother, the youngest one, who was thirteen, Jamie said, and whose name was Jake, giving a gentle shove when he bumped into her during some kind of a pushing game with another brother. It seemed to be the right approach.

'Sorry,' he grinned, 'it's Luke's fault.' Luke was fourteen and might as well have been a proper grown-up, Sarah thought, with his deep voice and salty, sweaty smell. Then there was one called Alan, the oldest by, Jamie said, four years and so far from Sarah that he may as well have been standing on top of a mountain, she thought. And there was a friend too, Ian; skinny and spotty, Sarah saw.

The brothers all looked like Jamie, the same combinations of blond, slightly stiff hair, brown skin and smudges of freckles. Only the mother was dark. The dad was blond too but without the tanned skin. He was red across the back of his neck, except for the creases within the fat of it which were white and stood out like line markings on a road when he stretched his head.

The dad didn't say much to Sarah, just 'hello', so that she didn't feel she needed to say anything except hello back. But he was very talkative with his own children, asking them questions about things they saw – tiles, boats, things they had read or should have read – as if it were a never-ending quiz.

'Who can tell me the name of the dictator of Portugal?' he asked at one stage, then was annoyed when no one answered him. 'Why do I pay for you to go to expensive schools if you can't answer a simple question?' he demanded as the older boy, Alan, rolled his eyes. Sarah saw the mother, Maeve, duck her head then and whisper into the ear of Jake, who had bumped into her.

'Salazar,' Jake shouted.

'You had help,' Simon answered, looking at his wife but not really angry.

'We could ask you questions too,' the middle brother, Luke, said. 'And bet you couldn't answer. Like, who wrote '911 Is a Joke'' and he started singing in an exaggerated American accent. 'I'll give you a clue: it's not Vanilla Ice.' The friend, Ian, sniggered with him and they both started walking in a slouchy way and waving their arms wildly at each other.

'Cheeky pup,' Simon said, and now he was angry. A bit, anyway. Until Jamie made up a rhyme about Salazar to distract him. Sarah wondered did she do it on purpose.

'There once was a dictator called Salazar,' Jamie said in a loud sing-song, 'Who spent too much time at the salad bar . . .'

This made her dad laugh and pull her head in towards his side as they walked. 'Not bad,' he said. 'So what's next?'

And Jamie faltered then, demanding, 'I don't know. What comes next?' so that Luke added 'His people got cross' and then, when they were all stuck, Sarah chipped in, so quietly that only Jamie heard her 'Because they needed a boss . . .' Whereupon Jamie shouted, 'That's good!' and repeated it, loudly, while they all cheered, even Simon, and let Sarah finish with 'So they got rid of that dictator called Salazar!'

Sarah couldn't believe she'd done it. It wasn't really any good – she had spent too much time alone making up little poems and songs not to know that – but she loved that she'd said it out loud, so someone could hear her, instead of in her head, the way she usually did, running entire conversations that would never be spoken.

They walked along a winding road that had shops and cafés and restaurants on one side and the sea on the other, flicking itself endlessly against the stone wall that halted it, as though it wanted to build enough momentum to get out. Sarah imagined it pouring up and over in one shiny mass, like honey tipped from a jar or a snake slithering out of a tub, and heading – where? To find more sea, presumably. Wasn't that what water did? Searched endlessly for bigger bits of itself? Like people, she thought suddenly. Looking to join bigger groups, noisier groups, where you could feel safe.

She was part of one of those groups now, she thought. Big

and noisy and complete in itself, not like the little group of three she was with her parents, where it always felt like there was a side exposed, through which came cold air and other people's cold looks.

There were little boats bobbing and clinking in the water, pretty ones in blue and green and yellow, with long, curved noses that reached up and out of the water towards the sky as though their faces were turned upwards to the sun. The noise they made with their bits of rope and metal as they rolled and righted themselves against the slap of waves cheered Sarah with its jolly regularity: *we're alright*, the clinking said. *We'll always be alright.*

It was hotter here than in the hotel, she decided. Or not so much hotter as stiller. Even though there were cars and little motorbikes that sounded like angry wasps and people in the shops, the village was asleep, and happy to be so. The hotel couldn't sleep. It was too anxious in case someone wanted something it didn't have. The waiters were always moving around so they didn't look lazy, and the guests were thinking about more things that they might need and ask for.

She tried to imagine what it might be like to live there, in that village, and couldn't. So she asked Jamie.

'You couldn't live here,' Jamie said, completely certain.

'Oh.'

'What would you do?' Jamie looked around. 'Where would you go to school?'

'Where the other kids go to school?'

'You couldn't.' Again that certainty. Sarah wondered was it because of the language – that they didn't speak Portuguese –

and wanted to try and explain that, in her mind, if you lived there, you would speak Portuguese because you'd be from there, but she found it too complicated so she said nothing and after a minute Jamie ran ahead, to her mother, leaving Sarah on her own at the back.

They walked as far as they could, out to the end of the little port where there was a jetty and on the other side of that were more fishing boats. These ones were bigger and rustier and stank of fish and rotted rope.

'It's a working village,' Simon said in satisfaction when he saw them. He was leaning far out over the low wall and his forearms were strong and covered in white hairs that caught the evening sun so that his arms shone, as if he was wearing armour, Sarah thought. 'A proper fishing village. Not just for tourists.'

They walked back and Simon let Jamie choose the restaurant, giving her no instructions about not too expensive or trying to direct her at all. She picked one where the front was painted sky-blue and pink, and when they went and sat down and were given menus, Simon said it was a good choice.

The unashamed favouritism he showed Jamie confused Sarah, who had no siblings but believed in the idea of parents loving equally. And being loved equally. Her own contortions to show no preference, to offer identical affection to her mother and father, were one of the most difficult parts of her life, one she assumed responsibility for as solemnly as if it were a job.

Sarah and Jamie sat at the end of the table, where Sarah expected they would be ignored and could talk just to each other, but instead the questions continued and now, it seemed, she was included.

'What do you like best about Portugal?' Simon asked.

Sarah thought for a long time. 'The pool.'

'That's not Portugal,' Luke said scornfully. 'The pool could be anywhere. It could be our back garden.'

'Except we don't have a pool,' Maeve said.

'You know what I mean.'

'Why shouldn't she like the pool best?' Maeve said. 'I'm sure Jamie does too.'

'Do you, Jamie?' Luke demanded.

'No.' Sarah wished and wished she had said yes. Had reached down into the place where Sarah felt she was alone and watched and joined her. 'I like the mini croissants for breakfast.'

They all laughed and Sarah felt Jamie had done even more than join her – she had laid a different trail and led the hunt away from her.

A girl brought them bread in baskets, and after she left, Luke said she was a looker.

'Don't tell us,' Maeve said. 'Where's the good of that? Tell her.'

'Or do you want me to tell her for you,' the brother called Alan said.

'Don't you dare,' Luke said, looking not scornful but alarmed now, and when the girl came back towards them, with wine and water, he left the table to go to the loo so quickly that Sarah knew he was afraid. When he came back, he covered up by teasing her. To show he didn't care.

'So, you're the new stray?' he said loudly, and when Sarah looked at him, he said, 'Jamie's always doing this. Picking up stray dogs and cats, and girls.' He pretended he was saying it as a joke, a nice kind of tease, but Sarah saw he was angry that he had been laughed at and wanted to take his anger away by hurting her.

Jake must have felt sorry for her, because he said, 'Give it up, Luke,' and started showing Sarah and Jamie things on the menu he thought they would like, but Luke carried on.

'She always has something,' he said. 'Once, we went to Greece and she found this cat, a skinny little ginger thing, and made friends with it and fed it every day. When we were leaving, she wanted to bring the cat with her and cried when she couldn't.'

'Luke . . .' Maeve said, like it was a warning, but Luke ignored her. 'Dad had to pay the man who owned the restaurant to take care of the cat.' He started laughing, looking around, waiting for everyone else to join in. They didn't.

'He said he would,' Jamie said, face getting red. 'He promised that he'd feed her. I called her Shadow.'

'Yes, I can just imagine that he took great care of her.' Luke laughed all the harder, making the word *great* sound like the opposite of itself. Jamie looked like she might start to cry. 'And now you've got a new shadow; only a girl this time.'

'Luke!' The warning note was gone from Maeve's voice, replaced with a coldness that made Luke mutter, 'I'm only joking' and something about 'people don't understand having a laugh . . .'

'Don't mind him,' Jamie whispered. 'He's like a rugby god at school or something. It makes him mean.'

The food came and it was awful. The fish had eyes and bones and a dry crispy tail and was covered in a greyish batter rather than appearing in neat squares covered with golden breadcrumbs. And the chips weren't chips – they were just thick lumps of potato, fried in oil that tasted strange to Sarah. She sat miserably, staring at her plate, until Jake noticed and said, 'Here, give that to me.' He took the plate and said, 'Now, don't look. Close your eyes for a minute.' When she opened them, her plate was back in front of her but the fish had been taken apart so that the head and tail were gone, bones too, and it sat before her with its white flesh exposed, so that it looked more normal. The chips looked the same but were fewer so that she felt she could make something of eating them.

'Vinegar,' Jake handed her a white jar with a spoon in it. 'They don't put it on chips here, just on salad, but sprinkle some on the chips and they'll taste more like you're used to.' His own plate was piled high with her unwanted chips.

'Thank you,' she said. Mostly, she was grateful for the speed and stealth with which he had acted, so that only the two of them were involved. The rest of the table were still busy with 'Can you pass me the salt' and 'Your chicken looks good'. She was especially glad Luke hadn't noticed. She knew he would have said something mean.

'So it was you who grabbed my leg,' Jake said then. Sarah looked up quickly, in case he was going to mock her.

'Yes,' she said, not knowing what else to add.

'I'm sorry I kicked you off. I didn't know.'

'It's OK. Jamie saved me.'

'Good for Jamie.'

CHAPTER 11

Trust Jake, Maeve thought, watching her youngest son awkwardly stripping Sarah's fish from its bones and arranging it neatly on her plate, his thin elbows sticking out on either side as he worked, like a grasshopper's knees. Trust him to notice and to do something kind. Luke would have ignored, or jeered, or, if it was something he wanted, reached across the table and helped himself. She smiled at Jake, who smiled back, rolling his eyes slightly at Sarah, now picking carefully at tiny bits of fish.

Looking around the table, Maeve was struck, suddenly, by the way Sarah seemed to fit amongst them, as if there was space just for her; for her size and shape and rather wispy personality; the way her own children moved up a bit, enough to make room for her amongst them.

She smiled at Sarah, and the girl, looking up suddenly and seeing, smiled back. It had been Sarah who had brought back the change from the ice pops earlier. 'Your money,' she said, holding out a few coins, sticky with heat and the melting pop.

'Thank you, Sarah,' Maeve had said. 'I know Jamie would never have remembered.'

'I remembered for her,' Sarah said, squirming a little with embarrassment and, Maeve thought, the pleasure that approval brought.

Simon called for more wine, ignoring the look on his wife's face that would have told him, in a way he couldn't ignore, that she thought he had had enough. He knew she wouldn't say anything there, in front of their children and their children's friends, but also that she would certainly bring it up later.

'You're too fat and you're drinking too much,' she had said just days before, with the bluntness that had first attracted him to her because it was so unlike the careful dissembling of the other girls he knew back then, who tried to make you work to find out what they meant. Maeve told you, and looked you in the eye as she did so. It was the way Simon tried to be in business and mostly was. But when the bluntness was harsh and turned on him, he liked it less.

She was right, he knew that – his own laboured breath after climbing stairs or walking uphill, his bloodshot eyes in the mornings as he shaved, told him the same – but he hated that she said it. Hated the way he must look in her eyes for her to say such a thing. And yet, hearing it now in his head as he avoided looking at her, he felt angry, the words *what right?* forming and running circles inside him.

He found himself thinking about Jamie's friend's mother. What was her name again? Mary? Marina? Something like that. There was a look she had – he'd known a girl like that once. Skinny. Tough. Sexy too.

Luke was jeering at Ian, who was technically Jake's friend – in his class at school – but had, this holiday, showed what Simon considered a deplorable tendency to suck up to Luke and be nasty to Jake. Ian wouldn't come away with them again, Simon decided. He was a spineless fool and a bad friend.

'What's so funny?' he demanded of Luke, who was still hooting with laughter.

'I'm just remembering Ian's "dive" off the high diving board,' Luke said, making quote marks in the air with his fingers. Simon was annoyed by the jeering and the stupid quote marks that were new and American and rude but in a flimsy, indirect way.

'And I suppose your "dive" was "perfect",' he snapped, doing his own quote marks with thicker, angrier fingers so that Luke stopped laughing and gave him a hurt look.

'I was only having a joke,' he said.

'Well, don't have nasty jokes,' Simon said. 'Not unless you can take getting nasty jokes back.'

'Simon…' Maeve said, so that he did look at her, and saw the expression that said *you've had too much to drink and you're being unpleasant*.

Sometimes, they were alien to him, these children who were his and whom he loved. They baffled him with their determined buoyancy, their vocabulary of rap songs and strange slang. They worried him – he couldn't see anything in them that reminded him of himself; not at their age, which he barely remembered, or any age.

Maeve had told him once how it worked with Luke – that each time he shouted or snapped at the boy, he drew further away from him, approaching again with even more wariness, cloaked in that self-serving bluster that Simon hated. 'So it's my fault?' Simon had asked.

'It's no one's fault,' Maeve had said, 'but you can mend this, he can't.' And Simon had tried, for a while, until he felt that trying got him nowhere and he had stopped.

When he saw his children, like now, sitting around him, over a meal he would pay for, making jokes that were foolish and pretentious, asking for food and drink with an assurance he had been years learning, he disliked them, but more: he feared for them. Feared that once his protection was removed, the world would simply swallow them up. All except Jamie, the child of his heart.

Or maybe, he thought, his gloom was because he was drunk and felt strange. That was how Maeve interpreted these moods when he spoke of them to her. 'You've drunk too much,' she would say, calm. 'You don't really feel that. You'll see. It'll be gone tomorrow.' And usually it was.

But before that, before the mood was gone, he would have snapped or, worse, shouted, the rumble of his anger crashing over them, pushing them down as surely as if they had been kittens and his the hand that rubbed their noses in whatever mess they had made. His anger exhausted him, just as it upset them, so that he swore he wouldn't give in to it, not again. But he did.

'Dad, can we have dessert?' That was Jamie, piping up from the end of the table; Jamie, towards whom his rage was never turned, who had never felt fear of him. Beside her, the friend looked scared, eyes as big as full moons. Jake, on the other side, hung his head over his plate which was full of fish bones and chips.

'Finish your dinner, Jake,' Simon said.

'I am finished.' Jake didn't lift his head as he spoke.

'You haven't. I don't take you to restaurants so you can pick at your food and leave half of it behind.'

There was a silence then and now the table was full of bent heads and averted eyes. Jake hadn't moved, so Simon leaned forward, shoulders hunched thick around his ears, ready to repeat his order, louder, when suddenly the friend, the girl with the full-moon eyes, said in a voice that was rushed and small and hoarse, more breath than voice really: 'They're mine. The chips. I didn't want them. He took them.' She looked at Jamie as she spoke, but her voice was loud enough, just, for them all to hear.

And in the air suddenly was relief that Simon couldn't interpret. The wine had blunted him, but he knew that he was at the centre of it somehow, him and this girl.

'Dad! Can we have dessert?' Jamie again.

Simon stared at Maeve, who stared back, a warning in her face, then picked up his wine glass, stained and blotchy with fingerprints, the rim greasy with the outline of his lips. Inside the glass, a tiny fly struggled in the wine, a speck of black in a sea of red. Still looking at Maeve, he raised the glass to his mouth and drained it, fly and all.

'Yes. Dessert!' he said, almost thumping the empty glass on the crisp cream linen tablecloth. 'Let's see if they have custard tart. The Portuguese are famous for custard tarts.'

He grabbed Maeve's hand and held it with both of his and she let him.

CHAPTER 12

Miriam and Paul sat facing each other over one of the small tables-for-two in the hotel restaurant. The room was badly lit, with strips of harsh light overhead that reminded Miriam of hospital corridors, so that she couldn't understand why the hotel didn't dim them. The lights were uneven and left patches of obscurity in which other diners moved occasionally, like something rustling in undergrowth. The room was quiet – it was grown-ups' dining hour – and Miriam decided she missed the earlier family sitting, where the roar of noise and endless negotiations over vegetables and ice-cream covered the poor scraps of conversation.

'If you're having the fish, we should have white,' said Paul, who was trying so hard to make the dinner an occasion because it was just the two of them.

'Whatever you like. I really don't mind,' she said, then realised it was the wrong response. That she should have pretended to care, should have bent over the wine list and made a show of choosing with him something perfect to match the food.

They sat at a window table and outside the slow descent of the sun from the sky made Miriam sad, as if it were taking her with it. In the sun's wake, the air changed to a thick orange, like marmalade that had been boiled too long, and there was a smell of burning that felt like it came straight from the weary sun itself.

She felt exposed and lonely and wished she were home. At this hour, she would have cleared dinner, made Sarah's lunch for the morning and be looking forward to watching TV. Here, because she had done nothing all day, she felt she deserved nothing, no hour or two that she could call a reward and feel she had earned, but she couldn't understand the source of her gloom. She dug around inside herself and tried to isolate what it was that was making her uncomfortable – almost physically so; she kept glancing over her shoulder as if something might sneak up on her – but could find nothing more than an unreasonable fear of the moment when the sun would finally disappear.

She wondered did it have to do with earlier when she hadn't been able to find Sarah, when she had raked through every group trying to see her and found only unknown faces, grotesque in their indifference, so that panic had bloomed – a panic that was itself a kind of recognition of every unquiet moment she had spent since Sarah's birth: *So this is how it happens*, she had thought deep within herself; *this is it.* As if the moment itself – the tragedy – were inevitable and only the time and nature of its arrival had been in any doubt.

She hated that her immediate assumption was not outrage, but *of course*. As if Sarah had never been hers to keep, and she had always known it.

And then she had found her, and the panic had slumped back down, like a dog expecting a walk, delirious with energy, when its owner leaves the house without it after all. She had felt weak in the aftermath, then exhilarated, with the words, *Not yet, Not this time*, running triumphantly through her. But maybe the panic had left some residue that crawled up into her throat now?

She put a hand up to the place where her neck and chest met, under the curve of her jawbone, as if she might be able to feel the thing there, whatever it was.

'Are you OK?' Paul asked.

'Fine. Hot.' She wasn't, but it seemed the right thing to say.

A waiter came then and closed the window behind her without a word so that Miriam thought of challenging him, demanding that it stay open 'to let in a breeze', then decided she couldn't be bothered. Maybe closing the window would shut out some of the anxiousness the evening seemed to bring. It certainly lessened the smoky smell.

She shifted in her seat to give herself more of a view of the room, less of the darkening sky with its fiery vanishing point. She wished Sarah were with them. Not that her chatter would have been distracting, because she didn't chatter, but because worrying about her and her happiness would have distracted Miriam from thinking about her own.

'We should have pretended Sarah was coming along and got a bigger table,' she said.

'I could ask them to move us,' Paul said immediately, looking around.

'No, it's fine.'

'What time is she back?'

'I'm not sure.. They didn't say. But it was after four by the time they finally left, so not for a while I'd say.'

'Right.'

Paul hadn't been happy when she had come back without Sarah, with no more than news of a plan he hadn't agreed to and didn't approve of.

'We don't know anything about them,' he had said, looking around as if information might be revealed to him; as if, Miriam thought, a man in a shabby suit and trilby hat might step from behind a tree with a notebook full of particulars. 'Why can't they just play here together? Why do they need to take Sarah off with them?'

Trying to explain, Miriam had found herself struggling, and so she got cross, snapping, 'Well, you're not exactly doing much with her, are you?' so that he had looked hurt and muttered, 'I brought us here, didn't I?'

She had tried to say something soothing then – she couldn't bear a row, not here, where there was nowhere to go except the small room they all shared on the third floor, with its windowless bathroom and uncertain extractor fan. 'They seem nice,' she had offered, although she wasn't at all certain that that was how they had seemed. Not nice, exactly. Something more energetic than that. 'They live close to us in Dublin.'

As if that meant anything. 'And I felt sorry for her – Jamie, the girl. All those brothers, and the brothers' friend, who has terrible acne.'

Paul shifted in his seat. He had once had 'terrible acne' and didn't like to be reminded of years that were still raw in memory. 'There's no one for Jamie to play with,' Miriam continued. Sometimes, she found, it was easier to pretend you were doing things for other people. The pretence protected you and made you look generous, whereas the truth of your own situation just made you vulnerable, to yourself as well as others.

'I wish they had been more precise about when they were coming back,' Paul said now. She could see he was ready to cast these people as careless and casual. 'We don't even know their second name.' Now he was casting her as careless too.

'We do,' Miriam said. 'The mother told me. It's O'Reilly.'

'What does he do?'

'I don't know. I didn't ask. They obviously have money, though. All those children, on holiday. And the friend. And when I offered to pay for Sarah, she said no, as if I was being crass by even suggesting it.'

'So she was rude?'

'No, not at all. Just, offering money was clearly the wrong thing to do. Actually, she's sort of magnificent.' Miriam felt embarrassed, because of how different this was to the usual conversations they had about the people they encountered.

'In what way?' Paul sounded suspicious.

'You just want to keep talking to her. Maybe it's her voice, the way it's so deep. But there's something about her, too.

Something, I don't know, warm and *reliable*.' She almost laughed at the unexpectedness of the word.

'Hmm.' He poured more wine into her glass, then into his own, and waved a hand for the waiter to bring another bottle. 'Well, I wish they'd hurry up. The maître d' told me there's a bush fire. Small, he said, nothing to worry about, but still.'

That must be the smell of burning, Miriam thought. Not a wood fire, for pizza or sardines, but a proper fire, gobbling up trees and bushes and spewing out black waste behind it. A fire that might gobble Sarah, take her away from them because they had failed to watch her.

'What would you like to do tomorrow?' she asked quickly, to get the thought from her head.

'I'm playing golf early.' He had the same images in mind, the same dread – she knew by the movement of his eyes, the way they flicked to the side of his head, desperate to see the door behind him but determined not to turn around and look. Neither of them would voice their fears. That was their deal. 'Then, maybe we could go down to the beach, see about hiring a pedalo for an hour?' he finished.

'There they are.' Miriam cut across him; didn't bother trying to keep the relief from her voice. She turned towards the group standing in the doorway of the dining room. In the midst of them, as though she belonged there, was Sarah.

'Sarah!' Miriam hated that she had lurched so quickly to her feet, that her voice sounded too full of relief. Sarah waved and ran over.

'There's a huge fire, we saw it. It's burning everything and it's so big that, even though it's dark, it's not dark where the fire is – it's light.' To Miriam's surprise, her daughter sounded pleased, not scared.

Miriam glanced over Sarah's head – a question – at Maeve, who had followed behind her.

'It's pretty big,' Maeve agreed, smiling, putting a hand out towards Miriam, reassuring, greeting. 'And burning very bright. We didn't go anywhere near it, of course. It's nowhere close to the road, or the hotel, but you can see it on the horizon.'

'It looked like a volcano,' Jamie said. 'Flames and smoke.' They were all clustered around the table now, telling Miriam and Paul what they'd seen, what they'd thought about it.

'I wanted to drive right up and take a better look,' Luke said. 'I'd still like to. Maybe I can get someone in the hotel to take me.'

'Don't be an idiot.' Jake said, ducking out of the way so Luke couldn't reach him.

'Have a drink.' Paul picked up the wine bottle, gestured towards Simon and Maeve.

'Why don't we move to a bigger table?' Simon said.

And so they did, all of them at first, then just the adults as the kids slipped off or were ordered to bed. The fire had given them excitement and drama, something to talk about and exclaim over. A sense of danger, but not too close; the cosy urgency of a disaster that wasn't theirs.

As if the fire were behind them, had herded them like forest animals into a protected clearing, they all moved tight in to one another, sat with dirty glasses between them and told stories of other fires they had known. Paul had once been on a camping trip that had nearly ended in tragedy when a cooking fire got out of hand; Maeve recalled her brother putting petrol on a bonfire when they were back in Kerry and singeing his eyebrows and eyelashes: 'They grew back longer than ever, so I wanted to do the same thing.'

These exchanges, the animation of flames and danger out there in the dark, sped them towards intimacy in the way that a polite evening of 'what do you do?' never could have, so that by the time they separated that night, Miriam knew several things.

She knew that her guess about Simon from breakfast – was it really only that morning? – had been half-right. He had said he 'worked in property' when she had asked.

'So you're a property developer?' She had heard this said before of various people, but none she knew well, and had no real idea what it meant. Something to do with doing up houses then selling them, she guessed.

'Yes,' said Simon.

'Well,' said Maeve. 'He does develop property, at the moment, but his background is law – he was studying to be a solicitor when I met him.' So, not a barrister, but close, Miriam thought. She could see this bit – the studying law bit – was important to Maeve.

'So why did you change?' she asked. They drank wine except for Simon, who was drinking whisky, of which he'd said, 'It's foul; I suppose they distil it here and pretend it's Scottish.' Apart from them, the room was empty. The tables-for-two had drifted off, Miriam noticed, some casting envious looks as they left at the raucous group they now were.

'I looked at my life and all I could see were decades of sitting at a desk, reading contracts,' Simon said. 'Trying to close gaps so tightly that nothing could get through. Always fencing off other people's deals – their jobs and houses and businesses. Always being the person to say no to risk.' He passed his hand in front of his face, as if to ward off something he didn't like the look of.

'The person who cautions caution?' Miriam asked with a smile.

'Exactly,' he said. 'I knew I couldn't stand it. So I left. My parents wanted me to finish my degree at least. Maeve too. But I knew if I did, they would find some way to persuade me to carry on, do the next bit too: "Just do your apprenticeship," "Just take this job, for a year,"' he mimicked although it wasn't clear who he was mimicking – his parents or his wife.

'Simon's dad was a solicitor,' Maeve said.

'And look where it got him,' Simon said bitterly. 'He was the perfect example of what I didn't want to be.' But after that, neither he nor Maeve said any more, so that Miriam had no idea what he meant.

'So what did you do?' That was Paul, leaning forward eagerly.

'I stopped going to lectures. I didn't do the exams. I didn't say anything to anyone, just bought a house with money my grandmother had left me, a rundown tip, sold it a few months later; bought another, sold it for more, and so on. When my class were graduating, and getting ready for two or three more years without a penny, I had made a quarter-of-a-million quid.' His voice was more matter-of-fact than boastful so that Miriam knew that had been only a beginning, that his ambitions had not stopped there.

'So, what? You bought the houses, did them up and sold them on?' Paul asked.

'It's not about doing up houses – putting up curtains and painting "statement walls", like one of those TV shows.' Simon flipped a hand, dismissive. 'It's about buying – land, buildings – in the right place. Then you don't need to do anything, except wait. And know when to move.'

Paul sat back, though whether he was discouraged or intrigued by this, Miriam couldn't tell.

Miriam also discovered she had been half-right about Maeve too – she had indeed come to Dublin from Kerry, had met Simon and married him. But she had come to study English literature, not nursing, and Miriam had been wrong in thinking Maeve 'never went home'.

'We have a house just outside Derrynane,' Maeve said, 'near where I'm from, and we go there every summer. As soon as we get home from Portugal, we'll go down.' She spoke with a deep longing that surprised Miriam.

'All of you?' Miriam asked.

'Maeve will stay there, with the kids, until school starts, and I'll join them at weekends. When I can,' Simon said. 'Maeve loves Kerry the way other people love animals or things they own. Every inch and corner of it. Her parents were English hippies, so they actually appreciated what the locals just took for granted.' He laughed.

'Just my dad,' Maeve said. 'My mother was proper Kerry.'

Maeve mended clocks. 'And watches,' she added when

Simon mentioned this. 'Anything that ticks. Or should tick,' she corrected herself.

'The house is full of them,' Simon said. 'Lying and standing around, like patients in a hospital, waiting for help. Grandfather clocks, tiny little watches, wall clocks, carriage clocks.'

'I do have a workroom,' Maeve laughed, 'but they migrate.'

'Why clocks?' Miriam wondered.

'I don't really know. They're so beautiful inside and so perfect in their make-up, I hate when something goes wrong for them. I like to set it right. Often it's a tiny thing. A cog out of line or dirt between the springs, something that can be easily fixed. I love the way something mechanical – gears and sprockets and tiny levers – can capture time; or rather, that we allow them to pretend they can.' Maeve sounded dreamy. 'They all have their own personalities. Some of them are bossy, always saying, "Hurry up!" Others are so meek, barely willing to remind us that time is moving on.' She laughed. 'I'm sure I sound crazy.'

'Not completely crazy,' Simon said affectionately, putting an arm around her.

'It's something about the order of them, too,' Maeve continued. 'All that measured ticking. The way they are smooth and oiled and follow their own logic. My dad didn't much believe in order and logic when I was growing up.' She laughed. 'In fact, he believed in the complete opposite. He hated plans and routine; maybe this is my reaction to that?'

Miriam knew that Paul was a little intimidated by Simon; she could tell from the way he became dismissive when describing his work as an engineer, the colleagues he liked but at whom he now sneered for Simon's benefit, mocking their caution and narrowness of ambition so that Simon laughed and urged him to have a 'belt' of whiskey.

And she knew that Simon found her attractive. It was the way he looked at her, longer than he needed to, the way he took her hand at one stage when explaining something about his work. It was in the heat of his hand, as though a fire burned there just for her.

Miriam was drunk, she knew it. They all were, Simon especially. But it wasn't just the drink, or the bush fire that seemed to wreathe them in smoke that both hid and revealed, casting shadows in which they seemed to dance for each other, projecting something different to each pair of eyes.

Her excitement came from relief too. The relief that had flooded her when she saw Sarah safe, matched then with relief that her daughter had someone to play with, had 'made a friend', all by herself. But, more even than that: it was relief that she and Paul need not continue the loneliness of their unspoken vigil for Sarah. That they need not, together, be a unit of three, weighed down by silence that was broken only by effort. They had joined up with a larger, noisier group; one that wanted them as much as they wanted to belong.

When they finally broke apart by the lift, they had a plan for the next day – they would go to the beach after breakfast where the boys could rent kayaks and the girls could go on a pedal boat.

'Once they're all gone, we'll have some peace,' Maeve said, yawning. 'I've been getting nowhere with my book.'

'Proust?' Miriam asked with a smile.

'Yes.' Maeve rolled her eyes a little. 'I bring it away with me every year and never manage to read any of it. It's as battered now as if I'd read it twenty times, from dragging it around Europe. The only reason I bring it is to give me an excuse to disappear for an hour or so every day. I open the book, begin to read and then usually doze off.' She laughed.

'Good meeting you,' said Simon emphatically, putting an unsteady arm around Paul's shoulder and looking at Miriam.

CHAPTER 13

By the time her mother said it was bedtime and asked would Jake take her up and make sure she brushed her teeth, Jamie was ready to go. Her eyes were sore, she'd been rubbing them with her knuckles the way her mother said not to, and she wanted to go to sleep.

Having a new friend had been fun at first – the boys had each other, even if Jake didn't really like Luke and now hated Ian – but then it tired her because Sarah wasn't much good at talking to anyone except her, so she had to say the things that Sarah said out loud so the others could hear them. And Sarah wanted to be beside her all the time, in the car, in the restaurant, when they walked along watching the sea. Every time Jamie ran in front or slowed down to stay behind, Sarah ran or slowed too, so that she was always there.

And she kept going on and on about Jamie saving her so

Jamie felt embarrassed because that wasn't the way it had seemed to her.

She had spotted her in the pool; had watched, curious, as the girl she'd seen at breakfast that morning swam along under water. At first Jamie had thought she couldn't swim at all because she was creeping round the side clinging on like a beetle Jamie had found in the water that morning. It had fallen in and would have drowned except it had a bit of leaf to hang on to. Jamie had lifted it carefully out, pleased with herself for noticing it before someone tipped it over.

The girl swam underwater, kicking smoothly, until she reached the steps beside where Jamie was sitting with Jake, their feet dangling in the water. She was trying to cheer him up after Luke had been mean to him.

She watched, only half paying attention, as the underwater girl reached the steps and put out a hand. She saw the hand get kicked away, and the girl turning round and round in the water, like their dog Taylor trying to get cosy in her basket at home. In all that blue, she was like a slowly spinning top.

'Luke's mean,' she said to Jake, 'just ignore him.'

The girl was still turning, and Jamie wondered was it a game she was playing. Then the girl had grabbed hold of Jake's foot. She gave him a fright. Jamie felt him jump beside her.

'What the . . .?' he said, then shook his leg hard, kicking the girl off. Jamie thought she'd swim away then but she didn't, she grabbed again and Jake kicked her off again, harder this time, annoyed.

Jamie watched as the girl let the power of the kick push her away from them and towards the middle of the pool, the deeper bit. Jamie found that she wanted to keep watching her, moving so peacefully along, slowly.

Jake was still complaining about Luke, so Jamie said comfortingly, 'You're right, I hate him too. I'll be back in a minute.' She jumped in, even though she didn't exactly know why, and swam to where the girl had drifted down like a drowned spider, in a little heap of legs and arms, and grabbed hold of her. Only when the girl began to splutter and cough and cry did Jamie fully realise what had been happening, and when she did, she was suddenly embarrassed, as if she'd tried to push in to someone else's party. She was going to swim away then, but the girl was hanging on to her hand so she couldn't. She stayed, and then the moment for leaving passed.

Jamie rubbed her eyes more. The room was too hot; they weren't allowed to open the windows, because there was nothing to stop them from falling out. 'So much for health and safety,' their mother had muttered when they first saw those windows.

She lay across one of the twin beds – Jake had the other one. She hated the scratchy cover so she'd thrown it on the floor, and every day someone tucked the sheets in really tight around the sides of the bed so she felt trapped and had to pull the top sheet out.

'Stop doing that,' Jake said as she dug her knuckles into her eyes. 'You'll make them worse. You've got smoke in them or something. Wash your face and they'll stop being sore.'

'I'm too tired.'

'Come on,' he ordered. 'Up. You need to do your teeth

anyway. Now, before you fall asleep.' Jamie, their mother said, fell asleep 'like other people fall down – sudden and hard'. She said it so often it was a family joke – 'Jamie's falling,' one of them would shout, in the car or watching TV, 'quick!' and Maeve would put a blanket over her, or scoop her up and bring her to bed.

'OK.' Jamie allowed him to drag her to her feet, then flopped forward as he pulled her towards the bathroom. 'Do you think I have to play with Sarah tomorrow?' she asked, not looking at him, over the wash-hand basin.

'Not if you don't want to.' He brushed vigorously.

'Really?' Then, 'Is it true I pick up strays?'

'A bit.' Jake found it very hard not to tell the truth. It made him blush and Jamie could see his face was going pink now.

They all teased her for being soft-hearted and feeding cats and stray things, Jamie thought, but her mum did it too. She'd given bits of her dinner to that cat in Greece, just as much as Jamie had. She'd give a secret look that said 'shssh' and then she'd put her hand under the table with a piece of fish or meat on it. Or she'd pass a plate to Jamie with a smile that Jamie knew meant 'here – but don't tell anyone!' and watch as Jamie fed it to the cat.

'What's a bit?' she asked.

'Jamie, you get carried away, you know you do. You make friends and then you get sick of them.'

'I never think they're going to hang around as long as they do,' she said. 'So, am I stuck with her now?'

'Look, she seems nice but you don't have to play with her

every day. Tomorrow, just stay out of her way for a bit and she'll get it.'

'OK. Maybe you and me can play mini golf? That takes ages.'

'Fine.'

Except that the next morning, by the time Jamie got up, there was already a plan and everyone loved it. They sat together at breakfast, as if they had all known each other for ever, and the plan, announced loudly by her dad, was that they were all going to the beach together. Sarah, when she heard, went bright red and said, 'Oh brilliant,' so that all the adults laughed, a lot, and Simon reached a hand out and messed Sarah's hair the same way he did with Jamie.

CHAPTER 14

One year later: Dublin, August 1999

'Here comes Shadowcat.' Jake was the first to look up when Sarah opened the kitchen door of 'Number Eight,' as they all called it to distinguish it from the other house in Kerry, 'Reevanagh', where Sarah had never been.

It had confused her at first, the different names, but after a while she started to understand. Number Eight was 'home' to Simon and the children, but not to Maeve, who meant Kerry when she said 'home', and not even Reevanagh but a different house entirely, where she had grown up. This was why they had titles for the houses, so they all knew where they were talking about.

There was yet another house, somewhere in Wexford, that they called 'The Van' because, 'It's a mobile home. Except it isn't mobile. It just stays in one place,' Jake had said.

'And rots,' Maeve added. That was because no one ever went there. Simon had insisted on buying it, but it was Maeve who decided when it came to where they all went, and she said, 'What's the point of going to Wexford when you could be in Kerry?' So no one went down, even when Simon complained about the 'bloody waste' and said it would end up being a home for rats and bats.

Sarah couldn't imagine what it would be like to have so many places that were all 'home' of some sort. In her family, when they said 'home', they all meant the four-bedroom house where they lived. Maybe it was a thing rich people did, she had decided. Because the O'Reillys were rich, like in a storybook. Number Eight proved it.

'Shit,' her dad had said the first time he dropped her there, a month or so after the holiday in Portugal – a month in which Sarah had slowly given up hoping that Jamie's mum would ring, the way she had said she would, so that her stomach had felt sick with excitement on that first visit, which had happened so unexpectedly: 'Sarah, Jamie's mum is on the phone and she wants to know if you want to spend the night at Jamie's tomorrow?' her mother had called up the stairs one evening, so casually that Sarah had run down to see if she was actually as calm as she sounded. Her mother's eyes were shining and she smiled so much that Sarah guessed she was more pleased than she let on. 'I think she'd love to,' she had said into the phone, watching Sarah.

'Shit.' Her dad never cursed and, that first day, Sarah had wondered if he had hurt himself. Then she realised he was looking at the O'Reillys' house that they had come to by driving in through some black metal gates that were open, then round a driveway curved like a bowl and out into a bit with gravel on the ground, big trees around it and a high red-brick house with a double flight of stone steps up to it and more black iron railings around them.

'Shit,' he said yet again, but this time more annoyed than impressed.

Inside there was carpet everywhere, not like their house which had what her mother called 'laminate', something that seemed to Sarah to mean 'pretend wood'. There were loads of rooms, with high ceilings and big windows, but Sarah found the O'Reillys didn't seem to bother with most of them. Mostly, they were in the kitchen, or the 'TV room' beside it that smelt of dog. Both those rooms were downstairs, almost underground. They didn't even use the front door much, except for Simon; instead, going in and out along the back hall with its jumble of wellies and hiking boots, and through the small back door where there were four mossy steps up to the back garden and a path that led round the front. The path was usually blocked with bikes, some new, some old and rusty, just like the back hall was blocked with boots. Maybe they were trying to barricade themselves in, Sarah had thought when she saw it first.

In the back garden was an apple tree so old it was covered in soft greyish-green fur, and a treehouse that had been built for Luke but was now Jamie's and had a ladder up to it that you could pull up behind you so no one else could get in. There was a dove house – called a 'cote', Jamie said – with white doves that made as much noise with their wings as with their cooing, and the grass was always covered with thick layers of fallen leaves that were wet or dry depending on the day, so that you could squelch or scuff through them.

Since the first visit there had been more visits, even a birthday party that had been loud and terrifying with Jamie's friends who ignored her so that Sarah had wished and wished she hadn't come, had stayed at home and celebrated another time when it was just the two of them.

But, by now, Sarah was used to Number Eight. Or almost. This time, Maeve let her in, hugging her briefly and saying, 'They're all in the kitchen,' then going out to chat to Miriam who had dropped Sarah and was coming back later, for the party, that night. It wasn't even a party to celebrate anything special, like a birthday. Just a party. 'Dad likes having them,' Jamie had said, as if that was enough of a reason.

Sarah walked through the hall with its high, curved ceiling, liking the way everything bounced in greeting as she went. 'It's the floorboards; they're uneven,' Jamie had explained the first time she commented on it. 'It makes the sideboards shake and then the things on them rattle.'

But Sarah had ignored the explanation, liking more the idea that the contents of Jamie's house were bobbing up and down, greeting her, like the cups and teapot in the *Beauty and the Beast* film Miriam had taken her and Jamie to see one time. Or maybe they were bobbing in time to the ticking sounds that came from all sides. Every wall and surface had clocks and watches, some broken, some fixed, some halfway between the two. There was a 'workshop' as Maeve called it – 'This is where Maeve kills time,' Luke said, and he laughed for a long time at his own joke, to which Maeve had answered, 'I'm not killing time, I'm saving time,' and then she laughed too – where the broken watches and clocks were meant to stay, but they didn't, they moved around the house, following Maeve, Sarah sometimes thought, silently begging her to mend them. And the fixed ones were supposed to be sold on, Jamie had told her, but often Maeve couldn't bear to part with them once she had put them to rights. And so they piled up, light reflecting off their round faces like so many small moons, their ticking and tocking building up, layer on vibrating layer.

'This house sounds like a bomb,' Luke had said once. Sarah could see what he meant.

'Hello,' Sarah said now, in response to Jake's greeting. 'Shadowcat' was what he had taken to calling her since the restaurant in Portugal when Luke had said she was Jamie's new stray. But with Jake, it wasn't meant meanly.

Sarah looked around. They weren't 'all' in the kitchen, she saw. Luke was there, petting Taylor, the surly brown retriever dog, the only thing he seemed to be nice to, and Alan, who hardly even came home now because he was at university, was there too, on the small sofa beside the Aga, reading a rugby magazine.

'Where's Jamie?'

'She's upstairs in her room,' Jake said, so that Sarah headed through the kitchen to go up the back stairs and find her. 'With Celine,' Jake added as she passed the table. He was eating cornflakes, she saw. Even though it was almost lunchtime. Sarah paused, then realised she didn't want anyone to notice her pausing, Luke especially, and carried on walking.

She went up the back stairs slowly, her bag trailing at her side. No wonder Jamie hadn't been there to greet her. Usually, she would have been on the front steps, or at worst hovering in the hall, maybe sitting halfway up the big staircase with its pale green carpet like grass, ready to shout, 'You're so late! Come on!' as soon as she saw Sarah. Sarah never was late – her mother made sure of that – but Jamie would begin waiting far too early, for everything – a trip, a treat, a game – demanding, 'Is it time yet? Is it time yet?' so that when it finally was time, she was convinced everyone else was late.

But if Celine was there, that explained it. Sarah had met Celine twice before, neither time for very long, but long enough to know that Celine didn't like her. That was so obvious to Sarah that she couldn't begin to work out what she thought about Celine. It didn't feel relevant – the other girl had got in there first and begun disliking Sarah so quickly that whatever Sarah thought just didn't matter.

'So you're the kid Jamie met in Portugal?' Celine had said the first time they met. She was lounging on Jamie's bed, on her stomach, legs kicking the air idly behind her. The way she lolled there, the few silent minutes it took her to acknowledge Sarah, said how comfortable she was and that Sarah was the intruder.

Sarah didn't like being called a kid by someone her own age. She wished she could stand straight, so Celine could see how tall she was, and snap back, 'Kid? Hardly . . .' – or something like that – but she didn't. Just stayed where she was, in what she knew her mother would say was a 'slouch', and muttered 'yes'.

'Jamie says she saved you from drowning?' Celine said then. She had pale blue, rather sticky-out eyes that seemed to goggle at Sarah. Sarah was shocked. Jamie had never told anyone about how they'd met except Jake, because he was there when it happened. Why would she tell this girl? Until that minute, she had thought it was their secret, a thing that bound her and Jamie to each other and gave their friendship power. She had loved that they had that, just the two of them, even though they never talked about it because Jamie didn't want to. Sarah had thought that was because it was something important. Now, she saw that Jamie was just bored by it, by the idea of it, by the way Sarah made so much of it.

And for Celine, clearly, it was a thing to laugh about. 'Jamie saving someone' was, to her, no different to 'the time Mrs De Rossa tucked her skirt into her knickers', or 'Angela Eggers picked her apple up when it fell on the ground and ate it, covered in muck'.

'Sort of,' Sarah had muttered, wondering when Jamie would come back. She'd gone to ask her mother if they could go horse-riding.

'Sort of?' Celine mocked. 'Hard to "sort-of" drown, isn't it?'

Jamie came back then and Celine shut up, but only for a few minutes. 'How come you don't go to St Assumpta's?' she asked. 'My mum says it's by far the best school in this part of Dublin.'

'I don't know,' Sarah said. 'I just go to a different school.'

'Celine,' Jamie said patiently, 'there are other good schools. You know there are. Come on, let's get our stuff. Sarah, Mum says to give you jodhpurs.'

And then, in the car, worst of all, 'Will Sarah be allowed to ride?' Celine asked loudly. 'Isn't it members only?'

There was a pause, and then Jamie's mum said, 'Don't be silly, Celine, of course she'll be "allowed" to ride.' She put such emphasis on the word 'allowed' that it was obvious what she thought of the question; Celine blushed and Sarah felt the same hot wave run through her, but of triumph not shame. Maeve caught her eye in the driving mirror and winked a tiny bit.

'Celine seems nice,' Sarah had said later to Jamie, after the horse-riding, when Celine had gone home and it was just the two of them. She hadn't meant it, not remotely. It was an exploration, the hesitant opening of possibility, a chance for Jamie to say, 'God no, she's horrible. I'm so sick of her,' but Jamie didn't. Instead, she said, 'She is,' then, 'let's go watch TV.'

'Sarah!' Jamie said now, 'I didn't hear you come in. We were trying out Celine's new compact disc player. It's got two sets of headphones.' She held up a tangle of wires.

'What are you listening to?'

'Backstreet Boys. They're amazing.' Sarah wished she knew something cool to say about them, but she didn't. Jamie was always miles ahead of her on music. 'It's because of my brothers,' she once explained. 'They tell me stuff I should listen to. But it's OK. I can tell you.'

But she didn't say anything like that now. Instead Celine said, 'What's your favourite track, Sarah?' in a way that told Sarah she hoped she wouldn't be able to answer. Everything, with Celine, was a dance of exclusion: conversations steered towards girls from their school Sarah didn't know – 'Did you hear what that kid in junior school, Amanda O'Hagen, got for her birthday? A Persian cat, completely white, with blue eyes'; sports she couldn't play – 'How's your tennis coming along?'; places she'd never been – 'Isn't Greece amazing?' So that somehow Sarah always felt on the fringes, as if she was on tiptoe, trying to see into the place where Jamie and Celine were.

''Get Down',' she said now, blessing the fact that she'd heard it on the radio in the car barely half an hour before.

'Oh. I hate that one. It's so commercial.'

'Celine, you said you loved it,' Jamie said, surprised, looking from one to the other.

Sarah dumped her stuff on the floor beside Jamie's wardrobe, which was huge and dark and old, so that the first time Sarah saw it she'd said, 'It looks like you can get to Narnia through it.'

Jamie had giggled and said, 'I know! I tried, so many times, when I saw that series first.'

But when Sarah said, 'You should read the book, it's much better,' Jamie's face had become stubborn and annoyed. She hated Sarah going on about books, because she had no interest in them, and so she had walked off.

Always, it was Sarah who wanted more, Jamie who got bored, or irritated, or tired of her company, so that she'd withdraw or go to find someone else – Jake, her mother, the dog, Taylor – to chat to, leaving Sarah alone, afraid to go down and look for her because the house was so big and she didn't yet know her way around it.

Jamie's mother seemed not to notice, or find it strange, if she came across Sarah on her own somewhere in the house. 'Oh, Sarah,' she would say, 'Jamie's outside,' as if it were perfectly normal that the two might not be together. Or she might find something else for Sarah to do – 'Come and help me pick up the fallen apples, then we can stew them. I know that sounds boring, but you'll see, it's surprisingly fun.'

It was fun and when they were finished, Maeve said, 'I think Jamie might be in the TV room. Go and see if you can find her.'

Like this, Sarah gradually got used to the idea that staying at Jamie's sometimes meant being on her own, and when Jake started giving her books he thought she'd like – '*Call of the Wild*, I loved it' – she would simply lie on Jamie's bed until Jamie came back for her.

'Hurry up, Bookworm,' she'd shout, sticking her head around the door, just as if it had been Sarah to disappear off without warning, and not her.

Now, Sarah spent a minute taking things from her overnight bag – pyjamas, toothbrush, hairbrush – in order to avoid being quizzed about Backstreet Boys.

'What are you wearing tonight?'

She had known this would be a question – now that they were nearly thirteen, those were the things they asked each other. And there was a party; of course it would be a question – but she hadn't expected that Celine would be the one asking it.

'Jeans. A red top.'

'Oh, a *red* top,' Celine mocked.

Sarah's height confused her. Jamie seemed to have grown all over, together, so that she was the same compact shape she had ever been, just bigger. She looked like herself and seemed to feel like herself because she threw on clothes without fuss, only now it was checked shirts and dungarees instead of tracksuits and T-shirts. She was as likely as ever to flip upside down suddenly, expressing the things she didn't, couldn't, say in cartwheels and handstands, bending her body back and forth like a piece of chewed toffee.

Sarah never felt she knew the length of her arms or legs. Every time she began to understand, they stretched out again, beyond her own reach. She was thin and white and long, so that she felt like a worm sometimes, unsure of how to move the furthest bits of herself. Clothes confused her because they never fitted properly, but even more than that, the idea of things suiting her confused her – the idea that there were clothes that looked nice on you and clothes that didn't, and that somehow you had to find the ones that did and learn to recognise them.

'You'll learn,' her mother said, laughing. 'Everyone learns. But it takes a while.' Sarah couldn't believe it had ever taken her mother any time. Or that there were such things as clothes that didn't suit her. Everything Miriam wore fitted her neatly, unlike Jamie's mum who wore T-shirts that were old and too short, so they sometimes rose up past her stomach when she stretched for something.

'Well, what are *you* wearing?' she asked.

'Pink and white stripy mini-dress with Converse.' Celine said it like she was showing a really great painting she'd made.

'Look, you can see them putting the marquee up.' Jamie,

bored by the conversation, opened the window so the sound of hammering came in. 'There's going to be nearly a hundred people.'

'My mother says it's going to be the party of the season,' Celine said.

'*My* mother says it's going to be a giant headache.' Jamie laughed. 'But I think she likes it really. She's been in a brilliant mood. She let us have Nutella for breakfast.'

'Who's coming?' Celine asked.

'Dunno. People,' Jamie said.

Having Celine around was like having a grown-up in the room, Sarah thought. Someone who asked strange questions, like 'who's coming?' and who you had to make conversation with.

When it was just her and Jamie, they spoke, or didn't speak, and it didn't matter. Sometimes they didn't talk for ages, then started again when there was something to talk about. It was nice. But with Celine around, Sarah felt self-conscious and she knew Jamie did too because she made an effort to talk about stuff Celine liked – who was in the charts and what girls they knew had done – and to be sort of polite to her.

'Can I borrow your Backstreet Boys CD?' Celine asked now.

'I'm sorry. I only just got it. You can borrow it next week,' Jamie said. To Sarah, if Sarah had dared ask such a thing, she would have just said, 'No.'

'So what are you wearing, Jamie?' Sarah asked.

'Jeans and a Nirvana T-shirt Jake gave me, but I have a new belt you can borrow, Sarah.'

'Thanks,' Sarah said. Belts were the greatest mystery of all.

CHAPTER 15

'Ready for this?' Miriam had asked Paul as they drove through the gently darkening streets, then past an inky sea that rippled like an oil slick and threw the lights of the city and the sky back, soft and fond, an admiring reflection. The O'Reillys lived close, but there was an upward evolution of privilege reflected in the surroundings as they drove; houses became bigger, set farther back in deeper gardens, with gates and high stone walls.

'I suppose so,' Paul had said. He had fussed about coming, spending too long choosing a shirt, debating which tie to wear, and Miriam knew he felt uncertain. She did too, but more than that, she felt excited.

'We won't know anyone,' Paul had said.

'We'll know Maeve and Simon,' she'd answered.

'Who will be too busy to talk to us, beyond saying hello.'

'We'll know each other, and we'll meet people,' she had said. 'There will be other people who don't know anyone too.'

She had been surprised all those months ago, when Maeve had finally returned her phone calls, made in the weeks after the return from Portugal. By then, Miriam had given up expecting to hear from her; had decided that, after all, theirs had been a holiday friendship, one destined to fade as fast as a tan, grow dusty the way seashells did when you removed them from the beach.

It had been, she tried to tell herself, perfect of its kind. A wonderful friendship, like a brightly coloured throw, across the two weeks. Those days that had started early, at breakfast, over coffee and pastries, when plans were made for what they would all do – visit a town, a beach, a hillside somewhere; plans for picnics or lunches out – and continued on, through swims and afternoon coffees, conversation and jokes. Nights were even better: dinner with the children, followed by drinks on the hotel terrace or some small restaurant by the sea while the kids did their own things. They had been drunk and silly and fond, and Miriam had found herself telling Maeve and sometimes Simon things she told no one else.

It was a friendship such as Miriam had never known, not as a child or during her two years studying accountancy, where the other students had mostly been older, many working as well as studying, inclined to rush off after classes and view their fellow students as competition rather than friends. Certainly not as an adult, when her friends had been largely dictated by where they lived and where Sarah went to school.

Those were friendships of convenience, of proximity, without any real beat to them, she realised, once she knew the warmth of something so different.

They had jokes, her, Paul and the O'Reillys – about a particular waiter, a dish, a funny thing one of the children had said – that were theirs alone, little tokens of good faith that they passed back and forth between them so that they became worn and shiny and precious. They also had a depth of charity together, a willingness to understand and be understood, that was first gratifying, and then necessary, to her. A way of talking that moved from light to dark and back again like a deft piece of music, so that Simon could tell her what it was, exactly, he had meant when he said, about his father, 'And look where it got him': 'He worked without joy, building up a firm of solicitors that had his name and he put off every other bit of his life to do that. And then he died, suddenly, at fifty-six, and when his partners went looking, there was nothing, just debts and bad investments that he had hidden. . .' And she had put a hand out and taken his and squeezed it, and then, moments later, they had both laughed, together, at something silly one of the children did.

It was the warmth of the nights, the way the humid dark drew around them, muffling the outside world where caution and restraint were things to hold on to. It was drink, yes – the bottles of wine, glasses of brandy and port, that began sometimes at lunch – but more than that, it was the appeal of togetherness that she could not resist and found difficult to forget.

They moved through the hotel, the towns they visited, as

a troop, a gang, one family. 'We're like a circus,' she had said one day to Maeve as they spilled out of cars and into a square that was deserted except for a few dusty pigeons scratching at the ground.

'Certainly a travelling show of some kind,' Maeve had agreed, watching Luke and Ian trying to push each other into a fountain.

'Does Ian often come away with you?' Miriam had asked then, having noticed how irritated Simon was by him.

'Recently he has,' Maeve had said. 'His mother is getting treatment. Cancer. There are younger kids, a sister and a brother. It hasn't been easy.'

She had, Miriam thought, something kind about her that was almost unreflecting – taking in waifs and strays in the same way she took milk in her coffee: because she could, because they were there. Miriam wondered briefly what that meant about Sarah, then pushed the thought away again. And yet it wasn't a type of kindness that made Maeve busy or interfering. The opposite in fact.

Miriam tried to learn from the surprising fact of Maeve's detachment from her children. She didn't rush to them or hover over them if they were hurt. Unless they came to her with their pains and problems, she ignored them.

'You should have put on a T-shirt when I told you' was all she said when Jake complained of burned shoulders; and, 'It'll be fine,' if Jamie cut or bruised herself.

'Independence is important,' she said when Miriam commented on the distance in her approach. 'They're better without my fussing at them. They need to work life out for themselves. That's what my dad always said, and I think he was right. Not that it isn't hard. I can't tell you how hard I have to work not to smother them.' She laughed. 'The clocks are a good distraction, I can squint and peer at them all I like, which stops me squinting and peering at the children. They need space and air to breathe and live and be themselves. To fall over and mess up and get hurt too.' Was there in her, Miriam wondered, the faintest echo of smugness? The unwitting complacency of a woman who had all the children she wanted, all strong and healthy and pulsing life with steady, regular beats? Who had never known what it was to try to hold onto something inside herself that could not be held?

'Anyway, once you have more than one,' Maeve said then, 'you can't keep watch all the time. You have to let them at it,' and Miriam had flinched at those words 'more than one', even as she told herself she was being too sensitive; that Maeve was right, and children were better not being too protected. Then, because she was curious, but also to pay Maeve back, she asked, 'But which one would you save, if you could only save one?' and was confounded when Maeve said with a laugh, 'I'd save Simon.'

Sometimes, to Miriam's eyes, the O'Reilly kids seemed wild, like the watchful cats that stalked the shadows of alleyways – rushing each other for scraps of attention, turning to hiss and arch over some small moment of maternal intimacy found and claimed. Turning and twining around the ankles of their calmly indifferent mother. Alliances would be made, then as quickly ditched, although a natural fault line seemed to carve out distance between Jake and Luke, who were never in alliance.

But in that bear pit, Sarah seemed to thrive. Her arms and legs grew browner and stronger, her voice gathered heft so that it could be heard, and she showed herself increasingly impatient with Miriam's care.

'I'm fine,' she snapped, blood running down her leg from a cut on the knee, when Miriam went to her. 'It's not sore.' And she dashed at the blood with an impatient hand then ran to catch up with the others. Miriam watched her go with relief and some small sadness that she immediately tried to cover over, like an animal burying something shameful.

At first Paul had worried about the cost of everything, counting and recounting the money he had set aside for these weeks, and trying to find clever ways to magic it further. But after a while, after low conversations with Simon that broke up if she approached, he had seemed to relax and when Miriam asked him, hesitantly, if they could afford the car hire or the day's excursion to a church the O'Reillys were planning, he had said, 'Yes, it's fine. I've worked it out,' as if it had been nothing more than a complicated puzzle that had a knack to it.

And so Miriam didn't ask again, although the feeling nagged at her that she should. Instead, she suggested excursions and paid for lunches with her credit card, insisting, 'No, no! Our turn.' Because by then, she had decided that these days were few and new and precious, and she would not make them in the image of all the other days, worrying about money and what they could afford.

And then, the return. There had been a week or so in which Miriam had restrained herself, and finally, when she felt enough time had gone by, she had made the call, and left a message with the woman who answered the phone – 'Can you just tell Maeve that Miriam called? I'm at home later if she wants to ring me.' And then, nothing. No return call. No hasty message or scribbled card to say 'Away, back soon, talk then' or whatever such a card might say. Just a silence that felt personal, even though she tried to tell herself it couldn't be.

After another week, Miriam had tried again – calls and messages could go astray, she told herself as she dialled, hand shaking slightly, trying to find the right voice in which to speak: the casual, pleasant voice of a friend who knows herself to be wanted. Another message, left with the same woman, presumably a housekeeper or some such. And more silence.

'When can I see Jamie?' Sarah had demanded. 'We said we'd meet – you said you'd arrange it with her mum.'

'Well, I'll try,' Miriam had said, 'but people are busy,' and when Sarah asked again some days later, days in which still no call had come, she snapped at her: 'Stop going on about it. If they want to see us, they'll ring,' so that Sarah had stared, face red and hurt, then pushed past her and run upstairs to her room.

It was what it was, Miriam told herself then. A holiday friendship. Of its time and place, and no more. Forget about it.

And then, when she almost had, Maeve had rung. Hearing her voice, Miriam at first had prepared to gather dignity around herself like a flag. To say, 'I'm just running out, I'll call you later,' in cool tones, and then not call. Not for a while anyway. But she didn't. She couldn't.

Maeve's apology had sounded like she meant it – 'I'm so sorry, really I am. I've been meaning to ring, but we went down to Kerry straight after coming back, and then the boys went back to school and getting all their stuff this year seemed worse than ever because they've all grown out of everything, but in different ways, so that Alan's old things don't fit Luke or Jake . . .' And within minutes Miriam was laughing and swapping her own stories and agreeing that, yes, she'd bring Sarah for a sleepover the next day.

That had been nearly a year ago. After the first visit, Sarah's stays became more frequent and longer, and Miriam found she had to talk herself out of her own reluctance to say yes when Maeve asked. Because for all that Sarah was so quiet, the house without her was more so, with an echoey emptiness like air that circulated too freely, without the mass of Sarah's form to navigate and slow it down. And yet yes was what she said every time – because of Sarah, the eagerness of her 'Can I, can I, please?' but too because of the intoxication of the closeness with the O'Reillys. Sarah in their house was a link between the two families, a rope-bridge that drew Miriam and Paul with it. And Miriam couldn't say no to that.

And with time, she grew used to Sarah being gone, to the house without her. It's good for all of us, she told herself. Maeve is right – they need distance, independence, to grow.

And of course every time she dropped off or collected Sarah was a chance, an opportunity. Soon she was having coffee with Maeve nearly every week, at one another's houses and in cafés. There were walks, and sometimes lunch, and now, finally, this: a party.

'You'll see,' she said to Paul now, taking his hand as the taxi turned in to the high stone gates of Number Eight. 'It'll be great.'

CHAPTER 16

Stepping out of the taxi, Miriam felt six years old again, the excitement fluttering inside her behind the ragged hull of her ribcage like rags in the wind, put out for gaiety.

'When was the last time you saw the O'Reillys?' she asked Paul now.

'I've seen a bit of Simon,' he admitted.

'What? When? Why didn't you tell me?'

'Just work stuff. A bit of business we might be doing together. I didn't think you'd be interested.' Which was, they both knew, a lie.

The house was lit like a cigarette, glowing bright in the dark as they turned in the gateway, and the door was wide open. Music came from somewhere within, and Maeve was standing there, waiting for them, waving and smiling as they walked up the stone steps.

'Thank goodness!' she called down. 'You're here.' As though

they had come a great distance, or navigated a treacherous path.

'I'll put your coats in our bedroom, in case you're looking for them later and can't find me,' she said, kissing Miriam and holding a hand out to Paul. 'It's a scrum, and there's every chance I'll be in bed by the time the last lot leave.'

'Sleeping on our coats?' Miriam asked with a smile.

'No, in the attic, as far away from the noise as I can get.' Maeve grimaced. 'I don't know why I said yes. Simon thinks it's a great idea. We used to do it every year, and then it just got so awful, I stopped. But he persuaded me…' She was wearing a long black dress, sleeveless, and so plain it was almost a vest, with an orange belt and high black heels, her hair tied up with an orange scarf. She looked tired and smelled hot, as if she hadn't had time to shower.

Miriam, in a white linen dress that buttoned down the front, felt cool and crisp beside her, so that when Maeve said, 'What'll you drink?' she asked for 'a giant G&T', instead of the glass of wine she'd planned on.

Inside, the house was, as Maeve had said, a scrum. A throng of people bouncing questions and jokes back and forth between themselves in small groups that became large, then broke off and dispersed, only to re-form elsewhere. It was like a lava lamp, Miriam thought – globules of humanity, running together then breaking apart, dragging bits of different blobs with them, then abandoning those when they found something else.

To her surprise, Paul seemed to know a few people. Men to whom he nodded in a way that was almost furtive, the tiniest jerk of the head so she knew that he didn't want to approach them. Not yet.

'Who's that?' she asked, about a man in a grey pinstripe suit, pink shirt and extravagant turquoise cravat to whom Paul did the head-jerk and who responded with a summoning wave.

'Mick O'Hagen. Another property guy. I met him with Simon. Simon says he knows more than the rest of us put together. The Man with the Midas Touch, he called him.'

'And that's his wife?' A carefully made-up blonde woman in a tight emerald green silk dress with a lace panel that showed most of her breasts stood beside him. It was, Miriam decided, a dress so tarty that only someone as unmoving as the blonde woman could possibly have worn it.

'Maybe, I don't know.'

It was, Miriam could see, a very good party. The right mix of people, of drink and food and music, in large rooms under high ceilings, with the poignant early autumn smell of wood fires and damp leaves coming in through open doors and windows. The party roar was that of a fast, expensive car, perfectly tuned and shown the open road. She just wished she knew a few people so that she, too, could be part of it all. She wondered where Sarah was. Perhaps the kids were in a different part of the house.

'Go and talk to Mick,' she said to Paul, because she could feel that he wanted to but didn't know how with her beside him. 'I'm going to ask Maeve something.'

She found Maeve chatting to a woman beside an open window. Outside, Miriam could see a giant white marquee with plastic windows shaped into classic Georgian arches, and remembered what Sarah had told her: 'There's going to be a huge tent. In the back garden. Jamie says she's going to try and sleep in it. She says her parents won't notice, they'll be too busy.'

'How's Luke's rugby coming along?' the woman – Anne – was asking Maeve.

'Good, but it's all he does,' Maeve said. 'His marks are terrible. I think he should play less this year and study more, but Simon doesn't agree with me.'

'Nonsense,' Anne said firmly, as though hers were the opinion that mattered. 'The rugby will stand to him. Throughout his life.'

'Well, he's hardly going to play professionally,' Maeve said, 'despite what he thinks.'

'I don't mean that,' Anne said. 'I mean in his career. Whatever he does.'

'Oh, surely that's all finished with now,' Maeve said with a laugh. 'Jobs in the bank because you played for the school team, like some kind of secret society made up of guys with broken noses and no necks?'

Miriam laughed. Anne didn't.

'It's not like that.' She sounded offended. 'It's an advantage, that's all.'

'I think reading a few books would be a bigger advantage,' Maeve said, but gently. She tried to introduce Miriam, but beyond a tight smile and wan hello, Anne wasn't interested and soon made an excuse to leave them.

'Her son is in Luke's class at school.' Maeve rolled her eyes slightly. 'And her daughter, Celine – dreadful name, like semolina – is a friend of Jamie's. She's good though with teacher's names and what the kids need to bring in for the start of term and stuff.'

'There is a place for that,' Miriam said comfortingly and was about to ask for a run-down on who was who and what to expect – the kind of cosy *mise en place* they had got into the habit of in Portugal; dissecting rooms, just like Paul and Miriam had always done, except that with Maeve it was funnier, less cruel . . . But then a man interrupted them.

'Corkscrew?' he asked, urgently miming opening the bottle of wine he held.

'Right,' Maeve said. 'Follow me. I'm sorry, Miriam.'

'It's OK, go. I'm going outside. I'll see you later.'

The window beside her was large and low enough to the floor that Miriam decided to avoid pushing back through the room and simply sat up on the sill and swung her legs over, grateful for the freedom of the linen dress, and was about to jump down, looking for a spot to land so as to avoid the plants beneath when someone below shouted, 'Wait!' and Luke came crashing towards her.

'Wait,' he said again, too loud. 'I'll help.' He trampled heavily on the plants Miriam had wanted to avoid so that the smell of crushed geranium rose up to her, sharp and reproachful on the night air. Beside the window now, breathing heavily, Luke grabbed for her hands. She let him take one but jumped lightly to the side so as to avoid landing too close to him. He was, she decided with a slight shock, drunk. His face was flushed red and he grinned broadly, exuberantly. 'Mrs Ryan,' he said, looking back over his shoulder at Ian, the friend who had been in Portugal, and making a clumsy bow that could have been mocking.

'Miriam,' she muttered.

'Miriam,' he repeated, still holding her hand, breathing into her face. The sweetish smell of booze and some kind of artificial orange juice was powerful and she tried to remember how old he was. Fifteen? Sixteen?

'Let me escort you to the bar,' he said. The surface was gallantry but there was mockery beneath; whether he was mocking himself, or her, or simply trying to cover his intoxication, she didn't know.

'Thank you, Luke. I can manage now.' She tried to sound cool and friendly, but knew that the way she snatched her hand out of the meaty heat of his was not that. His arm, as he let her go, brushed heavily against the side of her breast and her alarm was such that she began to say, 'Sorry . . .' although the offence wasn't hers; but she didn't finish, pulled up by the look of bland insolence on his face.

CHAPTER 17

Loud voices drifted upstairs from the hall, along with shouts of laughter and exclamations. Sarah fiddled with her hair and things in her bag. She didn't want to go down. This must be what dogs feel like at Halloween, she thought, terrified of noises and lights, believing them to have more power to hurt than bangs and flashes should.

She hated parties with people her own age – a raw awkwardness would land on her the second she arrived into a throng of those who were familiar, but now unfamiliar; wearing different clothes, in rooms and halls and houses she'd never seen before, with strange adults asking loud questions – 'Who wants to hit the piñata first?' – and behaving in ways she didn't understand, as if they were all lit up with a new fire that propelled them faster, more furiously, than usual, so that Sarah couldn't keep up or even understand what they all wanted.

How much worse would an adult party be, she wondered. There wouldn't even be the cover of party games, or a disco, or crazy golf, where she could hide for a while under the pretence of having a purpose. Instead, it would just be people standing around talking. Maybe trying to talk to her.

'Come on, let's go down,' Jamie said. 'I'm going to see if anyone gives me money. Some of the old guys do. They just hand you twenty euro because they don't know what else to do.' She went off into a fit of giggles. 'Sarah, if anyone thinks you're me and gives you money, for god's sake just take it! Don't go all moral and hand it back.'

'No one is going to think Sarah is you,' Celine said.

By the time they were ready, the hall was full of people. Sarah stopped on the landing below Jamie's room to watch them. The biggest rooms off the hall – three of them, that ran together through doors that could open wide so that the three rooms became one – seemed full too from where she stood: a brilliant, fizzing throng of faces and voices, the glitter of rings and earrings, the smell of cigarettes and the darker tang of cigars. In the background was music but not distinct, just a supporting net of noise for all these other noises.

The overhead lights were off, but there were lamps and candles on every surface, so the whole place was like a thousand tiny circuses, Sarah thought, bumping up against each other, but each with its own little spotlight, and its own performers. Men with deep voices and big hands, women in sparkly jewellery and dresses like rainbows. There was a smell that was of flowers and incense and spices and perfume all mixed together. She could smell the oranges that, directed by Jamie's mum, she and Jamie had stuck with cloves a few weeks before and left to dry out in the hot press. 'They smell like Christmas,' Maeve had said. 'Like presents and rich food.' They did.

Below her, all the little glittering spotlights and performers were joined together by webs of laughter. It seemed like everyone in that hall was laughing and laughing, as if the funniest joke in the world had just been told and Sarah had missed it, having arrived only for the bit afterwards where everyone fell about and couldn't tell you what was so funny.

She saw Maeve, moving from group to group, taking coats, offering drinks, passing on orders to the waiters in black jackets who wove in and out around her. Luke, Alan and Ian had been asked if they wanted to help wait – Sarah had heard Maeve suggest it, saying they would be paid – but Luke had turned it down.

'No way,' he said instantly. 'We've got better things to do.'

'Jake?' Maeve asked then.

'No, thanks. I'd spill something,' Jake said.

Stepping farther down the staircase, Sarah could see into the biggest of the sitting rooms. Simon was at the farthest end, standing almost inside the huge fireplace. Behind him a fire burned, and a log fell, sending up a shower of sparks as Sarah watched, a light patter of flame. Around him were men and women, watching, listening, tuned to the movements of his body and voice. The listeners seemed to grow taller, reaching up as his voice rose, then crouch lower as his voice dropped again, as if they were puppets, dangled by the thread of his voice and hands.

He looked up as Sarah came down and caught her eye. He winked and she smiled at him. Simon was someone she didn't, couldn't, easily talk to. But she liked being seen by him.

The band was outside in the marquee, Sarah knew, and she decided she'd make her way there. Jamie and Celine had disappeared, and it would be a good place to try and find them.

She should have been invisible, walking through that throng of older, more fascinating people who all knew one another, but she wasn't. First it was a man who handed her an empty glass and said, 'Same again,' before going back to the story he was telling, something about the races and a terrible bet he'd made. Sarah stood for a minute, wondering whether to ask him what had been in the glass, but didn't dare. Instead, she sniffed at it. A bitter smell, something sharp and sticky.

She hovered for a moment, edging from foot to foot, waiting for a break in his story so she could ask, but the break didn't come, and so she gave up and put the glass on a side table where it stayed, a grubby reproach, as she moved on.

As she wove in and out of the tightly packed rooms, Sarah tried to work out where her parents might be, so she could avoid them. She didn't want them to see her, all alone in this house where she was supposed to be such a friend.

The O'Reillys must have invited every single person they knew, she decided. Every single person anyone knew, by the look of things. Sarah felt bad, for a second, about her mother's excitement – 'Goodness! A party, at their house!' – now that it was so obvious that there was nothing special about the invitation. But she pushed the feelings aside. She wouldn't feel bad. Not tonight. Not when there was nothing really to feel bad about.

It happened a lot to her lately. That she would want to cry all of a sudden for no reason. Or not a proper reason. It could be the way her mother had folded a slice of fruitcake into a piece of kitchen paper and put it in her lunchbox, an unexpected treat. Finding it, the scene would recreate itself in Sarah's mind – her mother's thin hands, cutting, then buttering, then carefully wrapping the cake – and leave her with a thick lump in her throat, like porridge she couldn't swallow. She didn't know why. Something to do with the effort, the silent kindness, the futility of it. All the care and love that were laid upon her when she didn't know what she could do to earn them or be worthy of them. It was too much love sometimes. Especially times like this, when she felt that she had failed, by her solitude, again, and that her parents would feel the wound more deeply if they knew.

She lifted her head higher and pushed faster, determined to find Jamie and stay with her, even if Celine was there. She ate a mini sausage on a cocktail stick from a tray held in front of her face, and another that she grabbed from a table as she went by. There were tiny pizzas too – she'd seen them earlier – and wondered where they were now.

Around the edges of the rooms were old people, bent and seated, so that Sarah didn't dare sit and look around. They would talk to her, she knew, and she would have no reason to escape them, so she would be trapped. Better to keep moving. Look busy.

'Look at you!' a woman cried, blocking her way. She put

out a hand and placed it flat against Sarah's cheek. It was hot and dry. Sarah flinched. 'So grown up already! So big! I haven't seen you since you were tiny.' Sarah looked around her frantically. Clearly, the woman thought she was Jamie, but she hadn't actually said so, and so Sarah couldn't correct her. The rudeness, the presumption of doing such a thing stopped her. She stood silent, smiling, hoping it would be enough. It wasn't.

'What are you now? Ten?'

'Twelve,' Sarah muttered. 'Nearly thirteen.'

'I don't believe it!' The woman appealed to those around her, maybe for confirmation of her disbelief, or for their support that they, too, were astonished at this girl, this Jamie, being so grown up. They nodded, indifferent.

'The last time I saw you, you were this big.' The woman held her two hands horizontally apart, about the distance of a large shoebox. Sarah wondered why she did it that way. It was weird. As if Jamie had been a baby she had been made to hold. The woman's eyes were round and marvelling. She was wearing a shiny scarlet dress, a colour Sarah loved for its deep glow, but not on this woman, who was too big, so that the scarlet was stretched around and about her. She was like the big top, Sarah thought, gay and bright and huge and strange. She wished Jamie was there so she could have whispered that to her.

'Can I get you another drink?' she asked, desperate.

'Why, you darling! What a kind girl you are.' The woman leaned close in to her, as though to impart a secret, 'I'll have another white wine. But,' she paused, looking around in mock alarm, 'don't tell my husband!' she finished on a shriek. Sarah watched to see if anyone, a man, would hear and turn and pay attention, order her to slow down or even look disapproving. No one did.

'I'll be right back,' Sarah said. She fled to the kitchen. No one was there except black-and-white-clad waiters who didn't say anything to her, busy at their own dance of putting down and picking up. She went out the back door, into the garden.

It was easier there because although there were torches burning hard, pouring out black smoke and flickers of fierce light, in between and around them the air was wet and soft and almost dark, so that she could slip in and out and hardly be seen.

She found Jake on the old bench under the apple tree. He was drinking a Coke and gave her some.

'Are you having fun?'

'Yes.'

'Liar.' He laughed. 'You couldn't be. A load of old people getting drunk and telling each other how great they look. Where's Jamie?'

'I don't know.' She picked at a blistered bit of varnish on the bench. 'Off with Celine somewhere.' She didn't have to pretend with Jake.

'She would be. Celine winds her up like a clockwork mouse and Jamie runs and runs after her until she winds down. But don't worry, she'll get how awful Celine is one of these days.'

'Is she awful?' She was eager, too eager, for his answer.

'Of course she is. Celine's an idiot.'

Maybe, thought Sarah, but it hardly mattered. Not when you were that sure of yourself, so that everyone else was sure of you too.

Jake asked her what she was reading, and told her about a book he thought she'd enjoy, then: 'I'm going to get us something to eat. You stay here. Did you see any of those little pizzas as you came out?'

'No. But I looked. They're not in the kitchen.'

'OK. I'll try further in. Wish me luck!'

It was nice, waiting there for Jake, knowing he was coming back. 'I'm just waiting for Jake,' she could say, if anyone asked, and it would sound fine. Good, even. She could watch and not be seen, try and take in the hugeness of this party which already seemed to her to have been going on for a long time. The band were playing one of the songs her mother liked – 'The Sweetest Taboo' – except it was a man singing it, not the woman with the smoky voice, and he was trilling and frilling the edges of it in a way Sarah knew was awful. All the same, she was singing along, quietly, when she felt a hand sudden on her head, heavy as a blow, from the darkness behind her so that she sucked her breath back in, hard and sharp and loud, as if she was choking on a boiled sweet.

'What are you doing?' It was Luke, with Ian behind him, the usual jeer in his voice.

'Waiting for Jake.' Thank goodness she had something to say.

'Waiting for Jake to do what? Cop on and stop being such a loser?'

'He's getting something to eat. And drink.'

'Here. I've got something to drink. This.' He held out a clear glass bottle with a red label Sarah couldn't read because his hand was over it. In the bottle was a bright orange liquid.

'What is it?'

'Kool-Aid. You'll love it.'

'No thanks.' She didn't like the look of the bottle. Or the sound of Luke's voice. Least of all the sniggering of Ian and another guy she had only just noticed beside him.

'Oh, just drink it. We all have. It's fire water.' Luke laughed, loudly. His voice was loud too, Sarah noticed and she looked around, hoping to see Jake. Or Jamie. Even Celine. 'Come on.' He shook the bottle in her face, waggling it back and forth by the neck now. 'Come on!' Irritated, the way he was with Taylor the dog when they were out and she ran off and wouldn't come back when he called her.

Sarah took the bottle, unscrewed the top and sniffed. She smelled the fake orangey smell of one of those dilutable drinks her mother didn't let her have. Luke waggled the bottom of the bottle and tilted it towards her mouth. Her lips met glass and Luke stared at her as he pushed harder. Sarah angled her head back, away, but the liquid came up anyway and rushed around her lips and into her mouth. It was diluted orange, made without enough water so that it was thick and smooth and sugary. She swallowed, then more as Luke kept pushing the bottle at her. There was a burn to the sugary orangeness of it. She swallowed more, watching Luke watch her over the top of the bottle, then turned her head away so the bottle slipped and some of the orange spilled.

'Be careful,' he said. He raised the glass to his own lips then and drank deeply, then passed it to Ian. 'Get stuck in,' he said. After Ian, the bottle came back to Sarah and she drank more, and more deeply, but this time because she wanted to, not because Luke made her. There was something about the drink that heated a warm path down her throat and into her stomach, which she liked.

She sat back on the bench and watched Luke and Ian clowning round with their friend, who had a voice that went up and down like a see-saw, swooping from high to low and back again. They were shoving each other and shouting out lyrics to rap songs, Luke swaggering up and down, in and out of fire and shadow so that sometimes his voice came without him and sometimes it was with him as he punched the air and bumped shoulders with Ian.

They were like angry monkeys, Sarah thought, squaring up to each other, except that the anger wasn't real, just gestures and cries. More a dance that they did, showing off to each other.

The orange from the drink seemed to have bled into the air and things around her, or maybe it had seeped up from her stomach to her eyes like coloured lenses, so that everything she saw was orange. Fuzzy, orange and beating gently back and forth like a giant heart with her at the centre. It was nice, kind of warm. She wanted to leap around with the boys but the heart held her in its pulsing grip and she couldn't make herself move. The bench was soft now, moulding like clay to her back. She leaned farther into it, head slipping to one side, then farther as she began to slide downwards.

'Jesus Christ, Luke!' There was Jake, staring at her, a plate of cocktail sausages in his hand. 'What the hell?'

'What?' Luke came up close to him, head thrust forward, jaw jutting out. 'What's your problem?'

'What the fuck did you give her? She can't even sit up.'

'Oh, fucking relax, will you? It's just a joke.'

'It's not funny! Look at her!'

They were shouting at each other now and Sarah decided she'd better get away because it seemed to be her fault. She couldn't properly follow what was happening but her name kept popping up, said by first one of them, then the other, so that she felt she was watching a tennis match with her name as the ball: back, forth, back, forth. Whack, whack, whack. She tried to follow her name with her eyes, from one to the other, but her neck hurt, so she let herself slide all the way down and off the bench, then used it to help herself to stand. Her legs were wobbly and the orange fuzziness was worse when she was moving. It made her feel sick now, as if the orange was trying to come up and out from inside her. She steered herself towards the music coming from the marquee.

The entrance was crowded with people smoking but she pushed her way in. Then a man grabbed her as she tried to squeeze past. 'She'll tell us!' he said loudly, taking hold of her arm and drawing her towards him. Sarah couldn't remember how to resist. 'Won't you?'

'Tell you what?' Sarah muttered. The lights were too bright, hard white twinklings that confused her because she couldn't understand what they were supposed to be doing. There was a pattern to the twinkling, on and off, flicker-flicker, but she couldn't follow it.

The man was holding her arm too hard and the arm was telling her that it hurt, but only in the way that someone else might tell you about a pain they had; you knew it was there because they said it was, but you couldn't actually feel it.

'Tell you what?' she asked again.

'What the next generation intend to do about it?' There was meanness in the way he said this. As if it – whatever it was – was Sarah's fault, and he knew it, had had it whispered to him just minutes before by someone malicious.

'About what?' she asked.

'About the bloody mess we're in.' The man's voice went up and he waved his hand around in a broad sweep. What mess? Had she done something? She couldn't quite remember where she'd just been, where she'd come from. Maybe she'd broken something? Or knocked something over?

'Well?' he demanded.

Maybe he didn't mean her, maybe he meant the house? The party? The O'Reilly's? Everything?

'I think it seems really nice,' she said cautiously.

'Nice? *Nice?* Is that all you have to say about it?' He was angry now. She had angered him, but how she didn't know. '*Nice?*' Sarah wished he would stop saying the word. 'I told you,' he said to the rest of the group. 'This generation don't care about anything.'

She pulled her arm but he didn't let go. The men standing around started to edge back and one or two of them said, 'Forget it, Mick,' in voices with laughter in them. 'That's kids for you.'

'Mick, leave her alone.' It was Simon, suddenly among them, good-natured but firm. Firmer again after a moment when Mick didn't let go. 'Mick. Enough.'

'Kids,' Mick said, almost in surprise. He looked around, as though waking, and released Sarah's arm with such force that she lurched backwards and nearly fell. She looked at Simon.

'Thank you,' she whispered.

'Go on, scram,' he said, with a grin. He didn't seem to notice that she was sliding around inside herself, but he must have seen something because his arm came out and caught her, fast and sure, as she stumbled forward and vomited at his feet.

CHAPTER 18

The marquee was less crowded than the house and Miriam ordered another gin and tonic from the black-and-white-clad waiter behind the bar. 'Make it a double,' she said with a laugh, 'so I don't have to come back too soon.' He smiled, weary, indifferent, already moving off to the row of bottles behind him. She wondered should she have worn something else, something sexier. The white linen that had pleased her so much now seemed dowdy. All around her, women were wearing dresses that hugged and clung and plunged, in colours like an array of penny sweets. They looked tight and uncomfortable and hot, but there was a gay willingness too that she admired. It was, she decided, the modern equivalent of drawing lines up the backs of their legs the way French women had done during the war: a kind of determined vivacity.

On the other side of the tent, blocking the entrance so that those coming in had to sidle past him, crab-wise, was the man

Paul had indicated to her earlier, Mick O'Hagen. The stillness was gone and he was gesticulating, furiously animated, while around him a group of men wearing the same kinds of grey suits and brightly coloured cravats laughed and nodded. She wondered where Paul was.

She asked the waiter for a cigarette, then thanked him too much when he gave her a packet, even tried to pay him, so that he said, 'Don't thank me, they're not mine, they're on the house. I'm just handing them out.'

Feeling somehow slapped down, she went outside to smoke and found a heavy wrought iron table and chair, too low and uncomfortable, but in a shadowy corner that allowed her a view of the house and garden.

The band was playing 'Sweet Caroline' now, the singer giving it socks and she imagined couples dancing, men with their own wives and other people's wives. What might it be like, she wondered, to press up close against a man who wasn't Paul? And what might it be like to belong there, in that world? In that house? With those people? Would her life be bigger, grander, more vital and exciting, the way she imagined? Or would it really, after all, just be the same – a small life, with edges that were hard and so close together they nearly touched each other?

Every room in that house spoke of Maeve, she realised. Smelled of her, wore her colours – the touches of orange, fuchsia, purple and stinging yellow that were the flashes of her personality, like a hedgerow seen at speed from a moving car; a blur, in which a few bright spots stood out. The clocks and watches spoke of her, and to her; those that ticked and tocked, and, even more surely the silent broken ones – imploring her to notice, to fix them.

And Maeve, Miriam thought, responded to them in a way she didn't to her children: gently. The impatience that her children's moments of fragility brought out in her was set aside when the supplicants were made of delicate metal cogs and wheels.

And maybe mending clocks was more satisfying, Miriam thought. Do this, and that, replace this bit, and the reassuring tick told you you'd got it right. Unlike children who grew and changed no matter how much you loved the way they were; and learned to hide themselves behind a version of themselves that was badly, incompletely, made up, devised entirely to keep you out. How long, she wondered, since Sarah had told her anything that she didn't have to? Only rudimentary information – times, dates, requests for stationery – now emerged from the polite distance she had set up.

Sometimes, recently, she had come upon Sarah crying, or with the fat red eyes that said she had been crying.

'What's wrong?' she would ask, with alarm, with tenderness, with frustration.

'Nothing,' Sarah always said. 'Nothing.' As if she meant it. As if she didn't know what she meant.

When had her own life become so small, Miriam wondered, looking out into the dark? So small and neatly bordered, so that the idea of Sarah needing her less was frightening in ways she had not managed to understand. Was it the empty hours? The empty house? She could get a job, she knew that, or volunteer, or take up golf, although none of those things appealed. The real problem was the feeling of a chapter closing before she was ready.

When Sarah was a baby and Miriam had allowed the fact of her to expand and grow into every corner of her life and squeeze Paul to the very edges, she had not thought ahead to a time when Sarah would no longer want that place. Would instead shrink herself so as to occupy less than the fullness of her mother's life, because she wanted the privacy of her own.

Must she now try to encourage Paul back into all that empty space? How would she do it? Would he even want her to? She thought not – there had been a glow about him recently that she found easy to connect to the 'bit of business' he was doing with Simon.

If only there were more children for her to concentrate on. A younger brother for Sarah, a child who would still now need her.

'He only has to look at me and I get pregnant,' she suddenly remembered Maeve saying one night in Portugal, looking over at Simon and laughing a little self-consciously. Miriam, beside her, had flinched, as if Maeve had just flicked her with the casual sharp edge of a nail. *She doesn't know, how could she know*, she told herself instantly. But the night had been spoiled for Miriam.

'Miriam?' The sound of her name from the dark behind her made her jump. It was Simon. 'I think you'd better come,' he said. 'Sarah's been sick.'

*

Sarah was lying across three spindly white chairs, surrounded by a knot of people with glasses of water and concerned faces. Her eyes were unfocused and she was panting like an animal. Moving quickly to her, Miriam caught a whiff of vomit, and the same sweetish smell of alcohol and the something sticky and orange that Luke had had.

The girl was so obviously drunk that Miriam couldn't understand why no one had said anything – the various concerned meddlers had talked of the heat in the marquee, the excitement, the lateness of the hour but never of alcohol or intoxication.

'She's tired and over-excited,' a woman with two wings of poker-straight shiny brown hair hanging on either side of her face said, disapproving, almost as if it were Miriam's fault for not minding her better.

'It's too stuffy in here,' said another.

Miriam sat on one of the spindly white chairs and put her arm around her daughter, who now struggled to sit up. Her hair smelled so bad that Miriam was about to say this very thing – 'She's drunk!' – when she stopped and considered. To say it would be to accuse, to shout 'foul play', to demand, 'How is a twelve-year-old drunk? At your party?' and in doing so, she would be dragging Maeve and Simon into some kind of complicity with the outrage. Impossible to mention it without making it their fault. And so Miriam said nothing at first, just wiped Sarah's forehead and then the corners of her mouth with a wet napkin someone handed her, then finally said, 'I think we'd better take you home.'

Sarah was lying half-across her, too big to sit on her lap,

but too miserable not to try. At her mother's words, she tried to pull herself upright. 'I'm not going home. I don't want to.'

'Sarah, love, you need to go to sleep. In your own bed.'

'I don't. I want to stay.' She struggled away from Miriam, but slowly, like someone pulling themselves from thick mud or quicksand.

'Darling, it's not a good idea. You should come home.'

'No. I want to stay. You said I could stay. It's a sleepover.'

Sarah sounded tearful, her voice sharp with what might be building hysteria and Miriam looked around for some kind of help. Where was Paul? Could he not step in and help her solve this? There was no sign of him and she was about to ask, 'Could someone find my husband?' when Jamie said, 'I'll put her to bed. I'll take her straight up now.'

'And stay with her,' Maeve, who had just arrived, said firmly. Miriam noticed the girl beside Jamie – Celine, was that her name? Semolina? – rolling her eyes.

'Are you sure?' Miriam asked.

'Of course,' Jamie said politely.

'It's time for you to go up anyway,' Maeve said. 'You and Celine,' she added firmly. Celine, Miriam saw, rolled her eyes again.

'Please, Mum?' Sarah begged. And so Miriam agreed and helped Jamie arrange Sarah upright, half-supported, and watched them cross the lawn and out of sight into the pools of darkness that joined the dots between house and marquee.

'She'll be fine,' Maeve said, unable to quite meet Miriam's gaze. 'I'll look in on them later.'

'Come and have a drink.' That was Simon, concern and a faint stain of guilt on his face.

He and Miriam took drinks – whiskey for him, another gin for Miriam – back out to the table where she had been sitting and Miriam lit another cigarette.

'She'll be fine,' he said confidently. 'Sarah.' Then, 'How are you enjoying the party?'

''People Are Strange',' Miriam said in a sing-song voice.

'What?'

'It's a song by The Doors. But you know what I mean. I don't know anyone, and no one seems to want to talk to me much. I guess it's not really my world.' She shrugged. Simon looked upset, his own pleasure in the party spoiled.

'More fool them,' he said. 'I want to talk to you.' And he leaned in for what might have been a hug, except that Miriam turned towards him so that it became a kiss. Even then, she knew that if she hadn't so instantly kissed him back it would have been nothing, a slight embarrassment, a quick righting of themselves. But she kissed him as hard, much harder, than he kissed her and pushed herself towards him so that he held her close and carried on kissing her, and what, really, was nothing became a promise. A threat.

CHAPTER 19

On the way home Miriam watched early morning rain run down the taxi window, washing away the colour and sparkle of the night. Beyond the glass, greasy with the imprint of someone else's head, the world was flat and grey, like the headache building behind her eyes.

The thumping excitement of those moments in Simon's arms seemed a lie now, a trick. A thing that had never happened or that had happened to someone else. She felt as though she had watched the scene on a screen somewhere; his lumbering move in for a hug, her own snake-like wriggle that had inserted her body into the awkward space created by his so that they were kissing, at first politely, by accident, then, as if a light had gone on for both of them, much harder.

Why had she let him kiss her? Or made him, if she was honest? Was it to do with it being his party, his territory? The way everything around him hailed him as king, so that he was a fixed point where she had none? Yes, but it was other things too, pathetic things that she was ashamed of. The way everyone had ignored her, even the barman, that kid, who turned away from her weak jokes with more interesting things on his mind. The way it had been her daughter who had lain across those three spindly chairs, stinking of vomit.

It was also, she knew, something to do with the abundance of the O'Reillys; the way they spilled over – with money, with things, with flesh, with hair, and enthusiasm, and children. She wanted some of it.

The gap between her family and that of the O'Reillys, which had seemed to close in Portugal, had opened again, and become vast, that night. It was her empty days, the grinding fears around money, the years that moved forward and dragged her behind them; it was Maeve's voice saying, 'He only has to look at me and I get pregnant,' and the expression on her face as she said it.

Most of all, it was the careful reserve between herself and Paul that dug itself deeper within them both, year after year, so that he held her now as if she were glass and might break. All the times when she had cried and he had comforted her, when she had cursed her body and its messy failures, ending all her hopes in a rush of early blood, when he had stood by and promised her that it wasn't her, it was them both, or neither of them – those times had left a mark between them, roped them to each other in a way that was uncertain and tender and yet slowly scraped away at passion, honeycombing it and weakening it until it collapsed. So that now, when Simon reached, there was no opposite gravitational pull from home. From Paul.

It was all of that, and, as much as any of it, the rush of desire that grew thick and hot within her at Simon's touch, so that even though she had broken away first, said, 'We can't,' she knew well that if he had simply taken her hand and led her into some dark spot, without a word, she would have gone.

'You can't call me,' she had said as they separated, determined to be first to shut down something that was so obviously impossible. Knowing, too, that she had not the strength to expect or hope. That her days, already hard to fill, would become torment if she were now to add vigilance for calls that might not come.

'OK,' Simon had said, looking dazed. 'OK.'

'Tell me, exactly what happened with Sarah?' Paul asked now from the seat beside her. But because of what she had done, and because he had not been there when their daughter had been draped across her, stinking of vomit and booze, Miriam didn't answer his question.

Instead she said, 'She lets those kids run wild.' She needed to suggest something unkind about Maeve. Something that would rebalance the scales, because right now, all the wrong was on her side. 'Especially Luke. He's out of control. He was completely drunk. Or high. And whatever Sarah had, I'm certain he was the one who gave it to her.'

'OK, but they're *his* kids too,' Paul said reasonably.

'Well, I know, but, I mean, he works. She doesn't. She just lets them do whatever they want and never interferes. She says it's better for them to work things out for themselves. In fact it's just like a mini, South Dublin version of *Lord of the Flies*,' Miriam said viciously. 'With Luke in charge.'

'Well, that's never going to be good,' Paul said, with half a laugh, reaching for her hand. 'But all the same,' he added, 'shouldn't we have just brought Sarah home?'

'She wouldn't come,' Miriam said. 'You weren't there; she was about to have hysterics. What was I supposed to do?' The sharpness of her voice, the consciousness of his own failure to have been where he was needed, kept Paul silent. That, and the same knowledge that had kept Miriam from speaking up in the marquee: that to complain about what happened to Sarah would be to criticise the O'Reillys and the way they ran their house, their family.

'Maybe she spends too much time there?' he said instead.

'She needs friends,' Miriam said. 'Kids her own age.' What she didn't say – although they both knew it – was that they needed friends too. That the dazzle of Maeve, Simon, their children, meant there was no such thing as 'No.' Not when invitations to Sarah brought them along too.

'I suppose it's what kids do,' he said then. 'Experiment. Try things out. Alcohol, cigarettes.'

'Did you see them smoking?' Miriam asked sharply. She had left her own packet, the one the barman had given her, behind on the wrought iron table, as if it contained all that she had done wrong and could be neatly abandoned.

'No. I just mean, it's what teenagers do.'

'She's not a teenager; she's twelve.'

'Well, what do you want me to say?' He sounded irritated

then, dropping her hand and shifting away from her on the taxi seat. 'I think we should have brought her home.'

'Well, you weren't there,' she said again. The flat greyness, she realised, was inside her, not in the damp early morning. 'It wasn't a very good party,' she said, then, knowing she was being spiteful. 'I hope you enjoyed it more than me.'

'It was OK,' he said, cautious; 'some of Simon's friends are interesting.'

Hearing Simon's name from Paul's mouth made Miriam feel sick, so she opened the cab window quickly and breathed in the damp early morning air. It smelled of regret. Of something rolled up and finished, like a function room carpet.

She wondered whether to tell Paul about Luke helping her down from the window, brushing hard against her, but knew she would only be doing it to set a new fire, something to take her own gaze away from the one she had lit with Simon.

CHAPTER 20

It was so typical of Sarah to get sick, Jamie thought. If anyone was going to, it would always be her. Jake was furious with Luke, but it wasn't his fault. He hadn't made Sarah drink that stuff. Anyway, they all had a bit of it – it was a party. That was the point of a party.

Lending Sarah a belt had been easy. Standing up for her with Celine was easy too. She'd have done that for anyone. What wasn't easy with Sarah was being with her as much as Sarah wanted her to be. Realising that Sarah always wanted more. That no matter what Jamie did with her, or for how long, she would always want more. Extra. Reassurance that there would be a Next Time.

'When can I stay again?' she would ask as she left after a weekend, face all screwed up and worried. And when Jamie said, 'Soon,' the face would relax a bit. But only a bit. Times like that, Jamie had to remind herself that they did have fun together, of how Sarah could be funny, interesting, with her strange little games and the things she said and thought, so different to the things Jamie said and thought but the funnier for that.

But there were times, Jamie found, when she didn't know where she ended and Sarah began, or even if they were separate at all. It was like turning round and seeing yourself in a mirror you hadn't known was there. You got a fright and wondered, *Who's that?* And then realised, *Oh. It's me . . .*

Sarah wore her clothes, lay on her bed, hung out with her family, went where Jamie went, did what she did. She walked every step that Jamie walked, treading in her footsteps, sleeping beside her. She drank water from Jamie's bottle and tea from the mug Jamie had just used.

She even used Jamie's words. Like when Jamie started saying 'neat' because she heard it on a TV show and liked it, and almost straight away Sarah began using it too: 'That's so neat.' When Jamie said, 'Stop copying me,' Sarah had acted as if she was offended with Jamie for even suggesting she was copying: 'Everyone says "neat".' But it was a lie. Only Jamie had said it before Sarah started. And then Jamie had to make herself stop.

Celine said they should set a trap – make up a word, or give one a new meaning, like saying things were 'rage' when they meant great, and wait for Sarah to copy them, and then laugh at her. And when Jamie said, 'I'm not doing that, that's horrible,' Celine retorted, 'You let her get away with murder.'

And for all that they had fun, there were times with Sarah when Jamie felt prickly, like she was wearing a wool jumper with no T-shirt – all scratchy around the neck and wrists. It felt to her as if she was in charge of Sarah and of what happened to her and how she felt. As if everything Sarah did and felt was Jamie's to shape and decide, so that it was Jamie's problem if Sarah was upset. Partly, this was because Maeve had told her, 'When she's in your house, it's your responsibility to see she's happy.' But mostly it was because Sarah gave her that power, even though Jamie had never asked for it.

Her mum kept saying she should be kind to Sarah because, 'She doesn't have what you have. No brothers, only parents. She's lonely.'

But Jamie didn't think Sarah was lonely. She decided that she liked being on her own: she certainly didn't hate it the way Jamie did. Sarah could sit and read a book for hours on her own, and only if Jamie said, 'Let's do something,' did she stop.

It was funny with Sarah, Jamie thought. Her dad would say, 'She's so quiet, it's like she's not even there.' That was his reason for always inviting her. As if that was a good reason for inviting someone, Jamie thought! Surely the point of them was that they were there and you knew they were there and wanted them to be? And anyway, it wasn't true. Sarah might not say much, but you knew when she was there because everything was different. Only a little bit different, but enough to notice.

Taylor, the dog, didn't like Sarah. She ignored her. But Sarah didn't like Taylor either. Alan didn't notice her much, obviously – he didn't notice any of them much since he'd started college – but Luke and Jake were strange with Sarah around. Luke was even meaner – he teased her the way he used to tease that cat in Greece, putting a piece of string with a bit of fatty meat tied onto it in front of the poor little thing, to tempt it, and then jerking it away. Jake was the opposite: he tried to be kind. He was, Jamie thought, like her mum – he felt sorry for Sarah.

Sometimes Jamie liked it when Luke teased Sarah. It was nasty of her, she knew – her mother would have said it was 'cruel' – but she could see why he wanted to. She was like a scab you wanted to pick. It hurt you, but the urge was stronger than the pain. Jamie couldn't do it herself – tease Sarah like that – because she got that look on her face that said she was trying not to cry, and then Jamie felt terrible. But she let Luke do it and didn't always tell him to stop. She had let him give Sarah that Kool-Aid drink and didn't tell him not to. 'I'm going to feed this to Sarah,' he had said as he passed her on his way round the back of the marquee, shaking the bottle so the orange liquid rose up like lava in the clear glass.

'She won't drink it,' Jamie replied.

'Yes, she will.'

'Tell her it's orange squash. Her mum doesn't let her drink that stuff, so she won't know what it's supposed to taste like,' Jamie said in a rush.

Luke gave her a smirking look, and she hoped he wouldn't tell Jake what she had said. Jake would be furious. The exact thing that made Jamie want to hurt Sarah a bit was what made Jake protective of her. 'She's out of her depth,' he used to say. 'She hasn't worked it out yet. She'll find her feet eventually.'

For Jamie, wanting to tease Sarah was to do with Sarah being so quiet, sucking on her two fingers and staring, staring, staring. Not ever asking could she have something, always waiting till someone asked her and then saying, 'I don't mind,' or, 'If you like,' instead of 'Yes.' Jamie would tell Celine to stop, though, when Celine was being mean. Family, she knew, was different and Celine wasn't family, and Sarah sort of was.

As for what Sarah thought about Jake and Luke – she was clearly mad about Jake, following him around nearly as much as she followed Jamie, asking what he was reading and was it good. Luke, it was harder to tell. Sarah would just stare at him with those big round eyes, as if she might have to run away fast and didn't know what direction to go in.

Maeve liked Sarah, but then, she was always creeping up to Maeve. Going for little walks with her and asking about her family and where she grew up and the things she did as a child. Sometimes, Jamie thought, it was like she was Maeve's daughter too, as much as Jamie was. Even the fact that they both called her Maeve. For a while, Jamie tried saying 'Mum' the way she used to when she was smaller, but it didn't really suit the way 'Maeve' did.

And Maeve gave Sarah Jamie's stuff – Jamie's jodhpurs; her pyjamas when Sarah forgot hers; even Jamie's room. Sarah sat in there, reading, like it was her own room, so that Jamie couldn't go there to get away from her. 'She feels a bit strange,' Maeve would say, 'downstairs with all of us. Let her have your room for a bit while she's here. You have the whole house.'

Maeve had insisted Sarah come to Jamie's last birthday party – 'I don't think she's having one of her own; it would be nice to invite her' – but it wasn't nice for Jamie at all. Sarah clung on, literally hanging onto Jamie's arm or her sleeve the whole day. And when it was time for pizza and cake, her mum had put Sarah right beside her so that every time Jamie turned round, there she was, staring at her.

Jamie thought about the books Jake read, the ones about quests and sorcery and stuff – he'd made her read one once, saying she'd like it, but she hadn't. But there was a bit in the book, she remembered, about if you save someone's life, then their life belonged to you. Except she hadn't saved Sarah's life, even though Sarah said she had; she had just pulled her up in the pool. If Jamie hadn't done it, someone else would have. She didn't want Sarah's gratitude. And she certainly didn't want her life.

Being stuck up in her room while the party went on downstairs, loud and funny, had been awful. And all because Sarah was drunk and had got sick. Celine had been even more cross at being sent to bed than Jamie was, and so they decided to sneak down again once Sarah was asleep – which was pretty quick. She sort of passed out.

Once downstairs again, they had to stay away from the grown-ups or they would have been sent back to bed, so it was like being 'on manoeuvres', as Luke said, meaning some kind of army thing. They made a den behind the marquee and went on foraging trips to get stuff – drinks, pizza, cake – far more than they needed, because of how much fun it was, making their way through all the people without being seen.

Luke found cigarettes on a table and brought them back with him and lit one. They all had a puff, and even though Jamie thought it was gross, she didn't say so. They drank more of the Kool-Aid which had apple juice too in it now and, Luke said, whiskey, because he couldn't get hold of any more vodka and orange. After that, Luke got sick too and they all went up to bed.

But even though she went into her room so quietly, and Celine was quiet too, as soon as Jamie closed the door behind them, Sarah sat up in the pull-out bed and said: 'Where were you?'

CHAPTER 21

'God, I hate houses after parties,' Maeve said, piling dirty glasses on a tray. 'If we leave the windows open for a month, the place will still stink of smoke. Look.' She pointed at a plate filled with cigarette butts squashed onto half a leftover pizza. 'Who would do that? What foul people our friends are.'

'*Our?* You mean "your", don't you?' Simon said from the depths of an armchair. He was drunk and enunciating his words carefully, so as not to slur. He sounded, Maeve thought, like someone picking his way across a river, precise and unsteady, from stone to slippery stone. His stomach rose up, hard and round, in front of him and his legs were planted apart to make room for the bulk of it. She wanted to fall on her knees in front of him then, and beg him to stop drinking, to lose weight, to be again the man she had married, who made love to her anywhere he could, shameless and eager.

Now, he turned off the light even to walk from the bathroom to their bed, and would quickly pull the covers over himself. But she knew from experience that he would hear only her disgust and not the desire that still lay beneath it. And so she said nothing now.

But she planned to, as soon as the moment was right. Simon was like one of her watches, a solid antique one, well-made but now worn. He was predictable, obeyed the laws of his own dynamics. At times, things went wrong. But never anything that couldn't be easily fixed or replaced. And once he was running again, the reassuring tick-tock of his presence, solid, reliable, inevitable, unmovable, was the thing she measured herself by. The progress of his existence was logical and linear – not like the children with their chaotic unpredictability, which confused and wore her out. And because of that, even though she and Simon moved out of line with one another sometimes, like now, they could always, easily, find their shape again. She knew that; lived by her certainty of it.

And so she merely replied, 'No, no – *our* friends, Simon. For now, anyway. Until I find a burn in a rug or a red wine stain down the back of the sofa. Then, they're yours.'

'Just leave it,' Simon said, yawning. 'Gemma's coming in the morning.'

'I know, but I can't let her walk in to this. I'll do a dishwasher-load at least. Those barmen, bar boys really, were pathetic. They were supposed to do this, but you paid them too early and then they disappeared.' She started to laugh. 'In a puff of smoke, practically. I turned around, and they were all gone. I swear I saw a bottle wobbling on the sideboard where one of them had just abandoned it.'

'Oh, just leave it,' Simon said again. 'I'm going upstairs. You're making me feel bad.'

'Good,' she said. Then: 'I don't think the Ryans had much of a time, do you? Or at least, Miriam didn't. Paul seemed to be having fun.' She was stacking bottles, colour-coding them: green wine bottles together, white spirit bottles, small brown beer bottles. There seemed an awful lot of them. But she enjoyed the slow gathering and sorting, and the effect, almost like a mosaic, of the graded colours. She angled a lamp so that it cast its glow through the ranks of glass, like early morning in a church with darkness still massed inside it even as light began to split the windows.

'That's not your problem,' Simon said firmly, shifting in his chair. 'All you can do is give the party and invite people. It's up to them if they have a good time or not. Anyway, Paul certainly did,' he said with a laugh. 'Letting him at Mick O'Hagen is like letting a terrier into a barn full of rats.'

'Should you really be introducing Paul to all that?'

'I'm giving him a chance to make a bit of money, that's all. He could do with it.'

'How do you know? Did he tell you that?'

'No, but it's obvious.'

'What's obvious is that they don't have much money,' Maeve said, careful with the distinction, 'not that they want more. There is a difference, you know.' Saying it, she knew that he didn't know. For Simon, the idea of having less because you didn't want more, was strange and unconvincing, something to be suspicious of.

Sure enough, his response came quickly. 'That's nonsense,' he said, waving the idea away. 'And selfish. If I have the chance to do someone a good turn, I'll take it.'

'Well, I just wonder if it's a good idea. Sometimes it's better to leave people alone. To not be trying to drag everyone to where you are.'

'Neither a dabbler nor a meddler be?'

'Exactly.'

'OK, but it's not advice or interference; it's a chance for him to make a bit extra. I get the impression things are very tight. That car they drive . . . And the kid could be going to a better school. She's not doing well where she is. Paul said there were "difficulties".'

'I wonder is that the school though,' Maeve said thoughtfully. 'Or Sarah? She's a funny little thing . . .'

'Having the option to change schools if they want would be good for them.'

'Well, I suppose a bit extra can't hurt,' she said, not at all sure that she believed it.

'You're too country,' Simon said with a laugh. 'Suspicious of getting involved with anyone. You like a good strong boundary line!'

'It's not that. Or maybe it is . . .' She found it hard to put words on her belief, deep-held, that lives should not run too far into each other; should hold their separate courses and converge only to diverge again. She moved into the rooms beyond, gathering glasses and loading them onto trays, her voice coming and going under the high ceilings and through the smoky air.

'I know that's what you think,' he said. 'I was surprised you kept the friendship going.'

There where whispers in the glasses Maeve was picking up, tiny ghosts of voices, telling her what drinks people had drunk, what jokes they'd made, what lipstick or perfume they wore. She poured the dregs from each into an antique silver ice bucket one of Simon's cousins had given them when they were married, watching the liquid within swirl, contaminated, flecks of ash rising to the surface.

'It was because of Luke,' she said.

'Luke? How?'

'Just something he said reminded me . . .' Lifting the tray higher, she heard again Luke's voice, one Sunday evening before the boys went back to school, in the kitchen where they were eating macaroni cheese. 'Remember that weird friend of Jamie's,' he had said, looking around for a laugh. 'The one from Portugal. The skinny little cat-girl?'

'Sarah,' Jamie had replied, only half-paying attention. She'd named her as one might describe a dream, a thing that faded even as you spoke it.

'She was alright,' Jake said. 'Just a bit shy.'

'That's her,' Luke said, ignoring Jake. 'Sarah.' He dug at the dried-on macaroni cheese in the dish in front of him. 'Weirdo.' And in that minute Maeve, who had only barely been paying attention as she ran through the mental litany of *studs*, *trainers*, *mouthguards*, had seen again Sarah's face the way she had first seen it: the flickering shade of the tree that did not hide the look of wonder the child had turned on Jamie, and then her dismayed humiliation, so swiftly absorbed, when Maeve had seemed ready to reject her.

'Would you like to see Sarah again?' she'd suddenly asked Jamie then. 'They don't live far from us. You could have her over?'

'OK,' Jamie said.

And so Maeve had phoned, offering excuses that were true but a lie – yes, she had been busy, but, too, she had been pretty indifferent, ready to leave behind the short friendship – and invited Sarah over to their house to play. And she had felt good about doing it – as if it was the right thing – and that lasted for a while as she watched Sarah slowly settle into the house and find her place in it.

'The thing is,' she said now, 'it's hard for Jamie, staying friends when Sarah isn't in the same school, and when Jamie has so much going on with hockey and the horses and everything. And Sarah doesn't get on with her other friends.'

She didn't know what she wanted from the conversation, and was too tired to work it out, beyond a feeling that maybe Sarah and Jamie shouldn't any longer spend so much time together; that maybe they all needed to untangle a bit. The lines between them had become somehow muddled, like one of those 'follow the thread' comic book puzzles that led you through a knotted tangle, then emerged to link together unexpected objects, never the ones you expected.

Maeve picked up a tray, full now of grubby glasses, and started towards the door. The floorboards bounced and the glasses on the tray jingled, striking chimes from each other as though she were wearing harness and bells. She loved the way the house cheered her on, responding to every step she took, every surface she passed, with its own chorus of approval – creaks and bumps and gentle encouraging sighs.

'Perhaps we should all see each other less for a bit,' she said.

'I've invited them to Kerry with us,' Simon said as she passed the armchair where he sprawled.

'What?' She paused in the doorway, tray balanced against a hip.

'The Ryans. I said they should come down with us next year.'

'Oh.' Then, 'I wish you hadn't.'

'Maybe they won't come.'

'Maybe.'

CHAPTER 22

One year later: Kerry, August 2000

The drive had taken so long that it was evening now, the day shifting into a lower gear around them. Sarah felt as if she had never sat anywhere except that car, never breathed in anything but the stale smell of cheese and onion crisps. Taylor the dog was lying at her feet and beside her Jake read quietly. Jamie, on the other side of him, whispered sometimes to her brother and giggled quietly, ignoring Sarah.

They had left Dublin early, turning out of the iron gates of Number Eight while the morning was still slow and grey. Maeve, turning the wheel with one hand and holding a mug of coffee with the other, had said, with satisfaction, 'We'll beat the traffic.' Then, 'Well done, all of you. I'll buy you doughnuts when we get past the Red Cow.'

She had come into Jamie's room before the sun was properly up and opened the curtains briskly and Sarah, who had been awake for what felt like hours, had turned over, pretending to sleep still. She hadn't wanted Maeve to know she was awake, or about the pain in her stomach and the worry that scratched at the back of her throat.

It had all seemed so exciting the night before, arriving at Jamie's with her bags, packed for the weeks ahead with swimsuits and clothes, 'for every one of the four seasons', as her mother had said, while watching them being stowed in Simon's car with all the other bags.

'Wait till you see my Reevanagh room,' Jamie had said. 'It's got sideways windows in the roof and there are places you can't even stand up fully.' Sarah had felt she was starting an adventure, one that would show her something special and secret about this family, so that she would see them all more truly. They didn't know – obviously they didn't – how much she thought about them all when she wasn't with them. In the way she had once played with things she found – sticks, feathers, leaves, arranging them into families and making up stories about them – she now did the same with the O'Reillys. Placing and re-placing them in her mind constantly, in relation to each other and to her.

She made up stories in which Luke was nice to her, Jamie was always affectionate and happy, Alan included her in his complicated jokes (even though she didn't get them), Maeve and Simon paid her the same attention – as much; as little – they paid their own kids. In these stories, only Jake was the same as in real life: kind, careful, maybe even fond. She found herself spinning such stories endlessly. Sometimes she would do something daring, like rescue Jamie from a tree she had climbed or from a boat out in a high wind, ignoring the most obvious fact – that Jamie would never need rescuing, that she would be, had been, the one to rescue her. And each story ended in the same way – with all the family crowding round her, congratulating and thanking her, as they always did with Taylor when the dog dragged some stick or dirty jersey over to them to admire.

Other times, the stories didn't have her in them at all, because she couldn't think how to introduce herself, or what part she might play. In these, there was always something that the O'Reillys lacked, a sadness they were aware of but didn't know how to fill. So there was space for her in those tales, but her arrival was still obscure. She couldn't see how to bring herself into their life.

Perhaps the holiday in Kerry would show her where she came in, she thought, as she tried to settle in the pull-out bed in Jamie's room the night before the drive. But then when Jamie had fallen asleep, almost without even yawning, in the way that she did, Sarah found herself frightened, turning from one side to the other, unable to find a spot where she was comfortable, suddenly washed over with worries about going so far away from her own home. She was 'fretting', as her mother would have said, but she didn't know how to stop. Her loneliness was like a ragged doll or teddy, something tangible to be dragged along with her, and she longed to get in beside Jamie where the warmth of her friend's sleeping body and steady up-and-down breath would banish the feeling.

But she knew Jamie wouldn't want her. 'I hate sharing beds,' Jamie said, whenever it arose. 'Other people snore and move and their hair goes in my face. Or their feet stick into me. Yeuch. Feet!'

So Sarah stayed in her own bed, thinking of the ease with which Jamie slept, the same ease with which she inhabited her body, graceful and certain always, where she, Sarah, was awkward and agonised and still too tall for herself; thinking too of all the things that might go wrong in the coming weeks. Maybe Jamie would be in a bad mood with her when they got to Kerry and would stop talking to her, and Sarah would have nowhere to go. Maybe the whole family would get sick of her and wish she hadn't come. Maybe all her clothes would be wrong, and she would feel ashamed the whole time. Maybe everything she thought she knew about the O'Reillys was a lie, and when they were in Kerry, they would drop their masks and she would see that really they were cruel and hated her. Maybe even Jake would tell her to go away and look at her with Luke's eyes. And all the time her own parents would be in Dublin, hours and hours away from her. They'd be coming down later in the summer, but not for the first two weeks, and suddenly two weeks felt like a place that was long and flat and featureless and terrifying.

Her fear, then, was not a doll, but had become a live thing that had arms and legs which fitted inside her own arms and legs, and maybe even had a face, but not one she could see. It wriggled now inside her, as if she'd swallowed it.

'Are you sure you want to go so early?' her mother had asked. 'Perhaps you could wait and come down with us? Help us get the new house ready.' But the new house – bigger, shinier, closer to the O'Reillys and Number Eight, held no interest for Sarah.

'No, I want to go,' she had said. 'Please.'

She shifted again then, away from the wriggling inside her, as she remembered her own bravado with wonder, like it was an illness from long ago. She found that if she lay flat on her stomach, the side of her face pressed flat to the mattress under the pillow, the wriggling thing lay stiller.

She tried counting backwards from a hundred. She wished she were brave enough to go down to the kitchen and make warm milk. But even if she had dared run the risk of meeting someone on her way – 'What are you doing, Sarah?' she imagined them saying, Luke sneering, Maeve kindly, Jake curious – even then, there was the feeling that the house, by now so friendly to her in the daytime and most nights, was strange again, and its creaks and groans weren't familiar any more. Sarah's stomach hurt, with the kind of pain a hot water bottle could help, but there were no hot water bottles here. 'Jamie,' she tried, in a loud whisper. 'Jamie.' Nothing, just a deeper sigh from Jamie that said she had never known the terror of a night-time vigil over nothing.

Sarah fell asleep at last, but woke early, the pain still there, and she was still awake when Maeve came in.

'Ready!' Maeve said, shaking Jamie's shoulder gently. 'I'll make bacon sandwiches. We can take them in the car.'

'She always makes us leave really early,' Jamie said, head hidden under her duvet, once Maeve had gone, calling into the other rooms, 'Luke, Alan, Jake, come on!'

'Why?' Sarah asked.

'She says it's traffic, but I think she can't wait any longer. She's been looking forward and planning for so long. She starts filling the car a week before we go, putting in things she says we'll need. Dad takes them out again. He says we're no more likely to use raspberry vinegar in Reevanagh than we are here.'

Jamie's head was out from under the duvet and she was fidgeting with her lower lip. She did that all the time since having her braces put on, pinching the lower lip into a fish-face and shaking it to and fro. She said the braces hurt and made her mouth dry at night, so that in the mornings she had to unstick her lips from the metal.

'It's worth it for good teeth,' Maeve had said when she heard Jamie complaining.

'What's the point of good teeth when the rest of her face is such a mess,' Luke had said.

Jake had braces too.

'*Two sets?*' Miriam had whispered in horror to Maeve when she'd seen them. '*A second mortgage.*'

'Come on. Down! Now! All of you!' Maeve had called up the back stairs then.

'Better get moving,' Jamie said, swinging her legs out of bed. 'She gets furious if we delay her.'

Maeve had bundled bacon sandwiches into their hands then ordered them out the door and into the cars. Simon drove with Alan and most of the bags, Maeve took Jamie, Sarah, Luke, Jake and Taylor. 'She always goes there,' Luke had said, grinning, as he watched Taylor squeeze into the patch of space at Sarah's feet, enjoying the look on her face. 'That's her spot.' And Sarah, who was secretly horrified, fearing the sudden surprising wetness of Taylor's nose or tongue on her bare legs, had said nothing but had tried to cram herself into the very corner away from the dog. Luke then got into the front and pushed his seat back so that Sarah had even less space, but she didn't dare say anything.

'Leg room,' he said with a smirk, turning around to her so that his face floated, disembodied, between the two front seats.

Sarah hoped Maeve would notice what he had done, but she didn't.

The day had brightened briefly, then settled into a dull grey that grew thicker and deeper the longer they drove south-west, until finally, Sarah could see almost nothing out of her window except fuzzy lights that shone as if through cotton wool.

They had played games at first – memory games that she was good at, games of the imagination the O'Reillys were better at – and they'd eaten sandwiches, doughnuts, endless packets of crisps and bars of chocolate, until they mostly fell silent, stupefied by movement without engagement. They passed through miles and miles of land, which shook them off like drops of water from a smooth surface, pushing them ever forward, onto the next place. 'Not here,' the landscape said. 'Not here.'

Sitting beside Jake felt weird. Sarah tried to keep her arm and leg from bumping or brushing against his, after she'd done it once and turned and smiled and said she was sorry – and he'd looked surprised, as if he didn't know what she was on about. She didn't want to keep doing that, so she tried holding herself stiff and separate until her whole side ached and she finally had to give in. And when she did, lurching against him any time the car turned a corner, Jake didn't seem to notice, so that at last she stopped noticing too. At one point, he dug an elbow into her side and said, 'Look at this!' and showed her part of what he was reading so that she began to realise that it wasn't anything much, to him, to sit so close to her, and she stopped thinking about it.

Soon only Luke talked: about rugby – games played, won, lost, training sessions and what the coach had said about his chances. He kept on and on, a rolling wave of self-congratulation, until finally Maeve said, 'Maybe that's enough for now,' at which he at last fell silent in a sulk. Then he began to roll his window up and down, cold air snapping in and out, until she said, sharply, 'Stop that!'

Taylor stirred at Sarah's feet and she quickly lifted them, hugging her knees in to her chest, away from the alarming heat of the dog.

'Taylor, come here,' Jake said. 'You can sit on my knee.'

'It's OK,' Sarah said. 'She's just a bit heavy.'

'I know what she's like,' Jake said. 'She'll sit so close, it's like she's trying to sit inside you.'

Sarah found the idea revolting, but she nodded.

'She's lonely,' Jake said. 'Since Burton died.'

'What happened to Burton?' She had heard the dog mentioned before, but no details.

'He was Taylor's "husband". We got them together as puppies. Taylor and Burton?' Sarah looked blank. 'Film stars mum and dad like,' Jake explained. 'They were always fighting and leaving each other but they got married twice, so they must have liked each other too. Taylor was always snapping at Burton when he was alive and bossing him, but then he died and she's been sad ever since. She doesn't know what to do without him, so she hangs around with us more than ever.' He settled the dog on his knee. 'And she stinks.'

'But we love her,' Jamie said, dropping her face to the dog's head for a moment and resting her cheek against the shiny flat top. Sarah tried feeling sorry for Taylor for a moment, but she couldn't. The idea of a dog that felt sad was too strange and frightening. Did everything feel sad? Even things that should feel only hungry, or tired, or other physical stuff? And if so, did that mean that sadness was just the way of things? Not something that would pass, or could be grown out of, but something that would endure?

'Nearly there,' Maeve said then, half-turning in her seat towards Sarah. 'This is South Kerry now. My Kerry.' She began naming things, places they passed, spots on the road: 'That leads to Ballinskelligs. Bolus Head is up that way, where Seán Ó Conaill was born. That's the way to Loher stone fort. You'll catch a glimpse of the Skelligs soon.'

Bolus, *Skellig*, *Loher*, the strangeness of the words, the way Maeve said them, like a prayer, or a mother naming children, kept Sarah staring out the window, trying to see what Maeve saw.

The mist had lifted enough that the sky became two skies: a circle of silvery gold lit up the farthest corner where the sun was setting and sending up a final rush of light, and then the rest of the sky, which was thick and dark with dense tufts of cloud. Below, the sea was spread out like a piece of chain mail, seeming to ripple towards the lingering corner of light, as if that piece of shining sky were a hole into which all the water might pour and disappear. They were climbing now, the sea smoothing out beneath them, ripples erased with distance.

'Look, the Skelligs. There,' Maeve said, pointing out to sea where two jagged peaks reached up into the darkest grey of the sky. If the corner of light was sucking water towards it, Sarah thought, these two sentinels were holding it back. They were like firm stakes, driven into the sea to keep it whole and steady.

'Wait till you see them close up,' Maeve said. 'I know a man who'll take us out.'

'In a boat that rocks so much you'll vomit,' said Luke.

'Nonsense,' Maeve said. 'They're called Skellig Micheal and Skellig Beag.'

'She does this every time,' Jamie leaned over Jake to whisper at Sarah, rolling her eyes. 'Says what everything is, like we've never seen it before.' And Sarah, who felt suspended by every word Maeve uttered, as if each were a rung on a rope ladder she wanted to climb, was so relieved that Jamie was talking to her again that she forced a snigger and rolled back her eyes.

She looked out the window. It had begun to rain and she took in the darkening blur of hedgerows as they flashed past – a mass of feathery green with splashes of purple, orange, rose pink, yellow. These were the same touches of colour Sarah had noticed in Maeve's clothes, always to be found on a scarf, a belt, a brooch. She wondered if it was deliberate.

The radio was a low murmur beneath the noise of the car

engine, the tyres on the road and the sound of the wind as it blew against them. Sometimes Maeve would turn it up to listen to something she found interesting – the news, an interview – but mostly, Sarah thought, it was like the buzz of a distant bee. Dull and sleepy.

'Turn it up, Mum.' That was Jamie. 'I love this.' She started singing along to 'Freed From Desire', and then they were all singing together, except for Maeve, waving their arms around above their heads and shaking back and forth in their seat belts. Even Luke sang along and didn't say anything nasty, so that for once it felt like the four of them – Sarah, Jamie, Luke and Jake – without Maeve, or her parents, or other grown-ups, in a way that was new. Because it was not as if they had been left alone just for a little while; it was as if they were together, in a new, exciting place.

And then, 'We're here,' Maeve said, slowing and turning off the road and onto a pebbly path.

But the house was invisible still, completely surrounded by a ring of trees that leaned in towards it from the road, sparse and thorny branches that stretched desperately towards the few flickers of light Sarah could see, far beyond them.

'Oh, good,' Maeve said, 'Nora has been. The lights are on. There should be dinner. I wasn't sure she got my message.'

'Why do the trees do that?' Sarah asked, appalled by the wild angle of the leaning trees, the scrabbly brown branches ending in a few bits of evergreen. The way they looked like dogs on the end of a leash, straining hard to break their restraints.

'It's the wind,' Maeve replied. 'It blows from the sea, hard, all year round, so it pushes them and they grow away from it.'

'Prevailing wind,' Luke said with a yawn.

'They look like they're tied to something and trying to get away,' Sarah said.

'They do a bit,' Maeve said. 'And, really, they are. The wind here can be ferocious. They are trying to get away from that.'

CHAPTER 23

Simon and Alan had arrived before them and were unpacking, dragging bags and boxes from the wet gloom of the driveway and the quiet cars into the wavering square of light cast by the open front door. Stone pillars on either side were curved and austere, ordering Sarah to look up at the façade of the house above her, a dark grey that gave off no reflection, rising to a double row of big windows that were all shuttered, though gleams of fuzzy yellow escaped from around the edges and the centre of some, challenging the gathering dark, only for it to become wholly triumphant where it swallowed them up.

Somewhere behind the house there were the rough sounds of birds – rooks or crows – snarling at each other as they settled for the evening.

'You'll see it properly in the morning,' Maeve said then, walking past with a box containing wine bottles. Her voice was light and happy, like a cork bobbing on water.

Inside the door was a hall, straight and square and stern, with a floor of red and white tiles and a jumble of shoes and boots so like the one in Number Eight that Sarah wondered had Simon and Alan just loaded the car full and brought them all down. At the end of the hall was a staircase that rose straight up so that Sarah couldn't see where it ended. There was a smell of old books and cold wood smoke and damp clothes.

'Pooh.' Jake wrinkled up his nose. 'It always smells like this when we first arrive. It gets better.' He picked up a heavy copper bell shaped like a bulb that shone a dull gold colour and shook it. The sound was like someone dropping spoons down a well, Sarah thought; crashingly loud in the hallway.

'Maeve's cow bell,' Jake said. 'She rings it to get us up from the beach without having to come all the way down'

'I should just tie a rope to one of you and tug it,' Maeve said.

In the room to her right, Sarah could see an open fire burning hard and bright, as if to make up for the forlorn smell, and some fat armchairs in shiny pink and cream flowered material on a thick cream carpet. A deep window was cloaked in heavy gold curtains and there were little tables all around, spindly ones with twiggy legs, their surfaces covered in photo frames, books and a jumble of bits and pieces. She went in for a closer look. There were bits of driftwood, stones, pieces of smooth glass, shells, the jawbone of some creature, bleached white, with a few squarish teeth lying loose in the dried-out sockets. Also a piece of crispy seaweed, a rusty horse shoe. And, inevitably, pocket watches and small clocks, some ticking, some not.

Maeve came in and began poking at the fire. 'One of these days, I'm going to sweep the whole lot up and dump it back onto the beach,' she said as Sarah gently touched the jawbone. A log fell forward in a cascade of sparks and Maeve stepped back hastily.

'Don't you dare,' Jamie shouted from the hall. 'That's my childhood.'

'You can accumulate the debris of adolescence instead,' Maeve said. 'Old beer cans, cigarette butts, rolling papers.'

'So weird!' Jamie said. 'Come on, Sarah, come and see my room.' She grabbed Sarah's arm and pulled at her.

They went up the stairs at the end of the hall. A landing opened, broad and confident and rectangular, with doors off it, then a corner and more stairs up to a shorter, narrower corridor with just two doors, almost opposite one another. 'Bathroom,' Jamie said pointing at one. 'It doesn't shut properly. My room . . .' and she opened the other door.

The room was large and bare, with dark wooden floorboards and an old rag rug woven in circles of different blues in the middle. The ceiling sloped and the two windows set into it were uncovered: two blank panes like eyes, closed, that might flick open at any moment and stare at you. Behind them, a wind shook the house so the panes rattled a little.

'It's always windy up here,' Jamie said. 'Like being in a boat or a treehouse some nights. The room almost rocks with the wind. You can see the sea out there in the daytime.' She gestured towards the windows, relaxed, confident. Her room. Her view.

There was a single bed high off the ground with a shiny

brass bedstead, and laid across it, a quilt in different squares of brightly coloured cloth. Beside that was a big old chest of drawers in wood that was almost black with shiny handles, and on the other side of the chest of drawers, another bed, lower to the ground, pulled out of a small white sofa. It had a frilly white duvet and matching frilly pillowcase.

'That's your bed,' Jamie said, sitting heavily on the high brass bed and pointing at the other, 'and you can put your clothes in here.' She pulled open a drawer. 'You can have the bottom two and I'll have the top two.'

'OK,' Sarah said. She unzipped her bag and began taking out T-shirts, shorts, jeans, sweatshirts. Many new, bought especially for this holiday, in the way her mother bought so much these days. The sight of them, folded neatly, brought to her an image of her mother's hands, smoothing, shaping, hovering over this jumper, that pair of socks, choosing what to put in as she thought about what Sarah might need – considering the weather, the things Sarah might do, the places she might go. She imagined her mother, on her knees in front of the suitcase, mind bent on the business of making Sarah happy, trying to unscramble a dim future so that the things she packed might give comfort where she was not around to.

The image, in that house with its strange unwelcoming smell, left Sarah winded like a punch. She wanted to gasp for air and suck it deep into her lungs – but she didn't, couldn't. Not with Jamie there beside her.

She bent her head further and didn't know if Jamie had noticed or not noticed, when the other girl suddenly said,

'I'm done, I'll see you downstairs,' and jumped off her bed and headed for the door.

Listening to Jamie's footsteps thumping along the corridor, growing fainter and then silent, Sarah tried to still her breathing that sounded as if she'd been running. The voodoo panic doll she had created the night before wriggled again, wilder now, its hands at the insides of her eyes, trying to get out or drag her in. She got up fast, away from the case of clothes, and went to the bathroom Jamie had pointed out. She shut the door behind her – Jamie was right, it didn't close fully – and splashed water on her face, bent low over the stained white basin, then sat on the floor beneath it, tucked in the corner between it and the bath, with her knees pulled up to her chin because she needed to be in a space that was tiny, that could contain her.

The door burst open. It was Luke. 'Shit, sorry,' he said when he saw her, 'didn't know anyone was in here.' Then, 'What are you doing?' as he took in the small heap of her.

'Nothing.' She began to try and unfold. She saw then that her legs were shaking, and she didn't know how to stand upright on them.

'Here.' He held out a hand and she was grateful for the heat of it, the strength with which he grabbed hers. He pulled her upright but her legs still shook so she sat on the edge of the bath. 'What's up?' Luke sat beside her, close, so that the heat of him was still there. She leaned in towards it, unable not to, hoping he wouldn't quite notice, trying to draw the heat into herself so that it filled out the scrabbling and made it stop.

'It's nothing.' She didn't look at him, just stared at the rough pinkish-grey mat.

'Homesick?'

'I suppose.'

'You're just not used to it,' he said, staring at the mat too. 'It was the same when I went to school first. I hated it. But I can hardly remember that now. You'll be fine.' He bumped his shoulder against her briefly, in a friendly way, then stood up, held out his hand again and, when she took it, pulled her to her feet. 'Now scram. I need the loo.'

What was strange was that he was right. Suddenly she was fine. The scrabbly doll inside her lay quiet again, and she was able to go back into Jamie's room and throw the last of her clothes into the drawers and close them, knowing that when she opened them again, the clothes would smell of the house and not of her mother.

She went downstairs, thinking about Luke. His unexpected kindness had confused her. She had long ago decided that she hated Luke, and was happy to hate him, and now he'd messed that up, so that she'd have to think of him in a different way.

She got to the bottom of the stairs and realised she didn't know where the kitchen was. But she could hear Simon laughing, and so she followed that and found them all, warm and cosy, in a room with pale green walls, which had an Aga, like the one in Number Eight, and an open fire as well where logs were burning, so that it was warm and bright. Here, the house smell was laid over with the smell of cooking.

'Hi.' Jamie looked up and smiled when she came in, pulled out the chair beside her for Sarah to sit. 'Nora left lamb stew and apple tart. She makes amazing tarts. If we pick blackberries later on, we can ask her to make one with them.'

'Well, then, we're definitely picking blackberries,' Sarah said. She hated blackberries. Hated the hard little pips that got stuck between her teeth and the sweet-bitter taste. Most of all she hated picking them – they had spiders, even tiny caterpillars on them and she knew, just knew, that the bugs would go into the pot with the blackberries and they would all be cooked together and served up for her to eat, bits of spider in there with them. Her stomach heaved slightly and she pushed the image of spidery legs away. She would have agreed to anything Jamie wanted just then.

They sat around a big solid table, a little squashed, which Sarah liked, and Maeve dished up plates of stew with bread and potatoes.

'How's the new house?' Simon asked from the far end of the table. He sounded kindly, proprietorial. He had 'found' the new house, Sarah knew, the house her mother was 'getting ready' now, but she didn't know what his finding it meant.

'I've hardly seen it. They'll be moving in while I'm down here. It's bigger, though.'

'Good. It's a good house. In a good part of the city. Needs work, but it's all there.' Sarah could hear the satisfaction in his voice. 'You should have seen this place when we bought it,' he said then, leaning back in his chair. 'A complete wreck. Maeve didn't want to buy it. But I could see the potential.'

To Simon's left, Luke leaned back too, in a mocking parody of his father, with his hands crossed over his stomach that was pushed out to make it fatter. He made sure Simon didn't see him.

'It wasn't that,' Maeve said. 'I felt bad buying it, because of the Waldons.'

'Who are they?' Sarah asked.

'I used to come to this house when I was a child,' Maeve said, 'my mother was friendly with Patricia – Mrs Waldon – and it was a beautiful house. Then Mr Waldon died, suddenly, heart attack, and there was no money and Patricia stayed on but she couldn't mind the place or heat it and it all fell to bits, really. There were no children. By the time she sold, she was living just here, in the kitchen, and the room next door, where her bed was. The rest of the place was all closed up and empty.' She shivered. 'It was creepy, really. We'd visit, but we'd have to come in the kitchen door' – she pointed to a door behind Jamie – 'because the front door was so swollen and warped that it wouldn't open anymore.'

'It took for ever to set it right,' Simon said, looking around, pleased with what he had done. 'There's plenty of work still, upstairs especially, but we're getting there.'

'I felt bad,' Maeve said. She had not, as Simon had, skipped ahead to Now and the Future. She remained in the past, with loyalties and memories that Sarah felt were complicated. Behind her, a clock ticked, just a plain kitchen clock hanging on the wall, and Sarah wondered why Maeve hadn't brought in one of the fancy grandfather ones that chimed.

'About what?' Simon asked.

'Buying the place. Patricia moving out.'

'Best thing that could have happened to her,' Simon said.

'She was delighted. Bought a new-build flat in town and never looked back. No more rattling windows, no more damp, no more empty rooms and frozen pipes. I don't know why people stay on alone in these old houses,' he said, thoughtful now. 'They're family homes. They need activity, kids coming and going to fill them up. And money. A lot of money.' He smiled round at them all. Sarah knew that it was his money that he smiled about, and the way it could make a difference. She smiled back.

'She couldn't take her dogs,' Maeve said. 'To the flat in town. They were lurchers. They would never have managed in a flat.'

'They're buried in the garden,' Jamie said eagerly. 'I'll show you tomorrow. They have little headstones.' She said it like it was something cute.

'Made of slate,' Maeve said, like it was something beautiful.

'Best thing that could have happened to her,' Simon said again. He took one of Maeve's hands. 'You're being soft.'

'She loved this place,' Maeve said.

'And now we love it,' he said.

Sarah wondered did he really love it, or did he just love that it was his. Maybe there was no difference.

CHAPTER 24

Jamie could see Sarah was trying not to cry, or trying at least not to let Jamie see her cry, and she wished the chest of drawers was higher so she could lie down on her bed and Sarah would be blocked from her sight. That she could put on headphones, and the tiny sound of sniffing would be blocked from her. That Sarah's efforts to keep the crying hidden and secret were more bloody effective.

'So, what – she's your best friend now?' Celine had said when Jamie told her about the visit.

'No. My dad invited her. Invited all of them, her parents too. Mum hoped they wouldn't come, but they are.'

'It'll be fine,' Maeve had asserted when Simon said, 'The Ryans are coming', in a way that was a bit guilty. Jamie knew her father was feeling guilty because he did the same thing that she did whenever she felt bad about something she'd done and knew she shouldn't have – he rubbed the back of his hand over his nose.

'How long are they coming for?' Maeve had asked.

'A week or so.'

'Maybe Sarah would like to come down earlier,' her mum had said then, 'with us, when we go. I'll ask Miriam.' She'd looked tired as she said it, but had gone and asked anyway, without even checking with Jamie, and Jamie hadn't thought much about it – Sarah was coming to Kerry, it would be fine – until Celine started making such a fuss.

'So she's coming, and that means I can't stay at yours,' she said.

'But you've got your own house in Kerry.'

'Yes, but I always stay at yours.' Celine's voice did the thing it always did when she was cross. It went tight and thin like a big tired sigh.

It was so confusing. Jamie didn't know what exactly Celine was giving out to her for, only that Celine was certainly giving out and Jamie was defending, but she didn't even know what she was defending.

'You can still stay,' she said. 'Just not the whole time. We'll still do all the same things.'

It was a bit annoying that Sarah was coming. She wouldn't know anyone and she didn't know how to sail – Jamie knew that because she'd asked her – but Jamie still couldn't see why Celine was so annoyed.

After all, Celine could be pretty annoying too, always wanting to spend all her time with Jamie in Kerry, but never having any good ideas of what to do. 'God, that's so boring,' she said when Jamie suggested anything, like picking blackberries or going up to see the bull in the field across the road. On the beach, she wouldn't dig holes or dam the stream that trickled down from the hillside. Mostly she liked sitting in Jamie's room talking about the people they knew, which Jamie thought got boring after a while. She didn't know why Celine thought there was so much to say about people. Anyway, most of what she did say, Jamie had never picked up on herself.

'Have you seen how competitive Stephen and Luke are?' she'd say, and Jamie would have to admit that, no, she hadn't. 'You're hopeless,' Celine would say. 'You never notice anything.'

Sarah was pretty funny about Celine actually, and sometimes Jamie liked that. Like the time after the party, when Sarah got so drunk they had to put her to bed and Celine had been spitting fury, going on the next morning about how they had all got into trouble because of Sarah, and did she have any idea how pathetic she was?

'You'd swear it was your shoes I vomited all over,' Sarah had said. And Jamie had burst out laughing because Celine hadn't known what to say, and Sarah had looked at her, at Jamie, then and they both laughed so that Celine said, 'Pathetic,' again and walked out of the bedroom. Sarah always made Jamie able to be braver than she was, because she believed so hard in Jamie's bravery.

But now she watched Sarah putting her clothes away and her hairbrush and a tube of Clearasil on top of the chest of drawers – Jamie's chest of drawers – and suddenly she wanted to pull all the clothes out again and sweep her hand across the chest of drawers, so that the brush and Clearasil flew across the room onto the floor. She wanted a room that didn't have Sarah in it, that was hers alone like it always had been. Somehow, Celine or any other of her friends staying in that room didn't fill it up the way Sarah's presence did. It was as if she was drinking up the air, so that there was somehow less of it.

'Where can I hang my coat?' Sarah asked now.

'Downstairs. We don't keep coats in our rooms.' Jamie knew she was being mean. She knew that saying 'we' in that way was deliberate and showed Sarah that she wasn't part of the 'we'. It was exactly the kind of thing her mum had said to be careful about, but she couldn't stop herself.

Sarah's crying was always so obvious. First her face went really, really white, even whiter than it usually was. Then blotches of red started around her nose and moved up to her cheeks, and her eyes would go red, and then the tears came. There was no way to miss it, once you knew what to look for.

But still, Jamie pretended she hadn't seen. She didn't want to know what Sarah was crying about – whether it was because she missed her mum, or because she felt lonely, or because Jamie was being nasty. Maybe it was none of those. Or all of them. Sometimes Sarah got upset for no reason that Jamie could understand, because Sarah couldn't explain it herself.

'I don't know what it is,' she would say, her voice all hoarse with the effort of speaking. Jamie could hear the lump that was in her throat at those times, and could tell how much effort Sarah needed to put in to speak over it, as if she was having to push her voice up and over a hurdle. 'I just feel sad.'

'But you must have a reason,' Jamie had said the first few times, confused. 'Is it school? Are the girls being mean?'

'No. Not really. Not more than always.'

'So, what then?'

'Don't you ever feel like there's so much that is just sad about the world? Even the things you like, that make you happy? In a way those are even more sad, because they shouldn't be. And the people you love are all sad too, but pretending not to be for your sake and each other's sakes. All trying not to show it, when it's so obvious?'

'I don't know what you mean,' Jamie had said, making her voice as strong as possible. 'I don't know what you're talking about.' She hadn't, and didn't want to. She hated when Sarah talked like that, because of the possibility that Sarah would be able to explain herself well enough so that Jamie could understand, and then she'd start to see things the way Sarah did.

She was afraid that if that happened, she would feel again the way she had felt when Burton died and Taylor wandered around the house, with her head down, as if it was too heavy to lift up, and her big solid body thick with misery. Jamie had stayed away from her, because she didn't know what to do. They had all cried when Burton died, but it was like Taylor couldn't stop crying in her doggy way.

'Come on, Taylor,' she had yelled one day, throwing a ball into the back garden. She was so sick of the dog curled into the corner beside the Aga, wrapped around herself like her sadness was a bone she was guarding. But Taylor didn't move.

'Leave her,' Jake had said. 'She's not in the mood.'

'I'm sick of her,' Jamie had said, even though she wasn't. Really, she was upset by the way the dog was so completely sad – not sad one minute then happy the next, the way Jamie was.

'It's not your thing, is it,' Jake had said, and Jamie had agreed 'No. Not my thing,' even though she hadn't exactly known what he was talking about.

'I'm done, I'll see you downstairs,' Jamie said now, and she leaped off her bed and out of the door before Sarah could say anything to stop her; before she would have to notice the other girl's tears and stop herself.

CHAPTER 25

The next morning Sarah woke before Jamie to sunshine that spilled in through the slanted windows and fell across the floor, already bright and urgent.

She had gone to bed expecting to lie awake again, already planning what she would do, how she would manage. She had snuck up two biscuits with her in the pocket of her sweatshirt, because sometimes eating something helped distract her from not being able to sleep. But in fact, she got into bed and fell asleep in minutes, rocked by the buffeting wind outside that nudged the house in a friendly way.

And now that it was morning, she could no longer find her fear of the evening before. The house was new and welcoming, and when she looked out one of the windows, standing on tiptoe to see beyond the trees, she caught a flash of sparkling blue at the very edge of the horizon, where the sky swooped down to grab it, and she itched to get outside.

She knew Jamie wouldn't get up for a long time – she had started to sleep late and heavily in the mornings – but Sarah couldn't stay where she was. Not with that dancing bit of blue, and when outside was a place she had barely seen.

She dressed in jeans and a hoodie and went downstairs quietly, hoping to see nobody, hoping the front door would not be locked in a way she couldn't manage, so that nothing would delay or halt her. The house was silent, but Maeve was in the hall, putting on a long grey jacket.

'You're early.' She smiled up at Sarah as she came down the stairs. She had two flasks and a tea-towel wrapped around what smelt like warm bread. 'I'm going down to the beach. Do you want to come? You can learn your way around.'

'Yes, please,' Sarah said. Going with Maeve was even better than going on her own.

'Grab something from the kitchen,' Maeve said, 'there's apples and brown bread I just made, and we'll go. We can have breakfast properly when we come back.'

'I didn't know you made bread,' Sarah said, when she came back with an apple. Her mother made soda bread and had recently started a kind of seed bread that Sarah didn't much like.

'Only here,' Maeve said. 'And not very well. Here, put that on.' She handed Sarah a shiny olive-green jacket. 'That sweatshirt will never withstand the Kerry wind.'

'It smells of fish,' Sarah said, taking the jacket.

'There might be a mackerel in the pocket,' Maeve laughed, 'if one of the boys wore it fishing.'

Sarah patted each large square pocket carefully.

'Nothing.'

'Lucky!'

Outside was a day so new and fresh Sarah could feel it laughing with delight at itself. There was a clean-scrubbed clarity to everything, a sharp little wind and the sky was the modest blue of downcast eyes.

'Sometimes a really foul night produces a beautiful morning,' Maeve said, adding, 'but only sometimes. You wouldn't want to rely on that down here.'

Now that it was light and she was able to look calmly about her, Sarah could see that the house was halfway up a hill with fields around and behind it. There was a huge bush covered in deep pink flowers near the iron gate and at the back were tall dark green trees, where the cawing birds had sounded the night before.

The leaning trees looked less frightening in the daytime: not quite so much as if they were reaching desperately for the house so as to pluck something out of it – more as if they were huddled together to try and protect it. But she still didn't like them.

Halfway down the drive, Sarah looked back. In the morning sun, the house seemed to be weeping, pale streaks running down the rough grey stone from the shallow roof, cutting across the solid bricks like scars. There was no movement at any of the windows, just the blank stare of morning sun on glass.

The stony path of the driveway gave onto a narrow road banked high with hedges on either side, which led them downhill towards the blue scrap of water below.

'What do you all do while you're here?' Sarah asked Maeve, curious, trotting a little to keep pace with her.

'Different things. The boys and Jamie go to the beach. They all surf and sail. Simon and the boys fish. Jamie hasn't the patience for that. And I do as little as possible.' She laughed. 'Although it's getting harder. So many people come down. More all the time.' Sarah wondered was Maeve thinking about her parents. It didn't sound as if she liked people coming down. 'Really, I like to just be here, breathing the air. Smell.' She stood still a moment, hand on Sarah's arm to halt her. 'Breathe in. Deep.' She did just that, lifting her head into the wind and breathing deeply through her nose, eyes closed. Sarah did the same, almost rising onto her tiptoes as she searched the air for whatever it was that Maeve found there.

'Smell that?' Maeve asked.

'It smells different to Dublin,' Sarah said. 'Heavier. More full of things.'

'Exactly,' Maeve said. 'I think you could put me anywhere in Kerry, blindfolded, and I'd know where I was just by the smell of the air.'

They walked down, following the small road until it reached a larger road, as empty of cars as the first, then they turned off that onto a grassy track that led them through tall dunes with tufts of rough grass, and onto a beach that was wide and white and empty.

'We usually go round that way,' Maeve pointed, 'to the cove. It's emptier and better for surfing, although it can be dangerous for swimming. There are currents that come and go depending on the tide. There was a boy drowned here when I was a child, drawn out by the sea so far he had no chance to fight his way back. It was a warm day, and a crowded beach but no one missed him until it was too late. I wasn't here to see, thank God, but I heard later and I've never forgotten it.' She sounded, Sarah thought, still upset.

'The last years it has been much safer,' Maeve went on, 'but still, the rule is you never swim unless someone is with you. It's really the one hard and fast rule of being here. Got that?'

'Got it,' Sarah said. She knew she would never go in alone.

Midway across the beach, high up among the dunes, was a yellow and red hut with a flag waving from the top. 'Lifeguards,' Maeve said. 'I used to do that job, a million years ago.' They walked to the hut and she banged on the window. A guy wearing a faded red sweatshirt and red shorts came out. Sarah looked past him into the hut. There was a second lifeguard in there, who waved at them, and a couple of sleeping bags and some paperback books. Sarah waved back, wondering whether it would be nice, or lonely, to be holed up there all day with books and cups of tea.

'Sean. How are you? I brought you a bit of breakfast,' Maeve said, holding out the flasks and the tea-towel bundle.

'Thanks, Mrs O'Reilly,' Sean said. 'That's welcome.'

'How have you been?'

'Busy enough yesterday. There'll be more out today.'

'If it keeps up,' Maeve said. 'We'll be down later. I'll get the flask from you then.'

'Thanks again,' he shouted after them, the breeze taking his words and spreading them out into a fan-shape behind them.

They walked as far as the cove, where the wind was stronger and the waves higher, so that Sarah felt she was almost inside the roaring noise they created. It was smaller by far than the main beach, folded into a kind of semi-circle by rocks that were like arms wrapping around this bit of sand and sea. Inside the rock arms, the waves rolled in and out, in and out, dashing at the bit of beach, as if trying to pull it back out to sea.

Maeve leaned into her and said, close by her ear, against the wind, 'Unless you're starving, why don't we go back via the graveyard?'

Sarah said she was fine, although in fact as soon as Maeve said the word starving she realised that she was exactly that. They walked back the way they had come through the dunes, and then, at the road, turned the other way and up a steep hill to a small stone church and a field that lay slanted against the rise of the hill, dotted with tumbledown headstones. Once they were off the beach, the wind and the roaring sound died down. Sarah felt as if she had been shaken roughly, then set down again.

'These are my people,' Maeve said, pushing at the overgrown, rusted gate where it stuck against a tuft of wet grass. 'O'Connors, as far as the eye can see.' And indeed, every third or fourth headstone Sarah looked at had 'O'Connor' carved on it: Marys and Matthews and Paudies, with lives that were long and short and mourned by loving parents and wives and children. They had been living, and dying, here for more than a century Sarah thought, although some of the stones were so worn she couldn't read them. She had never thought of Maeve as old before, but suddenly she saw her as a tree, big and ancient, with roots everywhere, holding soil together, holding land and houses and people firm and upright.

*

Back at the house, the boys were in the kitchen with the radio on. The kettle was boiling on the Aga with a whistling sound, filling the room with steam. They didn't seem to notice that it was ready, rattling hard against the stove top, and Maeve crossed quickly to take it off the heat.

'Mum, Patrick's here,' Alan said.

She turned in a swift movement then and said, 'Patrick!' in a loud voice, so that Sarah, who had been about to go up and see if Jamie was awake, stayed where she was. Maeve was saying, 'How nice!' and hugging someone who stood up from the table to hug her back.

'This is Patrick,' Jake said to Sarah, pointing towards a young man with a brown face and brown hair that was messy, as if it wanted to be curly but hadn't quite managed. He had blue eyes, Sarah saw, the same blue as the jumper he was wearing, and very white teeth. She noticed teeth a lot. Maybe because Jamie went on about hers so much and left the coloured rubber bands for her braces around the place, and often had bits of food caught in the silver tracks that were disgusting, but Sarah tried not to dwell on that. This person could have been Luke's age, but he was much thinner and his face looked older.

'Hi,' she said, putting her hands behind her back and wiping them in case he expected a handshake.

'Hi.' He nodded at her. 'Friend of Jamie's?'

'Yes. Sarah.'

'Hi, Sarah.'

'Patrick!' That was Simon, bursting into the kitchen. 'I thought it was you in that dirty little car.' He laughed, delighted, and reached over to clap an arm around Patrick's shoulders. Sarah had never seen him greet any other friend of his children with so much enthusiasm – almost as if Patrick were a friend of his own.

'Are you driving?' Jake asked, fascinated. 'But you're not old enough.'

'Shssh!' Patrick put a finger to his lips and smiled at Jake. His eyes were sparkly. 'It's only when I'm down here, and as long as no one says anything. It's my uncle's car.'

'How is Pat?' Simon asked.

'He's good. The boats weren't out much last week because of the winds, but he's busy again now.' Patrick had stood up by then so that he and Simon were both leaning against counters, on opposite sides of the table. They were like two guys in a bar, Sarah thought, relaxed and interested in what they were speaking about.

'Patrick's uncle is a fisherman,' Simon said, in Sarah's direction but not exactly to her, more as if he was reminding himself of a thing he liked to hear. 'Knows more about boats than anyone I've met. But during the summer he becomes a fisher of men.' He laughed, then said, 'He takes people out to the Skelligs,' seeing Sarah's bewildered face. 'Tourists, not fish. You see.'

'Oh, OK,' Sarah said.

'How's home?' Simon asked then and the sparkle in Patrick's eyes shut off like a television at night.

'Fine,' he said. He flicked at a lock of hair, an action without any purpose that Sarah could see, so that she watched him more closely.

'You'll have some breakfast,' Simon said. 'I'm putting on sausages and bacon.' It wasn't a question – Patrick was already reaching for the packet of bread on the table.

'Hi, Patrick.' Jamie came in then, face crumpled and cross with sleep.

'Did you hear someone saying "sausages"?' Patrick asked, smiling at her.

'No, I heard someone talking such rubbish I thought I'd better see who it was,' Jamie said. She reached for the packet of bread, spread a slice with butter, then began sprinkling sugar on it.

'Sugar sandwich,' Patrick said. 'Very nutritious.'

'It's the Kerry air,' Jamie complained. 'I'm always starving here.'

They had sausages, bacon, fried eggs, tea, more tea, toast and jam. They ate for what felt to Sarah like an hour, passing things up and down the table to one another – 'Butter?' 'Anyone for mushrooms?' 'Any more of that home-made jam?' – talking constantly, over and around each other. Simon seemed determined to keep hold of Patrick's attention, asking him questions about boats and his uncle. Luke, Alan and Jake tried to butt in and interrupt, asking Patrick questions of their own – Had he seen Stephen? Did everyone still go to the cove? What was he doing later? – and he moved easily between them all.

'How old is he?' Sarah asked Jamie, quietly, because she couldn't work it out. He seemed almost like a grown-up in the way he spoke to Mr O'Reilly, calling him 'Simon', and not like it was hard for him to say, and talking about the weather and the season like an adult, and yet he had answers to all the boys' questions, which showed he was in the same gang they were talking about. It was confusing.

'He's fifteen, maybe sixteen by now,' Jamie said. She too looked for Patrick's attention, but in a way that said she knew she'd get it. She made jokes about him – even quite rude ones, Sarah thought, such as asking, 'Have you drowned anyone yet this year?' – and he teased her back: 'Do you still spend most of your time upside down?'

But, Sarah saw, he always stopped and listened to Jamie and often laughed, no matter who else he had been talking to at the time. His eyes sparkled even more when he looked at her, Sarah thought, as if Jamie was a brightly lit thing in a window.

When he left – 'I have to give my uncle a hand. I'll see you later at the cove' – a flatness fell down on all of them, so that the kitchen emptied fast. Sarah stayed to help tidy up, then went upstairs. Jamie was lying on her bed, staring at the ceiling.

'We'll go to the beach as soon as I can get up,' Jamie said. 'Luke and Jake have gone already. But I'm too full.'

'Have they gone to meet Patrick there?' Sarah asked. She was still curious about him.

'Eventually, but the others will be there already.' Sarah didn't know what others Jamie meant.

'Does Patrick live here?' she asked.

'No, but he's here more than the rest of us. His uncle lives here and Patrick stays with him a lot of the time. I think he used to live with him, but then he went back to his mum.

She's in Dublin. There's something wrong with her, which is why Patrick is here so much. I don't really know what it is. She's sick or something.'

'How long have you known him?'

'For ever. He's here every time we come down. Dad thinks he's great. He says Patrick has had a rough time of it and that he's got "grit".' She wriggled up to sitting. 'He says he wishes Al and Luke and Jake were more like him. He wants to pay for Patrick to go to college, but Patrick hasn't made up his mind yet. He says he might go into business with his uncle instead.' She stretched. 'Look, the sun's out. I think I can move again. Let's go. Everyone'll be there by now.'

But Sarah delayed getting ready until Jamie shouted at her to 'hurry up!' She hadn't expected there to be other people on this holiday, other kids. Vaguely, she remembered Jamie talking about her 'Kerry friends', and mentioning a few names – Stephen, Jill, maybe even Patrick – but not in a way that had made Sarah expect to actually meet them, do stuff with them.

She was terrified. Maybe they would be like Celine, cruel and superior, always looking at her from a place so far above that Sarah had to repeat everything twice because the distance between them was apparently too great for Celine to hear her the first time.

'What? What did you say?' Celine would ask, always surprised, as if a cat had spoken. And when Sarah repeated whatever it was she had said, it would sound even more stupid the second time. Often Celine wouldn't answer, as if it was too dumb to pay attention to anyway. If the friends were like that, Sarah decided, she would go home. Straight back to

Dublin and her parents. But then she imagined herself saying to Maeve, 'Can I ring my mum?' and Maeve asking, 'What's wrong?' and she knew she'd never be able to do it.

'Hurry up!' Jamie said again, from the doorway. Then, absently, 'You need a jumper. You'll freeze.' She was wearing crisp white shorts and a striped blue and white jumper. Her legs were brown – Jamie's legs were always brown – and she jigged up and down on the balls of her feet.

Sarah could see that, in Jamie's mind, she was already halfway down the road towards the beach, and moving quickly towards whatever group was there.

'Go ahead,' she said. 'I'll catch you up. I know the way.'

CHAPTER 26

The damned wind kept circling the house, pulling and banging at it, so that Simon gave up trying to go back to sleep and lay waiting, dredging up the energy that he hoped would get him from bed to bathroom. His head was clouded and he remembered the empty wine bottles he had planned on putting into the outside bin the night before. Had he done so? He couldn't remember.

He moved, aware that the space beneath him smelt bad, and wished he could open a window to clear the room. He wondered if Maeve had noticed.

Beside him, the bed was empty and the sheet crumpled. She was up already. Of course she was. For as long as they were there, she would be up and gone before him every morning, and in bed and asleep before him every night. 'I don't know why I come down,' he told her once. 'We might as well be in different countries.'

'Because you love it,' she had said. But he didn't. He had enjoyed buying the house, rescuing it from wreckage, overseeing its return to the kind of family home – comfortable, gracious – it was meant to be, even though Maeve had stopped him doing many of the things he wanted. 'It's out of keeping,' she had said, laughing at his idea of a jacuzzi, refusing to be persuaded, even when he tried to describe the joy of getting into it after a cold swim, of sitting in the hot bubbles with a glass of wine as the rain fell around them and the mist drew down. 'There would never be any room for us anyway,' she had said. 'It would just be full of kids all the time. You and I would be lucky to get five minutes at a stretch.'

She also said no to a gym – 'You have the whole of the mountains and beach to run around on' – and no to an outside 'den' with pool table and TV in the tumbledown shed. Even to his plans for the upstairs floors, saying, 'It doesn't need to be smart up there – it's just bedrooms,' so that by now he had lost his sense of purpose around the house and had drifted away from it, knowing it wasn't finished. Knowing, too, that he couldn't finish it.

Once there were no projects for him to focus on, he lost the reason for his visits and they became simply contingent on Maeve's wishes and plans, the dates that suited her. 'I can go up and down,' he said, 'arrange whatever suits you.' And he did go up and down, returning to Dublin for days at a time, but more because of the restlessness that wouldn't let him stay in Kerry than any real need to be at work.

He heard the sound of a car out the front then and turned onto his stomach, putting his head underneath the pillow so as to better ignore whatever early visitor had arrived to plague them.

He didn't know how their lives had become so sociable. The weeks in Kerry had at first been an escape – Maeve's from the city, his from work – but had now become something else. There had always been a few people to see, friends of Maeve's family and from her youth, but those were duty calls to be made in the first couple of days, so that the decks might then be clear.

When the children were small, they would see almost no one after those first days, and just move, day after day, from home to beach and back again, when it rained or got too cold. They would buy fish – mackerel and crab claws from the fishermen at the pier – and cook them together. They read and talked about what they read, and went for walks in the evening if Norah was there to stay with the children, watching the last, sometimes the only, gleams of light in the day rise up and fall back, flattening out until the sky became deep blue and then black. Back home again, they would make tea, try and tune the TV enough to watch a film and, often as not, give up on the scratchy reception and go up to bed, together, knowing that the next day would be the same, with only changes in weather to vary the timing of what they did.

But then came the new friends they made, summer people like themselves who came down for a few weeks every year, determined to 'get the best' before they went back to Dublin. More and more, the 'best' meant dinners and drinks and pub lunches, impromptu parties that ran late and at which Simon 'had' to be, so that he drank more, stayed up later and returned to city life feeling more choked and exhausted every year.

He had enjoyed it at first, the sense of liveliness, the company of others with their children, their dogs, their demands – the walks that had to be followed with a pint, and then another – but somewhere along the way he had stopped seeing the pleasure and felt more of the obligation. He couldn't say no, not when he was somehow central to it all. Many of these Kerry 'friends', now, were people Simon had made rich, or richer, and they wanted to celebrate that fact, reward him, thank him, but also – and this was where he felt exhaustion – to show how at ease they were with it all; how, really, they had always been meant for that life and that he, Simon, had only ever been a random instrument of fate.

'People hate you doing them a good turn,' he said once to Maeve. 'They won't admit it, but they do.'

'Perhaps,' she had answered. 'If they do, it's because they hate having to admit that they didn't always have what you gave them, or that they weren't always going to get it, one way or another. If they thank you, and mean it, then it means that they owe you. And everyone hates that.' Maeve was right. She was always right. Maybe, he thought, he should stop his forays into others' lives. Let them be. Keep himself to himself. But it wasn't his way.

Simon took his head out from under the pillow and heard Patrick's voice below. At that, he half-sat up. But the excited sound of Luke and Jake, answering Patrick, telling him things, bragging and swaggering for his benefit, held him back. The way his sons appeared so half-formed in his eyes, when he looked at them beside Patrick, embarrassed Simon. But what embarrassed him more were the comparisons he couldn't stop himself from drawing between them.

Patrick had so little, and yet he was himself so much. It made Simon feel guilty, and conscious of the contrast with his own sons – Luke in particular, who had so much and yet managed to be less than the sum of it all.

He remembered Patrick as he had first seen him, aged maybe four, concentrated and serious, on the kitchen floor of Maeve's parents' house. Simon knew enough by then of his background – the mother from up the road who had gone to Dublin and gone bad, the boy's back-and-forth between the uncle who ran boats and, when she was well enough to claim him, his mother – to have paid attention.

'Can you help me with this?' the boy had asked, looking up at Simon with a steady blue gaze. 'I got one side out but I can't get the other.' His speech was clear, the words distinctly spaced. He was holding a pair of Maeve's father's spectacles, from which he had removed one lens and was working hard on the second. Something about the small but efficient scale of the destruction, coupled with the child's innocence and determination, and the very directness of his appeal, had charmed Simon completely. Luke, just months younger, had little ability to ask Simon for anything. He whinged and sometimes howled, tantrums that took the place of speech, which had been slow to come for him.

'Let's have a look,' Simon had said, sitting down on the floor beside the boy. From there, he could see the line of grease under the cooker. Maeve's parents were getting old and their house, by then, was beginning to show it in dirt and neglect.

The boy placed the spectacles into his hand with complete trust and watched carefully, one elbow on Simon's knee, as Simon fiddled with the tiny rim screw.

'There.' Simon popped out the second lens. 'Now shall I show you how to put them back in?'

'Yes, please,' the boy had said, leaning closer.

In the years that followed, that combination – a serious mind and an appealing personality – would charm Simon again and again. The boy had no fear of him, asking for help and advice as he needed it. He approached Simon directly, sure of a welcome, whereas Luke would come to him at an angle, at first because he was wary of rejection, and later as if there was nothing Simon had that he could ever want.

As Luke became more distant from Simon – first a puzzle then a disappointment, so that even his voice, with the note of 'I' always in it, began to irritate – Patrick, more and more, occupied the space that Luke couldn't. Patrick was receptive, open, warm, where Luke carried always the ready hostility of anticipated rejection. With Luke, Simon felt angry, even bullying, so that often he disliked himself. With Patrick, he was the man he wanted to be – generous, capable, thoughtful – because that was what Patrick expected to see and came out to meet.

'Could we not put him through school at least?' Simon had asked Maeve when Patrick and Luke were both eleven. They were filling out forms for Luke's secondary school, the same school where Alan already was, and where Simon had been, although it was a place Simon secretly suspected would bring out all that was worst in his middle son.

Maeve had looked troubled, but finally said, 'I think it would be fair to offer.'

Patrick's uncle had been mostly silent as he listened to their suggestion – made by Simon over the phone so that, although he could imagine the man's weather-beaten face, the gentle nodding and thoughtful mouth pursing, he couldn't see it – and had said that he would leave it to Patrick to decide, even when Simon said, 'He's too young to make that kind of decision. You should decide for him. He can live with us at the weekends. You know we'd love to have him.'

And the uncle had said, 'You would, I know you would. But I'll leave it to him,' so that Simon hadn't know if the man was wise or foolish; brave or a coward.

And Patrick had said no. 'It's not the kind of school I want to go to,' he had said, looking at the brochure with its photos of playing fields and ancient chestnut trees, laid out below the school crest in swaggering red and the Latin motto that promised faithful hearts and true minds.

Simon, worried that the boy felt scared and was maybe unsure of the idea of himself in the green and pleasant land of the brochure, hadn't known how to reassure him beyond saying clumsily, 'We'd make sure you were alright,' so that he always afterwards wondered if he had failed the boy. Failed to convince him. Failed to persuade him that he could cope with whatever that school expected of him, and thrive there.

He had gone to find Patrick at his mother's house that day – a bungalow on the edges of the city with dirty fields behind it. A badly built house, he saw at once, that smelt of damp and showed patches of mould, thinly furnished with odd pieces of furniture, that spoke of neglect just as Patrick did. And he had left him there, after Patrick had said no, after he had handed back the brochure with its playing fields and pomposity that sat so improbably in that dank room, and shown Simon politely to the door. Left him in that house, with its smell of old cooking oil and mean coal fires. Without the light and heat that any growing creature needs to thrive.

Simon rolled over again and the memory of the smell in the house nagged at him. For years he had thought he could detect a whiff of it in Patrick's hair, on his jumper, even when he had been away from the place for a long, long time.

He turned onto his other side now, still unable to drag himself from bed although he wanted to be up, to be in the shower, washing his skin clean of the night-time sheen of sweat and anxious dreams. Every morning, now, was the same. The time it took to drag himself from night to day, from the person he was asleep to the person he needed to be when he was awake, took longer. He could do it, but it required more and more effort.

This year, it wasn't just the bone-deep exhaustion he felt at the idea of barbecues and sprawling picnic lunches involving heaps of stripy rugs and flasks and cocktail parties. And neither was it just – he cursed himself again – the stupidity of having invited Miriam and Paul.

'I wouldn't mind looking around down there,' Paul had said, barely a month ago, just when Simon thought the invitation, issued drunk after the party last year, had been forgotten. 'Might be a good time to buy something. A place in Kerry could be a good investment.' This, so soon after he had bought the new Dublin house, showed Simon something of the scale of Paul's ambition.

Simon had nodded and smiled and urged him to come, telling himself it didn't matter, that there were so many of them down there now – Dublin people with holiday houses – that Paul joining would make no difference, even though Miriam would be with him. They already knew others in that group, husbands who did deals with Simon, wives whom Maeve had introduced Miriam to. It wouldn't matter, he said to himself. But he knew it would. Of course it would. How could Miriam coming not matter?

'Don't let Jamie drop Sarah,' she had said out of the blue one day, lying on her back, slippery crimson bedspread pulled up to her chin as she watched Simon get dressed. 'Please,' she added then, softening the sense of an order issued.

'What do you mean?' he had asked.

'Just that. Don't let Jamie drop her. Please. The friendship means so much to Sarah. She's not very happy in school. Or anywhere, I sometimes think.' She turned away from him, head lying on one crooked bare arm. 'If the friendship with Jamie ends, she won't have anything much.'

'I'm sure there's no question of it,' he had said. Even though he suddenly recalled the odd hint from Maeve that, in fact, all was not well between the girls, although he couldn't remember exactly why.

'I know they aren't all that alike anymore. If they ever were,' Miriam had said. 'But please, just until Sarah settles down more. With other friends. Promise?'

'OK,' he had said, not quite knowing what he was promising,

or how he could do what she wanted. The children's friendships were no business of his, he felt. That was for Maeve to watch over.

But he had found himself saying to Maeve, 'Isn't it time we had Sarah over again?' whenever it occurred to him that they hadn't seen her in a while, even arguing with Jamie – the child he never argued with – when she said, 'Do we have to, Dad?'

'I don't see why not,' he said. 'She's no trouble.'

'She's no fun either,' Jamie muttered so that Simon snapped that she was being selfish and what would it cost her to invite the child. He could see Maeve watching him, perplexed, but when he appealed to her – 'You're the one who tells me how much it means to her to be invited' – she backed him up.

'Yes, Jamie. And you know you enjoy her company when she's here.'

All this made Simon pay more attention to Sarah when she was around. That was how he came to find that she watched him. Not just looked at, but watched, eyes following his movements: where he went, what he did, the passage of his thoughts written on his face. Watched them all, really. She made him think of a cat by a pool, watching the surface for anything gliding by.

He opened his eyes and forced himself up and out of bed. He wanted to see Patrick. Wanted to see how Luke compared to him now, after nearly a year apart.

CHAPTER 27

The beach was busy by the time Sarah got to it, the calm of the morning gone now as families gathered to swim and dig and drag each other through the surf. They had churned and scuffed the smooth wet sand of earlier so that it lay in messy heaps, while across the fine, dry sand were dotted checked rugs and the odd optimistic deckchair.

She could see the lifeguard hut, flag still fluttering wildly, lonely on its sand dune. Both guards were sitting outside now, backs to the hut, faces to the water, and Sarah began to wave at them, then put her hand down, embarrassed, when she realised they weren't looking at her and probably wouldn't recognise her even if they had been.

Sunlight glittered far out on deep water, but closer to shore the wind whipped up little choppy waves that slapped against each other, keeping the shallows in a constant state of agitation. The twitching and slipping of the water and the way the children ran in and out, alternately chased away and led on by waves, made Sarah think of some small animal leaping and nipping at their heels.

She put her head down and pushed into the wind, heading for the cove, pushing hard, too, against the feeling that told her to turn and leave, to allow the wind to send her back to Reevanagh and then all the way home to Dublin. She was astonished at her own daring. Astonished that she was there, walking towards her fear rather than curled up on the little white bed in Jamie's room with a book. Her sense of panic at what lay beyond the curve of rock and inside the arms of that little cove throbbed inside her like a second heart, only one that sat in her throat and beat back and forth like a bird against a window. She put a hand up to see if she could feel it through her skin, but from the outside there was nothing there.

Most of all she dreaded the moment when she would have to step into the cove entirely alone, when it would become a stage on which she would have to stand while Jamie's friends looked her over. She rounded the rocky corner and there they were, a gang of kids, maybe ten of them, her age, some older, none immediately younger. They wore wet suits so that they looked like seals, or selkies maybe, half-human half-seal, clad in rubbery black, some with the suits peeled down to show bare torsos. Their feet were bare, their hair tousled with wind and salt water and their faces burned brown by wind and sun. They looked alike, Sarah thought: a family or tribe. The same longish hair on all – boys and girls – the uniform wetsuits, but more, it was in the similarity of the way they turned to her – all together as if on a silent command, and yet somehow lazy, indifferent. A look that was a shrug as much as it was a question.

They had a fire going, more smoke than flame, and lounged around it on kayaks and surf-boards and blankets or with their backs against rocks. Someone had made a half-shelter with a cluster of stripy windbreakers and Jamie was sitting close into that drinking something from a flask, legs stretched out in front of her, beside a girl with long blonde hair tied up in a wet ponytail. The girl had the end of the ponytail in her mouth and was chewing it. Sarah imagined that it would taste salty, of the sea.

Sarah started to go over to them but stopped when she heard a voice saying, 'Who's that?' loudly, untroubled by the possibility of her hearing. She stopped, unable to answer, and it was Jake who said, 'That's Shadowcat,' and smiled at her.

'She's ours,' Luke added from over by a rock, and Jamie, who hadn't said anything, pulled at a corner of an orange towel and said, 'Over here, Sarah.'

'Everyone, this is Sarah,' she said when Sarah was sitting, knees pulled right into her stomach to make herself smaller. 'Sarah, this is everyone.' Bright eyes in brown faces stared back at her, a ring of wild animals beyond a camp fire, ready to run, not through fear of her, but because their curiosity wasn't sufficient to make them stay.

The second heart was still beating in her throat, a rapid pulsing. Sarah put her head back and dragged her shoulders up out of their hunch. 'Hi,' she said, looking round at as many of them as she could force herself to take in. A silence.

Then, 'Hey. I'm Stephen.' That was a boy with dark curls

and brown eyes, his wetsuit pulled down over a brown chest already showing a few dark hairs. He had a guitar beside him, with a bedraggled red ribbon tied to the neck. 'And this is Sylvain. He's my French exchange.' As if he were a pet, Sarah thought, not a person. The French boy nodded at her.

'I'm Jill,' the girl beside Jamie with the wet ponytail said. She held out a hand politely and Sarah shook it. The girl's hand was damp and cold, as if she'd handed me a fish, Sarah thought, and giggled. Jill smiled back.

'Siobhan.' That was a girl over beside Luke, who was doing something with a bit of rope. 'Do you want to help collect driftwood for the fire?'

'OK,' Sarah said, relieved to have something to do, grateful for the possibility of acceptance that was contained in the question.

'I'll show you the best wood to get,' Siobhan said. 'It can't be too close to the shoreline or it'll be wet and won't burn. You need to look up beyond the high tide mark.' She gestured to a ragged line of beach mess higher up the cove. Bits of dried-up seaweed tangled into driftwood, ragged plastic bags, all glued together with yellow foamy stuff that looked like the scum that formed on the bones Sarah's mother boiled up for stock. There was even a dead seagull, or bits of one, woven in and out of the debris.

Sarah stepped over the tide line carefully. The dried seaweed looked hard and painful to walk on; the dead bird looked disgusting. She picked up wood, then fed it into the fire, liking the way the sparks flew like insects and how the smell of the smoke surrounded her. She imagined herself as a witch, burning things with strange incantations to make magic happen.

'Once the flames die down a bit, we can put a pan on them and cook sausages,' Siobhan said. She was, Sarah thought, one of those bossy girls who always has a plan. But, she decided, as long as the plan had room for her, that was OK.

Luke, she saw, was equally bossy – barking orders about the exact height to which the dinghy needed to be drawn up the beach, as well as the placing of what he called 'boogie boards', and even the cleaning of the beach. The latter meant collecting the empty beer cans, cider cans, small, flat bottles of vodka, that were strewn about, tucked into crevices and rocky hollows. Many of them had leftover liquid and cigarette butts in them, and at one point Sarah picked up a can the wrong way and the remnants – stinking liquid, a few strands of tobacco, a wet filter – splashed over her hand. She went to wash it in the sea.

'Why do we have to clean the beach?' she asked Jake as she passed him. He was tying up a white plastic bag full of cans.

'We don't have to, we just do,' he said.

'Where does all this stuff come from?'

'Older kids use the beach at night. They light fires too – in fact that fire we have, it's pretty much constantly going. Us by day, them by night. They drink and smoke and leave all their mess here. Then we come and clean it up.'

'But why?'

'Because no one else will. So we just do.' He explained as if it was some kind of sacred law, Sarah thought. A thing that didn't need explanation, but just was.

There seemed to be many jobs to do, which was weird, she thought, seeing as it was a day at the beach. Once more, Luke gave them orders – about where to stack their stuff, how to build a better lean-to to shelter them all from the wind, even how to sit around the fire so as to keep the smoke out of their faces – so that, in the end, Sarah decided that he just wanted to see them all doing what he told them.

Grown-ups drifted in and out from time to time, with sandwiches and crisps and bottles of orange; and sometimes with questions – 'How many times have you been out?' 'What's the water like?'– and the constantly repeated instruction that they should go 'No further than the mouth of the cove, right?' to which they all chorused 'Promise!' But otherwise they were left alone.

'Where do the grown-ups go?' Sarah asked, after Maeve had passed through with slices of buttered fruitcake and more tea in a big flask that you had to pump rather than pour. 'Very good,' she said when she saw the neatly tied bags of empty cans and bottles. 'I'll take a couple of those with me up to the bin.'

'They stay on the other side, on the big beach,' Jamie told Sarah. 'We don't want them here. This is just for us. The deal is that we can be here as long as we obey the rules.'

'No going out beyond the cove! No swimming on your own!' Sarah declared.

'You got it,' Jamie said. 'Anyway they don't want to bother with us. They just want to go to the pub, or sit around and drink wine. Once we don't go near them, they forget all about us.'

At last even Luke seemed to have run out of jobs for them, and they all sat around the fire in the shape he dictated, and ate sausages that were burned and raw and too hot and delicious. They passed round the giant flask – 'It's an urn,' Jake said – and pumped the tea into mugs. It was milky and sweet, and Sarah thought she'd never had anything as delicious as those sausages, that fruitcake, that tea.

The sun was almost hot, although the wind made sure she didn't take her sweatshirt off, and the light danced on the waves as if the two – sky and sea – were endlessly congratulating each other, twinkling and nodding back and forth in mutual approval.

'Do you sail?' Stephen asked her.

'No.' It was Jamie who answered. 'She never has.'

'I can teach you,' Stephen offered.

'She can come out with me,' Luke cut in, so that Sarah didn't know how to say that she didn't want to, that she was terrified at the thought of going out into all that unstable blue. She hoped he would forget.

'When's Celine arriving?' Jill asked.

'The day after tomorrow,' Jamie said.

Sarah realised she had forgotten all about Celine. And it struck her at the same time that these friends were nothing like Celine, and then she wondered whether her arrival would spoil everything. Would she sneer and show all these new friends how pathetic Sarah was, so that they would wonder how they could ever have missed it?

Sarah took a bite of her sausage, which tasted thick and so undercooked that she couldn't chew through it and nearly choked.

'Oh God, not Celine,' Stephen, beside her, muttered. 'Maybe she can talk to Sylvain? She's always going on about how great her French is.'

'He's like one of the sad monkeys at the zoo, isn't he?' Sarah said, inclining her head towards Sylvain. 'The one that sits on its own and pulls all its hair out instead of playing with the others.' It wasn't what she had been thinking, not exactly, but she liked that Stephen laughed, so she ignored the little voice that told her she was being mean and that she knew very well what it was like to be the sad monkey and so she should go and talk to Sylvain. But she didn't. In case her doing so made the others recognise that she was like him – sad, alone. So she stayed away from him, and remained at the heart of the group, making jokes and laughing at jokes that others made, and promised herself that when she knew them all better, then she would be kind to Sylvain.

'He can't swim,' Jamie said. 'He's afraid of water.' Which meant, there, in that place, that he was out. 'He says he nearly drowned as a child and he's been scared ever since.' She looked thoughtfully at Sarah as she said it, and Sarah shuddered inside, again, the way she had so many times, at what might have been that long-ago day in Portugal. Not that she might have drowned – that was never what frightened her – but that someone else might have saved her. Or that she might have saved herself. Or never gone into the pool that day – or a thousand other possible outcomes that would have meant that she never met Jamie.

She had been frightened, the first time back to the pool in Portugal, but as she hesitated, she had seen Jamie fling herself in, shouting, 'Come on, race you!' and so Sarah had jumped in behind her, knowing to do it fast, without thought. And so she had moved past the place of fear quickly, like sprinting past a gate with a fierce dog behind it, before it could get her.

When they had finished their sausages, Stephen played his guitar and Jamie sang along with him. Afterwards she lay back on the blanket with her hands behind her head then and said, 'Play something else. Something not ancient.'

Here too, Sarah saw that Jamie was first. First to be called upon, spoken to, laughed with. 'Jamie, come with me.' 'Jamie, what do you think?' Even the older ones like Siobhan wanted her company, her good opinion. Sarah wondered what it would be like to be Jamie. To carry with her the welcome she expected to find everywhere. To have, as Jamie seemed to have, no expectations except pleasant ones, no fears except the most basic – that the sun might not shine and a planned day out would be ruined.

She lay back, trying to feel what Jamie must feel. That the sand beneath her was warm and giving; that the people around her would turn smiling faces towards her when she called on them. But she couldn't imagine it. She shifted a little closer to Jamie on the blanket, in case the feeling could be transmitted. It couldn't. Or not to her anyway.

Later Stephen tried to teach her how to surf, full of encouragement – 'You're getting it!' – even though she wasn't and knew she never would.

'I'm the wrong shape,' she said eventually, because he didn't seem willing to give up on her. Jamie, she could see, was exactly the right shape, and when she wasn't turning fast cartwheels or backbends, held her board easily and as if it were part of her, sending it wherever she wanted to go, jumping down lightly when she'd had enough.

'Come on, I'll take you out,' Luke said.

'I don't want to.' The sun had gone behind a cloud and now the water looked cross and dark, not dancing anymore.

'Oh, come on. Don't be a baby. Here—' He threw a life jacket at her, bright orange except where it was stained brown in sprinkled spots that looked like mould. 'Put that on.'

The boat was tiny like a toy, and so flat and low it was almost level with the water, so that Sarah didn't feel she was stepping onto anything that could keep her safe. She hated the way the tiny craft wobbled and couldn't be told to hold still. At least a horse just moved about a bit on four legs and you could see which way it might go. At least if you fell off a horse, you fell onto something you knew, something hard but familiar.

Luke got on behind her, causing the boat to tremble as though it wanted to shake them off, and pushed them out. The boat moved fast, slipping over the surface of the water as though pulled by an invisible thread out at sea. Luke did things with ropes and the small, stiff sail so that they zig-zagged across the bay. Sarah realised how different the sea was, once you were in it rather than looking at it. Out here, it was alive, every inch of it, pushing, pulling, moving; mocking and encouraging – *Go. Come back. Go. Come back.* She didn't like it. Didn't like the motion, the way it rolled and lolled. Or the sudden bumps as waves slapped them, or the way the boat shifted under her.

Out here, the gulls were different too. Patrolling what was clearly theirs, not sifting beadily through people's rubbish.

'When did you learn to sail?' she shouted over at Luke. The wind clawed at her hair and she felt her cheeks wobble.

'Years ago. Simon taught me. He wouldn't let me go out by myself until last year. He still says I'm not allowed to take Jamie out.' *So why are you taking me*, Sarah wanted to ask, but she didn't dare.

He asked her questions – about school, her friends, what subjects she liked – and she gave small, tight answers because she didn't trust that he wasn't gathering a store of stones he could later throw at her.

'You talk less than Jamie,' he said. Sarah didn't think that was true. She'd been noticing, and actually had lately realised, that Jamie didn't talk all that much, but she laughed a lot and smiled a lot, so that it seemed as if she was talking. And people talked to her, all the time, so even if she didn't say much, she was always surrounded by talk. Whereas she, Sarah, knew she was a different kind of quiet, one that people noticed and that made them uncomfortable. It was the same thing with their height. By now, Jamie had caught up, so that actually she was almost as tall. But Sarah looked taller because she was skinny, and her legs were too long, while Jamie was still sort of round and strong. And so people said, 'You're so tall' to Sarah and didn't say it to Jamie, but it wasn't actually true, it just looked like it was true.

However, there was no point trying to explain any of that to Luke, even if she had been able to. Anyway, he sounded pleased when he said that about her talking less than Jamie, as if he approved. It was because he thought she would listen more, she knew that, even though she didn't actually. Instead, she just let him talk on and on – more rugby, and the motorbike he was going to buy some day – and let it roll over her with the spray that came up over the side of the boat and landed so lightly on her that she didn't straight away notice how wet it made her.

They reached the mouth of the bay, where it spat itself into the open sea, and Sarah saw that out there, beyond, the waves were like a pack of snarling dogs, rolling in, hard and fast and dangerous.

'Let's go back,' she said suddenly. The spray had soaked her through and she was cold. Luke looked at her. Then he smiled.

'You know I could swim to shore from here?'

Sarah looked back at the beach, behind them. It looked very far, although when sitting safely on the sand, the cove hadn't seemed all that big. She doubted Luke could do any such thing, but all she said was, 'Oh.'

'And if I did,' Luke continued, 'how would you get back? You can't sail.' The idea scared Sarah so much that she answered angrily, in a rush.

'If you can swim it, so can I. I've got a life jacket. And then your boat would float out to sea and be lost.'

Luke laughed. 'Scratchy little thing, aren't you,' he said, looking at her. The sun came out then, although Sarah could see it was still running an obstacle course and would soon be smothered by another cloud. But while it was free, the bay was lit up by it, with a soft pinkish tint. They drifted, silent, for a moment. Even the wind dropped. Sarah turned her face upwards and closed her eyes. When she opened them, she saw that Luke was still staring at her.

'Won't we be late for Patrick?' she asked, realising that this was the best way to get him to go back. Sure enough.

'Fine, we'll go,' he said, and Sarah felt proud that she had been clever and had persuaded him.

CHAPTER 28

Maeve, walking back from the lifeguard's hut with the empty flask, wind whipping the dry dune grass against her legs, looked down to the cove below where the kids were scrambling around the stretch of beach, which was so changeable in size and ease of access, depending on the tide. Right now, the tide was far out and the bit of beach was large, easily reached by walking across wet sand and around the rocks. Later, when the tide came in – fast and certain, the way it did there – the beach would shrink and close itself off, so that you could only get in or out by climbing across raggedy barnacle-covered rocks that scoured like a cheese grater if you fell against them.

Scrawled on the rocks at the farthest edge of the cove she could still make out faint outlines of the words DANGER: NO SWIMMING that was repainted each year when she was a child, before some change out at sea, some swirling of sand and seabed, had brought alteration to the currents, meaning that now they lay farther out and the cove was safe. Relatively safe, she reminded herself. Not completely safe.

The day was so clear that the figures below were distinct but, in their pinpoint clarity, seemed more distant. Maeve watched Sarah arrive and stand on one leg, the other foot tucked behind her calf, until space was made for her. It took a moment, a beat, in which Maeve felt the girl's uncertainty as if it had been her own, then relief when she saw Sarah crossing into the circle.

The way they had spread themselves out across the bit of beach, colonising it with towels and sweatshirts and discarded wetsuits, spoke of their new independence. Of how they now expected to be left alone. She could hear Luke shouting instructions for a lean-to they were building, and she watched as the others, even Jake, did what he said without demur. That, she knew, would last as long as it took Patrick to arrive, and then the small army of underlings would gravitate towards him, abandoning Luke with exactly the same lack of any question as they now obeyed him.

And Luke would be annoyed, she knew, but comprehending, and he would fall in with Patrick's authority rather than set himself up against it. It was seamless, had been this way for years. Every tribe needs a leader, every leader needs a henchman, but the balance of power was a delicate thing, Maeve knew. Easily tipped, restored only with difficulty.

There was that poor French boy, Sylvain, was that his name? She must invite him over, talk to him, ask him questions. No one else seemed likely to.

Later she watched Sarah scramble onto the dinghy, Luke

behind her, then watched them speed across the bay, going farther and getting smaller. A tiny knot of worry in her stomach followed them, tugged painfully from within her, as if their boat had attached something to her insides. She walked almost to the edge of the dunes and sat down, staring out to sea. She saw the dinghy reach the mouth of the bay and pause there for a while. The sun came out and threw a veil of light over the surface of the sea. Even the rocks gleamed, sticky and wet, as though their surfaces were smooth rather than ragged. She watched the tiny boat as it bobbed in the mouth of the bay, saw it turn at last and watched them come back again.

CHAPTER 29

What should she bring? Miriam wondered, walking from her suitcase to her new wardrobe, so big it was practically a room all of its own, where her clothes – many of them new too – lay or hung in careful colour-coded piles, lending her a joy so intense she had to reach out and touch them, feel the soft give beneath her hand as she brushed it lightly along the piles and rows.

There was silk and cashmere and purest wool in an abundance she had never expected to know. It was the proof with which to remind herself, persuade herself, of the reality of their new life, and sometimes she wanted to get into the vast wardrobe, with its sliding doors and internal light switch, and sit amongst the clothes, breathing in the smell of the lavender bags tucked carefully between piles and running through in her mind, all over again, the distance they had travelled. 'Like Lotto winners,' she had said to Paul. 'People picked up by the giant hand of fate and set down somewhere better.'

'It's been work,' he had said, 'not luck,' looking serious, so that she had bitten back her first response, which would have been: 'Meeting Simon wasn't work. It was purest luck.' She could see that her husband had persuaded himself into a different version of the story of their good fortune. One in which he played a bigger part than Simon; one in which his own shrewdness had sized up opportunity and run with it.

Again she admired the spacious array of clothes, which lay in loose drifts like fresh snow, not packed and crammed tightly in the way her old wardrobe had been.

'You don't want moths,' the image consultant had said sternly, spacing out items carefully – one, two, three, four, then a disc of cedarwood, then four items, then more cedarwood. 'Once you get moths, you're finished.'

What will I pack? she wondered again. Jumpers, obviously, trousers. Dresses? Would they be going out? What else? Would she pack things she knew Simon liked? She didn't know, and the not knowing made her nervous.

What had surprised Miriam at first was the ease with which she slid between her selves. She would never have thought it possible that she could appear and disappear within the different bits of her life like a kind of cartoon witch. Popping in and then out again, without even a smell of singeing to show where the magic had taken place.

She found she could be 'normal' with Paul, to be as she ever was. She found no more fault with him than before, picked no fights, looked at him with no more distance than previously.

With Maeve, she was the same kind of friend she had ever been – relaxed, ready for whatever fun came their way, or, when it was just the two of them, for long intimate talks, walking or standing in each other's doorways, chatting as they came and went.

She moved in and out of these roles and places as she always had, and yet amongst them all there was now a new place with Simon, in which she was something else entirely.

They didn't meet often, there were few opportunities, and when they did, they talked little. They didn't have dinner or lunch. Sometimes they would order room service in a hotel and have a glass of wine or a sandwich, if the other was late. Mostly, they fucked.

Partly what drove Miriam's urgency was the strangeness of it all, the questions that hammered at her: *What are you doing? What are you doing here?* She watched herself, as if through a lens, preparing for these meetings. Showering, dressing in one of the sets of sophisticated, slutty underwear she now kept at the back of her knicker drawer, washing them herself by hand when the house was empty, drying them at the back of the hot press.

She watched herself putting on something neat and discreet over them. A grey or black suit, hair worn back in a braid or bun, so that anyone seeing her would not notice her, would think only 'meeting' or 'conference', as their gaze slid past and onto the next politely dressed corporate employee.

'Nice suit,' Paul had commented when he saw the first of these outfits hanging in their bedroom. 'Are you thinking of getting a job?' He had laughed, delighted that something they had once spoken of as a painful necessity could now be a pleasant joke.

'It's what women wear,' she had said, 'to lunches and things,' and he had said no more, knowing that their new social lives needed new clothes, suitable clothes.

They met, she and Simon, in bland hotels on the outskirts of the city. Commercial hotels, the kind of place where the chips were bad – thick-cut and under-cooked – and no one would ever go except for convenience. Hotels that looked as if they had taken all emotion and uncertainty out of their guests' lives, places of dependability and bland function: 'Stay with us and you will never be late for that morning meeting. The airport shuttle will arrive on time, your breakfast will be precisely as the menu describes it and your dry-cleaning will be impeccable.'

And into that established order, Simon and Miriam brought their own certainties. That, for example, as soon as the door shut behind them, they would undress – he fully, she down to the matching slutty underwear – and the pent-up anticipation of their days and weeks apart would throw them onto the too-neat bed quickly, before they changed their minds.

In that way – fast, urgent – they tried to ignore the enormity of what they were doing. They side-stepped the betrayals and turned their backs on the hurt they built on every time they met. They had agreed to never talk about Paul, or Maeve, or their children – and that left so very little that they didn't much bother. They talked about themselves and one another: *I like when you do this*; *touch me there*; *do that again, and harder.*

They made it expedient, and Miriam prided herself on keeping Simon, and everything they did, completely separate from her life with Paul and Sarah and Maeve; her life as wife, mother, friend. She did not look for Simon in Jamie's face when she saw the girl, or listen for a mention of him in conversation with Maeve. And because of that – the distance – she was able to stand in front of him in the harsh glare of hotel lights, turning around slowly so he could see her from every angle, and say, 'I want you to fuck me so hard,' looking into his face as she said it.

And afterwards, they would shower and dress and talk only of logistics – *Which direction are you going in? Did you park underground?* – and part with a careful peck on the cheek.

And Miriam did it that way because it was the only way she could. Because she knew the killer that proximity could be: the way that too much kindness, too much warmth and intimacy and telling each other the sad and shameful secrets of the heart, could eventually corrode passion, so that it became less and less and was finally lost – how the raw heat of base metal could turn into the oppressive gold of domestic intimacy.

And what was even more strange was the way they could meet then, as friends, with Paul and Maeve, and talk unconstrained about all those things they never mentioned when together: Luke's rugby; whether Jamie would go to the Gaelteacht and, if so, where she might go; house renovations and new cars and the thousand other little links they had all allowed to form between them.

She didn't know if Simon made the same calculations because they never spoke of it, but she guessed that he did. When he had called her after the party – weeks after – it had been without excuse or preamble. 'I know you said not to call,' he had said. 'But I have to. Will you meet me?'

And she had said yes, and made a plan with him, and had never once thought of saying no. It's medicinal, she told herself. I need to do this. Otherwise I cannot go on. She decided to think of it as a kind of blood-letting, a pressure valve on her life, no more corrupting than a massage or spa weekend.

And afterwards, she felt good. Relaxed and happy and pleased with herself for getting it so right. Until she began to count too minutely the days and sometimes weeks between calls, and remember his hand warm on the back of her neck or the rumble of his voice into her neck as he said something to make her laugh, more than the feel of his weight on top of her. Until she woke from dreaming of him and twitched away from the hand Paul had flung across her.

And when she found herself wanting to say his name, or listening in case Paul said it – not so that she could comment, but just to hear it spoken, the sound of it so familiar and so forbidden – she knew she was in trouble, and knew too that there wasn't anything she could do. That she had placed herself there in that very spot, as neatly as if she had plucked herself up and looked around for the most dangerous place she could find to set herself down again.

This was when she began asking Simon to do things for her. Little things, just so that she could ask and hear him say yes. At first, she kept it simple. 'Will you ring me tonight at eleven, just to say goodnight, not a word more?' 'Will you wear that blue shirt the next time we meet, so I know you prepared to see me the way I prepare to see you?' Because if he did those things, she knew, he would have to take something of her into his home. There would have to be a moment, however brief, in the morning, beside Maeve, when he would need to think of her and of their meeting and that thought would be there in the room with them, so that it was as if Miriam herself was in some way there, or a shade of her, between them,

And then she began to ask for things that were more complicated, and finally: 'Can you please make sure Jamie doesn't ditch Sarah, because it will break her heart?' And when he asked, in tones of confusion, why Jamie would do that, she answered, 'Because she wants to and I can see why – they don't get along as well as they used to – but please don't let her.' And he had promised that he wouldn't.

She did it for Sarah's sake – that's what she told herself. But mostly, she knew, she did it for her own. Because she wanted to lay some claim on Simon, even an indirect one, and because she was terrified that whatever she and he had would drift away to nothing if the girls' friendship did.

It was a harmless thing to ask, she decided. Even a good thing. She was saving Sarah from being miserable. Asking Simon to keep the girls close was a good way to keep all of them together. And keeping together was good for everyone, she thought, ignoring the little whispering voice that told her the matter wasn't hers to decide.

CHAPTER 30

Sarah wondered if Kerry had always been her place, even before she got here. Even before she really knew where it was. It was certainly her place now. She'd known it almost immediately – that first morning, walking with Maeve – and had it confirmed the first afternoon, on the beach, with Jamie's friends, who were so quick to become her friends. Even Celine hadn't ruined things.

Celine, when she arrived, had watched for a while. 'You're dug right in, aren't you?' she said.

'What?'

'Like a tick stuck into a dog, burrowing deeper and deeper, clinging on for dear life,' Celine said.

And then, as Sarah tried to think of something to say back, Stephen shouted to her, 'Do you want a go-kart race?' and, instead of answering Celine, Sarah had called back, 'Yes, coming,' and run off.

What was it? Was it them, or her? Was she different in Kerry, in ways that she couldn't see but that others could? It didn't matter. It was enough that, day after day, the magic lasted, until she began to depend upon it, build upon it.

It was different with Jamie too. She didn't feel she was always hurrying to keep up, or that Jamie had to slow down to wait for her. It was like they moved together at the same pace.

And when her parents arrived, Sarah could see they didn't belong, just as clearly as she knew that she did.

Not that her parents realised it themselves. They came, with too many bags and cases, early one evening, arriving, in a new silver car, just as Sarah, Jamie and the others were back from the beach. They were standing in the hall as she dragged a boogie board up the steps and kicked off her flip-flops, rubbing sand from the bottoms of her feet on the hall mat.

'Darling!' Her mother hugged her, then her father, tousling her hair that was so stiff with seawater and sand that his fingers got stuck and pulled it.

'Ow!' she said, jerking her head back and away.

The hall felt too small for all of them and the bags, but especially it felt too small for the conversation – 'How was your trip?' 'Did you get stuck in traffic in Adare?' – one that didn't know where to go, turning round and about the journey because it couldn't find a route through to anything better. Her parents kept asking her how she was and if she was having fun, and Sarah kept saying, 'Yes, it's brilliant,' wondering to herself what her parents expected her to say. She could hardly have said, 'No, I hate it,' even if that had been true, with everyone standing there. And she thought how stupid it was of them not to have seen that and asked their questions differently.

Finally Maeve said, 'Drink or shower?' and Miriam said, 'Shower first,' so that Maeve offered to show them their room upstairs. Sarah watched them, the backs of them, as they climbed. Her mother was wearing tight black jeans and boots with spiky heels. Her jacket was tight too, dark brown wool with shiny flecks. It had threads hanging down from the sleeves and all the edges. Sarah knew they must be there on purpose, but wondered why anyone would wear a half-ripped jacket. Maeve had on jeans, the normal blue kind, a crumpled white shirt and an old pair of navy Converse. Sarah imagined them being divided at the top of the stairs, sent different ways according to their outfits and not allowed to meet again until they had found common ground. She would go Maeve's way, she decided, looking down at her frayed denim shorts.

'So, Sal,' her father said, the old nickname jarring in that house where she was new, 'having fun?' he asked yet again.

Maeve and Simon never asked any of them if they were having fun. They asked specific questions: 'What are you taking to the beach?' 'Did you hear the wind last night?' 'Did you get to the top of Bolus Head?'

'I learned to sail,' she said, hoping that might give him something to actually ask about rather than all the awful 'having fun' stuff.

Luke, coming behind her then with an armful of wetsuits, said, 'You did not. You're useless.'

'Well then, you're a useless teacher, because it's you who taught me,' she flashed back. Her father looked startled.

Actually, Luke had been a good teacher, once she surrendered to the idea of doing exactly what he said as soon as he said it. The first time he told her to 'grab the boom' and Sarah had hesitated, worried by the weight of it, he had pushed her into the water. A hard shove that came unexpectedly so that the shock of falling and the shock of the cold had been almost simultaneous.

'You won't learn unless you listen,' he had said from the boat as she splashed around in water that was shallow, but she was no less indignant for that.

And so she had listened, and obeyed, and gradually had learned, enough anyway to enable her to step onto the boat without feeling that she was surrendering herself to a slyly wilful other.

'I hope they don't start fussing,' Sarah said to Jamie that evening as they got ready for bed. This, now, meant washing her face with a special cream to keep down the spots that flared up around her nose and chin, then putting more cream on the ones that had got through and stood out like tiny glowing bonfires. 'My parents, I mean.'

Jamie, who didn't get spots, just brushed her teeth and hopped into bed. 'They won't,' she said. 'You'll see. They'll all be even more busy now and won't bother with us at all. Luke says he's going to make a proper place in the cove where we can leave stuff instead of dragging it up and down from the house every day. He says that if we dig down under the rocks at the back, we can make a kind of cave and then cover it so no one but us will know where it is. Patrick said he'd help him. We'll be able to keep drinks and snacks and stuff.'

And the strange thing was that Jamie was right. The arrival of Sarah's parents, instead of reining in the freedom she had, expanded it. Maeve, who had sometimes asked, 'Are you warm enough?' or suggested that perhaps Sarah should wash her hair, now didn't, because after all Sarah's mother was there and so the job of doing those things was hers, if she wanted it. And she didn't want it, Sarah saw. Or, if she did, she knew that she couldn't have it anymore.

They had always had the days – herself, Jamie, Alan, Luke, Ian, Jake, their friends – to do what they wanted, but now they had the nights too. The grown-ups went to and from each other's houses, the pub and the one restaurant nearby that was any good – 'Not good, exactly,' Simon had said, 'but bearable.' So, beyond the occasional vague instruction – 'Not too late, now!' – they left them alone.

The world of the grown-ups and their own world drifted a little bit further apart, so that Sarah felt that she and the others had the keys to somewhere secret they could step into where they couldn't be seen or heard, and could play music and talk and play Truth or Dare. So she felt that she had stepped onto the shore of a new world, a place where they could make the rules, together, because they were the first to ever stand there.

Kerry with Sarah in it was fun after all, Jamie found. This was because Sarah was different there, as if she breathed in the air and it filled her out and made her stand up straighter. She didn't stare at the ground so much when she talked, and she was funny with everyone, not just on her own with Jamie anymore.

Jamie had thought she would be embarrassed by Sarah with her Kerry friends, as she was when Sarah was with Celine. That she would have to explain – 'Our parents are friends, and my mum says I have to invite her' – but instead, the friends liked her, straight away. And being liked, Jamie saw, was good for Sarah.

It made her better, less watery and creepy. Not, Jamie told herself, that she meant 'creepy' the way Celine used it, but creepy, as in creeping around things and people.

Sarah still did stuff like sneak biscuits up from the kitchen in her pockets instead of asking for them. But not so often. She didn't hang around in Jamie's bedroom on her own, afraid to come down until you went up and got her, and even then she'd walk so close beside you on the stairs and down the hall that you thought she'd end up tripping you over. She no longer jumped like she'd got a fright and move to stand in behind Jamie whenever Simon spoke to her. Mostly, now, she did normal things, like play on the beach and surf, or try to, because she was terrible, instead of sitting and staring at them all.

She tried hard with the surfing, and the sailing. Instead of saying, 'I can't, I'm no good,' and hanging her head and hinting, hoping, someone would save her by saying, 'You are; you just need more practice,' or something like that, she just kept at it, and she got a bit better even though she still wasn't good. And when the weird bits of her, that Sarah said were just because she was shy, weren't there anymore, Sarah was really good fun.

CHAPTER 31

Three years later: Kerry, July 2003

It had been hot for days by the time Sarah and Jamie, late and panting, sank down into their seats on the train to Killarney. Maeve had promised that 'someone' would meet them when they got there. The sky had stayed blue day after day until blue became its normal colour, and there was a feeling of everyone on that train willing it forward to its destination, so they could spill out onto beaches that had been made for just such days.

'Who'll be down?' Sarah asked.

'Jill and Stephen are there already, Siobhan's on her way. Luke and Alan are there, although Alan doesn't do anything with us anymore. Jake arrives later in the week. He's been on a trip to Cambridge with his Latin class.' Jamie rolled her eyes. 'Sylvain again, and I think Stephen has another friend with him this year, and Ian's coming. There'll be others. Some of the local kids come now too. Patrick's friends.'

'Right. More and merry,' Sarah said, holding hard to her determination to be glad about new people, not scared. 'I can't believe we've got a full six weeks. It's the longest ever.' Then, 'No more braces, I see,' as Jamie gave her a wide grin, showing her newly straightened teeth.

'Thank God!' she said. 'Getting those off was the best feeling in the world. Poor Jake still has another year. His teeth were worse.'

'I like your hair,' Sarah said then. Jamie had cut it short so that it sprang up into a tight mass of golden curls. She had kicked off her shoes and put her bare feet up on the seat beside Sarah. Her toenails were painted tangerine and she wore a silver ring on the third toe of her right foot. 'You look like one of those Greek statues of Pan or something. All you need are two little horns.'

'And pipes,' Jamie said. 'Your hair is nice too. Are you taller again?'

'I don't think so, I haven't grown in ages. Mum says I'm probably finished now. I hope so.'

'You've filled out too,' Jamie said, looking her over. 'You don't look so skinny anymore. In fact,' she laughed, 'not skinny at all on top. You used to be flat as a pancake. Now look at you!'

Sarah put an arm up to half cover her chest, then laughed. 'I know. There goes my modelling career.' The year before, they had joked that Sarah, with her height and skinniness, could be a model, while Jamie could be an acrobat.

'You look better,' Jamie said, looking her over. 'It suits you.' Then, 'How's school?'

'It's fine.' Sarah shrugged. They didn't talk about school, carefully, deliberately didn't talk about it, because of how much Sarah wanted to keep it – school – apart from these summers. Her parents had tried to move her, suggesting sending her to St Assumpta's with Jamie, but Sarah had refused. It had been her first act of open rebellion, the first stubborn planting of her feet in soil and refusing to be dragged further. 'I won't go,' she had said. 'I like it where I am.'

She didn't – that was a lie. They all knew it was a lie, but it was one she stuck to. Going to St Assumpta's would be bad, she knew that. Whatever she had learned to be in Kerry, Sarah knew she couldn't be it every day, in a school uniform, in front of Jamie and her other friends. In front of Celine, who would have a chance to sneer and push and watch Sarah fall, again and again. Because Jamie wouldn't help her, she knew that. It wasn't Jamie's way.

And so for the sake of the summers, Sarah stood against her parents and continued in a school where group loyalties and allegiances had formed long ago, and did not, any of them, include her. She had no friends, but by now she had no enemies there either, had weathered the storms of her early years so that she was left alone. And alone was fine, because she had Kerry.

These days, she and Jamie hardly saw each other during the year, although Sarah lied to her mother that she did, and Jamie lied too. She knew that because one day she had come home to find Simon leaving her house – 'Just had to drop something for your dad,' he had said; then, 'I hear you're going to Kildare with Jamie at the weekend,' and Sarah had said yes, even though she wasn't, hadn't heard from Jamie in weeks. What had been in Kildare, she wondered now. With Jamie, it could have been anything – a party, a festival, a horse show, a lie.

'Is your parents' Kerry house ready?' Jamie asked. 'My dad says he found you a great plot, close to Reevanagh.'

'Yes. But I'm still staying at yours.'

'Of course,' Jamie said. *Of course.* Sarah bent down to tug at the bottom of her jeans, so Jamie wouldn't see the flush of joy spread across her face.

'Dad says he'll never ever do a build again,' Sarah said, sitting upright again, eyes flickering at the rapid passage of outside – trees, houses, hills, horses – flashing past. 'He says it took years off his life.' But she remembered the way her father had said it, how proud he had been and how much he had exaggerated the difficulties to try to hide that pride. 'And he said that Patrick's Uncle Pat was amazing and he could never have done it without him.'

Jamie, she saw, sat up a bit straighter when she mentioned Patrick's name, then asked, 'Did you see Patrick?'

'No. Just the uncle. We went down to look at the house a few weeks ago, to make sure it was all done, and he was there. But he said Patrick was in Dublin, with his mum. Do you not see him when he's in Dublin?'

'No. Dad does sometimes, I think, but we don't.'

'Why?'

'I don't know. I asked Dad and he said that it was Patrick's choice.'

Sarah was at once curious, compelled by the idea that

Patrick, too, kept Kerry separate. 'Is his mum still sick?' she asked, wanting to know more about him. The way Patrick seemed, of all of them, to inhabit two worlds, the grown-up world and theirs, made her want to watch him, to understand how he did it. And why he did it.

'Actually, she's not sick; she's an alcoholic,' Jamie said, voice bloated with the importance of the word. 'Dad just said she was sick when we were younger because we wouldn't have understood. Patrick takes care of her. Or he tries to. Dad says it's almost impossible.'

'Oh.' Sarah tried to imagine it. She took the can Jamie passed to her and had a swig. She had seen her mother drunk – at parties, sometimes in the afternoon after she'd come back from lunch somewhere – and she knew the signs. The voice that was louder than normal; the affection that was more pronounced but too volatile, with its swift, unpredictable changes – the annoyance that would come fast and hard, if Sarah ducked the protestations of love or exaggerated expressions of interest. 'Fine,' her mother would snap, in a too-sharp voice, sometimes with a pronunciation that wasn't exactly hers, that had crept in with the lunches and the new house. 'Just ignore me then!'

What might it be like to have that every day? To be constantly stepping around it? Drunk people were unpredictable, Sarah knew, and she had heard that they could be angry too. Even violent. She tried to imagine Patrick, always in charge, always the one to be listened to and consulted, trying to 'take care' of a woman Sarah saw as shouting lewdly at him, spitting curses with her face twisted with rage, alternating this perhaps with an affection that was cloying and clumsy. She tried to imagine it, but she couldn't. 'Poor him,' she said. The idea that Patrick was someone to feel sorry for was new and uncomfortable. It sat all wrong beside her wish to simply admire him.

In Killarney it was Luke who met them at the station door, ignoring their struggles with bags and Jamie saying, 'Why are you here?' until she asked a second time, louder: 'Why are you here?'

'Because I'm giving you a lift, and – oh, yeah, by the way, you're welcome,' Luke said. He was taller and his shoulders, in a faded pink T-shirt, had the thick fleshiness of a bull or draught horse. Because of them, his neck seemed shorter, as if some of it had vanished into the shoulder flesh. His face was already dark brown from the sun, and his lips were red and shiny as if he was wearing lip gloss.

'I thought you weren't allowed to do long trips?'

'As long as I don't go over the speed limit, Simon says it's fine.' They put their bags into the car – Maeve's car, not Simon's, Sarah noticed.

'We need to get some stuff,' Luke said.

'What stuff?'

'Sleeping bags. Supplies.'

'Why do we need sleeping bags?' Jamie asked, adding, 'I hate when you do your whole "I've got everything planned, just do what I say" act.'

'For the beach. It gets cold at night.'

'Are we allowed down at night now?' Jamie asked, all excited.

'Yes. As long as we're all together. We're supposed to be home by midnight but they never check.'

They bought green sleeping bags, rolled like caterpillars, from a shop that sold camping stuff, then went to the supermarket, where Luke said, 'You two wait here. They'll never serve me if they see you kids.'

So the two girls sat on a low wall in the sun and Jamie took her shoes off again. 'I'm not going to put them back on all summer if it stays like this,' she said.

'It won't stay like this,' Sarah said, because she wanted it to, so badly. 'It can't. It never does.' She leaned back, head against the warm brick behind her.

'It does sometimes,' Jamie said. 'There was a summer when I was a kid, it didn't rain for sixty days or something. Maybe it'll be one of those.' She stretched her head out and back behind her, letting it loll down between her shoulder blades.

'Do you think Luke will get served?' Sarah felt nervous of the idea. She hadn't drunk since that night at the party, the night of the 'Kool-Aid', when she had been sick on Simon's shoes. All she remembered of it was a series of images that slid like ghosts in and out, leaving her with no firm impression of what had happened, just vague outlines that blurred and obscured and rubbed each other out faster than she could read them. She was scared of another night like that.

'I don't know. He looks so old now. I haven't seen him in ages – he doesn't come home at weekends anymore. He stays at school or at friends' houses. And they're less strict down here.'

Luke did get served, coming out with two bottles of vodka. 'It's the easiest to mix,' he said with authority. 'Stephen's getting beer, but we didn't want to buy the hard stuff in Molloy's, in case Ed decides to grow a conscience and tell the Ps – parents,' he added, seeing Sarah look confused. 'No one is going to mind about beer, but they might get edgy over voddy. Mind you,' he said, giving Sarah a long look, 'you could nearly pass for eighteen, and Ed's not going to tell on you. Wouldn't know who to tell. Your parents are new.' He said *new* in a way that said it was something to be laughed at. And he looked at her again, like she was something he might store up for later. Sarah felt her face go red.

Luke made a great play of rolling the windows right down and turning the radio up full blast as they drove out of the carpark. Two girls wearing the cream and brown uniform of the supermarket, hair scraped back into high ponytails, faces orange with make-up, watched him as he did a flashy reverse with one hand, the other angled out the window of the car, then gave him the finger as he shouted, 'Not bad for culchies,' at them.

'That was rude,' Jamie said.

'True, though,' he answered, 'especially the blonde one.'

'They were both blonde,' Jamie said.

'What?'

'They were both blonde.' She turned the music down. 'Do you even know your way back from here?'

'Course I do.' He was annoyed, Sarah could see that, and so he drove fast, far faster, she was sure, than the speed limit, whatever that was, going around corners in a way that made the car wobble, and once nearly running straight into a car travelling in the other direction. Sarah caught a glimpse of a man, face drawn back in horror, behind the wheel of the other car, before Luke righted them and swerved past. 'Bloody tourists,' he said.

But he slowed down after that, thumping his hands on the wheel in time to the radio as they sang along to whatever was on. 'Kerry FM,' he said. 'Years behind Dublin radio. Which is a good thing,' he added, turning towards Jamie, 'before you start having a go at me.'

He lit a cigarette, telling them, 'Roll all the windows down or Maeve'll smell it and kill me,' then passed it to Jamie beside him. She pulled hard on it.

'Drag?' she asked Sarah.

'OK.' Sarah took the cigarette, feeling its unfamiliarity between her fingers, and raised it to her lips. She didn't know what to do and found herself blowing through it. The tip glowed red and a flake of ash fell off and drifted down to her bare leg.

'Suck, don't blow,' Luke said. She looked up and found his eyes watching her in the rectangle of the driver's mirror. Still looking at him, she took a drag, pulling the smoke into her lungs, then coughed. She thought she might get sick. 'You'll get better at it,' he said.

Sarah handed the cigarette back to Jamie, who took another drag and held the smoke in for a moment, breathing out in a steady stream that she angled upwards so that it curled around either side of her nose and on up. Where had she learned to do that, Sarah wondered. And when? Jamie had her feet up on the plastic strip under the windscreen, waggling her toes in time with the music.

'So, what's it like this year?' she asked Luke.

'The cove has changed shape again,' he said. 'It's bigger and there's more dry sand because the tide isn't coming as far in. There's more room to store our stuff. The cave survived the winter. There's even a packet of biscuits one of us must have left last year. Custard Creams.'

'I left those,' Jamie said. Sarah didn't believe she had, but knew Jamie wanted to claim a part of what was treasure to all of them – the knowledge of that secret spot.

Sarah watched the landscape outside the windows move from light greens, long grasses and supple trees to the darker, denser, more concentrated incarnation of nature that was their part of Kerry. The fields seemed to shrug off a farmer's care and the trees turned squat and huddled together, although the hedges burst into life that was like song. It was a landscape that was lush and barren at once. 'They grow stones out here,' she remembered Simon saying once. 'Fine big stones.' He laughed and pointed at a rocky mound surrounded by short, thick grass that was the intense uniform green of glass bottles. 'Those are burial mounds,' Maeve had said.

The leaning trees at Reevanagh were more desperate than ever, Sarah saw, when they reached the house. They had grown, and the twitch of their outermost branches was now closer to the upstairs windows. Closing this gap seemed to have given the trees greater urgency, a yearning that was worse than before.

The front door was wide open and Taylor came slowly down the steps to meet them, Simon behind her. 'How was his driving?' he asked Sarah, leaning in to hug her and inclining his head towards Luke, who paused in the doorway, vodka bottles bundled under his top, waiting for Sarah's answer.

'Very good,' she lied.

'As if you'd tell me if it wasn't,' he said, shaking his head. 'You're like the Baader–Meinhof gang or something, all covering up for each other. Anyway, welcome. Maeve's down swimming, she said to tell you she'll be straight back.' He hugged Jamie, resting his forehead against hers for a moment, then hugging her again.

'Or we'll go down?' Jamie said. 'I'm dying for a swim. Sarah?'

'Definitely.' It was what they always did as soon as they arrived. The first swim. The first immersion.

'It's how I know I'm really here,' Jamie used to say, once they were fully in the water, heads properly wet – they had to dive right under for it to count. 'Maeve says it's a baptism.'

'Baptism with fiery water,' Sarah had said. 'A cold that burns.'

'OK,' Simon said. 'She's at the big beach. Sarah, when are your parents down?'

'Tomorrow,' she said. But he had turned in to the house and wasn't listening. As if he knew already.

They changed into shorts and T-shirts over their swimsuits. 'Jesus, your boobs are huge,' Jamie said to Sarah. 'You look like you're going to fall over.' She stared down at her own, flatter chest and said, 'Lucky you,' with a laugh, but not as if she meant it.

At the beach, they met Maeve coming out of the water, wet and goose-bumpy. 'It's gorgeous,' she said, shaking water from her hair. 'The nicest swim I've had this year. The next few days look good too. Make the most of it.'

Make the most of it. It was what everyone they met said. As if an urgency had infected all of them, a need to eat and drink outdoors, together, witnesses as each day drew itself up to full height then sank slowly back, satisfied, into the rounder glow of evening through to a twilight that was mysterious and precious.

By the time she and Jamie got back to the house, friends of Maeve and Simon had arrived and they were all sitting in the back garden, around a new marble-topped table that had thick, curly iron legs. Sarah still wasn't sure who was who – she knew Stephen's mum was called Jean, but hadn't worked out which of the made-up ladies she was. She knew his father was the man with the pipe because Stephen had pointed him out, but she had no name for him. Then there were Jill's parents and Siobhan's mother – her father lived in Spain with someone else – and a couple who had younger children Sarah didn't know. All together in a group, they were so noisy and their questions so terrible – 'Aren't you tall?' 'Whose daughter are you?' – that she tried to make herself invisible and slip by without being noticed.

Mostly it worked.

'They're so pissed, we could all disappear off the face of the earth and they wouldn't even notice,' Luke said, bringing another bottle of white wine in a silver bucket out to them, on Simon's instructions.

'Good,' Ian said when Luke came back. A year hadn't improved Ian at all, Sarah decided as she put butter on a slice of white bread. His spots were worse than ever. Why didn't he do something about them? Her own were mostly gone now. She felt triumphant suddenly, as if she had been challenged, but had won.

'So what's the plan?' she asked, as if the plan were something to do with her.

'Beach party as soon as it gets dark,' Luke said. 'We've already hidden the vodka and beer in the cove, so all we need to bring down is orange juice, or whatever you drink with your vodka?'

It was a question, and Sarah didn't have an answer, so she said, 'Orange is fine.'

But in spite of her resolve, Sarah's nerve wobbled in the end and she was late down to the beach. She stayed behind alone, because she didn't know what she would find there. The house was empty by then. Maeve and Simon and all the rest had gone to Stephen's parents' house, leaving behind them a table full of empty glasses and bottles, cigarettes stubbed out on saucers or thrown onto the ground.

'I'll tidy up a bit,' she had said, wanting time.

'You don't have to,' Jamie had said. 'Nora will come in the morning.'

'I don't mind,' Sarah said. 'I'll see you down there.' She cleared the table and stacked the dishwasher and set it, then went up to her and Jamie's room, where her little white bed was strewn with clothes she hadn't put away.

She did her hair in a ponytail, then let it hang loose again.

She put on lip gloss, liking the sticky feel and strawberry smell, and thought of not going. *I could stay. I could say I fell asleep. That I didn't mean to, but I just did.*

But she knew that if she did, it would all be over. The call of the darkening sky, the knowledge of what was even now happening at the cove, reached to her. Something was changing, she knew that. As if a portal had been set up down there on the beach through which they would walk, together, into somewhere new.

The whirring, flickering excitement that had kept them busy all day, making sure they had enough wood for the fire so that they would not run out, hasty conferences and decisions, orders – to get, find, bring down batteries, marshmallows, snacks – pulled at her. She knew that if she didn't go now, they would not wait and she would never find them again. They would be gone from her as surely as the travellers in stories who followed fairy music and vanished into mountainsides. Everything they had done that day, everything she heard and felt and smelt in the evening air, told her that.

And so she pulled on a pair of white Converse and went downstairs and out the front door, closing it behind her. The rooks in the trees behind the house were busy with their querulous evening routine, cawing and bickering, but without their usual conviction, Sarah decided. It was too beautiful for that.

The light was ink dropped into a glass of water, swirling clear and deepest blue, and she stepped out into it, following the last rays of the sun as they slid behind the straight line of the sea, and walking down to the road, then the dunes and across to the cove. Tiny birds sped low over the sand and stiff grass, on a final reconnaissance before dark, and she could feel the night creatures ready to creep forth as soon as they retreated. The light faded faster than she had expected, and by the time she reached the rocks to scramble over, it was almost silvery.

CHAPTER 32

The cove was the violent gold of a strong-burning fire, high and bright enough to make the black surface of the water shimmy like an oil slick and throw lurid shadows behind them. Around the fire someone had laid out rugs and even cushions, taken from their parents' houses. There was a smell of burned sugar from the marshmallows and lanterns with flickering candles, tiny lights dwarfed by the setting sun.

'Sarah!' voices called to her from shadows; dark shapes leaned forward to the fire so that faces were lit up, one after another: Stephen, Jamie, Jill, even Sylvain was there, looking pleased to see her although she couldn't imagine why.

'Sit here,' that was Luke, sprawled on one of the sleeping bags they had bought in Killarney. She sat. 'Drink this. Vodka and orange. There's one with blackcurrant too but you said you prefer orange.' She took a sip, then another. It tasted fine, better than the Kool-Aid concoction. Better than she remembered it anyway. She took a bigger swig, watching the flames dance upwards into the night air.

'Here . . .' It was one of the lifeguards from the hut, Sean. He handed her something shaped like a cigarette but clumsy and baggy, without the hard sleekness of the one Jamie had given her earlier.

'Thanks.' She took the thing, remembering to 'suck, not blow', but did it carefully this time so that she didn't cough. The smoke stung her lungs and tasted different but she held onto it and let it out in her own time. 'Good girl,' Sean said. She tried to hand it back to him but he said, 'Pass it on,' so she gave it to Luke.

They danced around the fire, whooping, with the music from the two portable CD players as loud as it would go. Stephen had worked out that if they played the same track on both machines at the same time the sound was louder and better, but of course no matter how many times they shouted, 'One, two, three, play!' there was always a time-lag, so that instead of one synchronised whole, they got two slightly off versions, which was much funnier: listening to two different versions of Basement Jaxx, singing 'You used to be my Romeo', at odds with one other.

'Like singing rounds in school,' Sarah said and Jamie laughed.

The fire had died down and Luke began jumping over it, daring anyone to follow him. At first no one would, except Jamie, who took a giant run up and leaped across the hot glow with a scream. After that they all did, although Sarah noticed that Ian jumped sort of sideways over the smallest blaze. 'Cheat,' she said scornfully. 'Chicken.' He gave her a nasty look.

'Bitch,' she heard him mutter under his breath. She knew that he was enjoying saying it, liking the sound of it, the way he felt as he said it, because he said it again, louder. 'Bitch.'

She ignored him but Jamie heard and threw a handful of sand at him. 'Don't say that,' she said, 'not every girl who slags you off is a bitch,' so that Sarah threw her arms around her and hugged her.

'I love you. I really do.'

'Idiot,' Jamie said, but she wrinkled her nose in the way that said she was glad, and hugged Sarah back. 'Here, have a swig.'

Jamie was better at the drinking and smoking than Sarah, by far, calling for 'more voddy' if the bottle stayed away from her for too long and hanging onto the joint – Sarah had figured out that's what it was with a sudden tingling thrill of recognition – for so long that Jill, beside her, said, 'Stop being a hog, Jamie, pass it on.'

At some point Patrick arrived with more beers and a friend called Seamus who, after looking around for a few minutes, said to Patrick, 'You weren't lying about this lot,' so that Sarah wondered what Patrick had said about them.

There were new people this year, some of whom Sarah was introduced to, and others not, and where this would usually have bitten at her – Who were they? What did they think of her? Was she supposed to say hello to them, or not say hello? – now she found she didn't mind, and just smiled at them, passed them a bottle or a drag or took whatever they passed her and sometimes made a joke, and they did the same back. Easy, no effort.

So this is what's it's like, Sarah thought. This is what everyone else has always understood, and I am only understanding now. She wondered why no one had ever managed to explain it to her. She thought of her mother, trying so hard to tell her: 'Other people aren't thinking about you, pet, they're thinking about themselves. There's no need to be so self-conscious.' *Self-conscious.* One of those words that had become her, wrapping itself around her like cling film, so that she couldn't tear it off or even see much beyond it.

And anyway, it wasn't true. No one who had ever walked into a school hall full of girls who knew you and half-knew you could believe they were thinking only about themselves. That razor-sharp flash of appraisal, the speedy calibration of where you belonged – *if* you belonged – and the way this was communicated silently, the way birds communicate, so that the entire group turned, as one, away from you.

If only her mother had been able to show her *this*, Sarah thought, looking around the campfire; had stuffed *this* under Sarah's skin so that she could have known what it felt like and, once knowing, could have reached for it thereafter.

Well, I have it now, she thought, hugging the feeling to her and reaching up into the air with her arms as if she could have hooked the sky and pulled herself towards it.

Everything was different that night, but most of all the difference was in them and between them, all of them, Sarah realised. The looks that lasted for longer and the way they sat close together, arms and knees touching as if carelessly, by accident, but not.

Stephen kissed her, suddenly, without warning, pinned his mouth to hers and wriggled his tongue frantically against her closed lips. That, like the joint, was new too – something she had heard about but never done. She knew Jamie had, Celine too, because they talked about it – sounding, Sarah had thought, ancient and wise as they discussed different boys and the way they kissed, or 'shifted', as they said. 'He puts his tongue so deep into your mouth, it's like you might swallow it by mistake,' Jamie had said about one guy she and Celine both knew.

'I know.' Celine made a face. 'The first time with him, I thought I might choke.' They seemed to have 'shifted' lots of the same boys, so they compared notes, the way they used to about riding horses – 'Chestnut is a brute, don't let him get you near a fence or he'll brush you off.' Now it was, 'Angus is a creep, he puts his hands up your top straight away.' And Sarah had felt left out, again – another thing they had together that she didn't have – irrelevant in her lack of experience, the way she had nothing to throw into the conversation, no sophisticated mention of things she secretly thought sounded disgusting.

'Luke's a good kisser,' Celine had said then, and Jamie said, 'Eugh!' as if she was going to be sick. 'Way too much info.'

Sarah had listened to them talk and said nothing and when Celine asked, 'How many boys have you kissed, Sarah?' she said, 'A couple,' and then, 'You wouldn't know them,' hastily, before Celine could quiz her, knowing well that Celine didn't believe her and that Jamie probably didn't either.

Celine was coming down the next day, so Sarah let Stephen kiss her, even though it felt wet and sloppy exactly as she had thought it would, but also alive and alien in a way she hadn't expected, a living tongue working hard inside her mouth. She knew that Jamie saw them, because when she opened her eyes, Jamie was grinning over and when she saw Sarah looking at her gave the thumbs-up. Then Jamie was kissing Patrick, the two of them standing up, with Patrick's arms wrapped tight around Jamie. That shocked Sarah, because of the way Patrick seemed like a grown-up. But no one else appeared to notice much or mind so she tried to see it differently.

Someone got sick then and the one called Seamus laughed and said, 'Kids!' in a mean way but Sarah didn't care because it wasn't her, and when the vodka bottle came round again, she took a deeper pull this time, swallowing fast, then slugging again. The wind and the waves and fire crackling were all encouragement – to stay, to do what they were doing, do more even.

It got darker and the fire got lower and the batteries on the CD players ran out, so they shouted for Stephen to play the guitar – 'Give us a tune, give us a tune!'

'Come and sit beside me,' Stephen had whispered as he passed her to get his guitar, but when she tried to get up, Luke, beside her again, took hold of her arm and pulled her back and said, 'There's room in here.' He was half inside the green caterpillar sleeping bag, leaning back against a rock, legs covered. So she got into the caterpillar with him and he made room so that she sat between his legs. She could feel his breath on the back of her neck as they sang Nirvana's 'Smells Like

Teen Spirit', and when they joined in with the chorus it wasn't petulant, the way Kurt Cobain sang it, it was a demand, an ultimatum to the universe not to let them down. And Sarah, who had never imagined she could feel like that, sang the loudest of all.

'Look up,' someone said then. Sarah thought it was Jill. She turned her head upwards, following with her eyes the sprinkling of tiny sparks from their fire that were pouring upwards, reaching towards the thick black night above them dotted with pinpoints of light; they moved and regrouped even as she watched them, changing places, redistributing themselves, deliberately confusing, it seemed, so that no matter how hard she stared, she couldn't work out where anything was.

'It was like tiny holes in the sky, letting light in from somewhere else.' And she tried to imagine the 'somewhere else', a place filled with light so intense it could push its way through the barrier of an entire sky and down towards that beach – but she couldn't.

Tilting her head so far back, staring at those tiny pinpricks of white light, had made her dizzy, so she closed her eyes and fought down the sudden nausea that pushed at her.

Stephen was playing something quieter they didn't know the words to and they all leaned back or lay down and Sarah leaned farther back into Luke and when his hand moved around her waist and up, across the bare skin of her stomach and over the outside of her bra, she did nothing. He paused, hand on her breast, hot through the cotton, then pulled the sleeping bag higher up so that it was almost at her chin and began to squeeze her breast, lightly at first, then harder. The other hand came up too so that he had both of her breasts and was rubbing against them. She stayed still, still, as if she hadn't noticed, as if the hands were somehow an accident; and perhaps he too had not noticed what they were doing, and to draw his attention to them would have been rude, like telling someone they were spilling tea from a cup they had not seen tilt, knowing they would right it as soon as they saw what was happening. But Luke didn't stop.

If he had asked, she would have said no. If he had tried to kiss her, she might have pushed him away. But like this, she didn't know what she could do. There had been no request, no moment she had recognised where she might have refused. So she did nothing and the hands continued, moving in under her bra now, then fumbling shakily with the back of it to undo the clasp so that her breasts were in his hands without the cotton barrier, and the heat of the contact was shocking, as if he had held his hands to the fire before transferring them to her. They felt alive in a different way to the rest of him, as if they were working alone and independently.

Stephen was still playing the guitar and Sarah was half-asleep, despite the movements of Luke's hands and the deepening of his breath into her neck. The things she had drunk and smoked worked together to subdue her now rather than elevate her, and she felt a long way out, closer to the steady wash in and out of waves than to the sharp crackling fire and sound of Stephen's voice.

Luke shifted behind her, pressing deeper into the back of her and she could feel the muscles in his thighs against the outside of her thighs. His breath was faster now and the hands were moving everywhere: to her stomach, her waist, up across her back and down into the waistband of her jeans.

Still she did nothing. She didn't know what she was meant to do. Looking around, nearly everyone was part of a couple, kissing, or just sitting with arms around each other. Jamie and Patrick had disappeared. Luke had managed to get the button of her jeans undone now and the zip down. His hand, hot as a burning coal, moved into her pants and again he wriggled himself closer into her. With sudden astonishment she realised she could feel a thick bulge at the back of her and between his legs, and wondered where it came from, how long it had been there.

She stared at the fire, now a subdued glow pulsing beneath its ashy coverlet. Luke's hand felt like a wild creature, digging furtively, for what she didn't know. She didn't know if *he* even knew, except he must have done because when she moved – uncomfortable with the angle she was sitting at – the hand moved too, deeper into her and her body had no idea what to do with it, whether to accept it or reject it, or even how to do either of those things.

He pushed himself against her harder and then harder still. And then he stopped with a giant sigh that blew across her neck and along the side of her cheek, and sank back against the rocks behind him. After a moment he leaned forward again and kissed the side of her face, curving round her neck to peck it the way a seagull might peck swiftly at a piece of forgotten bun or sandwich. The wet imprint his lips left behind felt cold in the night wind.

It was dark, the fire had gone out, and Stephen had stopped playing and disappeared.

Luke leaned back again and pulled her against him.

Sarah must have fallen asleep then because when she woke, it was nearly dawn and her neck hurt. The light was dirty and grey, the same colour as the ash from the fire that had blown across her so that she felt she had perhaps died a long time ago and been buried. The waves were stronger now, crashing onto the beach with fury, and out to sea she could hear the mournful shriek of gulls forced into a new day.

She got out of the sleeping bag carefully, so as not to wake Luke, and poked the fire to see if there was any light left, but there was nothing but forgotten ash and half-charred sticks there, so she set off to walk up to the house.

CHAPTER 33

Kerry wouldn't have been Miriam's choice – for her, 'holidays' meant leaving the country and going somewhere hot, but now they had built this house – 'an investment' Paul said – and Kerry was where Maeve and Simon and everyone went, and so Kerry it was.

'It would be quicker to fly to the Algarve,' she complained to Paul as they packed the car. Was it really possible, she thought with a secret thrill of delight, that she was bringing three suitcases for a two-week stay? And that the suitcases alone cost more, by far, than her entire holiday wardrobe of just a few years ago?

'The roads will improve,' Paul said confidently. These days, he believed everything would improve. Miriam had seen his 'projections', as he called them, that began small and ended in millions, with huge gaps in between that she didn't see could be filled. 'In a few years, we'll be up and down in no time.

And anyway we can sell the house if it doesn't work out,' he went on, making space in the boot for a crate of wine. 'We've made money on it already.' That was how he talked now, as if everything had a price, belonged in a grid, and it was just a question of knowing how to move up and down that grid.

'In that case, you owe me a decorator's fee,' she said. It was the kind of thing the other wives said, with laughter and clinking of glasses, meaning, *I'm as big a part of his business as he is, he just doesn't realise it; I'm the brains, he's just the muscle.* And maybe these women were, Miriam thought, getting into the champagne-coloured car with its cream leather seats that had made her want to cry actual tears of joy when they chose it – but she certainly wasn't. She didn't do anything with Paul's money except spend it. She wondered for a moment if that was a bad thing, whether she should be more 'instrumental' in the acquiring of it, then chucked the thought into the back along with her handbag and quilted jacket.

At least it looked like good weather this year, and of course they had their own place. She wished they didn't, though.

Staying with the O'Reillys had been cosy and fun. Waking up every day, meeting in the hall to go for a quick swim, or in the kitchen for long breakfasts and plans to be made and remade depending on the weather. 'I'll take the girls horse-riding this morning while the boys are out with Simon, then we can meet back here for lunch and all climb Bolus Head in the afternoon.' The kids came and went, mostly doing their own thing, although Jake, always the one to stick closest to his mother, sometimes joined them.

They walked up hills and mountains and along beaches,

stopping for pints in warm pubs, shopping quickly, because, 'Nothing kills my dream of Kerry faster than a supermarket,' Maeve said, stocking up on the biscuits, crisps, sausages and orange squash the kids devoured. Normally, Miriam would never have let Sarah eat so much 'rubbish', but, 'It's the Kerry air,' Maeve said. 'They're always starving. It's the only way to keep them fed.'

They cooked on alternate nights, mixing up couples so that she and Simon were paired together, and had glasses of red wine in the kitchen as they chopped and stirred and sliced. He was an exacting cook, she found, refusing to let her cut corners the way she usually would have.

'Not fine enough,' he'd say, looking at the onions she had chopped. 'Not nearly fine enough.'

'He's a slave driver,' Maeve said, putting her head round the door and laughing. 'Why do you think I picked Paul? You'll be lucky to get mashed potato and gravy when it's our turn.'

With music on and the door shut and just the two of them, it was almost like they were a couple, Miriam had thought, finding that there was a quiet eroticism in being close to Simon like that, sometimes almost touching him, seeing him as he was at all the hours of the day, but without allowing herself to give in to the expression of it.

Because he was firm about the rules.

'No,' he said, when she followed him out into the garden one evening where he was throwing eggshells into the compost heap and pressed herself against him in the dark behind the end-wall of the house, 'Not here,' and even when she took his hand and guided it under her skirt and between her legs, he still said 'Not here,' and set her gently back from him by the shoulders. 'We have to wait,' he said.

And so she obeyed him and didn't try to find them sly moments together for sex that could have been hurried and urgent and almost angry, because that was how she felt when she saw the way he was bound and knotted into his family life, not tied loosely the way she had hoped to find him. Instead, she made herself take a deep breath and allow the pace of things to be set by him, and she tried to enjoy the closeness, the moments alone together over the kitchen counters, Bach playing behind them, as he talked about how long to boil stock and the best way to dress rocket leaves.

And if one part of her sank into dismay that he was able to hold back, resist, set rules and keep them, the other part knew he was right. They had sworn they would not do anything destructive. That they would be 'kind and careful', as he said. 'We don't want to hurt people.' And even though he hurt her by the very fact he could say that, and mean it, she agreed immediately. 'Of course we don't. We must be very careful.'

'How does it end between us?' she had asked one afternoon as they lay in bed, some months after that first Kerry holiday.

'Why are you asking that?'

'I'm just curious.' She had tried to sound 'just curious'. 'I can't see how it ends, when I play this – us – out in my mind. We're careful, so we won't be found out, unless we stop being careful. And we won't. And if we're not found out, then what? I mean,' she leaned up on one arm, looking down at him, tracing with her eyes the broken veins in his nose and over his cheekbones, 'we're not going to throw a bomb into this and insist on "being together"?'

She put emphasis, even irony, on 'being together', to disguise the fact that it was a question, then steeled herself to hear him say, 'No, we're not going to do that,' exactly as she knew he would, and choked back her misery when he did.

'So,' she continued, 'then what? How does it end?'

'Maybe it doesn't,' he said, putting an arm up to draw her down to him.

'Everything ends.' She lay her head on his chest. 'It's just a question of how and when. But you won't pension me off with a gold watch and a certificate of faithful service one of these days?'

'Never.'

'I'll miss staying at the O'Reillys,' she said now to Paul as they drove through the changing, deepening greens and golds of fields and woods. 'It's been fun, the last years.'

'Yes, but this year we can entertain them,' said Paul. 'It's about time we showed them reciprocal hospitality.' Since when had he started saying things like 'reciprocal hospitality', Miriam wondered. And how on earth could he think Simon and Maeve cared about that? 'I'm looking forward a few good parties in the new house,' he continued. 'The jacuzzi needs an outing. That was Simon's idea. He's hoping to persuade Maeve to let him install one at Reevanagh. I told him he should go ahead and do it anyway; surprise her.'

'She'd hate that,' Miriam said.

'That's what Simon said. I suppose with a woman like Maeve, you don't do things without her agreeing.'

The admiration in his voice annoyed her. And so she tried to hurt him, and said, 'What's the point of having a house with six bedrooms, when it's just the two of us and our own daughter won't come and stay with us?' and didn't try to disguise her hostility.

'Leave her be,' Paul said; 'she's that age.'

'But I miss her.' Miriam dropped the antagonism.

'I know. So do I. But she's close, at least, so we'll see her every day, and better this than having her sulking with us.'

'I suppose so.' She knew what he meant – *at least she's not on her own. At least she's with a friend. At least she has a friend.* It was what Miriam thought too, it was why she had agreed, but still she felt Sarah's eagerness to leave them in a way that was personal and intense and sore.

'How can you bear it?' she had asked Maeve, hearing Alan talking about finishing university and moving abroad.

'God, I can't wait,' Maeve had said. 'I'm living until it's only me and Simon again. Just a few more years.' She had laughed.

Maybe that was the problem, Miriam thought. Maybe she wouldn't have been able to wait if it could have been her and Simon too. Maybe it was a house alone with Paul that was the problem. Nonsense, she told herself. She and Paul got on perfectly well together. And they did, except that Miriam hardly knew who he was anymore.

His clothes were new – so were hers – but the way he spoke was new too. He still had his engineering job, but he had an office at home now and made phone calls in the evenings, to

Simon, to Mick O'Hagen, to 'contacts' in Bulgaria, when she was watching television on the new flat screen he had bought and hung on the wall, as though it were a painting. She would tuck her legs up under her on the new dove-grey velvet sofa for the watching, with a glass of white wine and the fire on if it was cold, but the TV was at an awkward angle, and she felt somehow staged and uncomfortable.

Around her, the creams and golds of the room would blur into a soft mass that she knew would defy her no matter what she did – scream, curse or cry; all raw emotion would be absorbed into this place of sullen glamour she had accepted for herself.

'Who are you talking to?' she'd ask Paul.

'Our Bulgarian partners,' he'd reply.

'Partners in what?'

'An apartment block we're building on the Black Sea. We have half the apartments sold already.'

'The Black Sea. Sounds horrible,' she had said.

'It's going to be the hottest resort in Europe soon. You'll see.'

If water had a smell, in a large enough body, then so did money, she decided now as they drove. A lake, a river: these were the kind of sums Paul now dealt in, or claimed to deal in. It was a smell of cologne, of cigar-soaked wood and linen tablecloths; of satisfaction. A smell she associated with Simon, a whiff of which she now at times caught on Paul, so that she became disorientated. This kind of wealth was a look too: eyes that didn't stay still, always flickering, assessing, narrowing and widening over endless mental calculations.

Miriam's phone rang. 'Hello?' She let her voice rise up, interrogative, even though she knew who it was; had seen Helen's name.

They chatted about various friends, slow and idle, like a waiting motor. 'I saw them at Gavin and Tracey's on Saturday,' she said of one couple, then realised she had mentioned the party three times now, although Helen hadn't been there, and that each mention had been a slow, cold, purposeful squeeze, inflicting pain. She wondered when she had become someone she would once have disliked? Was it when she lost her job as mother and found that she had hours to fill every day, so that she needed to find social engagements, commitments, and then make them – or try to make them – something others might want? When had she begun to look for a sense of her worth in the things she had that others didn't? Was it because of Simon, and the affair that didn't have a name, only places and boundaries, rooms in which they met, things they did, things they didn't do? Maybe that was the poison that allowed her to be so frozen now, in a way she never would have thought possible.

It was early evening when they arrived in Kerry, the day's heat fading fast around them, vanishing into a mist that crept in from the sea. The new house felt strange and unfinished, even though they had gone through the 'snag list' a hundred times with the builders. It sat in its plot like a scar through the landscape, the earth around it turned over to show an underbelly that was somehow obscene despite all the careful attempts to create a garden on top of the churned soil. The disruption to the land felt like a trauma, and Miriam felt responsible.

Inside, the house smelt of cement and cold walls and glue. It was so new and shiny, all the marble and reflective surfaces they had chosen somehow standing back, holding off a welcome, as if giving their new owners a once-over.

'Put the fire on and I'll open a bottle of wine,' Paul said. 'Lucky we brought down a take-out – I can't see us cooking tonight.'

Or any night, Miriam thought, looking at the huge cream Aga, the expanse of gold-flecked marble and the bright spotlights set into the kitchen ceiling, and contrasting it in her mind with the O'Reillys' kitchen, the soft green walls like moss and the jumble of boots and dog leads; pots simmering; Simon cleaning mussels in the sink while the kids recounted their days.

Maybe if we'd had a family, Miriam thought. One child isn't a family. One child is a child just waiting to leave. Waiting to find more life and fun and freedom somewhere else, to swap the careful contours of an uneasy three for something loud and noisy and comfortably sprawling. Who could blame them? Who could blame her?

'I'll ring Maeve,' she said. 'We can make a plan for tomorrow. It's going to be another gorgeous day. We should invite them all here for lunch.'

CHAPTER 34

When she woke properly, the broad bar of sun slanting across the end of her white bed told Sarah it was late. She turned to look at Jamie's bed – empty when she had come in out of that forlorn dawn – and saw the top of her curly golden head. She must have arrived after Sarah, either so quiet, or perhaps Sarah had slept so deeply, that she hadn't heard her.

She lay still and listened to the house. It was quiet, without the usual sounds of radio, doors banging, people calling to one another.

'Jamie,' she called. Jamie didn't stir.

Sarah's pillow smelt of wood smoke, and her feet and bare legs when she swung them out of bed were filthy, flecked with smuts from the fire.

'Jamie,' she called again. 'Jamie, are you awake?' Jamie mumbled something and dug her head deeper in under the duvet. 'I'm going to have a shower,' Sarah said. Still no answer.

The bathroom door stuck, despite Simon's promises to get it fixed – he never came that far up into the house; only when they reminded him did he think of it – so she pulled a chair across it to hold it closed and got in under the jet of hot water. She washed her hair, then the rest of her with lavender soap, scrubbing off the smell of smoke, the smuts and smears of charcoal, the sticky places on her arms that might have been spilled vodka and orange and that had green fibres from the caterpillar sleeping bag clinging to them, as if she had begun to camouflage herself in spots but never finished.

Through the small bathroom window, the sun ordered her to hurry up. She thought back over the night before, which returned in flashes so that she could consider each piece, handle it gently from every angle, before setting it down and moving to the next. The fire, the dancing, the passing of bottles and joints. Had she really smoked weed? She put a hand up to her mouth, as though her lips might feel different. They didn't, but the dirty taste at the back of her throat was some kind of proof. The flashes that included Luke were harder to look at. She felt sick but didn't know why and found she couldn't remember the sequence clearly; couldn't even be certain that she hadn't dozed off and imagined everything.

She looked down at herself, naked, clean, water streaming over her like a torn veil, over the swelling of shoulder, hip, knee, over the tan lines on her arms and stomach, the varying shades of white and brown and red that told the tale of T-shirts, swimsuits, her new bikini.

She looked down at the dark vanishing point between her legs that had seemed to call to Luke, guiding his hand in some silent urgent way that even Sarah couldn't hear. None of her looked any different, although if she closed her eyes, holding tightly to the shower rail because closing them made her dizzy as if she would topple, the ghostly scrabble of his hand was still there on her, in her.

After, she went to the tiny mirror above the sink to look at her face, turning it this way and that, but she could find no difference there either. A few more freckles, dark smudges under her eyes, but otherwise it was the same face she had consulted so many times before; had studied and tried to catch in different expressions, hoping to learn what she looked like to others. What they saw when they looked at her; what her mother saw that made her say, 'You're beautiful'; what her teachers saw when they asked, exasperated, 'Are you even listening?' What Jamie saw. Celine. And Luke. What he had seen last night that had made him move towards her like that.

Wrapped in a faded purple towel, Sarah sat on the edge of the bath, remembering the time she had sat there with Luke, her first night ever in Reevanagh. She remembered again the clawing of the voodoo panic doll and the way it had nearly pulled her inside out. She remembered how Luke had been kind then, or at least not horrible, and wondered if that had been the start. Or had it been when he picked them up from the train station yesterday – only yesterday? – and told her she could pass for eighteen. Had that meant something? Had there been some kind of code there, for what had happened later by the fire, that she had not understood? A 'yes' that she had said by not saying 'no'?

She wished she could ask Jamie: question her and compare

notes, like it was an exam where she could see if she was studying the right thing: *Is this what we are doing? Is this where we are? The page we are on, the lesson we are learning?* But she couldn't do that. Not until she understood what it was that Luke had seen, what he wanted. What, now, she was to him.

Back in the bedroom Jamie was still asleep, even shaking her shoulder didn't wake her, so Sarah got dressed, fiddling with different T-shirts, different earrings, to delay going downstairs. She put the clothes from the night before, crumpled, filthy, ugly now, into the laundry basket on the landing below, and wondered would she ever wear any of them again.

The kitchen was empty and hot. There was a smell of toast which told her someone had been there already; that she was not the first up. A bluebottle hurled itself against the window in fuzzy, bumbling fury – but when she opened the window, it wouldn't fly out. She flicked it with a dishcloth, hating the light thump of contact with its buoyant body.

'Hello, Taylor,' she said to the dog, to break the silence of the kitchen before it choked her. Taylor raised her head and thumped her tail once, before sinking back onto her paws.

'That dog should be called Patience,' Simon had said the day before.

'Or Vigil,' Maeve said. 'Poor Taylor. Waiting and waiting.'

And Sarah had felt sorry for the dog, so that now she went over and stroked her head. 'There's a good dog,' she said. Taylor thumped her tail again but otherwise ignored Sarah, so she poured herself a bowl of cornflakes and sat, feet up on the chair beside her, eating. She found she was ravenous and had poured herself a second bowl, was even thinking about frying bacon, when she heard the front door open and the sound of someone crossing the hall. Her heart started to thump then, in case it was Luke, or Maeve. She suddenly realised that to see Maeve would be strange now too, because of what Sarah knew that she didn't.

But it was neither of them: it was Jake.

'Hi!' Sarah waved at him happily. 'You're early.'

'I got the first train. Dad collected me. He's gone to see Pat about the boat.'

'Well, it's great that you're here. How was the Latin trip?'

'Brilliant.' He told her a little – about Cambridge and how he hoped to go there to study, about debates he had taken part in, and then asked, 'What have you all been doing?'

'Not much,' she said. 'The usual.' She found she couldn't look at him and distracted herself by putting butter on a slice of bread, then sugar.

'Still with the sugar sandwiches?' he said. 'I'm making coffee. Do you want some?'

'OK.' It was, she decided, time to put away childish things and grow up.

'How do you take your coffee?' Sarah had no idea. She'd never drunk coffee before. 'With milk?' she hazarded, then added two spoonfuls of sugar after taking a sip. Like that, it was delicious. Almost like coffee ice-cream.

The kitchen filled up. Maeve came in next, straight from the beach, saying, with a laugh, 'You've already missed the best of the day'– but because Jake was there too, Sarah didn't mind and didn't feel she was in the false position of knowing what Maeve didn't know; wouldn't like to know.

Jamie, unusually, was dressed when she came down. Normally, she could spend half a day in her pyjamas. 'Patrick's calling here before he goes down to the cove,' she said. She was sparkling like a piece of cut glass held up to light. 'He says he'll take me out to check his uncle's lobster pots.'

'I've already offered to buy any lobster he brings up,' Simon said, coming in through the back door. 'God, it's hot out there. Even the wind is hot today.'

Sarah stayed, had more toast and another cup of coffee, afraid that if she left, she might meet Luke in some corner of the house where they would be alone.

When he did come in, face still swollen with sleep, he ignored them all at first, not answering even when Simon said, 'Good of you to join us' in a sarcastic voice. When he did begin to talk, his voice was hoarse, but he was the same as ever, teasing Jake: 'The lamest trip of all time – a Latin trip. What did you do, dress up in togas?'

'Can we borrow your surfboard?' Jamie asked him.

'Why?'

'So Sarah can use it. The one she had last year got lost. Someone left it on the beach and it got washed out to sea.'

'Typical Sarah,' Luke said. 'You're like blood group AB. The universal recipient.'

'Luke, don't be rude.' That was Maeve.

'Wow, you actually remember some biology?' Jake said. 'Good for you.'

But Sarah could tell – she was practically an expert in Luke's teasing – that he didn't really mean it; was probably trying to be funny. And so she knew that everything was back to normal and that the night had never happened – not really, or not in real life anyway.

But even so, when, a bit later, Jake said, 'Does anyone want to cycle to Valentia with me?' she didn't say yes, although a year before she would have done. She said nothing, and no one else said anything either, until Luke announced to everyone, 'We're going down to the cove,' emphasising the 'we', so that Jake wasn't in it. And even though Sarah could see Jake was hurt, she didn't offer to go with him. Neither did she say, 'Come with us,' because she didn't yet know what she would find there, at the cove. Jamie and Luke didn't say it either, so Jake set off on his own, hurt and pretending not to be, while they took drinks and packets of crisps and went towards the sea.

Jamie walked ahead with Patrick, and when he put his arm around her, she leaned into the side of him so that he wobbled off balance for a moment.

'What'll your parents say when they see that?' Ian asked. It was exactly what Sarah had been thinking.

'Nothing. They think Patrick's the best thing ever,' Luke said. 'If they could swap me for him, they would in one second.'

'Anyone would swap Patrick for you,' Ian said, shoving Luke, because, Sarah could see, he was embarrassed at what Luke had said, or rather, the way he had said it.

Last night's fire was a chilly, blackened ring and they didn't have the energy to revive it, so they sat with their backs to it, faces to a sea that was pale and smooth. They were tired and the day was as lazy and languid as they were, without even the usual Kerry breeze to nip at their edges and keep them in shape. So, when someone produced a joint and Sarah took her first drag, it didn't feel there was far to fall.

Afternoon came and made the air thicker so that it seemed like there was no line, now, between it and the sea. There was a violet shadow on everything and the water lay clear and still, with only the tiniest of waves reaching up from the shore towards them.

Celine arrived, climbing over the rocks towards them, reproach written in the lines of her back and shoulders. 'I called to the house,' she said to Jamie. 'No one was there.'

'I guessed you'd know to come here,' Jamie said lazily. She passed the butt of the joint she was smoking to Celine who, Sarah saw, took the tiniest of drags before passing it on.

'We called to your house on the way too, Sarah,' Celine said then. 'My mum says it's very South Dublin.' She smirked.

'What does that mean?' Sarah asked.

'You know,' she waved a cigarette around, expansive, dismissive.

'No, I don't.'

'Very new. Very shiny.'

'But it is new,' Sarah said, confused. 'It's brand new.'

'Yes, and looks it.' Celine laughed. 'Shiny-shiny. Full of shiny people. *New* people.'

'Celine…' Jamie said.

'What? You know it's true.' She shrugged, irritated by Jamie's failure to respond, and began to tell them about a party she'd been to in Dublin.

But for all her bitchy posing, Celine wasn't part of them,

just as Jake hadn't been. Sarah saw it immediately, and saw that Celine knew it too. With the clarity of exhaustion and maybe the weed she had smoked, Sarah looked at Celine properly for the first time, noticing that beneath the confident voice and snappish assertions, the well-cut hair and stylish clothes, there was a strained look to her bony face.

She's not pretty, Sarah thought in sudden exultation, seeing how this changed everything. *She's not as pretty as I am*. 'Who's for a swim?' she asked suddenly, knowing that around her would be a chorus of yeses.

'Me!' Jamie stood up and started pulling off her T-shirt then stepped out of her shorts. 'I can't be bothered with togs today,' she said as she walked towards the water. She took her bra off, dropped it behind her then stepped out of her pants.

'Good idea,' Stephen said.

And because the air was dark enough, thick enough to screen them, to blend them, because she felt as if really there was no difference between herself and the land, sea, air around her, Sarah said, 'Me neither,' and then they were all pulling clothes off and heading for the water. Except Celine, who stayed on her towel as if it were an island.

'Isn't it gorgeous?' Jamie asked, floating languidly. 'Like swimming through satin. Evening swims are the nicest.'

'Yesterday, you said morning swims are the nicest,' Sarah said and they both burst out laughing. Sarah wrapped a wet arm around Jamie's neck and when Jamie didn't say, 'Get off,' or shake herself free, Sarah leaned down and kissed her, on the mouth, standing naked in the evening water that swirled around them like a bolt of pale blue silk. 'I do love you,' she said.

'Idiot,' Jamie said again, with the same affection as the night before, and Sarah was the first to move away.

Afterwards they wrapped towels and rugs around themselves and stayed like that, drying gradually, not talking, until, on the darkening air, came the sound of a cowbell from up and far away.

'Maeve's bell,' Luke said. 'Dinner.'

CHAPTER 35

'It doesn't look like Kerry anymore,' Maeve said, leaning out of the bedroom window. 'Or not my Kerry anyway. It's like Tuscany or somewhere like that. The fields are all yellow, like the straw that sticks out of a scarecrow's arms and legs.'

'Makes a nice change from forty shades of mist,' Simon said, still in bed, voice thick with sleep and last night's drink.

'I like those forty shades of mist. There's something weird about this, don't you think?'

'It's perfectly normal,' Simon said. 'Just because you get one heatwave in ten years, doesn't mean global warming.'

'I didn't say it was global warming,' Maeve said. 'Just that it's weird. It's like living in a different country, being a different person.' She leaned further out, elbows on the very edge of the stone ledge, staring at the familiar undulations of hills and fields now appearing in front of her in strange colours, like one of those famous landscape paintings – Van Gogh's *Landscape at Auvers in the Rain*, or Degas's *Landscape with Hills* – but painted by someone else, someone with a different palette.

The air told of dry grass and hot, hard earth, and Maeve wondered how much rain would be needed for it to smell damp and thick and many-layered, to smell of home again. Around her, the house too was different. Heat had made it swell up like a rotten limb, so that doors stuck and hinges creaked, protesting the warped shape of things. The door to the upstairs bathroom didn't close at all now, and Jamie had told her that Sarah was so nervous about using it that she had a stomach-ache.

'She can use my bathroom,' Maeve had said.

'She doesn't want to do that,' Jamie had said, with *obviously* underwriting every word.

Turning back to the room, Maeve said, 'Better get up. The Kerry carousel waits for no man.' The 'Kerry carousel' was what she had taken to calling the manic round of entertainment they were launched upon, driven in part by the new predictability of the weather, the possibility of making plans and those plans coming to fullness, but in part too by other things she was only beginning to puzzle out.

There was something new among them, she decided as she packed for the day's outing. Something sharp and goading that put heat into them all.

It was a kind of madness that swirled around and made them come up with new, extravagant ideas, trying each day to better the day before.

Maybe it was money? There was more of it, for all of them, that year, so that it became a sound to be heard, a whisper in all they said and did. A glow of easy confidence that lay over everything, like a clean tide sweeping over an empty beach, washing it with possibility, washing it free of consequence. The money would protect them all, animate them all.

Maybe it was Miriam and Paul's new house – now that they had their 'own place', as they put it, they could not be stopped, leading the charge in every kind of plan and scheme: 'To pay you all back,' as they insisted gaily to Maeve and Simon, 'for the hospitality of the last years . . . Sure, the house was built for entertaining!' And indeed it was, with its cavernous open-plan living room in which sound travelled in hard clusters – so that being there with more than a few people, Maeve thought, was like being struck around the head.

Today the plan was a visit to an island, one just a few miles offshore, where they could swim and picnic. They'd go there in Patrick's uncle's boat.

So, what was it, Maeve wondered, as she stuffed sunscreen and a book she knew she would never get to read into the bag, that had infected them all? Where had this new urgency come from?

Jamie stuck her head in the bedroom door just then. She was wearing a red towelling dress that was too short, belonging to last summer, and blue flip-flops.

'Have you seen Sarah?' she asked.

'She's still in the village with Luke,' Maeve said. 'They're getting batteries or something.' Jamie didn't wait, and Maeve doubted she had even heard her. It was as if they now lived on parallel frequencies, where Jamie could stand and watch her mother's mouth move, even nod in time to the rhythm of the words, but hear nothing.

Maeve knew the island they were planning to go to: she'd been out to it before, though not for years. She remembered it as a quiet, almost sad place, as if it took seriously its own solitude. She wondered what it would be like, invaded by them all with their flasks and plastic cutlery. She must make sure they didn't leave a single thing behind, not even an apple core. That would, she felt, be an insult – like presuming someone wanted your company just because they were on their own.

Under the new regime with its new energy, places she knew and loved and turned over in her mind during the long months when she was away had become nothing more than backdrops or focal points for their excursions. A mountain pass that, to her, was sacred became just somewhere they could arrange for seafood platters and pints of Guinness to be served, to celebrate the reaching of it.

And even the reaching was often a cheat, done by pony and trap, say, with a crate of wine in a car behind them. 'We should walk, at the very least,' she had said, just the day before.

'It's too hot,' Miriam had complained, fanning herself exaggeratedly.

Maeve was about to insist, when she looked at Simon and took in the high colour of his face, and so instead she said, 'Fine, go in the trap. Simon can go with you. I'm going to walk.'

'I'll walk with you,' Paul said. And he did, spoiling her ascent with his talk of the new house and the things they still needed to get for it. 'We haven't seen the right kind of light fittings at all yet,' he said, so that she couldn't follow the steady drone of the hedges and swish of dry grasses in the skittish wind the way she wanted to.

'Does it really matter?' she asked at last.

He stopped for a minute, then began to laugh. 'No, of course it doesn't. Doesn't matter a damn. Thank you for reminding me of that.' He took her hand then. 'Thank you for many things,' he said.

Maeve, embarrassed, pulled at her hand and said, 'Don't be silly; you don't have to thank me for anything.'

'I do, and I'm aware of it and I wanted to you know that,' he insisted.

And Maeve, afraid that he would begin to list the things he wished to thank her for, said nothing but began to move off.

'Wait,' he said then, 'just a minute,' and he leaned in towards her awkwardly, as though pushed, embarrassed but intent, moving close towards her face, her mouth. And Maeve, fighting an urge to laugh, had turned her cheek fast and said, 'Honestly, it's nothing. We'd better hurry; they'll have eaten all the nice bits on the seafood platters and left us with the smoked mackerel.'

'It's like the last days of the Romanovs,' she'd complained later to Simon. 'A never-ending round of entertainment in odd places, driven by boredom and because-we-can, and secretly by fear.'

'It's fun' had been his reply. She had wondered whether or not to tell him about Paul, but she didn't know what there was to tell – had it been a pass? Probably. But she had never been someone to gather proofs of her appeal and submit them, in evidence, to her husband. She decided to say nothing. Poor Paul. What had he been thinking? She must make sure not to sit next to him on the boat.

Through the window, Maeve saw Patrick arriving in his little blue car. Instead of working on his uncle's boat and dropping in and out of their lives, Patrick, Maeve found, was now always with them.

'How is it possible?' she had asked Simon. 'I thought he needed to earn money?'

'I have an arrangement with him' was all Simon would say. By which Maeve knew he was paying him – of course he was, and willingly. She knew Simon would have given Patrick far more than he would ever take, and she had learned not to feel that as an insult to their own sons.

Downstairs now, Simon was shouting orders about food and what they needed to bring. 'Patrick,' she heard him roar, 'come and help me with the steaks. If we marinate them now…'

Even over the noise of the boat engine and the smell of the oil, Maeve could feel the beauty of the morning, lying quietly beyond the disruption they brought with them. The sea was smooth, as though a quilt of pale blue satin had been laid across it, quieting the chop and roll of the waves, and the sun that slanted across it was already warm and certain.

'We may never get this again,' Miriam, beside her, said.

'It would be a sin to waste it,' Maeve agreed. That too drove them, she knew. The certainty that they were blessed, but momentarily only. That they had somehow chanced upon a run of days, made up and ready, for who knew what, and had been allowed to use them. Like finding one beautiful painting in a shop full of junk, and being told it cost the same as the other, terrible paintings. Then allowing yourself to buy it and walk away with it under your arm, knowing it was wrong and a mistake, but doing so anyway.

Miriam leaned back against the boat rail, pulling her baby-pink cashmere wrap tighter around her. 'Is it too early for a glass of wine, do you think?' she asked. She was wearing flip-flops with heavy glittery stones studded into them, so that her perfectly pedicured toes lay like tiny pigs in a sparkly basket.

'Too early for me.' Maeve laughed.

Miriam called the same question over to Jean, whose son Stephen was on the boat too. Jean laughed and said, 'Never!'

That was part of the mix too. Drinking, which started early and went on late. Drinking, which fuelled the urgency, but was also fuelled by it. For underneath everything else – the weather, the new money, the booze – what drove them, Maeve saw, was the too-rapid run of time and the way it stood, now, poised to take everything from them – so that they sped up, dug deeper, spent more, while it was still theirs.

Because what she had started to understand was that the shocking contagion of their teenage children's coming-of-age was the real force that animated them all. The electric currents that ran between the young people – invisible, irresistible – spread out into the air in their wake and alarmed their parents into a late, jerky dance. Watching their children plunge into life, like gulls dive-bombing – hurling themselves at and through the surface with abandon – had stirred the air around them. It was the overspill of that energy, the drops shaken loose by their transit, that Maeve and Simon and Miriam, Paul, all of them, were maddened by.

It was change – change that was rapid and violent, that gave off a gunpowder smell. That, and the silent knowledge of their own impending losses. *They will take everything we have*, Maeve thought. *All of it, without reflection*. It was a thought that both cheered her and depressed her. She didn't mind for herself, but she minded for Simon, minded terribly. If she could have denied Luke, Jake, any of them, for Simon, she would have; she knew that, and was glad that the power wasn't hers.

She saw it in the way Patrick looked at Jamie and the way Jamie, now, looked back. That was why Patrick was there. He might accept some of Simon's money, little enough, Maeve was sure, but he wasn't there because of it. And Sarah, still quiet, still watchful, but watched now too. By Stephen, by Sylvain, the French boy. By Jake, and by Luke too, she feared, wondering how such a primal battle could end. Maeve had looked at Jake and seen that he had arrived too late. That something had happened in the days before his arrival which meant there was a line he could not cross. She had seen him try, the first day, with questions and suggestions – 'Does anyone want to cycle to Valentia with me?' – and seen the hurt on his face when no one spoke up and said, 'I'll come.'

There was a new assurance in the way Sarah sat and stood and waited, as space was made for her. And Maeve was happy to see it, even if it came at the cost of harmony between her sons.

'Good for you,' she'd said to Sarah that day, passing close to her. The girl looked surprised, almost guilty.

'For what?' she asked, darting a look over Maeve's shoulder.

'Just good for you,' Maeve said, passing on.

'We're here,' Patrick called down from above them. He was wearing faded jeans and had already removed his white T-shirt. His chest and arms were brown and strong. 'Isn't he beautiful?' Miriam whispered beside her, and Maeve felt suddenly certain that they should not all be there together; that the lives of old and young should run more separate. And for the first time ever, she longed for the summer to end, the heat to end, for them to be back in Dublin, where they could all fall into the distinct grooves of their different lives.

The tenderness Maeve felt towards Simon persisted, while they unloaded the boat and explored, choosing a shady spot on the only beach the tiny island offered, where Simon dug a hole and lit a fire and ordered them all around as he prepared lunch.

'Steak,' he said. 'Just as easy to do over an open fire as on a barbecue at home.' Except that it wasn't, and the flames wouldn't behave for him so that he became annoyed as the day crept towards its hottest and least forgiving point.

'Damn thing!' he cursed at the fire. 'Keeps going out.' He drank beer after beer, kept cool in a rock pool, and his face got redder.

'Go and see if you can help him,' Maeve whispered to

Miriam. 'I've tried, but he won't let me.'

'OK.' And Miriam was tactful where Maeve had been direct, asking Simon to show her how he did whatever it was he was doing, so that he agreed and then allowed her to distract him when she said, 'A watched potato-in-tinfoil never cooks,' with a laugh and led him for 'an explore' around the island. Maeve, her feet in the rockpool with the beers, watched them go with relief. When they came back, Simon looked less angry.

'You could build a couple of houses round the other side of the island,' he said. 'There's a perfect, naturally sheltered spot.'

'You'd need a helipad.' Paul sat up, alert suddenly. 'I doubt a boat would get you here reliably during the winter.'

'That could be done,' Simon said, 'easily.' It was what they did now, Simon, Paul, their friends – remade the world around them to suit their image of themselves. They built imaginary houses and shopping centres on every scrap of land they found, debating numbers and materials as fiercely as if the project were actually real, actually theirs.

'You'd ruin it, completely,' Maeve protested.

'You wouldn't have to. You could landscape the helipad and position it so you wouldn't have to see it from the house,' Simon said.

'But it would still be there,' she said, 'and landscaping it would only be a lie. You'd do what those awful people who design gardens here do – import a load of plants that don't belong, because they grow fast or something. I saw a house the other day, just past the pier, where the owners had planted bamboo. Bamboo!' She looked around, indignant at the absurdity.

There was a pause. Then Miriam said apologetically, 'We

put some bamboo in. To screen the jacuzzi. Anything else will take years to come up.'

'Oh. OK. I'm sorry—' Maeve gestured helplessly. 'I didn't realise…'

'Perhaps we can dig it up once the hydrangeas reach full size,' Miriam said.

'Nearly impossible to dig up bamboo,' Maeve said, but quietly. 'It travels like wildfire.'

'We should eat,' Simon said. 'The potatoes are done.'

They ate, then swam. Miriam stripped down to a turquoise bikini, which suited the leanness of her figure. Her hair was longer these days and streaked with delicate slivers of blonde so that it caught the light and shone brightly. Her perfect nails and glowing skin suggested the discreet help of good salons.

'You're much better at all this than I am,' Maeve said to her, trying to make up for the bamboo comment.

'All what?'

'Going to the hairdressers, getting your nails done.' Maeve waved a hand, taking in the full extent of Miriam's efforts. 'Buying clothes. All of it. I can't ever be bothered.'

'Don't you see?' Miriam said, 'You don't need to. You always look amazing.'

'Kind, but not at all true,' Maeve said, and it wasn't, she knew that. She had put on weight, around her middle, so that everything she wore now fitted badly, was too short or too tight. Her usual walking and swimming didn't seem to be working for her any more, and she had begun to wonder could she take up running, although the inanity of it depressed her.

'You have to keep up,' Anne, Celine's mother, had said to

her briskly barely a week before. Maeve hadn't been sure if she meant her specifically, or all of them.

'Keep up with what?' Maeve had asked.

'The men,' Anne replied. Then, when Maeve looked baffled, Anne added briskly, 'If Simon is going to move up to the next level, you have to be ready to go with him. You have to keep up your end of the bargain.'

'What bargain?' Maeve had wanted to ask, but didn't, because she knew what Anne was getting at and couldn't bear to hear her say it. This bargain – it was something to do with a wife reflecting the status and wealth of her husband, creating homes and buying clothes that gave an accurate picture of his worth to the world. As if his money were a theatre set, and her job was to dress it.

Instead, Maeve said, 'We never made any bargains,' and changed the subject. She didn't believe Simon wanted that of her. That wasn't, ever, how they had been together.

She watched him walk towards them, a plastic tumbler of white wine in his hand. He was wearing navy shorts and a white collared T-shirt, and the heat was making him sweat. There were damp patches under his arms and he wiped his brow with a silk handkerchief – yellow with blue dots. Maeve wanted to take his hand and lead him into the water where it would be cool, then bring him home, away from all of them, and take him to bed for love and sleep and the kind of quiet, intimate conversation they had not had in too long. These days, there were always phone calls to make; trips to Dublin for meetings; places in Prague to fly out and assess; deals to watch over. But she knew if she tried to take him away, he wouldn't let her. He'd insist they had to stay, had to 'see it through'.

Luke came past them then and said, 'You're looking hot, Mrs Ryan,' to Miriam. And even though Maeve knew he was trying to be funny, was trying to flesh out the larger distances of his new world, spread thinly between childhood and adulthood, she wished he wouldn't. Simon, who had heard him, looked furious and a few minutes later Maeve saw him run past Luke, down on the beach, and shout, 'Race you to the rocks,' once he had given himself a decent head-start.

Even so, Luke caught up with him easily and would have passed him by if Simon hadn't put a hand out and grabbed hold of his T-shirt, pulling Luke back so that he fell, hard. Simon ran on, as far as the rocks, and called back 'Beat you!' triumphantly. He was breathing heavily and had to lean over, hands on his knees, to try and catch his breath, which eluded him for so long that Maeve didn't know which of them to go to first, son or husband.

'You cheated.' Luke was furious. His face flushed red and Maeve could hear tears in his voice.

'Fair and square,' Simon called back, trying to laugh. 'Fair and square.'

'It wasn't. You cheated!' Luke's voice was higher now and everyone in earshot had stopped to listen and watch. Maeve went to him.

'Let it go,' she said.

'I will not! He cheated. He cheated!' The anger was strong, but the hurt was stronger.

'He didn't mean to,' Maeve said.

'Of course he did,' Luke said, 'but you'll never admit that.' He walked off and Maeve watched him go, seeing in him, despite the thick-set shoulders and pumped-up biceps, the aggressive way his thigh muscles rubbed together, the child he had been. She would have to talk to Simon. But not now.

By the time Patrick said it was time to go, and Maeve had picked up every scrap of rubbish, even the potato skins, Simon was thoroughly drunk. He insisted that Patrick sing as they drove the boat back, and Patrick, after a moment, obliged, but quietly, singing 'My Dark Rosaleen' as if he had been entirely alone. Maeve joined in with, 'Shall glad your heart, shall give you hope, Shall give you health, and help, and hope, My Dark Rosaleen!'

The rest of those in the boat were silent, almost without breath, until they finished singing, then they clapped and cheered and Simon came and sat beside Maeve, and put his arm around her and his head close to hers, so she could smell the booze on his breath and feel the sweat still on his brow, even though the evening was cooling around them. He muttered, 'I'm sorry, my love,' into her ear, so only she could ever have heard him. And Maeve put a hand up and pulled his head down onto her shoulder and said quietly, 'I know.'

Beneath the noise of the engine again was the gentle sound of waves slapping at the hull of the boat, like hands passing them forwards, hand to hand to hand, to shore.

But when they got back to the dock, Simon was loud and insistent again and said they should all go for dinner. Miriam and Paul said yes immediately. 'The perfect end to the day,' Miriam said, and Jean agreed: 'Exactly what I feel like too.'

Maeve, exhausted, longed to go home but couldn't say anything. She missed the days when the children were small and she could have used them as an excuse to leave. Now, the children – she still had no better name for them – were the worst offenders. 'Yes, please,' they chorused, 'please, please, can we?'

Late and tired and knowing their parents were drunk and distracted, they were less discreet than earlier. Jamie openly leaned in towards Patrick, who, Maeve felt, almost trembled with the effort of not putting his arms around her. Stephen bid for Sarah's attention with everything he did, like a puppy doing tricks, Maeve thought with a smile, and Luke sneered at him for it in a way that told Maeve much.

'I think we should all go home,' she said, but was merrily shouted down: 'It's such a gorgeous evening!' 'We're on holiday!'

And so they piled into the bar and Simon ordered more drinks, then food, then yet more drinks, until at last it was time to go. 'I think you should leave the car,' she said to Simon, taking his arm. 'We can come and get it in the morning.'

He gave her a look, as though he suspected a trick, then said, loud and carefully, as if she didn't understand English. 'You can drive my car and Luke can drive yours. Can't you, Luke?'

'Can't I what?'

'Drive back.'

'Of course I can,' Luke said. Outside, in the dim outdoor carpark, his eyes glittered like a cat's in the reflected yellow light of the pub windows.

'Right,' Simon said. He handed him the keys, still slow and careful, as if Luke might not know how to take them. 'Half of you come with Maeve,' Simon continued. 'The rest go with Luke. Sure you're up to this?' he asked then.

'Of course,' Luke said again.

Maeve looked from one to the other. 'I'm not sure this is a good idea. It's late and dark and a long drive. Luke hasn't driven at night before.'

Luke, chewing gum, put an arm round her and said, 'It's a good idea, Mum. It's a brilliant idea.'

And then as they moved towards cars, calling, 'Goodnight, see you tomorrow,' Simon shouted out suddenly, 'Patrick, I don't want you hanging around with this lot too much.' He was swaying, holding onto the open door of the car. His eyes were bloodshot.

'Whatever do you mean, Simon?' Jean said with a little laugh that snagged on the air like a ragged nail on sheer tights.

'What I said,' he snarled at her. 'Stay away from them, Patrick. You're worth the lot of them put together. They'll do you no good. Bunch of spoiled pups.' He looked at Luke as he said it. 'You're better than the lot of them,' he said again, mournful now.

'Thanks, Simon,' Patrick said, 'I know who to put as a reference if I'm ever looking for a job.' He said it easily, to make them laugh, to disperse the tension, but he went to Maeve and said, quiet so the others couldn't hear, 'Would you like me to drive him?'

'It's OK,' Maeve said. 'I'll get him home and he'll be fine.' Then, loudly, 'Who's coming with me?'

'I am,' Jake said. 'Ian, you come with us.'

'Patrick says he'll drop me,' Jamie said.

'Fine,' said Luke. 'Sarah, can come with me.'

Sarah moved towards him, like a sleepwalker, Maeve thought, then stopped as her mother said, 'Sarah, love, wouldn't you like to come and stay at the new house? You haven't spent a single night there. You can meet up with everyone tomorrow. Or Jamie can come and stay with us too.' Miriam smiled round, another amusing plan in the making.

There was a silence then, in which everyone waited for Sarah to speak, and when at last she did, her face was pink in the uncertain light and she said, 'It's OK Mum. I'll stay at Jamie's. It's easier. My stuff is all there.'

Miriam looked crestfallen and Paul moved closer to her.

'Well, come on then,' Luke said. Then, to Maeve, 'We'll follow you. But don't wait for us.'

CHAPTER 36

The speed of those weeks took Sarah by surprise. The way they advanced without check, running one into the next, so that they came in and out of focus, like a Ferris wheel moving lazily past chaotic colours, stopping at high points. A succession of days that swung gently in bright sunlight and hot winds, and nights that were humid.

The only limits seemed to be their human ones – how tired they were, how drunk or stoned. The grown-ups set no realistic boundaries – 'Don't be late,' they said, never clarifying what 'late' was, or what the consequences might be. And money did not stop them either.

'Your turn,' Luke would say, to Stephen, or Jill, or Siobhan, or Sarah. And whoever he picked out had to choose a parent – the more generous, the least observant – and ask them. Luke took charge of this money, doling it out as required – for booze, weed, pills now sometimes too, which Seamus bought and distributed, making, Sarah suspected, a tidy profit on what he gave them. She heard him once, whispering with Patrick, who was saying, 'I wouldn't,' to which Seamus said, 'What harm? It's not like they'd miss it.'

When the adults left them for long periods, they would hand over yet more money, never checking first if it was needed, and make what to Sarah were ridiculous statements. 'You're to look out for each other,' Jean would say. 'We trust you,' said Miriam, smiling round at them all.

Her friends made her mother nervous, Sarah could see that, so Miriam covered up with more friendliness than was necessary; more than the other mothers showed. More, and maybe of a different kind. Once or twice Sarah had seen Seamus nudge Patrick, or mutter something to Luke about her mother that made both of them snigger. She knew what it was they whispered, could imagine the sort of thing. Miriam was younger than the other mothers, and she dressed better too, especially now there was the money. But, Sarah thought, she dressed too much like her and Jamie and Jill and Siobhan. Miriam, in a tight pink T-shirt with 'Rockstar' picked out in rhinestones on the front, tight white jeans and huge sunglasses, could so easily have been wearing clothes borrowed from any of the teenagers' wardrobes.

'When she says they trust us, she really means, "We can't be bothered to check up on you",' Jamie whispered to her then, so that Sarah laughed.

As well as the cove, they went to Sarah's, to Jamie's, to the pubs in town that would serve them. Or at least, those that would serve Luke, Patrick, Seamus, Siobhan, and turn a blind eye to the extra drinks – vodka and red lemonade, whiskey and coke – they'd carry outside for Sarah, Jamie, Jill and Celine. Leaning against the windowsill, half-caught between the stillness of the town at night and the noisy warmth of the pub, the girls would pretend to hide their glasses if the barman came outside to where they stood, in the square of yellow light that spilled out of the pub's window.

'It's like living in a next-door world,' Sarah said to Jamie. 'They all see us – our parents, the other grown-ups – but they look through us or away, like they don't want to have to do anything about us.'

'Of course they don't,' Luke, listening in, said. 'They can't do anything, so they pretend we're not here. Or at least, not doing anything we shouldn't.'

When the grown-ups did talk to them, they were obsessed with 'What next?' Sarah decided. 'What year are you going into?' 'What will you do after that?' 'Have you thought about post-graduate courses?'

'As if we care,' Jamie muttered to the others, after one quizzing session from Jean. 'We're on holiday.'

Luke was doing the Leaving Cert that year and planned to 'study law in Trinity', he told Jean.

'If you get the points,' Simon snapped from across the room. He was trying to persuade Patrick to consider Trinity also, with his support. 'It'll be like a bursary,' he said. 'You can even pay me back if you want. Consider it an investment,' he tried, in a last ditch attempt. But Patrick just smiled and thanked him and said, 'It's not what I want.'

'Why don't you just take it?' Jamie asked him one day.

'I don't want to. Going to college is a waste. I know what I want to do, and delaying for four years while I hang round Trinity in a velvet jacket isn't part of the plan. That might suit Luke' – he smiled over – 'but not me.'

'Well, why not just take the money then?' Jamie asked. 'Simon doesn't care. He's dying to give it to you. You could take the money and enrol and then just not go, do your other thing.'

Patrick looked at her.

'You'd rip off your own father?' Seamus asked. 'You'd try and tell someone else to? You really were right about this lot' he said to Patrick. 'They're something else.'

'I don't notice you complaining when we pay for *your* drinks,' Jamie said.

'Yeah,' Sarah agreed, but secretly, she was shocked. She knew Simon had plenty of money – and that her parents did now too, because of Simon. His generosity had always been as much part of him as his blue eyes and the smell of cigars that hovered about him – the way he insisted on 'taking care' of every bill, as if it were something ailing that only he could cure. But Jamie's suggestion bothered her – the casual dishonesty of it; the way she didn't seem to know there was anything wrong with what she'd said.

Jake didn't come along with them much, preferring, he said, to stay home, or swim at the big beach. Celine did, but she remained a little on the outside, clamouring for attention that wasn't offered willingly by any of them. She's like an annoying child, plucking at our sleeves, Sarah thought, feeling warm with the knowledge.

Mostly, it was Luke's attention that Celine sought, and Luke who withheld it the most. And because of that, as well as so many other things, Sarah sought his attention too – played for it, stretched for it, pretended to be indifferent to it.

Because of the heat, because Jamie was happy with her and wanted her close, because of those things and more, what Sarah had thought belonged only to one night, by the fire – with the light of elsewhere pushing through the tiny pinpricks in the black sky – turned out to be movable; could follow her, and take her with it. The hand, Luke's hand, could reach for her, and find her where she was. She learned this two days after the party at the cove.

'Someone needs to buy charcoal,' Simon had called from outside at the back, where he was firing up another barbecue.

'I'll go,' Luke said. 'Sarah, you can come with me.'

'OK.'

It was the short hour before dinner and they were just back from the beach. Jamie and Sarah were slumped on the sofa, Sarah with a copy of *Vanity Fair* Jake had brought back from Cambridge, while Jamie was reapplying varnish to her toenails, in navy blue this time. She wore a pink fluffy hoodie that was Sarah's, and the foot she wasn't painting lay, bare and brown, on Sarah's knee. 'Get me a packet of crisps,' she said. 'Salt and vinegar.'

'We need butter,' Maeve called from the kitchen. 'And lettuce. Get the frizzy kind.'

'And more wine,' Simon said. 'Just tell Ed it's for me.'

'Like I always do,' Luke said, in a voice that made Simon look at him for a moment before going back to the barbecue.

'He must think you're a world-class alco by now,' Luke muttered, loud enough for Sarah and Jamie to hear, too low for Simon.

Jake, reading at the table, looked up. 'That's not funny.'

'Nothing's funny to you.'

'Nothing *you* say,' Jake agreed. 'You never have understood that nasty doesn't mean the same as funny.'

'Come on, Sarah, let's go,' Luke said. And Sarah went with him. She wondered whether to roll her eyes at Jake, to show him that she agreed with him and that she was going with Luke only because she didn't know how not to, but Jake had bent his head over his book and wasn't looking at her.

'Did you write any of that down?' Luke asked in the car.

'No, but I'll remember. Jamie wanted crisps. Then butter, fizzy lettuce and wine.'

'Frizzy, not fizzy,' he said, with a laugh that was friendly rather than mocking.

The sky was huge still as they drove down the small road, rattling over the uneven surface with its central line of weeds and grass, to the bigger road.

They had gone only a half-mile or so, when Luke pulled into an overgrown laneway and stopped the car beside a five-barred gate. The ground sloped up to the gate and beyond, so that the sea was invisible, hunkered down below the skyline. The blue of the sky met the green of the grass, air to land without the interruption of water. The car windows were down and the sound of birds, happy with the day's progress, drifted in.

'Why are we stopping?'

'The view,' Luke said. He sounded strange. Sarah looked

around. There wasn't any view, just the too-tall grass on either side and a muddy patch inside the gate in front of them that bore the prints of many hooves and pats of cow dung. The weeks without rain had sucked the ground dry, so that instead of a wet churn of mud and shit, there was a hard-baked surface on which the pats had landed in distinct spheres, ejected with force so that they showed whorls and smoothly concentric circles. They were a greenish-brown, the colour of oxidised pennies, and sent up a strong smell.

Sarah was about to say so, and suggest they go, when Luke leaned over from his seat and pressed his mouth to hers, hard, and left it there. When she didn't do anything, but stayed still as if silence and stillness could protect her, he moved his body farther in towards her, across her, and pushed his tongue in between her lips. It was, she thought, like someone picking up your hand to shake it, ignoring the limpness, the lack of engagement. He chased her tongue around for a while and, when she still did nothing, moved one of his hands to the back of her head and pushed her mouth closer in to his. With the other hand he took hers and placed it in his lap, over the hard lump in his jeans, then used his hand to push her hand against him, tongue moving more wildly inside her mouth.

The drone of flies buzzing above the shit made her slow, as did the effort of staying away from what was happening, of skirting over it in her mind. She forced herself to stay distracted, connected to the outside, to the breeze that stirred the trees, the fly that landed on the front windscreen and stayed there, busily rubbing its legs together – rather than to what Luke was doing, with his body and hers.

His breathing got faster and then stopped, at last, and he leaned back so that her mouth was free, her hand was free. The smell of sweat in the space between them remained, so that Sarah rolled the window down further, trying not to see the wet stain on the front of his jeans.

In the silence, the birds sounded loud and a car going by on the road behind them gave her a fright. She had forgotten where they were, that they had shopping to do, commissions to execute.

'We'd better go,' she said, 'they'll be wondering where we are.' They wouldn't, she knew that. Trips into town took 'as long as they took', depending on who went and what was needed. But she needed to say something quickly that would force the day back to normal, that would stop Luke saying anything about what had just happened. Because if he did, then it would be true and she would have to say something back, and she didn't know what that could be.

'OK,' Luke said. 'I suppose we had.'

And they drove to town, shopped, drove back, with the radio on and talked, or didn't talk, about plans for an island picnic in a few days when Patrick could get his uncle's boat, about what they might do later, and sang along to the songs that came on the radio. Luke was in a good mood, laughing, chatting almost eagerly, without put-downs or sarcasm, so that Sarah matched her mood to his and the drive was fun.

And after that, when stopping in lay-bys and rutted tracks became a pattern, this became a pattern too – that they never spoke of what they did there. In the days that followed, days that were golden and blue like a princess in a fairytale, he would do this – stop the car once out of sight of the house, pulling into an overgrown laneway or field gate, and then he would reach for her, take her hand, draw it towards him, draw her towards him.

And Sarah, she did nothing. She didn't resist or say no, ever, and she wondered why not. Partly it was the silence – he didn't say much, was neither rude like he usually was, nor polite as he might have been. He was awkward and embarrassed too, she began to learn, and so somehow it all felt unreal. But it was also the way that each time she didn't say no made it harder to do so the next time. As if by not saying no, she had said yes, and that each yes was a guarantee of more yeses.

And, if she was honest, it was better than nothing. Being wanted was better than not being wanted. And he did want her. 'I think I might be addicted to you,' he said one day, staring at her, his face only inches away so that she could see the faint freckles on his nose and cheekbones, the sheen of sweat on his upper lip and the almost delicate stubble below. He said it, not as if he liked her, though, but instead curious, almost angry. She did not reciprocate, could not, but she was glad that he had said it.

She didn't enjoy what they did, what Luke did. But she didn't hate it either. It was something to do, a secret to make her feel she was more than the others. At first, she stayed still and passive, then she found that if she did something, anything, it passed much quicker, and so she learned the timing of it all, the moment to speed up, hand or mouth, or when to utter the sounds she forced herself to make, to bring it all to its messy conclusion.

She also found that if she turned up the radio, she was distracted and minded less. And with the bit of herself that stayed apart and watched, she noticed things, sounds, smells, so that ever afterwards, certain songs – the Pussycat Dolls singing, 'Don't Cha' – or the smell of cow parsley, or the fabric softener Maeve used, made her think of these moments with Luke that were furtive and unacknowledged and strange.

The only complaint she made, could make, was the mess. 'Don't you have any tissues?' she asked, wiping her hand on a patch of grass beside the car that was dry and scratchy.

'Sorry.' The sound of that word from his mouth surprised her. And a day after that, he said, 'Here,' and handed her a packet of baby wipes. 'You can keep them in the glove compartment.' It was as close as either of them came to acknowledging what happened between them, or admitting that it would happen again.

CHAPTER 37

With the others, Luke was his usual self, snapping out instructions and orders the same as ever, teasing, jeering, but he showed favour to Sarah in small ways. If they played rounders and Luke was captain, he picked her first, or at least second, saying that she was fast. He passed cigarettes, joints, cans, to her, and made sure someone always bought the blackcurrant cordial she had decided she liked best with vodka. And once, when Celine asked him outright to take her out in the boat, he said, 'I'm taking Sarah. She still needs to learn to sail,' so that every bit of it was worth it, Sarah decided, looking at Celine's face and the annoyance on it, which she instantly moved to hide.

Celine's revenge came later the same day. 'You make such a gorgeous couple,' she said to Jamie, inclining her head towards Patrick, loud enough that Sarah couldn't pretend she hadn't heard. 'He's so mad about you. Anyone can see that.'

It was perfectly true, but Sarah hated Celine for saying it. She hated that Jamie was part of 'a couple', while she was, what? She didn't know. She hated that Jamie could take Patrick's hand and put it to her face, that he stroked her hair, whispered in her ear. She didn't want to do any of those things with Luke, but the fact that she couldn't – and knew she couldn't – upset her. She imagined the look on his face if she were to take his hand, raise it to her lips and kiss the back of it, as Jamie did with Patrick, the way he would snatch it from her, hard as a blow, and the cutting things he might say.

Every time she looked up, she found his eyes on her, looking at her, into her. But she didn't know what his eyes meant. Sometimes she thought they meant he hated her. 'Addicted' wasn't a very loving word, she knew that; it was an angry word almost. And whatever she was, she wasn't Luke's 'girlfriend' or anyone's girlfriend, although she thought Stephen might like her to be his. And so she felt humiliated, even though she tried to tell herself that this was just a different way, her and Luke, and a better way because it meant they didn't have to do everything together, the way Jamie and Patrick now did, always walking hand in hand and going off alone together.

Yet because she felt humiliated, she wanted to reach out and break something that someone else – Celine, Jamie – had. Funny that friendship should have made her greedy, Sarah thought. If anyone had ever asked how she would feel if she was made a part of the group around her, instead of standing always on her own, she would have said 'happy', but now, it turned out that having meant wanting more. More than Celine had. More even than Jamie had, just for once.

When Sarah had had nothing, she wanted little. Now that she had a lot, she wanted more. And, she told herself, she could have it – should have it – because for so long she had not had anything. She began to judge the distance between Jamie and herself, the gap, and understand that she might be able to bridge it, close it.

It was as though Luke had infected her, somehow poisoned her, so that now, when she looked at everyone around her, she saw their faults and failures, magnified. It's just that I'm growing up, she told herself, I'm more aware now. But it wasn't that.

Looking at Maeve, she could not stop the meanness: *She's getting fat. Her clothes don't fit her. Why doesn't she lose some weight? Or buy new clothes, at least?* Her own mother, so trim and chic, wasn't spared either: *She looks like a rake, hard and thin. And that laugh… And why is she nasty to people now? She didn't used to be. Now she's like Celine: she says things purposely to show people she's better than them.*

Her father, Sarah saw, had disappeared under the weight of his new sense of purpose and his new busyness. Only Simon was the same, except that now, with her new eyes, she could see he was worn and tired and overweight in the way other people were thin – because he was ill and exhausted. She wondered why no one noticed.

She saw Jamie too and saw the glow of happiness from her love for Patrick, which lifted her up from within, made her light and floating like a balloon, bobbing along a little above them all. And Sarah hated her friend for this. She wanted to scratch at the balloon so that it burst and let Jamie back down with a thump. Back down where the rest of them were. Because

Jamie being so much in love with Patrick meant Jamie was less interested in Sarah. And Sarah was afraid of how far up Jamie might rise, how far below she would leave Sarah.

Because of all this, she was glad to hear the beginnings of arguments between Jamie and Patrick. It was a tension that didn't last, but didn't disappear either, surfacing at times and in bursts, then dying down again.

'What is it?' she asked, after Jamie came back from one of their walks, looking cross, and flung herself down on the rug beside Sarah.

'It's Patrick.'

'I guessed as much. So, what about him?'

'He wants to do . . . stuff.'

'What kind of stuff?'

'You know . . . I don't mind kissing, that's nice, though not for as long as he wants to do it for. And even when he puts his hand up my top, I don't mind, but all the other stuff . . . yeuch!' Jamie said. 'The worst is when he takes my hand and tries to make me do stuff to him.' She made a face. 'And then when I won't, he says it's fine and he doesn't mind waiting – but I can see he's annoyed. He says he isn't, that he's just frustrated, but that's worse.' She rolled her eyes. 'And he goes on and on about it, saying, "What about this? And that? Can we do this?" And he tries to make deals: "I promise I won't do this if you let me do that . . ."' She broke off, disgust across her face as if it had been thrown there.

'What kinds of things does he want to do?' Sarah was curious – here, finally, was something to use as comparison. But Jamie wouldn't say.

'You know the kind of stuff.' She waved her arms in front of her, as if shaking something unpleasant from them. 'The stuff guys like doing.'

'Can't you just say no, and tell him to stop going on about it?'

'I try and he says he will, and usually he's good – but then we're alone together and he starts up again. He says he can't help himself, that I drive him crazy.' She didn't sound even a bit proud, as Sarah would have been. 'And he's not like himself then. It's like he's a zombie, and just obsessed. He keeps coming after me.' She giggled a bit. 'It's like *Night of the Living Dead* or something, with the zombies all going, "Brains . . . brains . . ." Except it's not brains he's interested in.'

'That's guys,' Sarah said, conscious of how knowing she sounded, and trying hard to keep the note of weariness in her voice. 'Why don't you just let him?'

'No way.' Then, after a moment, 'And he says I have a bad attitude to money.'

'I think we all do,' Sarah said. 'But you a lot more, because you've always had lots of it. I still remember when we didn't, when we couldn't afford things, and my parents used to argue about it. But that's not your fault,' she added.

'Patrick says it makes him feel bad, the way we are with money, and that Seamus hates us for it, but if I try to pay for him, he gets furious.'

'I understand that.'

'You can?'

'Yes, it's obvious. He's a guy.' Sarah sounded knowing again.

'I don't see it like that. It's just money.' Jamie made an

emptying motion, as though tipping out a tub of dirty water. 'I can always get more; he can't. It doesn't matter.'

'I think that's what he means about having a bad attitude,' Sarah said.

'I suppose so. It's annoying, though. Anyway,' she changed tack, 'what about you and Stephen?'

'What do you mean?"

'Well, he likes you, he told me he did. And you've snogged him . . . so,' she gave Sarah a look that sparkled again, 'what's happening there?'

'Nothing. It's not, you know . . .'

'You don't like him?'

'Not like that.' It was true, she didn't, but she might have gone out with him anyway – instinct told her that he would be pliant, biddable – but she couldn't, because of Luke. And Stephen seemed to know that, even though everything was secret and no one said a thing. He hovered, but only if Luke wasn't around, and he didn't pursue anything.

After that, Jamie went off alone with Patrick less than before, or invited Sarah to go with them, so that often it was just the three of them, and Sarah could see for herself what they were like – the shocking harmony that she hated, and the way it could splinter suddenly. Which she liked.

Patrick disliked her being around; she knew that because he didn't hide it. Not that he was horrible – it was more as if he forgot she was there, so absorbed was he in Jamie and everything she did, every word she said. And then he would look up and see Sarah, or Sarah would say something to Jamie, and he would see her properly, and his face would change and be more stern and grown-up and distant again, losing the bright look it had when he spoke to Jamie or she to him.

At first Sarah tried to flirt with him a bit. It was, she told herself, to make him like her more, for Jamie's sake, because then it would be easier. But Patrick didn't see any of the new her; he didn't see what Luke saw, or what Stephen saw. He looked at her and he saw the old Sarah. Plain, boring, quiet Sarah. He wasn't interested in her. His eyes flicked past her and, she knew, her voice came to him as a subdued murmur, indistinct, uninteresting.

He couldn't bear to be out of touching distance of Jamie. He needed to always have an arm around her, a hand on her, a leg flung across hers, so that one day Sarah said, 'Gosh, he's so desperate!' And Jamie flushed red and said, 'He isn't!' but in a voice as if she was very tired.

'Sometimes I wish the summer would end,' Jamie said to Sarah in their room later that evening. She was lying on her bed, music playing, and the air was hot and dusty enough to choke them. 'Maybe Dad's right. Maybe six weeks down here is too long.'

CHAPTER 38

This year was different, Miriam found. Simon no longer kept the boundary walls in place. He kissed her, put his hands on her, when they might have been seen – by Paul, by Maeve, by anyone. So reckless was he that at first she wondered if it was the risk that excited him, the possibility of discovery? If it was, she decided, that was OK. She could let herself be excited too by the danger; could do that thing people did with danger – see only the excitement and stay blind to the actual penalties of discovery. But soon she realised that it wasn't that. It was as if Simon couldn't help himself, as if he couldn't make any awareness of the risk stick, so that his appreciation of all he – they – had to lose became clouded and uncertain, insufficient to keep him from her. But, as well as this, he seemed unable to stay away because he was drawn to the comfort of her *Yes* as surely as cold hands to a warm fire.

He was drinking more and was forgetful – not in the

old, grand way of 'what does it matter?' but in small things that, reading the twist of fear on his face, Miriam could see disturbed him because of their pettiness.

'You can't have forgotten butter!' Maeve would say. 'It's the thing you went to get.' And Simon threw it off with a laugh, saying, 'I have to go out again later anyway,' as if he had meant to come away without it. But Miriam saw that he hadn't, and that the knowledge of this bothered him.

From being a good drunk, he became a messy one – either because he started earlier on the sly or moved faster than the rest of them, or because his body, under strain from the size of his stomach, the redness of his face, dealt less efficiently with what he put into it. Always the entertaining one, now, Simon could be boring, even boastful, repeating stories she had already heard, and which had no real point beyond showing off about a clever move on his part, a daring game-of-poker piece of bluffing.

He was angry too, losing his temper – with Luke mainly – more often and more openly than before. Once, he had roared at Luke for careless driving, telling him, 'I don't care what you do to yourself, but as long as you have other people in the car with you, you just watch out!' and Miriam had seen tears in Luke's eyes which shocked her. She had allowed herself to believe that the rows between father and son were somehow choreographed: she had thought of them as a play they put on together, a pantomime they both enjoyed – 'Authority Defied', 'Impudence Challenged', and not as the real state of their relationship. And it upset her to see that in fact there was no enjoyment, just hurt on both sides that was growing deeper.

She wanted to tell Luke that Simon loved him and didn't know how to show it, because Simon had told her this. He had told her too that Luke annoyed him, worried him, and that he hated himself for revealing both those things but never love. But Luke wasn't the sort of person you said such things to. He was, she thought, a kind of terrifying half-creature, with the frame and voice of a man, the appetite of a man, the tread of a man, but the soul, still, of a boy. He leered at her, and at her daughter – Miriam had seen the way his eyes followed Sarah, his squashed-down rage when she spoke too long to Stephen or Jake, flirting with that mixture of innocence and intent that told her age as surely as an ID card would have done. But she could tell that he was lost too – confused, no doubt, about everything.

'I think it's time Sarah came home,' she said to Paul, thinking of Luke. 'She hasn't slept a single night at the new house. We aren't here for much longer. A few nights with us will do her good. She looks tired. Under the suntan and the freckles, she has black bags under her eyes. They all do.'

'I'll talk to her,' Paul said. 'I think you're right.'

Miriam wondered whether others noticed the changes in Simon or if was it just her. Did Maeve notice? She didn't say anything, but she behaved towards him with such gentleness, despite his increasing capriciousness, that Miriam thought she must have.

If ever there was a time to break with Simon, Miriam saw that it was now, when, although he couldn't say it, he so badly needed her to, if only to take something out of the overcrowding of his life; now, when the fun had gone from their affair, and it was serious, far too serious. And yet she didn't. Couldn't. And she knew it was a mistake.

She saw them all as if in a film or a photograph, poised at the top of a mountain, about to tumble down through stiff grass that would not cushion their fall, but would scratch them and roll them further down the baked, steep ground, to land in a heap at the bottom. When Jean said, 'Simon's found a pub he says makes the best Irish coffees in the country – the guy uses cream from his own cows apparently – and we're all going later,' Miriam thought of the dog, Taylor, old now, slow, and the way she would walk back and forth across the kitchen, from door to basket and back again, unable to settle. 'She's so used to begging us for walks, she doesn't know how not to,' Maeve had said, 'even though she's too tired now to go.' That, Miriam thought, was like Simon – still making plans, dreaming up schemes, even though he was too tired to enjoy them: old habits died hard.

But they went to the pub anyway, because that's what they did, and had so many Irish coffees that they were wired, all of them, somewhere between drunk and high. There was music – a group of traditional musicians happy to play as long as the drink flowed. They all danced, Maeve well, the rest badly, so that she was in constant demand as a partner, with Paul, and with the other men, locals presumably, who drank at the bar.

Only Simon didn't ask her – 'I'm not dancing,' he said – but he watched her and, Miriam saw, Maeve knew that he watched, and because of that, she danced for him. Whoever her partner, it was Simon she moved for, Simon she looked at and, when the music ended, Simon she walked over to, leaning down to whisper something in his ear that made them both laugh, as she trailed a hand across the back of his neck. It was, Miriam suddenly realised, unmistakably the walk, the trailing hand, the voice, of a woman who knows her husband still desires her.

Why should I be surprised? she asked herself, locked into the threadbare toilet of the pub and trying to prod and jeer herself out of her misery. *Of course he does. What did I expect?* They had never spoken – she and Simon – of what happened, for either of them, in their own homes, with their own spouses. But because Miriam had gradually put space between herself and Paul, so that now they lived together but separately – it was what her conscience demanded of her, that she have one lover, not two, even if it was the wrong one – she had allowed herself to believe Simon had done the same.

That night, Simon drove her home from the pub, his hands shaking slightly on the steering wheel after all the coffee and whiskey.

'Do you, still . . . with Maeve?' she asked, watching the headlamps pick out the road, inventing it anew by bringing light to it. Behind them, dark swallowed everything as soon as they passed it, returning it to formless confusion.

'What?'

'Sleep with her?'

'Well, yes, sometimes . . .' He sounded uncomfortable. 'I never said we didn't. But not like you and me. We don't do the things that you and I do.'

It was that, more than anything, which made Miriam feel worthless. A whore, someone to do tricks for him. Not his wife, who didn't need to.

CHAPTER 39

The kindness had gone out of Kerry, Maeve decided – burned up and scorched, along with the grass.

There was dire talk in the town of farmers who had fed the whole of the winter allowance in hay to their cattle already, because there was nothing left in the fields for the poor beasts to graze on. Streams and marshy spots that Maeve had known from childhood as rushing and sparkling, or oozing mud, were dry and hard. Even St Brendan's Well on Valentia Island had retreated so far below its normal level that no water was visible, just a faint damp smell, a reminder, so that she wanted to lie on her stomach and scrabble in the earth for more of it.

And everywhere was crowded with people who had come from Dublin, Cork and beyond, drawn by the good weather, the novelty of a heatwave that had become something to marvel at, travel for. Weekends were the worst – the beach crowded and chaotic – but even the weekdays were busier than she had ever known them to be. People filled the beaches and walked two-abreast along the narrow lanes, so driving was dangerous and slow. Sometimes they would find that they knew these people, when a shout – 'Simon!' 'Maeve!' – came at them, followed by excitable chat: 'We just came down for a few days, we couldn't resist. The weather!'

There were more and more of them – noisy, possessive newcomers – so that Maeve felt squeezed out and claustrophobic, as if there wasn't enough air for everyone and they had taken her share, breathed it in and used it up. The places she loved disliked the intrusion; of that she was certain. Under their bleached blanket of dry earth and yellowing grass, they had retreated deep into themselves, sulking, brooding, waiting for wet and cold winds and the peace of emptiness.

Because of the crowds, she and Simon and the rest of their group had retreated from the main beach to the cove, where the faint 'Danger: No Swimming' sign and scramble of sharp rocks protected them from the casual picnickers and visitors. Their children had complained, 'You can't, it's our place,' but not as if they meant it, and they had laid boundaries, drawing a line in the sand down the middle – 'You go this side, we'll stay on the other' – that had made them all laugh.

The cove was small, even though the tide was out, and because Maeve was tired of the antics of her friends, she watched the children, the young people, in their growing glory. She watched them play, and try to stop themselves playing when they remembered their dignity that was new but precious. She saw the new certainties and newer uncertainties in the ways they spoke to and touched each other; the roughness that hid tenderness, the often-shifting patterns and lines of connection between them – between Luke, Sarah, Celine, Stephen, Jamie, Patrick. How these were erased and redrawn as fast as she thought she had understood them.

'What's interesting at that age is that there is no difference between love and lust,' she said to Simon, beside her on a rust-coloured blanket.

'Isn't there?' He was reading a newspaper and barely looked up.

'No. Or at least, not that you can work out. It's one and the same thing. Don't you remember?'

'What? Being seventeen, eighteen? Not really.'

'No, I suppose you don't,' she said. Then, watching Patrick and Jamie walk down to the water together. 'What about those two?'

'I'm sure it's nothing.' He sat up. 'They're too young. Patrick has too much to do. He's told me his plans, for the boat and the business, and they're good plans. He's not going to be distracted from them.'

'I'm sure it *is* something,' Maeve said, 'and I don't think it's a good idea. He's too old for her.' Even at a distance, the intensity Patrick turned on Jamie couldn't be hidden. Nor could the layers of Jamie's reaction: pleased; confused; wary. 'Or she's too young. I'm not sure which it is.'

'There's only a couple of years between them, but for his sake, I hope it's nothing. Now, anyway. Later, it could be something.'

'Did you give him money? For the business?'

'He's adamant that he won't take it. He says he'll go to

the bank. That all he needs is a small amount, to convert his uncle's boat and buy a second one. He says there are so many tourists wanting to go to the Skelligs now that they could make three sailings a day if the weather let them.'

'Well, it will be better for him if he gets it going without your help,' Maeve said wisely. 'Better for him and Jamie too. If there is a him and Jamie.'

'I knew you'd say that.' Simon lay down on the blanket. 'I still wish he'd take the money. I'd rather he was in with me than a bank. There will be uncertain years in the beginning, and banks don't always understand that.'

The children – she must stop calling them that – were playing volleyball now, Patrick with close concentration, Luke diving and falling showily as he returned the ball. Jamie, she saw without surprise, played effortlessly well, Sarah badly, with a lack of co-ordination to her gangly limbs that was like a calf scrambling awkwardly, desperately, to find its first feet and follow a mother that has begun to move away. Not that her ungainliness stopped Stephen, who had joined the game now and was trying to show Sarah how to serve properly, guiding her arms and hands with his. Sarah was making no effort to do what he indicated, but she was laughing up at him, her face bright and animated.

'I'll have to get Sarah's hair cut before school starts,' Miriam said, sitting down beside her and Simon, wet from the sea. 'If anyone can get through those knots, that is. They all look untamed, as if they've been living wild on the beach.'

'I suppose they do,' Maeve said, watching the volleyball.

Patrick was shouting instructions to Jamie, which she was ignoring.

'They've grown too,' Miriam said, 'especially Jake. He's nearly as tall as Luke now.'

'He's getting more sleep than the rest of them,' Maeve said, wryly, conscious that Jake was still on the outside, was only there at the cove with them that day because she was. She watched as they ran down to the water, screeching about how hot it was, and threw themselves in, flopping down, then rising up to splash one another. She watched Luke dunk Stephen, hold his head down for such a long time that she nearly got up to go and see, then saw him letting go. Stephen lurched up out of the water and shouted something she couldn't hear, and Luke shrugged, turned away. She must tell Luke to be more careful.

Later, as the tide rolled in, squashing them onto a dwindling patch of sand, she and Simon and Miriam divided up tasks for the evening. For the first time, Maeve felt the exhaustion of effort, hating the isolation of the house and the drive that had to be accomplished day after day, perhaps twice or even three times a day, to fetch and carry what they needed from town. The wearying sameness of it all struck her unexpectedly. 'Simon, I'll go into town if you like and get the chicken,' she said, to spare him. 'What else do I need?'

'It's OK,' Simon said. 'I'll go.'

And Miriam said, 'I'll come with you. Paul's still playing golf.'

'Fine,' Maeve said, 'I've got my car. I can bring all this back up to the house.' Perhaps, she thought, she would get an hour, alone, uninterrupted. She thought longingly of her clocks, missing the feeling of clarity that came over her when she was lost among ratchets and balance springs, absorbed in the joy of each tiny part working in precise harmony with the next; big and small, all equal and necessary.

'Jamie,' she called, 'Sarah. I can drive you back if you're ready to leave.'

'OK.' Jamie came over, Maeve saw, dropping Patrick's hand.

'Just help me pick all this up, will you?' Maeve asked.

'Why do you take everyone else's litter?' Jamie said. 'It's not like we don't have enough of our own. People should take their own crap.'

'But they don't,' Maeve said. 'They just leave it, and I can't bear that.'

'I think it's great you do it,' Sarah said. 'I'll help. We all used to do it, years ago, didn't we? Cleaning the cove?'

'No scrap left behind,' Jake said.

'Exactly,' Sarah said. Jamie kicked at an empty crisp packet then, when Maeve looked at her, bent and picked it up.

Walking back to the car, bags and baskets and blankets between them, Maeve, who was carrying a bundle of rubbish to the carpark bin, spilled the remains of someone's chocolate milk over her arm. 'Dammit,' she said, holding out her dripping hand. 'Disgusting.'

'That's what you get for being a goodie-two-shoes,' Jamie said.

'There's a packet of baby wipes in the glove compartment,' Sarah said.

'Oh, brilliant. Did you put them there? That was clever of you,' Maeve said.

'Luke's idea,' Sarah muttered. Her cheeks flushed red as she spoke and her eyes darted sideways. 'I'll walk back up,' she said then. 'Once I don't have to carry anything, I'll be as quick as driving will be. Mum wants me to spend a few nights in the new house. I suppose I should. I'd better get my pyjamas.'

Maeve got more time with her clocks than she had expected. The house was silent. Jamie had gone with Sarah. 'Maybe I'll stay in the new house with you,' she had said. 'See what it's like to sleep in a princess's boudoir for a few nights, instead of a tree house like the attic.'

'Yes, do!' Sarah said.

'Sarah's parents might like to have her to themselves for a while,' Maeve said to Jamie, but Sarah instantly chipped in.

'They'd love it if Jamie came. Just a couple of nights.'

So Maeve laughed and said, 'Really, not even a night apart?' She went to her workroom and shut the door, closing herself in to the gentle, sleepy ticking, eyes fixed on tiny golden wheels and the exact placing of a pinion. By the time she heard the front door slam, it was late and almost dark.

'You were ages,' she said to Simon, with Miriam behind him, as she came down the stairs.

'We stopped in O'Shea's for a pint,' he said.

'You'd better be careful.' Maeve laughed. 'You know what they're like around here. One drink and you're having an affair.'

And in the pause that followed, there in the hall that was dark because she hadn't yet turned the lights on – in the silence between dropping a stone down a well and the stone hitting water – she knew. Something. Nothing exact, but something.

'Well, I'd better get that chicken on,' she said.

CHAPTER 40

Every day was sunny and every day she and Sarah were friends, Jamie thought. They knew how to do things together now, and they liked the same things. Before, Sarah used to try to like things Jamie liked – and Jamie would see her, watching, trying to understand what she was supposed to do and look like, and copying that. But now they were together, doing the same things: getting drunk and high, chatting and making jokes. It was like they had a ball and were chucking it back and forth, back and forth, knowing the other one would catch it, and everyone else watched and laughed because they were so good at it.

Jamie knew they were leaving the others out, but she liked it and knew that Sarah did too. Celine especially was being left out. She still said Sarah was creepy, the same as she ever was – but Celine, Jamie decided, was wrong and jealous.

They were both obsessed with Nirvana, and made Stephen

play 'Teen Spirit' again and again on his guitar so they could sing along. He was sick of it and said it was never much of a song anyway, but he did what she and Sarah said, because when they were together like that, everyone did what they said.

'You're formidable.' That's what Jake said about them, and he was right.

But it was also because Stephen would do anything Sarah said. He was nuts about her. She said he wasn't, but that was just because she didn't want to admit it. Jamie knew he was, because she recognised the look on his face – it was the same as the one on Patrick's face when he looked at her.

It's like they want to eat us, she thought.

She loved Patrick, but she knew she didn't get that look on her face when she stared at him. It even scared her a bit. Patrick always wanted them to go off on their own together, but Jamie preferred when they were with the others. When it was just the two of them, it was different. It got too hot and the way he stared at her and breathed so roughly scared her. Sometimes he just wanted to lie close beside her or on top of her for ages, and it was fine at first but then she got sick of it and didn't know how to say that.

Maeve had asked her if there was anything she wanted to talk about and Jamie had said no. And even when Maeve said that if anything 'got too much' for her, she should tell her – but she didn't. She had Sarah to talk to. Sarah got it.

And Sarah said if she saw Patrick trying to go off on his own with Jamie, she would make up a reason why Jamie couldn't go. That was part of Sarah being different, coming up with plans like that, which were quick and clever.

The time Sarah kissed her, that was different too. She never would have done that before. She used to be embarrassed even about getting changed if Jamie could see her, and made Jamie shut the door when she went to the loo, even though Jamie said, 'I don't care if you hear me wee.'

And then she said, 'I love you,' and kissed Jamie, on the mouth. She was smiling when she did it, so her mouth felt funny, and instead of kissing her heavily and pressing forward, the way Patrick did, Sarah kissed her lightly and pulled back a little so that it was Jamie who pressed forward, following her, following her mouth, liking the shape of it, the taste of it. Sarah broke the kiss then and laughed.

They all noticed Sarah was different. Luke slagged her, same as ever, but there was something else there too. And the time Stephen flirted with her when they were playing volleyball, showing her how to take shots, later, when they were swimming, Luke jumped and dunked him but then he held Stephen's head under water for way too long. Like, really long, and when he let Stephen up, he was choking really badly and Jamie thought he might have been crying because his shoulders were shaking. But his face was wet anyway so she couldn't tell if there were tears, and he said, 'Fuck's sakes, man,' and was really angry. But Luke just looked at him and said, 'What? *What?*'

'Is it to get away from Patrick?' Sarah asked. 'Coming here with me?' They sat on her bed – which was a double, larger even, and covered in a squashy pink satin quilt – in a room that was just as Jamie had described it: a princess's boudoir, with gilt-edged mirrors and floor-to-ceiling built-in wardrobes with curly gold handles.

'A bit,' Jamie admitted.

'Do you not want to see him?'

'Not for a little while anyway. It's too much,' Jamie said. 'I feel crushed by him, by how much he wants to be with me. I love him, I really do, but I don't know what to do anymore. I think he'd marry me in the morning if I said I would.'

'I think he would too,' Sarah said.

'And I want to marry him too. But not now. I wish it could just go back to the way it was.'

'You never can go back though, can you?' Sarah said wisely.

'Let's open the window and we can have a fag,' Jamie said. 'Or a joint. I've got some weed. No one will smell it if we wave towels around madly afterwards like fans.'

That night Luke called for them in Maeve's car and they went into town, to O'Shea's, Jamie and Sarah waiting outside while Luke went in. 'I don't know why we bother anymore,' Jamie said. 'It's not like anyone cares what we do.'

Patrick and Seamus arrived, then Stephen and Jill, Sylvain trailing behind them. Stephen had his arm around Jill and avoided looking at Sarah, so that she finished her vodka and orange in one gulp. Jamie, beside her, was drinking just as fast.

'Another,' Jamie said, putting her empty glass down on the windowsill where it clinked against the stone.

'I'll get them,' Patrick said.

'Let her go herself,' Seamus said. Patrick ignored him.

Later, when Luke went in, Sarah went too. Luke's eyes were

slightly crossed and his words ran a little into each other. The barman wouldn't serve him.

'You've had enough,' he said. 'Go on home, all of you.'

Luke leaned heavily onto the bar. 'Do you know how much my dad gives to this town?' he asked. 'Every charity raffle or sponsored bloody walk for the GAA' – he said 'Gaaaa', like a baby being sick – 'he's the first person anyone comes to and he never says no. He digs deep, deeper than anyone else, I bet.'

'Your father is a fine man,' the barman said. The implication was so clear Sarah was almost winded by it.

'Come on, Luke, let's go.' She tugged at his arm and he allowed himself to be pulled away. Almost at the door she looked back, an apology, a roll-of-the-eyes ah-forgive-him glance at the barman, but he didn't meet her in indulgence and just stared back, stony-faced.

Siobhan and Celine had arrived now too, so they all went to sit on the bench in front of the library, daring each other to drink neat vodka from the bottle and walk the little walls around the carpark backwards, sideways, running, hopping. Anything that felt like it would kill the boredom, the tension, of having nowhere they wanted to go.

Jamie was still drinking heavily, pulling hard at the vodka bottle and grabbing every joint that went around, so that Sarah wasn't surprised when she began to slur and stumble. Not even when Jamie leaned over, almost politely, and was sick behind the little wall. It was as if it surprised her, this stream of stuff pouring up and out of her.

'I think I better go home,' she said, voice muffled behind

the hand she held in front of her mouth, as if to stop another wave of vomit.

'I'll take you,' Patrick said instantly, holding a hand out to her.

'No, it's OK. Luke can. Can't you?'

'Oh, let Patrick,' Luke said. 'I've been drinking.'

'No,' Jamie almost shouted. 'We've all been drinking. Can you not just do this one thing for me?'

'OK, OK,' he said, making 'calm down' motions with his hands. His arms, muscled and brown in a yellow T-shirt, looked powerful. 'I'll drive you.'

'Will I come, Jamie?' Sarah asked, half-hearted. 'You'll have to wait for me to finish my drink though.'

'No, it's fine. You don't have to. I'm just going to go to sleep. I'm tired.' Jamie released the words one by one, as if her jaw ached.

'If you're going to mine, the door's open,' Sarah said. 'Go on in. There's no way my parents will be there, not for ages. And I'll see you later.'

'I'll be right back,' Luke said, to Sarah, although he pretended it was to all of them.

Patrick, who had stood silent so far said, 'Why don't we go down to the cove? Seamus scored some pills, right, Seamus?'

'Right,' Seamus said.

'OK,' Luke said. 'I'll meet you all there.'

'Sure you won't come?' Patrick said to Jamie, quietly. 'Or let me drive you back?'

'No.'

Sarah didn't want to go either, but there wasn't anything

else to do and so she went. The cove was scrubbed of colour, bleached silver in the moonlight with spots of deep brown and black, like the moulding back of an antique mirror. They didn't bother trying to light the fire, just sat around the blackened pit, not talking much. They took the pills, washed down with cans of cider, but even that failed to bring them any of the fuzzy goodwill Sarah was used to. Everything was spiky and cold, she decided, like climbing over jagged rocks.

'She cried all the way back,' Luke said, when he returned, dropping down onto the sand beside them in an attitude of weariness. 'Wouldn't say what was wrong. Nearly snapped my head off for asking. People shouldn't drink if they can't handle it.'

'I'm going for a walk,' Patrick said. The edges of what Sarah saw had blurred by then; Stephen was playing his guitar quietly, just for Jill, and Luke looked over at her in a way that was too focused, intense, so Sarah jumped up and said, 'I'll come with you.' When they were out of sight, she put her hand on Patrick's arm and when he stopped and turned towards her, she kissed him. He did nothing at first, then he kissed her back. But only for a moment, then he started to pull away.

And because of everything – because of Celine and 'You're such a gorgeous couple.' Because of Luke saying 'I think I'm addicted to you,' but as if he hated her; because of Jamie always having more, and now having a place for just her and Patrick where there was no space for Sarah. Because of the way Patrick looked at her and didn't see her as she now was, and wanted to be, just saw the old Sarah. Because of school and the girls she would have to go back to in just a few short weeks, as if waking from a mad but wonderful dream into a reality that was familiar but hateful, Sarah didn't let Patrick pull any farther away. Instead, with what was now almost instinct after all those times with Luke, she followed his mouth with hers, then reached her hand down, to his belt and then his zip. And he didn't move, but stayed still, sluggish, like a fly before a thunderstorm, drugged into heaviness; caught in the amber of her willingness and experience.

Patrick walked her home and between them was silence. The silence of embarrassment, at what they had done, at having now swapped dark and shadow and furtive movement for the light of a torch and the occasional glowing window. But also the silence of regret.

Patrick's footsteps sounded muffled, as though he had tied rags around his shoes, and the drag of his feet was such that Sarah knew only a sense of courtesy kept him beside her.

'Will you be alright from here?' he asked when they reached the driveway of the new house. Behind Sarah, the porch light was on and her way was clear.

'Yes,' she said.

'OK. See you.' And he was gone, moving fast, back the way they had come.

She had no idea what time it was, and crept through the silent house, wondering if her parents were home and asleep or still out. She thought about going into their room, the way she had as a child, to check on them, reassured by the heaped shapes under the bed covers and the slow rumble of their breathing. But she knew that couldn't comfort her now. The power of reassurance was no longer theirs.

Already the time with Patrick seemed dim, like part of a film she had watched or a song she had heard. Whatever had fuelled her had receded and all she could think about now was what Jamie would say. And what she would say to Jamie. What could she say? That she had been drunk? High? They were all both those things, often. These could not be excuses. But perhaps Jamie would never know? No one had seen them, although Sarah had heard Luke calling her name from the beach, below where she and Patrick lay in the rough dune grass. They had paused, together, frozen for a moment at the sound of his voice, torn by the wind, and Sarah had wondered if Patrick would draw back, move away, leave. But he didn't and after a second or so he had lain down again, pulling her on top of him. But his eyes were closed and his face screwed up, as if resisting the wrongness of what they did or maybe already sickened by it.

Afterwards, he was polite and careful, helping her with her clothes, standing patiently while she tied her laces, taking too long because she didn't know how to look at him or what to say. And every bit of him so obviously wanted to be gone, to never have been there. It wasn't like with Luke, a silence that could be covered with talk of shopping or what they might do later. With Patrick, there was no breaking the silence. It lay between them like a giant lake, smooth and treacherous.

In the bedroom, one of the small pink-shaded lamps was on, and Jamie had left a note on her bed, a picture of a sad dog face, with the words, 'Sorry I got sic' and many 'x's for kisses.

Sarah locked the door of the ensuite and ran a bath, because it would be less noisy than a shower, then climbed into bed. In bed, she lay and listened to the sound of Jamie breathing, the steady in and out which had been a backdrop to so many nights now that it could have been the wash of waves down on the beach, or the rhythm of her own heart.

Maybe she'd never know? Sarah knew she would find it easy to keep the secret, if she got the chance. She would never blurt out a confession, never look for forgiveness, never feel the need to gloat aloud. If the others asked what had happened to her, she could say that she got bored and went home. Or that she too had got sick – that maybe it had been something they ate and not vodka? – and that she had been right behind Jamie. They would believe her; why wouldn't they? And Patrick could tell his own story, make up his own excuse. And he would respect her, owe her, for her silence.

Jamie was up first and didn't bother asking about the night before. She was twirling and singing in the kitchen by the time Sarah got down.

'Your parents buy better breakfast than mine,' she said. 'Four types of muesli. And the fancy granola.'

'Well, there are fewer of us,' Sarah said. 'In your house that would last about five minutes.'

'So, plans?' It didn't surprise her that Jamie didn't ask about the night before. Jamie never cared about things that happened without her. She always looked forward, and not back.

'Not sure,' Sarah said cautiously. 'I might need to do stuff with my mum.'

'Well, let's have a swim first.'

'OK.' There would be no one at the cove that early, and that was good. Sarah knew she could tell her lies only to one, maybe two people, at a time, not to everyone together in a group staring at her. She shifted on her chair at the thought and felt her breath thicken in her chest, clumping between her ribs so that she pushed her bowl away. 'I'll get my togs.'

CHAPTER 41

The day was fine again and Jamie was glad. She couldn't understand why the grown-ups had turned against the good weather, muttering about 'needing rain', and 'it's not normal', the way they now did. As far as Jamie was concerned, it could be like this every day for the rest of time. Typical grown-ups, looking for reasons to worry and fuss. She wouldn't be like that, she decided. She and Patrick wouldn't be like that.

The back door was open to the sunshine, so she saw Patrick as soon as he came round the side of Sarah's house. He looked tired and she wondered if he had been out in the boat already. 'Hey!' She stood up to go to him, kiss him, but he stepped aside, warding her off with his arm, keeping the table between them.

'I need to talk to you.'

'OK.' She sat down, pulling her mug towards her and looking at the cold tea. Lines of milk swirled through it like veins.

'It's about last night.'

'Yeah, sorry about the vomiting.' She smiled. 'And not letting you drive me back. I just thought I'd be better with Luke.'

'It's not that.' He sat then and started talking, but his voice was low and there were so many breaks in what he said. He looked at the table not at her so she had no idea what he was on about and was about to say, 'Whatever, let's go for a swim,' when she realised that there was a name in amongst his words, and he kept repeating it. 'Sarah.' Sarah's name. So she began to listen more closely, to the gaps as well as the words, and stop her mind from wandering to the day outside. Bit by bit, like being shown flashcards one at a time to make sense of, she saw images. Dark and shadow and a hand taking his, lips finding his, more hands. Sarah's, but his too.

'I don't want to hear,' she said, covering her ears.

'You have to. I have to tell you.'

'You don't.'

But he told her. A confused story full of things that meant, 'It's her fault, not mine,' even though he didn't use those words. She wished he would talk normally. Or better still, not talk at all.

The day was still beautiful but now he had ruined it. The plans she had begun to make when she saw him at the back door – a boat, a hike, cold beers, sandwiches – had to be put away, put right away, and in their place were new things that she did not like at all, but that he would not spare her.

'I have to tell you,' he said again, ignoring the fact that she did not want to be told.

It was, she decided, a pathetic story. The kind of story a child would tell – 'I couldn't help myself'; 'I couldn't resist' – with little rivers of blame under the sorrys: 'You made me'; 'You didn't stop me.'

And when it was all done, when she was a piece of paper Patrick had torn up and scattered, so that she didn't know where to find any of the bits of herself that he had pulled apart so as to start trying to reassemble them, Jamie didn't know which was worse – knowing that he had cheated on her, or knowing that he and Sarah had done it together.

She looked up then and saw Sarah standing in the doorway, face white, mouth moving, but making no sound, so that she was like a doll or a puppet.

'Where did you learn to do all that?' Jamie asked her. She really wanted to know. When, how, had Sarah gathered the knowledge that had fitted her out as this siren Patrick spoke of, this temptress who couldn't be refused? What had Jamie been doing while Sarah learned these things? Who had taught her? Maybe she just knew them, in the same way Jamie knew how to turn cartwheels and back flips – like her body had the knowledge long before it was asked to use it. Thinking about Sarah was easier, much easier, than looking at Patrick, talking to him.

Sarah didn't answer and she didn't stay in the doorway. She turned and ran from it, and Jamie realised she was in Sarah's house and needed to get out of it.

'I have to go. I have to go home.'

'Jamie, please. Say you forgive me,' Patrick said.

'But I don't forgive you,' Jamie said, almost surprised that he would ask or expect such a thing. 'I don't.'

'You have to.' He was spluttering now. 'I didn't mean it. I love you. I don't know why I did it. Please, Jamie.'

'You should go away, Patrick.'

Luckily Sarah had gone out or at any rate wasn't sitting in the bedroom when Jamie went to grab her things, and Sarah's mother surfaced only as Jamie was coming back down the stairs with her pyjamas bundled up into a knot in her arms.

'Morning!' Miriam called to her, emerging fully made-up, wearing a pale green silk kimono painted with pink blossom. 'Another beautiful day!'

'It needs to rain,' Jamie said, loud and abrupt, head down, almost pushing past her to reach the stairs first, get down them and out the door before Miriam could ask any questions, make any more stupid comments. Sarah's mother was an idiot, she decided. Like one of those painted boats that were no use for anything except short distances, bobbing up and down on the water, empty, their masts jingling gaily.

Patrick was at the gate; he hadn't gone like she'd asked him to.

'I can drive you back,' he said.

'No, you can't.'

So he followed her home, walking close behind her, picking up her toothbrush when she dropped it, saying nothing. His face, when she allowed herself to look at it, was so miserable that she just felt more anger towards him. He did this, she thought, he messed up and ruined everything, and now he made her feel almost sorry for him. Made it seem as if it was her responsibility to mend him. She wanted to kick him.

'I wish you'd go,' she said. 'You're not coming into the house.'

'Can I come later?'

'No.'

She got through most of the day by saying she had a headache and wanted to lie down, but by late afternoon the news, some version of it, was out. She wondered where it had come from? Who told who? Or had it just been figured out, the way things were, by a creeping kind of osmosis?

Maeve came to her first. 'Can I come in?' She knocked gently.

'OK.'

'How's your head?'

'Still sore.' The gratitude Jamie felt at Maeve allowing the fiction to continue, even for a few more minutes, needed to be expressed. She grabbed Maeve's hand – cool, dry – and held it to her cheek.

'Do you need anything? Luke's going into town.'

'No, I'm fine.'

'Patrick called.'

'Oh.'

'I told him you couldn't be disturbed.'

'OK. Thanks.'

'What do you want me to say if he calls again?'

'Same. I can't be disturbed. Not by him.' Her voice was croaky because of the lump she had to talk around. It hurt, like trying to push through a gap that was too narrow.

'OK. And Sarah?'

'Same. Please don't let her in.' There was a pause then, and Maeve smoothed the sheet around Jamie's bare shoulders.

'I don't know if I can do that,' she said cautiously. 'By which I mean, I don't know if it would be right for me to do that.'

'I hate her.'

'Jamie, I know you're upset now, and I know – or I guess, anyway – some of what has happened, but you've known Sarah a long time. Perhaps she has an explanation you haven't heard? Or even just an apology.'

'I don't care what she says or how sorry she is, or says she is. I never want to see her. I hate her.' It felt good, saying it, believing it.

'No guy should come between friends,' Maeve said.

'Why not?'

Maeve left then, after pulling the blind a little farther down and opening the window wider. Jamie knew Sarah would be back, maybe not that day, but soon. *No guy should come between friends.* Maeve believed that, and she would try to make Jamie believe it. But we're not friends, Jamie thought. We were never friends.

Luke was next, pushing open the door and standing over her, his voice loud and full of demands. If she really had had a headache, he would have been torture, she thought.

'That guy is an asshole,' he said. He sounded so angry, and Jamie was pleased that he took her side so completely. Pleased, but surprised. She had expected Luke, so impressed with Patrick, so adoring of him, to try and persuade her to forgive – because it would suit him, Luke, far better.

'He is,' she agreed.

'As for her, stupid little bitch.' That was better. Hearing

Sarah cursed and despised was everything Jamie wanted in that moment. She sat up.

'Stupid, stupid, stupid bitch,' she agreed. 'Sneaky, creepy cow.'

'What actually happened? All we know is they went off together. Celine saw them,' Luke said. Once more, Jamie was surprised. Luke never cared about *what actually happened*.

'I don't really know. I didn't listen. He went off, she went after him, he says it was her, that she made a pass and he couldn't resist and that it was a moment of madness.'

'Right. Fucking stupid bitch.' His anger was so strong that it was giving her a real headache, so she lay down again. 'I think I'll try and sleep a bit now,' she said. 'My head is really sore.'

'OK. And don't worry – I won't let either of them near here.'

CHAPTER 42

He had missed his cues, Simon realised. He had believed he could make it alright, and he couldn't. He had missed the turn in the road that would have brought them home.

He was broken, and he couldn't go to Maeve to be fixed. She knew – he knew she knew – about Miriam and about him. But she didn't say anything, only, 'I'm sick of the heat. I wish it would rain,' looking at him like he had that power and was withholding it. 'It's not summer anymore,' she said, 'it's autumn. The weather just doesn't know it yet, but the days are shorter and the leaves are starting to turn.'

There wasn't a place he could go or a thing he could do that would get him away, get him the peace he craved and that he had done so much – so very much – to destroy. Always, now, whatever he did was, for some reason he didn't understand, the opposite of what he needed. He complicated things, crashed into things, so that his life became fuller and thicker and more clogged, like a mill wheel that can't turn because the water it moves through is foul and polluted.

But he would put it right, he swore to himself. He still could. All of it.

The house swirled around him, with doors that opened and closed as the family came and went. Everywhere there were plans, and plans for more plans. He and Maeve on one set of tracks, round and round, the young people on another, weaving in and out. Only Jake had seemed distant, slower than the rest of them during those weeks, watching the others but pretending not to, watching particularly as Luke took Sarah with him to town and the cove.

'I'll let you drive my car if you want to go off,' Simon had said to Jake, finding him on the front steps with a book, head down and shoulders hunched, as Luke roared off down the drive in Maeve's car, scattering gravel behind him. 'I'd never let Luke so much as sit behind the wheel.'

'It's OK, Dad, but thanks,' Jake had said and gone back to his book.

And now there was a problem between Patrick and Jamie that all could see but no one spoke of. Jamie, his youngest and dearest, face shut with fury and misery, saying, 'I'm fine,' whenever asked and, 'No thanks,' to anything suggested.

She moved back from Miriam and Paul's so that the disentanglement between the families was begun and perhaps it was a good thing. But before the break could take hold, Miriam had another request.

'Don't let Jamie drop her,' she asked, as she had asked before. 'Please. I don't know exactly what's happened.' She shrugged. 'These stories are always so garbled, it could be anything, really. But they aren't talking, and I know Sarah will be heartbroken if this is the end of them. So please. Will you try?' She looked up into his face, with the full knowledge of everything he owed her in her eyes.

'I'll try,' he said, knowing that it was beyond him. Knowing that he would ask Maeve, and that, even now, after what he and Miriam had done, Maeve would do what she could.

But he couldn't give his full attention to even that. There was so much to do, more all the time. Money, he found, had its own pace, its own rhythm. Money took you with it. Swept you up like a wave, and it was hard to get off. There were so many deals, phone calls, sums to be divided and multiplied, plots of land to be considered, sites to be looked at, propositions in Prague and London. Pies that needed his fingers in them.

There was Mick O'Hagen, always on the phone. Paul now too, and others, with questions and suggestions that needed his attention.

Money had its own pull, its own magnetism. But he should have known that.

Patrick, when he came to Simon, said, 'I'll take that loan.' He stood on the doorstep, unexpected, refusing to come in. It was evening but still hot, and the air around Patrick was like a dry cough.

And Simon, despite the feeling that told him this was not good and was a sign of something that was trouble, said, 'I'm glad.'

'I thought you would be,' Patrick said.

'What made you change your mind?' Simon asked, knowing he should not.

'You did.'

'I persuaded you. Good.'

'No. I saw you.'

'What do you mean?'

'I saw you. And Miriam. Outside O'Shea's.' And when Simon said nothing, because he had nothing to say, Patrick continued, 'I never envied you the big house and the fancy cars and the holidays in Portugal. I never cared that you all had money to throw over a cliff if you'd wanted. I envied you your family. You had each other and all I had was my uncle. I used to leave this house in the evening and walk away, or drive away, and I'd look back and the lights would be on and you'd be in the kitchen or somewhere, all of you, having dinner or making it, and talking to one another. All of you. Together. And you just threw that away,' he said, almost in wonder. 'As surely as if you'd lined them all up, all your family, and shoved them, one by one, into the sea.'

'What about Jamie . . .?' Simon asked. He meant, *Have you told her? Does she know what I have done?* but he couldn't say it, and so Patrick answered the question he had heard, not the one Simon had wanted to ask.

'I cared for all of you, as if you were mine.' He wouldn't say Jamie's name. Maybe he couldn't. 'That's why I didn't want your money, ever. Because I knew – my uncle told me, but I knew anyway – that if I took the money, I could never be in there, in the warm kitchen, with you. And I wanted that more than anything.' His voice trailed away and he looked past

Simon, over his shoulder, as if at that scene he had conjured up, saying goodbye to his place in it. 'Now, though,' he gave a shrug that was as indifferent as he could make it, 'I figure I'll take the money, because there's nothing else.'

'I'll put it into your account tomorrow,' Simon said.

CHAPTER 43

You could know, or you could not know, Maeve told herself. And she chose not to know – chose deliberately and carefully, having weighed up all the options.

She had looked at the cards in front of her, cards printed with lurid images of Simon and Miriam, and considered them all. Questions ran through her – *What, exactly? For how long? Where? When?* – but she realised that eliminating each possibility, one by one, until the correct answer was left, would only make her more unhappy.

Because, what did it matter, really? What could knowledge change? She had been betrayed, that she knew, by the person she loved most. And who loved her most: she did not doubt that part of it. So what else was worth finding out? Did she want to know what Miriam wore? Where they met? The positions they chose? What they said to each other?

Yes, she did, all of it. But she wouldn't. It was all the power she had left: not to ask. Not to know. Do not snoop with that tiny key, she decided. Stay on the other side of the door. And so when Simon came to her and said, 'Can't you do something about Jamie and Sarah?' she didn't question why he asked, or even allow herself to wonder. 'OK,' she said. 'I will do what I can. I've always been good at mending.'

'You have,' he said.

She went to Jamie who lay in bed again, not crying but worse than crying, staring dry-eyed at the wall in front of her. 'No guy should come between friends,' she had said.

'Why not?' Jamie asked. And Maeve had no real answer – after all, why not indeed, part of her wondered.

'Friends are more than boyfriends,' she tried, knowing that wasn't always true. But what was true was that Jamie was too young for this to be the tragedy she painted it, and Maeve, for her part, was too old, and the awful symmetry of their misery coming from one family was too much, and so she wouldn't allow it for either of them.

Patrick called round, just once more, and accepted Jamie's refusal with a haste that was, Maeve decided, even sadder than if he had remained, arguing, on the doorstep. He went back down the front steps almost before she had finished saying, 'I'm sorry, Patrick, Jamie says she won't.' As if those were the words he had expected, the words he felt he deserved. He looked thin and beaten and entirely without the confident grace she had always seen in him.

Over the next days, she tried again with Jamie, and then yet again, because Simon asked her to, and when she finally said, 'There is nothing more I can do. She won't,' he was annoyed.

'This is ridiculous,' he said. 'They're kids. How can it matter so much?'

'She's not making this up,' Maeve tried to explain to him. 'She's not being dramatic. She's hurt. By the two people she loved; not one, both. It's too much.'

But he wouldn't listen. 'They're kids,' he said again. 'It's ridiculous.'

In the days that followed, Jamie let go of the headache story but stayed close to the house and back garden. Luke did too, and Jake came and went at his own pace, so that often it was the three of them and there was a sort of togetherness between them that hadn't been there in the weeks before. Jamie was surprised the others didn't come – Stephen, Jill, Siobhan. Sylvain called once, but he was looking for Maeve. Something about a map he wanted to show her. Celine came often, even though Jamie didn't much want to see her.

Jamie didn't have the words to express even to herself what she felt. She supposed it was pain, but that didn't work. That was a word associated with skinned knees and the time she got her braces on – not this thing that had no location, no point to press and of which to say, 'There it is, that's the source of it.' Before, she had run away from anything that made her feel the way this did – worried and confused and hopeless. She had skipped away from Taylor's heavy head and misery-thickened body; from Sarah's face in red-and-white blotches; from the occasional look Maeve gave Simon when she thought he wasn't looking. All those, the sore points of her life so far, had been easily banished by noise, laughter, a game, a plan. But now she couldn't get rid of the feeling. It followed her, waited for her, dogged her footsteps. It lay behind doors and around corners, taking her almost by surprise. *Oh, there it is*, she thought. *Of course. I had forgotten.*

It made her heavy. She no longer turned cartwheels or stood on her hands because she couldn't. The ground dragged her towards it in a different way now, as though she and it were magnets, drawn close together, so that all her effort went into staying upright with nothing left over for playful tumbles.

So this is what it feels like, she thought, trying to be interested in what was a new sensation. *This is pain. This is heartbreak.* But the cruel trick of this thing that held on to her was that she could never see it straight. It slid around the edges of her vision, bigger, and yet smaller, than she could grasp. Soon she began to forget the cause, the why, of it all. She just knew that it was, and would always be. She even began to forget that this was new, an interloper. The feeling settled within her, like a dog that shakes itself and lies down to wait, and after a while she didn't even notice that it was there.

Maeve tried again, as Jamie knew she would. 'Friends are more than boyfriends,' she said. And when that didn't work, she – again – recounted what Jamie had come to think of as 'The Sad Story of Sarah': 'She doesn't have brothers and sisters, so she never learned about how to behave with others the way you did. She's lonely, and you are the best friend she has. She relies on you.'

But for once, Jamie refused to listen. 'I don't care,' she said. 'I really don't.'

That was when Simon got involved, cajoling her, the way he used to when she said she didn't want to go swimming or to play a match, with certainty and charm. She had never said no to him before, she realised, feeling just how much most of her wanted to say yes – to smile up at him the way he was smiling down at her and say. 'OK, fine!' and watch his smile grow bigger, feel his hand reach down and rub her hair with rough approval.

But she didn't. Not even when he said things like, 'Poor Sarah. You have so much, could you not be a little bit kind to her?' Why did he even care, she wondered? Just because he wanted all the grown-ups to carry on getting pissed together as usual and not have to feel embarrassed because their kids weren't friends anymore. That, she felt, must be it.

'No, I couldn't,' she said.

'At least tell me what happened,' he said then and she could see that the effort of asking, of listening, was hard for him.

'No,' she said.

Then Luke joined in, saying, 'Why should she? Sarah doesn't deserve it.'

That was when her father lost his temper, shouted at her, called her 'selfish' and 'obtuse', which she didn't understand but figured that it meant more or less the same as selfish, except maybe a bit mean too. Her father, who never shouted at her, who never looked at her with irritation, his face red and furious at a will as strong as his own now bent in an opposite direction.

'I won't,' she said. 'You can't make me.' And because he couldn't, and knew that no one could because she was like him and he could not be made to do anything either, he shouted again, on and on, the way he sometimes shouted at the boys, but never had before at her. It was, she realised, like having things thrown at you – the angry voice that kept coming, as though it was full of stones, or a strong wind with hail in it blowing in your face. She put her head down and resisted.

She let him shout and said nothing, knowing he would calm down and come back later and pull her onto his knee and say how heavy she was now and that he was sorry he had lost his temper. He would say he was so sorry and could she forgive him, with a smile that said he knew she already had. And she would pretend she couldn't and then say, 'Oh, OK, if I have to!' and he would hug her hard, and that would the end of it.

Except he didn't.

He walked around her, avoided her, for so long that she finally knew he would not.

CHAPTER 44

What was weird, Sarah thought, was that she didn't lose everything immediately. Jamie stopped talking to her, obviously, and so did Luke, and Patrick had gone by the time he'd walked her home that night. But everyone else stayed, or sort of stayed.

That first day, she didn't know what to do and so she hovered, at the new house, then down at the cove, empty when she arrived, so that she wondered if she would be alone there all day and how she would bear it. But Stephen and Sylvain appeared, then Jill, then Siobhan, and no one said anything, except the usual things, not even when Celine clambered over the rocks and said, loudly, importantly, 'Jamie isn't coming down today. Or Luke. They won't be coming down as long as she's here.' And she had pointed to Sarah, who waited for the others to turn and point too, to jeer and curse her and drive her away.

But they didn't. They kept doing what they were doing and after a moment Stephen called over to her, 'Throw me that rope, will you, Sarah?' and she did – badly – but he caught it and said, 'Thanks,' and Celine looked at them all for a few moments then said, 'Fine,' and turned on her heel.

'Why don't we see if we can go horse-riding later?' Sarah said then, as loudly as she could manage, because she wanted to see was it actually true, would they really let her stay? Had they understood?

'Good idea,' Jill said.

Later, Jake came down, on his own, his face full of uncertainty.

'I thought I'd see how you were getting on,' he said.

Sarah could feel the others behind her, listening hard, and so she responded, 'Great. We're going horse-riding later. Do you want to come?'

'OK.'

She felt like a general then, marshalling an army, bending it to her command. It was a strange, dizzying feeling and she had to keep testing it, looking for the limits. She went to the big beach, knowing Maeve wouldn't come to the cove, not that day, but found her, dried, ready to leave after her swim, wet towel and togs in a straw basket.

Sarah made to call to her but the words disappeared in her mouth, so that when Maeve turned around, there was a moment of fright and confusion. Sarah was too close, and Maeve had turned too fast, a sudden whirl that brought her to within just a few inches of the girl, so that they both stumbled and Maeve nearly fell. She stepped hastily back.

'Sarah! You startled me.'

'Sorry. I didn't mean to.'

'How are you?' Maeve's voice was hesitant, like the cries of the gulls that came and went around them, near and far at once.

'I'm OK.'

'That's good. I must be getting back,' Maeve said.

Sarah put a hand out, ignoring the slight twitch of Maeve's arm, and said, 'Wait. I just wanted to say . . .' She fell silent. She waited for Maeve to say 'Yes?' gently, and then continued. 'I know Jamie's upset with me. I don't really know why. It's something about Patrick, but I didn't . . . I don't . . .' Again she allowed herself to fall silent, for Maeve to speak.

'I'm sure it will all be fine,' Maeve said. She gently unpeeled Sarah's hand from her arm. 'It will blow over.' Her voice was distant now, the call of gulls far above.

Simon, calling to the new house a few nights later, was more blunt.

'I understand my daughter is being difficult,' he said, as Miriam looked on from the couch in the sitting room, legs crossed in front of her, a tall glass in her hand. Sarah was shocked at his saying that, shocked at the disloyalty, because it wasn't like the rough way he usually spoke about Jamie, so full of love and pride that the roughness was there only to hide those things. Now, he sounded tight, as if he meant it.

'It's OK,' Sarah said.

'It's not,' Simon said. 'But she'll come around.'

That was when Sarah first understood that she could do it.

And even then, she didn't know exactly what it was that she could do, just that something had shifted. That she wasn't the one hanging on any more; that even if Jamie left her behind, she wouldn't be on her own. There would be others. They wouldn't be Jamie, but they would be there.

What was strange was the way that made her feel. There was a glow of triumph, but something else too that made her feel a bit sick. Like she had pushed against something that should have been solid but it had dissolved under her so that she fell forward and her stomach dropped away as if she was in mid-air.

The next day, Patrick called to the house, rang the doorbell but refused to come in.

'You have to tell her it was you,' he said when Sarah went out.

'It was you too,' Sarah reminded him.

'But it was mostly you. You know it was. You have to tell her that.' He wanted to shake her, wanted to grab her by the shoulders and shake something out of her, into her – she could see that as clearly as if he had said it.

Around them was a wind that was warm and gentle, a wind to encourage rather than nip and tease. She could have done what he asked, she saw that. Played the heroic part he offered her, of self-sacrifice and truth – and that would have brought her gifts too, of approval and gratitude. But she didn't. Why should she, she thought? She might have started it, but he had been more than willing. 'I'm not going to,' she said. 'It isn't true.'

She didn't see him again after that, although she ran into

Seamus in town later that day and he said, 'I knew you lot were bad news, but I didn't think you'd be this bad.'

Jake had said Jamie was mad, and Simon said she was being 'difficult', so that when Sarah thought about her, as she constantly did, she thought of her with an angry face, and of the flare of her temper that had always impressed Sarah with the certainty of its rightness.

But then just a few days later, as she came out of Molloy's shop, she saw Jamie, alone, in the back seat of Simon's parked car. And Jamie had turned away immediately, but not before Sarah had seen her face. And it wasn't angry. It was sad – so sad that it looked as if it was made of wax that had melted slightly, blurring the edges, dragging it all downwards.

She wanted to hammer on the window then, until Jamie had to roll it down or she would have broken it; she wanted to say, 'I'm sorry. I'm so sorry. I didn't mean to. I don't know why I did it.' But if she did that, she would have to go back. Back to the old Sarah, the quiet, despised Sarah. The Sarah who dragged 'shy' around with her like a leg brace, so that it slowed her, fitting her to its own warped pace. That was the Sarah who no one liked, no one looked for, no one reached for. She would have to erase the new Sarah, rub her right out, in an effort to please Jamie, and then she could never be her again.

And Sarah couldn't do that. So she didn't bang on the window. She walked on, as if she hadn't seen Jamie. As if she had never known her, and, even, there was a little bit of her that was proud that she had such power – the power to wound Jamie, to hurt her so badly. She who had never had power before.

*

'I want to go back early,' she said to Miriam when she got home. 'I need to get stuff ready before school.'

'OK. I'll drive you,' Miriam said. 'I want to leave too.'

'No, I'd rather take the train. I get sick being in a car so long.' It was a lie, but she couldn't bear the hours alone with Miriam, the many questions, or a silence that was worse than questions. 'You can leave at the same time and meet me at the station in Dublin.'

On the train, Sarah stared out the window, trying to work it all out: the last couple of days; her leaving. It was hard. Normally, she had looked at Jamie and that told her how to feel and how to act. Now she couldn't do that. It was strange and, under the strangeness, the panic doll that Sarah thought she had got rid of was twitchy again, opening and closing its fingers in a way that Sarah didn't like, scratching at the inside of her.

It was still hot and the land they passed through was dry and dusty, so that the 'good weather' was no longer good. Now it was relentless, and needed to break. That was how the grown-ups talked about the endless sun that had been a miracle and was now a problem. 'Needs to break' – as if it was an evil mirror. Or a huge wave crashing down on them. Was it really only five-and-a-bit weeks since she had sat on that same train, with Jamie, going in the opposite direction?

She moved around so she wasn't looking out the window at the blurry trees and houses going by because they confused her and made her dizzy, but instead at the inside of the train carriage and the other people, reading and messing with their phones.

She thought how dull and ordinary they looked. Fat, or thin, with greasy skin and hair and boring clothes. Some were sunburned but not in the way Sarah and her friends had been burned that summer – shoulders red because they had spent too long racing boats across the cove or surfing the endless roll of waves so that you stopped, finally, because you couldn't go on, and never because you had reached the end. These people were burned, banally, because they had fallen asleep in a park or forgotten to put on a T-shirt.

She despised them because they couldn't see how different she was. How different the place she had come from was. She despised the way they turned the pages of their magazines or stopped the trolley attendant and bought a Snack bar to go with their cups of tea. *Imagine living like that*, she thought. *Imagine that being your life.*

I won't let it go, she thought, only half-knowing what 'it' was: them, she supposed. All of them, the things they had done and been and must continue to do and be.

School would be different that year, she suddenly knew. Because she was different. The crazy heatwave had been all for her, she saw that now. The sun, day after day after day of it, had soaked in, right in deep inside her, and changed her. It had been a spell powerful enough to burn through all the stiff layers of her and expand something deep down.

And the spell had been made stronger by what she had done to Jamie, in a way that meant it was almost too powerful now.

All the way home from the station, her mother, who met her with the car, asked the questions Sarah had feared: why had she left early? Had anything happened? Was everything

OK? And when those – general, scattershot – questions failed completely to get her the answers she wanted, Miriam tried again, with smaller, sharper arrows: how was Jamie? Had she seen her? How was Luke? When were they back in Dublin?

And if there was more than nosiness in her questions, a wanting to know that had more than curiosity to it, Sarah chose not to see it. Her mother's problems were not her problems. She could leave them alone. And if her mother was unhappy – why should she be, and yet there was something pinched around the edges of her face? – then Sarah could choose not to see or know it.

That was what she did. She answered Miriam's questions in the best way she could, directing her mother far away from where she was trying to go. No, she hadn't seen Jamie but she would, she was sure. Luke too. They would all be back in less than a week; she'd see them then.

And maybe she would, she thought. After all, things did blow over. 'Jamie will come around,' Jake had said to her – the only time he spoke directly about the row. 'She gets really mad, but never for very long. You know that.' Neither of them mentioned Luke, or how mad he was.

And if it didn't blow over, Sarah knew, she would be OK. She sat up straighter in the car seat now, gazed at the faint outline of her reflection in the window and tilted her head, chin up. She would still be her new self, because if that self could come through these days, then it could survive anything.

I did it, she thought. I never thought I could, but I did.

CHAPTER 45

Five years later: Dublin, October 2008

Sarah checked she had everything she needed: bottle of wine, flowers, copy of a book that had just won a literary prize. She knew Eilish would never read it, but it was important to turn up with the right things.

These dinner parties had taken the place of pubs and clubs, because her friends felt themselves 'too old' now for that kind of thing – meaning strangers and crowds and pushing and sometimes fighting and vomiting. But it was like playing at being grown-up and secretly Sarah thought the evenings boring. The first half, anyway, when they all self-consciously talked about politics and plays. Later, someone would bring out a bag of coke or 'pure MDMA' and they would get wasted and dance and it would be more fun, but, to Sarah, also empty. There never seemed to be a point, beyond the being wasted. They never did anything, changed anything, started anything – and the cold emptiness of the next day, alone in her apartment, or with the duty of Sunday lunch with her parents – held her back more and more from throwing herself into the nights.

Those Sunday lunches made her impatient and cross, but she hadn't yet found a way to kill them off. Listening to Paul talk about his deals, watching Miriam's face for more signs of the 'work' she now had done, regularly. As if, Sarah thought, it was a job, this 'work'; something her mother had committed to and had to turn up for.

Miriam had hidden herself more and more: behind her clothes, behind the bacteria she injected into her face that gave her a beautiful, mask-like quality that Sarah half-envied, yet half-hated, because of the way it made her mother impossible now to talk to, because the face gave so little away. Whatever Sarah said, her mother looked at her with that air of faint, bland curiosity. Most of all, though, Miriam had hidden herself in conversation that was light and amusing and impersonal, and rippled out of her in a steady, distancing stream as if her two arms were held out, palms up, to stop any approach, any intimacy. She never asked about Sarah's life, beyond the physical circumstances of it – 'Did you go to that film?' 'Will you come with me to the Brown Thomas sale?' 'Are you going skiing this year?' It made being with her exhausting, because if they were alone together for too long, Miriam would start to speed up, the deliberately banal questions and comments coming thicker and faster, in case silence should fall between them; in case Sarah would begin to ask her own questions.

And maybe it was contagious, her mother's careful indifference, because Sarah found that she too had smoothed over parts of herself. The imagination that had always threatened to swamp her, with images of things she craved, things she feared, so that sometimes she hadn't been able to remember which bits were real and which made-up in the fever-dream of her too-active mind, was quieter now. More biddable. And that was a relief, but sometimes she felt it was a loss, too. Imagination, Sarah thought, must take its energy from wanting. The more you wanted, the wilder it ran. Once you got – or gave up – it settled.

'You're first,' Eilish said now when she opened the door. 'Come and have a drink. Prosecco?'

'Lovely.' Sarah hated Prosecco, its aggressive tickle and faint smell of vomit, but again, it was what they did. There always seemed something to toast – an engagement, a new job, a promotion, another degree, and 'bubbles', they agreed, were 'just right'.

'You're so lucky,' Miriam had said about all this, 'such a dynamic time of life. So much going on.'

Maybe she was right, Sarah thought, but it didn't always feel that way. There were long days and weeks that felt like moving through a sluggish river, with no rush or sparkle of water. Ahead was always possibility – she might excel at work, or move abroad, or meet someone – but somehow these things never seemed to come closer: they just shimmered there in the distance, kindly illusions that allowed her to believe in them. Or if they did approach, become real, their glow faded as fast as it took for Sarah to reach for them.

Eilish's apartment was many floors up, with one side of the living room made all of glass, so the city stretched below them like a fisherman's net, the first twinkling lights of early evening caught like the reflection of tiny stars. A long white sofa stretched across the other side, with a crimson velvet throw across it like a splash of blood. On the walls were framed Art Deco posters commemorating famous train journeys: Paris–Lyon, Londres–Vichy. Eilish, Sarah knew, could no more have afforded the apartment than Sarah could hers. Behind both of them was the security, the muffling blanket, of their parents' money.

'So who's coming?' Sarah asked.

'Everyone who was at Nick's last week,' Eilish said, 'plus a couple of the old college lot, and a friend who's just back from the UK. It'll be fun.'

She said it firmly, as if to squash any doubt. Not that Sarah cared; 'everyone' may as well have been 'anyone'. Then, 'Have you thought any more about Tuscany this summer?' Eilish asked. 'We need to decide on the villa quickly.'

'Yes, fine. Whatever you think.' Sarah was glad to be asked – sometimes she wondered would that ever go away? The swooping feeling of relief at being included? But the holidays had become predictable too. 'Such fun,' Miriam said. 'Tuscany, at your age, with your friends.' Trying hard to keep the note of wonderment out of her voice – that Sarah should have friends, should be invited on holidays.

'Everyone' arrived, girls in tight jeans and sparkly tops, guys in jackets they soon discarded. A group gathered around Sarah, asking her things, telling her things, listening for her answers. And she answered, and asked, and listened, but through it all, she was bored, and the faint sawing edge of her boredom cut away at the corners of her mind, leaving them uneven and raw. The buzzer went, loud behind her, and because Eilish was busy, because it gave her something different to do even for a moment, Sarah pushed it and said, 'Yes?'

'Hi, it's Jake.'

'Come up.' Sarah pressed the buzzer and went to open the door, to stand there, staring into the empty hall with its too-white strip lighting, waiting for the lift to open. She stood and watched, as the party continued behind her, attention turned away from her now, and waited. It wouldn't be him, she told herself. There were so many Jakes. He didn't live in Dublin. It would not be him. The lift doors would open and a man she didn't know would step out and she would smile and say, 'Eilish is in there somewhere. I'm Sarah,' and she would go back to the group she had been talking to and continue discussing Tuscany and whether it might be fun to hire a convertible.

She had half-turned to go back inside, because what was the point of standing there, when she heard the ping and the whoosh of the lift, and so she turned back again. And it was him. Jake. Walking towards her, looking at her but not seeing her, because on his face was a polite smile and he was holding out a bottle of wine in a shiny paper bag with rope handles.

'Jake?' He came closer, still smiling, and then he saw her, saw that it was her, and the smile dropped and he stood still.

'Sarah? What the hell . . .?' He just stood there so that she didn't know what to do. Move forward and kiss him, the way they did then, on the cheek? Put out a hand, to shake, to draw him forward? To hold him away?

'Ah, Jake, you made it.' This was Eilish, now behind Sarah. 'Come on in. You've met Sarah? Jake is just back from Cambridge where he's been finishing a master's or something dreadfully impressive.' She laughed, a little tinkle, that told Sarah she liked Jake.

'But I know Sarah,' Jake said. 'From ages ago.' He said it to Eilish, but it was Sarah he stayed looking at.

'Oh. How nice,' Eilish said, but not like she really thought it was nice.

They went inside then, and the party was different after that. It had a point, Sarah decided. Not a point as in a purpose, but an actual point, a sharp spur that followed and poked at her, moving her on and forward, because every time she looked up, Jake was looking at her. And even though she tried not to look at him, she always knew exactly where he was. When he began to speak, she was already listening, having felt the intake of breath that said he would.

He was different, she saw immediately. The braces were gone, and the spots, and his hair was darker, but it wasn't that. It was in the way he sat and stood and leaned forward and the things he said – not very much, but clearly, and in a way that made other people stop their own talking and listen to him.

He was broader than he had been and looked, she realised with a sudden lurch of her stomach, more like Luke. Except for the mouth. Jamie's mouth.

She was so quiet during dinner – she, who was so often the centre of animation – that the girl beside her asked, 'Are you OK?' as Eilish was clearing plates for dessert.

'I just need some fresh air. I'm going to pop out to the

balcony,' Sarah said. The smokers were already out there, in a noisy knot at one end. Sarah walked to the other end, sat on a pale blue wooden chair beside a matching table on which Eilish seemed to have arranged her pot plants to die. There were peace lilies, aloe vera, a few ferny things, all brown and withered looking. She began picking at the dried bits of a fern, crumbling them off in her fingers, liking the parchment feel of them, staring out at the lights of the city: there were more of them now, brighter in the gathering dark.

'Eilish doesn't seem to have green fingers,' Jake said, behind her. His voice was deeper than it used to be. Of course it was, she told herself. He was older. They were all older. 'Can I sit down?' he said when she didn't answer him.

'Sure.'

'So?'

'So?'

'I can't believe it's you. How do you know Eilish?'

'We work together.'

'So you're a solicitor?'

'Yes. Well, an apprentice, loads more exams to go.'

'Do you like it?'

Sarah simply shrugged at the question, wishing he would stop. Stop asking the questions everyone asked, anyone could ask. They weren't the questions for him.

She remembered an afternoon with sun so bright it made him squint, a crease right between his eyebrows, and the smell of woodsmoke and burned fruitcake on his clothes.

'What about you,' she asked. 'What are you doing?'

'I've finished my master's, in history, and now I'm back, to get a job. If anyone gives jobs to history students.' He laughed. He was, Sarah realised, far more relaxed than she was, and that annoyed her. This wasn't the way it used to be between them. She turned and smiled deliberately at him,

'Of course they do,' she said. 'If it's you, anyway. Did you like Cambridge as much as you thought you would?'

'Yes, at first. But I started to miss this place after the first few years. It's very different, over there. People are very different. I missed my friends. My old friends.' He looked at her but she couldn't be sure how much he included her in that. Was she an old friend? Or just someone that he used to know.

'And is being back among them' – 'them', not 'us' – 'living up to your expectations?' She couldn't ask him any of the things she really want to know – how is Maeve? And Simon? How is Jamie? – so she stayed on safe ground.

'So far. It's nice being home.'

'What about Kerry?' she asked. 'Have you been down?'

'Yes, it was almost the first thing I did. Only Maeve goes down now. The others are too busy.'

'And is it the same?' *Do you not remember*, she wanted to shout at him. *Do you not remember the way the sand felt between your shoes and your feet, bare because you hadn't bothered putting socks on? Do you not remember the way the light changed every moment, so that you would bend your head to do something – tie a rope, pull up a boat – and when you lifted it again, it was as if there was a whole new day in front of you? Do you not remember what it felt like to be so exhausted from surfing you couldn't drag yourself up the beach to your towel? And if not, why not? Did those things happen? Or did I just dream them?* It was her most secret fear – that she had dreamed it all.

But she didn't ask anything like that. She couldn't. Partly because she didn't know how to – there was no bridge across the distance between them that she could have used to get to him, to ask – but also because maybe he didn't remember. Maybe those weren't his memories, even if it had all been real. He hadn't been with them so much, not that last summer, and she was afraid to remind him of that. Most of all, she was afraid that the person she recalled as Jake in her mind was actually Luke.

'Almost exactly the same,' Jake said. 'That's the amazing thing about it. It never changes. A few more houses – really fancy, grand ones – but that's it. Do your parents still go down?'

'No. They sold the house almost immediately. It was the "new house", and then it was the "old house", and never anything in between.' She laughed, even though she had been shocked when Paul told her they were selling, shortly after she had come back that last summer. Shocked because she had known then that it was final. There would be no reconciliation. Everyone who had said Jamie would 'come round' had been wrong. She would not come round, and she would slam the door behind her, leaving Sarah on the wrong side.

'How are your parents?' he asked politely.

'Fine.' What else could she say? *They walk around each other as if there are holes they might fall into. They talk to each other politely, but I can't remember the last time either of them laughed at something the other said. They both think I will take the other*

one's side and so they are polite now with me too, careful, in case I ask what's going on. But I don't ask. I'm afraid they will tell me.
'I think my dad still sees a bit of your dad. But they don't all hang round together so much. Not for ages now.'

'Right.'

'Is Luke's cave still there?' She felt rather than saw the change in him when she said Luke's name.

'I don't know. I didn't check. I barely went to the cove. There's a new gang of kids who go there now. I stayed more on the big beach.'

And then Eilish stuck her head out the balcony door and called, 'Dessert!' and Jake stood up, to go back inside, and Sarah wondered frantically how she might stop him, keep him . . .

'Could I ring you?' He said it almost as if he hadn't made up his mind, was wondering aloud to himself. But she didn't care.

'Yes,' she said quickly.

'Tomorrow?'

'Yes.'

That night, Sarah slept badly and didn't care, because it was excitement, not drugs or worry, that kept her up, caused her to wake many times. And each time she woke, she checked to see if the excitement was still there, shining inside her, and it was.

Because even though Jake had been so much absent that last summer, still he was part of it, and part of all the other summers. He was part of Maeve, and Simon, even Luke. Mostly, he was part of Jamie. Which meant he didn't belong to the Now of her life, the boredom and sameness of those dinner parties and lunches and days at her office. He didn't belong on what felt to her, so often these days, like an empty stage, because the audience she had played for – the audience she had chosen in Portugal when she was eleven years old as the only one that mattered – was gone.

All these years, since Kerry, she had continued to feel, in one small part of her, as if she'd been thrown out of Paradise. And now, the way back in was open before her.

Seeing him had brought it all back – the wild, unexpected fun she used to have with Jamie: zipping across the bay on a surfboard, dragging at the sail as the wind tried to snatch it from you, snatch you both and throw you over its shoulder. The smell of salt dried onto hot skin, the taste of burned, raw sausages, of cigarettes and sticky blackcurrant vodka, hair so thick with sand it broke combs, and with it, the heat, the heart, the raw feeling of fear and adrenalin and anticipation. Those nights when your stomach turned to liquid because the air was clear and violet and humming with possibility, like the beating of insect wings. When a song could open up the universe and a look could thrill you through.

CHAPTER 46

'Please don't tell them it's me.'

'But why not?' Jake asked.

'I'd rather they didn't know. A surprise.' Except it wouldn't be that, or not exactly, Sarah knew.

One half of her wanted Jake to tell them, prepare the way, so that they could be ready, as she would be, after all this time. But the other half wanted to see the looks on their faces. And feared that Jamie, if she knew in advance, wouldn't be there. 'Just tell them you're bringing a girl home. Surely that's enough of a surprise for the moment.' She smiled at him.

'It sure will be. Maeve is always trying to get us to bring people to these Sunday lunches – she's says it's the only time she and Simon get to actually see us these days, and they want to know what's going on in our lives. But Luke is the only one who ever does – and only because it's another way of showing off. Anyway, with him, the girls change so fast that Maeve told me she hardly makes an effort anymore because she knows they won't be there the next time.'

'Does Jamie never bring anyone?'

'The odd waif or stray; usually someone she's been out with the night before who's too hungover to get home. Or has no home they want to go to. So they sit there, the two of them, falling asleep into their plates, stinking of booze and cigarettes, while we all pretend nothing's happening.' He laughed.

So, you're the new stray. Luke's voice, sneering at her, in the restaurant in Portugal. *Jamie's always doing this. Picking up stray dogs and cats, and girls.*

'Never a boyfriend though,' Jake continued. 'Or girlfriend.'

'Why girlfriend?' Sarah asked.

'Well, apparently there are girlfriends too.' He sounded faintly awkward. 'Sometimes. But we never meet anyone. Maeve thinks Jamie's afraid to bring anyone she cares about home. In case . . . well, I don't know why.' He looked uncomfortable then and went back to his first question. 'Can I really not tell them?'

In case they're like me, Sarah thought suddenly. 'No. It's better, trust me,' she said. She sounded like she knew what she was doing. Had a plan. But she didn't, beyond feeling that letting Jake's family – Jamie's family – know in advance that she was coming would not be good.

'What does Jamie do now?' she asked.

'She studied development and is, apparently, "about to" go and volunteer for a conservation project in Vietnam or Thailand or somewhere. Mostly she just parties too much and lectures us on everything we're doing to kill the planet.'

His description was pitched for her laughter, but there was confusion there in his voice too.

He had rung her the day after the dinner party, just like he had said he would, and they had met, for coffee, and then a drink, and then more drinks, and then they had fallen into the familiarity of every day, every night, every weekend so that Sarah's life, instead of being something she worked at carefully to keep full and interesting, became those things without effort on her part. Became something else too – something that felt settled and right and dependable – but still they didn't tell: not her parents, not his.

'Not yet. They'll just spoil things,' Sarah said, kept saying, when he suggested she come home with him or call by Number Eight to collect him in her new powder-blue Fiat 500. And then, after nearly six months, he suggested Sunday lunch – 'We eat in the dining room these days, not the kitchen' – but as though he expected her to say no. Except she said, 'OK,' and then, 'but don't tell them.'

And now, walking up the stone steps of Number Eight again, she thought she might fall over, or vomit. So intensely was she thrown backwards, into the past, that she lifted her legs higher than she needed to, to get up those steps, because her body believed itself to be that of a child again. Even before the door was opened, she thought she could smell the lavender beeswax and dust and dried flowers, the imprint of the house that gathered most intensely in that hallway; and she could hear the insistent ticking of Maeve's clocks.

She grabbed Jake's hand and was about to say, 'I can't, I can't. Let's not,' when the door opened in a rush and there was Maeve, who said, 'Hello, darling' to Jake, then turned to Sarah, hand outstretched, then stopped, and stared. And stayed silent so long that Sarah wished that she had after all made Jake leave with her before the door had opened. Finally Maeve said, 'Sarah?' but it was a question.

'Yes. It's me. Hi.' Sarah stood awkwardly on one foot, feeling as if she was being introduced to this forceful woman for the first time, except that now it was Jake beside her, not Jamie. She pulled him closer with the hand that held his.

'You've changed your hair,' Maeve said, then followed up with, 'God, what am I saying, of course you've changed your hair. It's been so long. But why…? I mean, are you…?'

'The girl I said I was bringing to lunch? Yes,' Jake said. 'Sarah. She's my girlfriend.' The pride in his voice stood there in the doorway beside the three of them.

'Well,' Maeve said. 'Well.' And only then, made bold by the uncertainty in her voice, could Sarah see her properly. She looked older, her hair mostly silver now, and more tired, faded even, so that for a moment Sarah wondered why she had wanted so badly to come back. And then Maeve smiled, a different smile, not the polite one of a moment ago. A smile that said not just that she remembered Sarah, but that she remembered details about Sarah, moments with Sarah – early morning walks in Kerry while her family still slept, a trip to the graveyard where her people were buried, conversations and cups of tea and board games. And, yes, the last days and Patrick, and fear of what Jamie would say – all that was there too. But even so it was a smile that Sarah felt wrapped itself right around her, close and warm.

'You'd better come in,' Maeve said.

Sarah wondered would Maeve stall them somehow, give herself a chance to go ahead and prepare the rest for what was coming, for who was coming. But she didn't. Led them straight into the sitting room that Sarah had always thought of as the garden sitting room, because that was where its large windows looked – back, not front. Before, this room had been a creamy pale pink with deeper pink in its cushions and lampshades. Now, it was white and orange with a floor that was polished wood rather than soft carpet, and the sofa, instead of being old and squashy, was long and hard and shiny with steel, so that walking into it was like being promised something – a hand held out – only for the promise to be snatched violently back. Sarah felt dizzy for a second at the wrongness of the room, then, hearing Maeve say, 'Look who's here,' she clasped her hands together to stop them from shaking.

Luke, on the sofa, looked up slowly, lazily. Jamie, at a small table with a deck of cards, didn't look up, not until Luke said, 'Jesus Christ!' loud and angry. But Sarah wasn't minding him. She watched Jamie. Watched as she raised her head in a rush at the loudness of Luke's voice, looking first at him, then in the direction he faced, so that her eyes travelled towards Sarah even as Sarah stared at her face. And Sarah saw the look that crossed it – as if Jamie had bitten into something bitter, her mouth suddenly flooded with sharp disgust.

Jamie shook her head, literally shook it, as though to clear some treacherous vision, then looked again.

'What are you doing here?' That was Luke, with a hostility he didn't bother trying to hide.

'She's with me,' Jake said.

'She's Jake's guest,' Maeve said. 'Guest', Sarah noted, not 'girlfriend'.

'Hi.' Sarah did a sort of half-wave at them all. 'This is weird, right? How long has it been?' As if she didn't know, almost to the hour.

Still she looked at Jamie, waiting for her to say something. Jamie said nothing. She was, Sarah saw, no longer round and brown and sturdy. She was thinner, paler, with shadows under her eyes and around her mouth which emphasised her cheekbones and made her look, Sarah thought, older than she was.

But still there was that hair, an arrogant, unrepentant halo, and those eyes, blue like the deepest seawater.

'Not long enough,' Jamie said then, so that Maeve said, 'Jamie!' and then, to Sarah, 'Come and meet Vanessa,' leading her towards the long shiny sofa where Luke was sitting.

If Jake looked more like Luke, Sarah thought, Luke looked less like himself. He was fat now; the slabs of muscle from his rugby-playing days had slid together and softened, and his hair was moving backwards from his forehead at the edges so that his face looked half-dressed, vulnerable. Beside him was a girl who was blonde and tall and almost pretty.

'Nice to meet you,' Vanessa said, holding out a limp hand that Sarah took pleasure in squeezing too hard so that she snatched it back. Doing that took some of Sarah's nerves away, but only some.

'Where the hell did you two find each other?' Luke asked, looking from Sarah to Jake. As if they had done something shameful, like scrabbled in a dustbin, or met down a dark alleyway.

'At a party. A mutual friend,' Sarah said. She didn't know what else to say.

'Would you like a drink?' Maeve asked. 'A glass of wine? It seems funny to be offering you wine,' she smiled at Sarah, 'but I suppose you're an adult now.' Sarah remembered the taste of vodka and blackcurrant off Luke's mouth, and turned away from him quickly.

'White wine, please,' she said.

'OK, what would anyone else like? Lunch will be ready in about ten minutes,' said Maeve.

'I'm not hungry,' Jamie said.

CHAPTER 47

At first, Jamie thought she had made a mistake, hadn't looked properly at what was in front of her, but she had and then she realised it wasn't just the seeing. It was a feeling too. There was a sudden full-stop, like when a glass breaks and everything goes silent on an inhale for a second. That was even before Luke shouted and gave her a fright. She already knew something had happened, had been disturbed, but she would never have imagined what.

Sarah. Not just Sarah – Sarah with Jake. Like a couple. Sarah. Sarah with her big eyes that looked more normal now because the rest of her face had rounded out. Sarah with new hair, more blonde in it, and blow-dried so it was swishy and shiny to her shoulders. Sarah in a short black dress with a sequined collar and black patent leather heels, like she'd just come from a meeting. Or a funeral. Sarah, all composed, holding her two hands neatly clasped in front of her like she was about to say a prayer. So different. So sleek and chic, asking politely, 'How long has it been?' as if they had all had tea together once upon a time. But the same too. Those hot, eager eyes, staring at Jamie and staring at her, like she needed to see through her or inside her.

Jamie had expected to run into her over the years, had prepared herself for that – at a party or in a pub, a sudden face-to-face, and had long ago worked out how she would be: perfectly polite, and distant, and then gone immediately. But it hadn't felt as if Sarah could ever be there, in that house, because to be there she would have to be invited, and no one would invite her. Except now they had, and there she was, smiling at them all, shaking Vanessa's hand and asking Maeve about the garden. *The garden!*

And for all that seeing her like that was awful, Jamie didn't leave straight away. She thought about it – just getting straight up and walking out – but she wanted to see what this Sarah was like, to hear how she had grabbed hold of Jake, and so she stayed.

She'd heard bits over the years, mostly from Celine who seemed to know some of Sarah's friends, and who still disliked her more than Jamie secretly felt was Celine's right. After all, it wasn't Celine she'd betrayed.

'She hangs with a very show-offy crowd,' Celine said. 'New money. You know the sort of thing.' Like they should be ashamed of the shininess of what they had. Jamie thought that was stupid – Celine really was pretty stupid – but she wanted to hear the things she said about Sarah. At first. Then she didn't. Because it was never the right thing. She wanted to hear that Sarah had dropped from sight, had been seen alone and miserable somewhere, had embarrassed herself horribly in public. But it was never that. Instead she seemed to have friends and places to go and a job and good hair. So Jamie stopped asking. And bit by bit she sort of forgot. Except that now, when she saw her again, Jamie realised that she never had forgotten. That every line of Sarah's face, every ripple in her voice, was familiar, even the bits that were changed, because she could still see and hear what had been there.

She watched as Sarah answered Luke's angry questions as well as she could. Watched her bend and try to pat Taylor and laugh a little, as if she didn't mind when the dog moved away from her. Good old Taylor, Jamie thought. She never had liked Sarah.

Jamie watched, and she tried not to think about Patrick, but now that Sarah was there, in front of her, he wouldn't stay away.

She would forget – for days, weeks, maybe even months – until she remembered again, what it felt like to be with him. To be the person he saw when he looked at her.

She understood him better now, she sometimes thought, after all the years apart and without the dazzle of him in her eyes. And she understood what had happened between them better – the frustration he felt, the terrible failure of resistance, the truth of his apology. She got it now in a way she hadn't, couldn't have, when she was younger. But that only made her hate Sarah more. After all, if he was less guilty, Sarah was more so.

And now here she was: a reminder to Jamie of how much she still missed him. Missed being with him. The fact that Simon, and Maeve, missed him too made it worse. She knew they did, Simon especially. Sometimes he asked, 'Heard anything from Patrick?' in a hearty way that did a terrible job of hiding how badly he wanted the answer to be yes. And when Jamie said no, he would say, 'No. I suppose you wouldn't,' as though it was a small thing, a whim, to have asked at all.

Sometimes, he was the one to have news. 'It's tougher for Patrick and his uncle now,' he had said just a few weeks earlier, sounding worried. 'I hear from Pat sometimes. You have to have a licence to go out to the Skelligs. It's all been clamped down on.'

'So why don't they get a licence?' Jamie had asked, pretending not to be paying too much attention.

'They can't. There are very few, and they've gone, Mick says, to guys who are owed favours. So that's cut their business model in half. It's a worrying time. For everyone,' he added. But Jamie hadn't wanted to know.

'Whatever,' she said, knowing how much he disliked that word, her use of it.

She watched now, and listened, and then, when Sarah took hold of Jake's hand and said something about what they planned to do later, she decided she had seen enough. 'I'm going out,' she said.

But Simon came in as she was leaving and stopped her – 'Don't be rude,' he said. 'Your mother has cooked for you, and I haven't seen you all week. You'll stay,' so that it was an order, not a request.

He didn't seem surprised the way they had been to see Sarah there in his house, just asked how her parents were and said he'd seen her father recently. The worst of it, for Jamie, was that he was clearly charmed by this new Sarah. By the fact that in her solicitor's job she worked with guys he knew and was able to be funny and even a bit malicious when she spoke about them. Sarah, who had never been able to string two words together in front of Simon, now chatting easily to him, making him laugh.

'How is Dominic?' he asked her over lunch. Dominic, it seemed, was a partner at the law firm.

'He's fine,' Sarah said. 'Still on the three-day week.'

'There's a lot to be said for it,' Simon said. 'Get a job where someone will pay you to play golf.'

'After decades in which you sweat blood for them and have no relationships that aren't transactional,' Jake said.

'True.'

'Mick O'Hagen was in the other day,' Sarah said. 'The way they all hover around him, it's like the king has come to visit.'

'Well, they know that if Mick is in, the rest will follow,' Simon said wisely. 'Anyone who's not with them already.'

'Sounds like you're a bunch of tame pen-pushers for property developers,' Jamie said. 'Which is about as credible as being fleas on rats.'

'As credible as anything else,' Simon said. 'It's a job. Which is more than you have, missy.'

'I don't want a job,' Jamie said. 'There isn't a single job I can think of, except being a postman, which is ethical. And I don't want to be a postman.'

'And aren't you lucky you can afford to be so high-minded?'

'My uncle was a postman,' Luke's girlfriend said and then, when they all turned to look at her, 'now he works in a bank.'

'Right,' Simon said, with a wink at Jamie. 'See, even postmen get sick of ethics in the end.'

But she refused to wink back, and so he turned again to Sarah. 'What about Dominic's wife, Elaine?'

CHAPTER 48

'You'd better come in.'

After all, Maeve thought, what else do you say to the stranger, the half-stranger, on your doorstep? 'You'd better come in.' Even if part of you knows that bringing this person in will bring trouble.

The look Jake gave her, the gratitude in it, made her think she'd done the right thing. However, the looks from Luke and Jamie showed her that, after all, she had been wrong. But by then it was too late, Sarah was in, and she couldn't ask her to leave, and so instead she watched her, carefully. Watched throughout that lunch and all the lunches that followed.

She was so different. Of the old, hesitant Sarah there was little trace, except that she sometimes still blushed red, broken up with patches of white that appeared at the sides of her nose and across her cheekbones. Maeve presumed this meant she was upset or flustered, but clearly Sarah had become skilled at otherwise keeping such feelings hidden. The new Sarah was precise and definite, like someone had gone over the old wavering outline of her in a bold black felt-tip pen.

Watching, Maeve saw that Jake was besotted, that he had allowed the tiny flame from long ago to burn high and hard, but she saw that Sarah cared for Jake too. That was also part of the girl's new definition – before, when Maeve watched them all, as teenagers, she had never known what Sarah felt about any of them, except Jamie, whom she clearly loved with the kind of passion most people only know once or twice in their lives. Now, she didn't hide what she felt – reaching over to put a hand on Jake's hand, allowing her eyes to follow him when he left a room, waiting for him to return.

And Maeve noticed things about Jamie now too. Things she hadn't noticed before, or hadn't allowed herself to notice. She saw that Jamie was less than she had been – this was especially clear beside Sarah, who was now more, rounded out by everything she had become. Jamie, on the other hand, was thinner, yes, and, if not quieter, then certainly more serious. But it was more than that, Maeve began to see, as she compared the two and remembered how they had been. Jamie was no longer first to say yes to anything, everything suggested. Often now she said, 'No thanks,' or hung back instead of pushing herself to the front as she once would have, carried ahead by her enthusiasm for whatever it was that was offered, even small things, like toasted cheese sandwiches or a trip to the petrol station.

The weight of her was less now, the steps she took within the world were lighter, fewer. Now she was still, where before she had been in motion; indifferent, where she had been curious. The changes were subtle, only really visible beside Sarah, this new Sarah – but when exactly had they taken place, Maeve wondered.

That night, Sarah went over the day in her head, again and again, trying to see it from all angles, trying to see what she had not seen in the moment. To understand so that she might predict, and be ready for whatever might come next.

'I think that went well,' Jake said when they left, and Sarah hadn't known if he really thought so – how could he? – or if he just was trying to cheer her up. Or worse, was he trying to persuade himself?

'I'm not sure,' she said.

'It did. I mean, everyone was surprised. Luke and Jamie especially, but now they know, they'll come round.' It was, more or less, what everyone had said about Jamie all those years ago – 'She'll come round; she'll get over it.' They had been wrong then and, Sarah knew, they would be wrong now.

Because, for all that Jamie was changed, she was more like the sixteen-year-old she had been than Sarah was like her younger self. Sarah had seen that when Jamie talked to Maeve, to Luke, if not to her. It was as if Jamie had pulled closed a door between them, so that whatever Sarah did on the other side of it was invisible and unimportant to her. Jamie might be thinner, more frail, but the certainty of her own rightness was still with her. And within that there was no place for allowing Sarah in.

'What will you do if they don't – come round?' she asked.

'They will.'

*

But they didn't. Sarah went back, many times, with Jake and sometimes without him, and a kind of holding pattern emerged. Maeve would answer the door – somehow, it was always Maeve (she wondered if Jamie kept watch from an upstairs window, and even tried, once or twice, to look upwards and see if she could catch a glimpse of her) – and welcome Sarah and ask about her work or her plans, and Sarah would tell her and Jake, if he was there, would hover, pleased. Sometimes Simon was there and he would ask too, after Dominic, others from the law firm, and Sarah would do her best to make him laugh. She saved up amusing anecdotes for those days, little stories of who had been in, what had been said, she would trot them out, and Simon would laugh, and all would be pleasant.

Except that somewhere else, in the room itself, or the house, Jamie would be silent and watchful and furious.

'Does Jamie talk to you when I'm not around?' Sarah asked Jake after one Sunday lunch.

'Less than before,' he admitted.

'Doesn't it bother you? You were so close.'

'I don't like it,' he said. 'I wish it would all stop, but I can't make her. It's up to her. She'll get over it. She's just spoiled and used to getting her own way.' Jamie *was* spoiled, Sarah knew, always had been – it was one of the things Sarah had always secretly loved about her: that bred-from-birth assumption that she could get away with anything, would always be wanted, be welcome. But she didn't think that being 'spoiled' was Jamie's problem now. In fact, in a funny way, even though it was her Jamie was so rude to, so hostile towards, Sarah also felt as though she was the only one to properly understand her. It was, she decided, a weird feeling.

'But don't you miss her?' she asked Jake.

'No. She's behaving badly.'

But if Jamie wouldn't speak to Jake anymore, she was closer than ever with Luke now, the two of them united in silent eye-rolls and sneers at everything Sarah said. They didn't say anything that Maeve or Simon could hear, but just sat together on the orange sofa or at the end of the table and chatted and sniggered together, and whenever they were asked what about, they'd say, 'Oh nothing, no one you know.'

That ganging-up with Luke, Sarah saw, hurt Jamie's cause with Simon and with Maeve. Jamie alone in her dislike of Sarah would have had to be listened to. Jamie together with Luke was something else – difficult, unreasonable.

'We shouldn't go to the house so much,' she tried saying to Jake.

'But my parents love having you,' he insisted.

They didn't, Sarah knew. How could they, with so much animosity around her? And yet, she couldn't stop herself, not for long. She was drawn back, again and again, because each time she hoped the outcome would be somehow different. That she and Jamie would swap one of those looks, those smiles, that said it was just the two of them, and that two was all they needed. That Luke would somehow forget how much he hated her and go back to treating her with the lofty disdain of before, would call her 'Shadowcat', with no more than his usual rudeness or jeering.

But these things never happened.

One day, when, for a moment, it was just the two of them in the sitting room, Jamie asked her, 'Who even are you?' then answered her own question: 'You're like a shape-shifter.'

'You know, I am trying,' Sarah said. It was the first time she had directly approached Jamie.

'Well, you should stop then, because there is no point.'

It was soon after that that Jamie announced she was, finally, going to Vietnam. 'For a year. There's a conservation project I want to work on. Something *useful*.'

'So, what? You're just going to push off and leave the coast completely clear so Sarah can continue sucking up to Maeve?' Luke asked her, and Jamie shrugged.

'Well, what else am I supposed to do? I can't stay here and stand guard. Anyway, she's like a creeping fog. She gets in under doors and through cracks in windows.'

'Well, thanks for helping out,' Luke said.

'You hate her as much as I do,' Jamie said. 'Why?'

'She's a creep.' But it wasn't just that; Jamie knew it wasn't. Yes, he hated Sarah, that was clear, but now he hated Jake more. And even though he hated Sarah, he couldn't ignore her. He hated her in some way that meant he couldn't leave her alone.

What Jamie didn't say to him was that she had to leave, to get away – to Vietnam or anywhere else – because seeing Maeve, Simon, Jake, and even Luke, she felt like her nose was pressed up to the window of her own family, who had their backs to her and were all looking, captive, at Sarah.

CHAPTER 49

The house should have been happier with Sarah back in it, Simon thought – but it wasn't.

It wasn't that he'd missed her, just that nothing at home had felt right these last years, and he had thought, somehow, that Sarah being back might change that, might mend whatever trouble had come upon them when Sarah and Jamie fell out. But here she was, and that was wrong too. She was with Jake, not Jamie.

'Don't you see,' Miriam kept saying emphatically in the weeks that followed Sarah's reappearance, when both families knew of the relationship. 'This is how it was always meant to be. Jamie was just the beginning. This is the real deal. This is how it should be.' She was delighted, as though vindicated in something he, Simon, had denied.

But Simon wasn't sure. He could see how happy Jake was – happier than Simon had ever seen him – but he could also see Luke's anger rumbling beyond that and gaining force as the days went on. And the way Jamie was moving backwards, away from Sarah. Away from all of them.

Or maybe it was just him. Just the way he felt.

There was something coming. A reckoning, Simon knew. He could feel it. He himself, Paul, Mick O'Hagen – they were all flying too high, lifted on warm currents of conviction. As if nothing could ever go wrong, and could only ever get better. That's not how it goes, he told himself. But he couldn't make himself believe it.

He worked too much, travelled too much, planned too much, promised too much.

He hadn't broken with Miriam. He had meant to, had sworn to himself that he would; he had even played out the conversation in his head – the sorrys, the explanations, the guilt-sharing: *we both know this is what has to happen.* He had told himself that it would be hard, but he had looked forward to life on the other side – the simplicity of one life, not two. The freedom from guilt, the ability to look at Maeve straight on and tell her he loved her, without the note of apology that had crept between them in recent years.

But it didn't happen like that. If Jamie hadn't thrown off Sarah, he could have broken with Miriam. He could have stood to mess her around in one deal, but not two. It wasn't fair. And so, he didn't break when he could have, and then he couldn't anymore.

Ever since that row in Kerry, when he stormed and shouted at Jamie and demanded she do what she would not do, there had been a distance between him and his daughter. Nothing obvious, nothing that could be seen head-on, but something. The breaking of that perfect bond that had been theirs. He had let her down, and he had not been sorry when he should have been. He was sorry now, but it was too late. They had rebuilt things, but around a fault-line that trembled still between them.

He had tried asking Maeve – *what is this?* Because she would know. She always knew.

'She was in love. Her heart was broken. By Patrick, by Sarah too. It was too much,' Maeve said.

'But she'll get over it?'

'Eventually.'

What he hadn't asked Maeve was how much of Jamie's upset was his fault, and because he didn't ask, Maeve didn't tell him. But they both knew the answer – some, anyway. Patrick and Sarah had let her down, but Simon had too, and maybe that was worse.

And now Jamie was leaving. She said she wanted to travel, to see more of the world before settling down, but Simon didn't believe her. He knew her, and so he knew she wasn't being pulled by what was in front of her: she was being pushed, even if she didn't quite know it, by what was behind her.

'You could come with me,' he said. 'On some of my trips. See New York. Prague.'

'No thanks, those places don't interest me. I want to go and see if I can do something useful. Not property deals.'

And so he had said OK. Of course he had. What else could he say? And maybe in a year she would come back and she would know what she wanted. And maybe by then he would know how to say he was sorry.

They met rarely, him and Miriam – less than before, because he travelled more – but they did still meet. And not always at her insistence. And then, after those times, he would go home to Maeve and stay close to her because she – the person he had wronged the most – was still the only one who could make him feel right.

Maybe that was penance enough, he thought, knowing that nothing could be penance enough. His remorse came to him in the language of his childhood and his church, both now remote from him, and therefore empty. Words only. His remorse was something he thought, not lived. He could not suit the deed to the words.

Sometimes it seemed to him that Sarah was the child he and Miriam never had, a kind of half-promise-made-flesh between them. And because he disliked the thought, and disliked the feeling even more, he was kinder to Sarah than he would usually have been.

CHAPTER 50

One year later: Kerry, August 2009

'I don't think you should go,' Miriam said.

'It's the last time,' Sarah said.

'I know, but even so.'

'I have to,' Sarah said.

And Miriam didn't say what she felt – *you can't go, it isn't right that you are there* – because she couldn't. To say that meant she would have to say more: why it wasn't right; what it was that wasn't right about it. And she had spent too long not saying any of those things. She and Sarah were polite and distant these days; the anxious closeness of their early years was gone, and it had left so little behind it. Just as when the tide retreats, the sand between was scrubbed clean.

And maybe Sarah did have to go, although Miriam hated the idea. Some things you couldn't grasp until you saw them.

If she had seen Simon dead, maybe she would be able to

believe it – but she hadn't, and so she couldn't. She went to the funeral, of course, but so did everyone. She didn't go to the house. No one did. Mostly, they didn't go because it was 'too sad', but in Miriam's case, she didn't go because she understood that Maeve's tolerance was now at an end. It had lasted the span of Simon's life, and that was enough. In death, it was finished. So Miriam stayed away from the house and now that Sarah was going to Kerry, to the other house, she wished she would not.

Simon had died as he had lived – in a rush. Heart attack, they said, massive and immediate. *He didn't suffer; he didn't know* – the usual words that are spoken at such times, passed around like a plate of iced biscuits, for comfort, for reassurance.

The shocking thing, Miriam found, was that she didn't care. Or rather, she corrected herself, she cared only that he was dead. Beyond that, she found, nothing much mattered. She did not need to see Maeve to feel her grief. She felt it as closely as if Maeve had stood beside her and screamed it into her face.

She would leave Paul, because she had to, and he would think it was because of the money, but she didn't care about that either. No one had money now. They had debts, empty holes where money had been, holes that were deeper and wider than could ever have been filled, even by the money they had once had, so that Miriam didn't understand how any of it had worked. The madness had passed and the pieces she picked up didn't fit.

'I feel like the fisherman's wife,' she said to Paul.

'Who?'

'The one who started in a pigsty and became Pope and ended up back in the pigsty.'

'Hardly a pigsty,' he said, aggrieved. They got to keep their house. They were lucky. 'I got out early,' Paul had taken to saying, as if he were smarter somehow, had seen what was coming. He hadn't, Miriam knew: he'd just had better timing.

At first he had refused to believe it was all over. 'It's a blip,' he said, grey, in those first days when news, like despatches from a battlefield, began to travel, and passed through the ranks of the wounded and shell-shocked, back behind the lines. Only when Simon died did Paul understand that it wouldn't all be OK.

And when they found there was nothing left of Simon's money, or very little – that he had gambled big in those last months in an effort to make it alright, and that he had lost – Miriam said to Paul, 'What will you do about it?'

'What do you mean?' He was shifty. His conscience must have told him what was coming.

'I mean, what will you give them?'

'I don't have anything to give.'

'You have enough, and you owe them. You owed Simon and now you owe Maeve.'

'I'll see what Mick says.'

'No. Tell Mick what you're doing and that he has to do the same.'

In fact, Paul wasn't lying by much when he said there wasn't anything to give. There was little enough. Miriam had seen the accounts, and knew how to read them, thanks to her accountancy diploma. If he gave to Maeve, there wouldn't be anything left for her to take away with her, Miriam knew, but that was OK. She'd manage.

Taylor, the dog, was dead too and Maeve had to try very hard not to let the words 'Everything dies, everything is lost' form themselves in her head and rattle around like dried sticks. Taylor had died just days before Simon, who found her in her basket one morning, cold, curled meekly around herself as though trying, in death, to be the smallest, the least inconvenience she could be.

By then it was all over, and Simon knew it, although he had not told Maeve. She knew it too, the signs were everywhere, most of all in the broken trail of their friends, but she said nothing either. The frantic months of always peddling faster, harder, were finished, and Maeve, who had watched Simon trying to save what could not be saved, was glad. Now he could be quiet, she thought, now he could rest. She didn't care what they had lost – most of it, she guessed, maybe everything even – because she had never cared about what they had. She worried for the children, of course, but part of her thought, too, that it was time for them to take responsibility for themselves. They never came home, not Luke nor Alan nor Jamie, but they took the money that Simon sent them, without thanks or acknowledgement.

'I'm a fool,' he said to her that night, late, after he buried Taylor in a hole he himself had dug, in the wet earth of the back garden. Maeve had gone downstairs to see where he was, why he hadn't come up, and found him in the sitting room, with only firelight and a small lamp to chase away the shadows. He sat in a wine-coloured leather chair with high wings so that she couldn't see his face clearly. Only in the cut-glass tumbler that dangled loosely from the hand that lay across the armrest was there any movement; he turned it this way and that, to catch the light from the dying fire.

'You're not a fool,' she said, crossing to him, kneeling beside him.

'I am. The others haven't come as badly out as I have. They were clever. They put bits aside or in other names. They'll be OK.'

'Just because they're sneaky doesn't make them smart and you a fool,' Maeve said. 'It just makes them sneaky. I bet they didn't tell you what they were doing.'

'No. I thought we were all the same. But I've failed you. And the children.'

'You have not,' Maeve said. 'You never could.'

She told him how much she loved him and how she wanted nothing but him and that he must not worry, they would be fine. But it wasn't enough and barely a week later his heart gave out, because, Maeve thought, it was broken. Broken by his failure, broken by Miriam and her refusal to let him go, broken by Taylor's death, broken by being his father's age with, now, his father's life. Broken too by all the years of being what everyone else needed him to be; being the energy, the soul, the fun, the point of every day out and night out; and the many plans and propositions, all pulling and pulling and pulling at him. And maybe she was part of all that, she thought. Maybe her love for him was part of the pulling too? Worse, maybe her silence about Miriam – her refusal to let Simon see that she knew – had made him work to keep a secret that had already escaped? All these years she had known and said nothing, because she didn't know what to say, couldn't bear to make her humiliation into truth by speaking it. And, too, because she believed in him and believed that he would make it right in the end, and not because he had been asked by her. And so she said nothing, out of love and her own reluctance, ever, to interfere. But maybe that too had been part of the strain? The too-great effort of Simon's life that had strained it to breaking point?

In the days after his death everything was confusion, when what Maeve craved was silence. And the worst of it was the reckoning – what was lost, what was left. Paul tried to give her money. He said it was 'owed' to Simon, and came from Mike O'Hagen too. But the idea of it crushed her.

'No, Paul, I won't.'

'But it will save Reevanagh. You love that house.'

'Yes but I'm not taking it.'

'Why?'

But she couldn't tell him why – that his money was blood money. Because it came from Miriam too – so all she said was, 'Because I want you to keep it.'

He went away then and she knew he wouldn't come back. That he would be too ashamed by his own feeling of relief that she had said no. He would never risk visiting her and seeing the changed circumstances of her life, in case these ate away at him and his sense of relief.

She was glad. It was funny, she thought, how simple things

could be if you let them. If you didn't interfere or try to mend what shouldn't be mended. If only she'd always lived by.

Everything, now, was effort. Especially the things that should have been effortless. Making a cup of tea was OK – it had rules, an order. Breathing was not. Filling her lungs with air and expelling it became something she had to fight for. There was a band halfway down her chest so tight she couldn't breathe past it. Like someone had buckled her into an ugly, ungiving harness. Her breaths were shallow, panting, and so she never felt she had enough air.

Sleeping was not effortless either. Now, she slept by accident, in the afternoon, in a chair or sofa. Not at night, in her bed. Their bed.

She went to Kerry, to Reevanagh, for the last time, and there it was even worse. She couldn't find her way around the house anymore. Or maybe it was that she couldn't remember what she had set out to do, why she had moved from sitting room to kitchen, so that she would stand, bewildered, at the door, looking around, hoping something would tell her why she was there. Her feet would carry her upstairs, to their bedroom, with a purpose that seemed urgent but would abandon her on the threshold, at the door, leaving her confused and upset.

She toured the house, checking all the rooms, even Jamie's attic room, several times before she understood that she wasn't looking for storm damage or broken shutters. She was looking for Simon, and he wasn't there. She thought she caught a hint of him when she pressed his pillow to her nose, but it was gone even as she pressed deeper, trying to find it, to isolate it so she could keep it with her. The more she tried, the less there was there, so that she felt she was chasing him on the wing. That was when she moved downstairs to her workroom and made a bed among the clocks, in case their ticking would drown out the sound of her heart thumping heavy in her chest. It didn't but it was better than the black silence of her own room.

She was strict with herself, because she had to be. Eat now, she told herself. Go outside. Walk. Swim. Eat again. And so she got through the days. Her concentration was bad, so she could not read or mend watches. Without those things, the days were a succession of long empty hours. Funny how there used to be never enough time, and now there was too much of it.

It would be worse when the children arrived, because they would watch her and she would have to try. The children – she still called them that, even though there was now no one to share the calling with; no one else on earth for whom they were that. She thought of Taylor the dog, leading only one half of the life she had lived with Burton. The smaller half. And Maeve resolved that she would live both halves. She would live Simon's life too. To make up to him for having lost it.

CHAPTER 51

Packing Reevanagh would be horrible, Jamie knew, but the boys were there, all three of them, and they would help. Even Luke would help. Because they understood without saying that Maeve could not help them, that they had to help her, and help one another.

Maeve had been down there, alone, for over a week now. She had left soon after the funeral. After the days she spent with Mick O'Hagen and Paul and other men in grey suits, who had, behind closed doors, 'filled her in' on 'the situation'.

'Stop sugar-coating it,' Jamie had heard Maeve snap, her voice high enough to travel through and around the closed door. 'Just tell me what I have and don't have.'

Very little, it turned out. But not nothing. Reevanagh would have to go. Actually, there had been a choice – Number Eight or Reevanagh – but there was no choice really. 'You all need somewhere to live, to base yourselves as you come and go,' Maeve said. 'There is no point me being down here. I need to be in Dublin.' And when they protested that, no, she should be where she wanted to be, she said only, 'I've made up my mind. Reevanagh goes.'

'But you love Kerry,' they said.

'Yes. And Kerry will still be here to love in a few years when you are more settled.' That, more than anything, showed Jamie that everything had changed.

She would have to move back from Vietnam – 'I can't afford for you to stay out there,' Maeve said – but Jamie had already known that. The endless return journey with its long lay-overs, because she had booked in a rush and had to take what was available, had given her time to dwell on what waited for her. A home without Simon. A world without him. There were times on that journey she felt she was tripping, lost in the super-strong plant stuff she had once taken in the jungle. The stuff that stripped you bare and sent you to wander in the world and out of it, so you didn't know if the monsters that came to you were real, if the people you met and spoke to were alive or had ever been.

'My father is dead,' she wanted to say in explanation to the woman beside her, the man at the check-in desk. 'My father is dead. There is no corner of the world with him in it any longer. Everything he knew and was, and everything that I was with him, is gone.'

'I don't have anything now,' she wanted to tell the people in the Amsterdam café where she got coffee at 4 a.m., and stared out through the thick glass into a dawn that crept up with stealth, then chose not to go through with it, slinking back into a dull grey instead of bursting forth with morning light. 'I don't have anything that is mine. Everything is gone.'

And as she fought to keep the words inside her, she knew she was selfish and childish and, yes, she had lost, but so had they all. Especially Maeve.

She also knew that she couldn't be, any longer, as she had been. The indulgence of her rows and her sulks, her refusals to listen or understand or ever see anything except what her own eyes showed her, all that shamed her now. A year away from home, and the sharp goad of loss, showed her that.

The first thing Maeve said when she opened the door to them was, 'No swimming at the cove this year. None at all.' Her voice was anxious. The anxiety of loss, of more to lose. 'The storms have shifted the seabed and the current has got very bad again. Nora says it's very dangerous now, and that the county council are going to close it off at last.'

She had made a bed up for herself in the room beside the kitchen that had been her workroom, surrounded by her clocks and watches. 'I can't sleep upstairs,' she said. 'I can't sleep here either, but it's better. At least I don't turn and expect to find him beside me.' It did not look as if she had been anywhere near the rest of the house. The upstairs rooms were shuttered still and smelt of damp and neglect.

'Patrick came,' Maeve said. 'He says he'll come back and help.'

'How was he?' Jamie asked.

'He looked tired. Older.'

'How's his business?'

'It will be OK. He says they'll get through, and that Simon lending him the money saved him. That if he'd gone to the bank, after the downturn and what happened with the licences, he'd have lost both the boats.'

'So Simon did him a good turn?' Jamie said.

'He did.'

'I'm glad.'

'He said he would call to see you all,' Maeve continued. 'He said he would like to.' And Jamie's heart, even after all the years, swelled thick for a moment and her chest went tight.

'I'd like to see him too,' she said suddenly, and knew it was true. Patrick had loved Simon, as much as any of them. To see him now, speak to him, would mean a chance to share a loss that was too great for either of them alone. 'I'm going to ring him later.'

'Do,' Maeve said. 'Do.'

They walked through the house, deciding what to pack, what to discard. 'I don't want any of the furniture,' Maeve said. 'It can stay. Whoever buys the house can have it. And the fittings and stuff. I don't want any of it.'

'Shouldn't you take an inventory at least?' Alan asked.

'No. I don't care about it. But I need you to dig up the slate gravestones in the garden, Mrs Waldon's lurchers. I'm taking those. They can go into the garden at Number Eight, with Taylor.'

'I'll do it,' Luke said.

'I'll help you,' Jake said.

'I don't need help.' Luke's anger – with Simon, even now, with Jake too because of Sarah – was something Jamie understood. It felt familiar to her, like a coat or jacket she had also worn. But he threw it on more boldly than she ever had, even now when they tried to speak kindly or at least quietly to each other. It was an anger that would burn him up, she knew. But there was nothing she could do.

In the sitting room, Maeve pointed to the pile of stones and shells, the sheep's jawbone and twisted bits of driftwood, dustier, more faded now. 'You need to take those down to the beach.'

'I'll take them,' Jamie said. She walked down the small road to the big road. It was cold and a wind was blowing briskly, keen to strip the trees of their leaves and move on into autumn. She crossed the big beach, empty. The lifeguard's hut was closed, the red and yellow flag had been taken down. The wind slapped at her, instructing her to turn back. She climbed across the rocks to the cove. The sea was grey and the waves rolled briskly onto shore. It didn't look dangerous, Jamie thought. There was a light out beyond the mouth of the cove, a glimmer of sun shining onto the sea below, lighting it up like silver.

She tipped the little pile of objects down by the shoreline and watched as the waves came in and out over them, brightening the shells and stones, washing off the dusty coverlet of years on a sitting room table, so that they woke with an answering gleam, blending now into the slick and glowing stones and shells around them, all the same glistening wet.

She walked around the cove, marvelling at how small it was. She looked for signs of their parties, their fires, themselves, and there was nothing. The little hidey-hole they had made beneath the farthest rocks was gone, collapsed by the wind and tide or destroyed by some later incarnation of the group they had been.

She sat still and tried to hear their voices, the sound of Stephen's guitar, the scrape of Luke pulling the boat up above the high-tide mark, Patrick singing 'My Dark Rosaleen'. There was nothing, not even ghosts. *You don't get to keep your ghosts*, Jamie thought, *just as you didn't get to choose what you lost.*

She tried to find Simon there, among the wind and wild dunes, but there was nothing of him. Maybe it was the wrong place to look.

I miss being happy, she thought.

CHAPTER 52

Jamie and the boys went to town to get boxes and begin the packing, and Maeve started taking packets out of the kitchen cupboards. Sarah arrived, the sound of her little pale blue car in the driveway first, then she was pushing through the front door with a carrier bag full of food.

'I got a few things. I'm sure no one's in the mood to cook.' She set the bag down carefully. Inside Maeve could see silver-topped cartons and a baguette. Trust Sarah, so smooth and competent, to bring what was useful. Jamie had brought home dirty laundry and grief that had no outer edges, just travelled on, without limits, sickeningly, into the space around her.

She had so much, Maeve thought, looking at Sarah, who was now tidying cartons into the fridge. Plans – she and Jake talked of marriage – a career, money, self-belief. A father.

Jamie, her own daughter, had so little. None of those things. Not much of anything, really. And it was because of Sarah.

Jamie, so thin and tense and angry. Luke, angrier still, with Jake, with Jamie, and with Maeve too, because she had not been able to soothe him. And angry most of all with Simon, for so long before his death, and in a way that could never now be mended. Finally, Jake, so besotted that he was bewitched, almost indifferent to the anger and pain around him because he could see only her. And at the heart of all of it, Sarah.

Always Sarah. Sarah aged eleven, standing on one leg, shoulders burned and raw, meeting no one's gaze, waiting silently to be taken in, begging to be accepted. And Maeve had accepted her. Taken her, absorbed her into the warmth of her family. She had stood by while Sarah grew fat on that warmth, and while the rest, Maeve's own children, had grown thin.

Sarah, clutching and taking. Clutching at Jamie, choking her, stifling her. Taking Patrick, taking Jake, taking Simon from Jamie, taking Luke from them all. Taking and clutching and keeping.

'The others are out. They'll be back soon,' she said to Sarah now.

'OK,' Sarah said. She ran a hand through her hair. It fell back, smooth and shiny, into its honey-blonde waves. 'I might go down to the cove for a swim. The first swim. A baptism, remember?' She tried to smile, was maybe trying to create warmth from shared memories, but it came out too hesitantly, like Maeve was someone she was afraid to approach.

And in Sarah's face, suddenly, Miriam's face. Then Simon's voice: *I've failed you* and with it a throbbing in the air around her that was thick and confused and driving and then finally silent.

'A swim?' Maeve said. 'Good idea. You do that.

EPILOGUE

The town was quiet and half the shops were shut already. The season was nearly over. It had been a disappointing one from the start. The rain had been bad that year and many of the Dublin folk had left early. There would be no more coach tours, and so there was no point in being open.

Jamie, Jake, Luke and Alan went to the supermarket for cardboard boxes and packed the car tight. The owner helped them. 'Let me know what else I can do,' he said, squeezing Jamie's hand when she thanked him. 'We'll see you back soon.'

'You will,' she said. He went inside and Jamie said, 'Does anyone want a quick drink before we go?'

'I wouldn't mind,' Luke said. 'It's years since I've been into O'Shea's.'

'Jake?'

'No thanks,' said Jake. 'Sarah's due to arrive about now. If I leave quickly, I might get back to meet her.'

ACKNOWLEDGEMENTS

No book gets written – not by me, anyway – without a great deal of input behind-the-scenes, around-the-scenes and beneath-the-scenes. This input comes from my wonderful family and many amazing friends. I hope you all know who you are, and what you mean to me (if you don't, ask, and I will tell you at length…)

My mother, who both terrifies and inspires me; my brothers, Michael, Liam Francis and Myles; my sisters, Bridget and Martha. There hasn't been a moment of my life that you have not made better, by your wit and kindness and generosity. Also your savagely high standards and refusal to pretend you like things when you don't. It isn't always easy to take, but it certainly makes me try harder.

My husband David, children Malachy, Davy and B: you aren't just my inspiration and motivation, you're my everything.

My extended family on every side: Finn, John, Paula,

Mark, Peter, Allan, Caroline, Aisling, Ann, Patrick, Frank; life is very much a group effort. I'm so glad we are all part of the same group.

And then there are the people who had a direct impact on this book. First, my sister Bridget, to whom the book is dedicated. I always marvel at my own bravery when sending you a draft of something new (it can feel pretty much like buckling myself into stocks, ready to be pelted with rotten fruit and jeered; not that you do that, but neither do you hold back...) However, the upside – and it's a huge upside – is the exhilaration when you like something, and the complete faith I have in your judgement. Thank you for reading this, for your excellent comments.

Ciara Doorley, my editor at Hachette Ireland. You are always the ideal balance between encouraging and demanding. This time, your immediate and wonderful enthusiasm for *The Outsider* was such a massive boost. Finishing a book can be a bit flat and angsty; getting great feedback transforms that.

Susan Feldstein, who did a clever and sensitive edit; Joanna Smyth, who answers my many tedious questions with grace and patience; Breda Purdue, Ruth Shern and Elaine Egan; John Coffey, who does his best to keep my online existence in someway relevant. Jonathan Williams who has been my agent for five books, and always a wonderful friend, champion and mentor. Josepha Madigan, friend and shining example.

Louise O'Neill, whose generosity to fellow writers is amazing and exemplary, and up there with her immense talent. Ditto Sinead Moriarty, who writes, and supports other writers, so beautifully. Annemarie Casey O'Connor, who knows this world inside out and keeps me sane in it.

Brendan O'Connor – I can't believe I keep asking you to launch my books, and even less can I believe the way you always have something new and brilliant and funny to say. Sarah Caden, Mary O'Sullivan, Anna Coogan, Gemma Fullam, Chloë Brennan, Madeleine Keane, Dave Conachy, Cormac Bourke and all my pals at the *Sunday Independent*, for years of support and fun and friendship.

All the lovely people at Annaghmakerrig – for the peace, the creative space, the delicious food and good company.

Fionnuala McCarthy: I can't believe a chance lunch encounter (thanks also to lovely Andrea Smith for inviting me to that lunch) and engaging chat ended in your reading an early draft! Sorry! And thank you for your brilliant comments, and, most of all, your huge encouragement.

Orlaith Hanrahan, for reading this, for being blunt and brilliant about it, and for lending me clothes (lucky for me you have a wardrobe as big as your heart!)

And especially everyone who has ever told me that you have enjoyed my previous books. It still amazes me that something that begins in solitude and sometimes frustration can then go out into the world and be read and loved and understood. That, more than anything, is what keeps me going.

Finally, I loved writing this book, in part because I loved writing about Kerry, and trying to capture the way I feel about it. Kerry means far more to me than simply a place to go. It is where my father is buried, in Cahirciveen, and it is the landscape I walk in my mind, the air I breathe in my imagination, whenever I need to escape what's immediately in front of me.

In an exclusive all girls' secondary school, they become friends. They choose the same university, and through smoke-filled nights, lectures, sexual encounters and first loves, their bond deepens: a friendship which seems like it will last for evermore.

But then, at an end-of-year party, something happens which changes everything ...

Afterwards, they drift apart. Now Stella, a lawyer in New York, lives for her work; Laura, a struggling journalist in Dublin, is still waiting for the scoop to kick-start her career; while Amanda, broken and beautiful, lives a life of slow decay in London.

Then the phone call comes which brings them back together, to the friendship they swore would last, and the night when it all went wrong.

The Privileged is a haunting tale of friendship, loyalty and how one decision, one night, can decide the future.

Also available as an ebook